Hard Knox

Hard Knox

Pursuit of Vengeance

A Harding Knox Novel

L.E. Rogers

ISBN-13: 9781494880729
ISBN-10: 1494880725

Cover by: Rudy Balasko
ShutterStock #8621157

Available from Amazon.com, Kindle and CreatSpace.com

Info@lerogerscrimeworks.com
www.lerogerscrimeworks.com

— For my life and their love —
Bette and Marilee

Acknowledgements

I SHALL ALWAYS be grateful to Meg Price and Ruben Colon. Harding Knox would not live among these pages if not for you; a story that begins in a cemetery, and later crashes onto the shores of the Great Lakes. A new project has found life and you both remain at my shoulder through each paragraph.

An appealing aspect of writing is research. Although, many contributions are regrettably set aside to accommodate structure, pace and plot, research forms a web upon which a story is formed. Thanks to Minneapolis PD Investigations Division Commander Eric Fors, and former colleague, Michael Ridgley, both resources to a great police agency and city where the world of Harding Knox exists.

Motor vessel Captain Russell Achzet traversed the Caribbean islands and America's Great Loop. Thanks for the navigation points for *Superior Star*. As well, the technical information contributed by Kenneth Glina, American Steam Ship Company, provided a sense of scope and structure to float *Superior Star* down the Saint Louis River channel.

A special acknowledgement goes to my wife, Marilee, and to Professor Ron Sharp, PhD and his gracious wife, Inese.

Every story has an ending. Mr. Ryan Beamer, Ariel Bridge Supervisor, City of Duluth, Minnesota added context to a location that figured large to the conclusion of Hard Knox.

Retired New York State Police Investigator Chris Murphy provided the artwork on the closing page. He is now gone, and sorely missed, as is author Andrea Galabinski. I am grateful for her generous time, and encouragement, as I am to Lisa Wroble.

Thank you all for your contributions.

PROLOGE

Beyond the windows of the car paraded a blur of black wrought iron pickets in a fence that provided a boundary of sorts between the living and the dead. A turn off Thirty-Sixth Street led Sergeant Harding Knox, Minneapolis Homicide, onto the grounds of Lakewood Cemetery.

The late afternoon reflection of headstones and tree-shrouded knolls floated across the windshield of the blue Ford Taurus, boughs of giant ash and elm hung naked in the clutch of winter's cold grasp. A crust of snow covered the rolling landscape, remnants of a late March storm. Knox glanced stoically at the high ground, lichen mottled crypts and snow capped monuments stood hauntingly against a slate gray sky, immortality for the famous and infamous alike, if only in stone.

Lower, on gentle slopes, headstones flanked the terrain beneath the barren, aged trees. On the most ordinary landscape under forlorn, flat markers rested those less privileged in life. Regardless of one's mortal status, death was the inevitable ticket of admission to the marble orchard, some victims of murder.

Knox slowed at a place now painfully familiar. Messages crackled from the police radio but faded like white noise into the background. Only the loss of Lara and finding who killed her mattered.

Her headstone rested near the lane. Polished Verde granite, it stood amidst a stand of ash in windswept silence. Knox padded slowly through the ankle deep snow then stopped before her plot.

"I'm back," he said, succumbing to the want of being near her, even in the bitter cold. "I was driving by from the Third, thought I'd stop for a few minutes. I've got an off-duty gig tonight with the Skipper and Swede, something to keep me busy." Of course, *she* could not hear his words, or feel his sorrow.

Lara Conlon-Knox, her name carved in stone, her essence etched into Knox's soul. Gone, the feel of her fair skin, her supple body, the fragrance of her. Lost, the impish glint of her green eyes, her teasing smile. Taken, the touch of her lips sealed in a coffin buried in frozen earth—*Oh, God.*

Knox hunched his broad shoulders against the cold, pushed his hands deep into the pockets of his long winter coat. He glared upward, "Jesus Christ, why?"

It had been a month since she had been run down in the heart of the city, crossing Fourth Street at Hennepin Avenue. Knox, with his partner Swede Lundgren and fellow detectives had trudged through back-street bars, searched the wrecks of automobile body shops and worked informants to find the perp. The struggle to hold together what remained of his life seemed otherwise without meaning.

Karl Krieg, Commander of the Detective Division, had served only to hinder Knox's struggle. An acerbic bureaucrat, Krieg's lifeless, dead-eyed gaze, fixed behind the lenses of steal-rimmed glasses, accompanied a dispassionate expression of sympathy. "I understand your grief," Krieg said, impassively.

The chair creaked under his weight as Krieg leaned forward. "Regrettably, there are no further leads, and the increase in homicides compels me to transfer your wife's case back to Traffic Division. I understand your need to pursue this further, Knox, but I can't permit your grief to get in the way of professional objectivity, to get in the way of the job. Therefore, you are to pass on anything you have to Traffic, period."

A raised eyebrow accentuated Krieg's officious demeanor. "I know the proclivity you have to push the edge of the envelope. Do not go there, Knox. There may be repercussions

Knox stood among the graves, resentful of the reproach that swirled through the air on a gust of cold wind, and burrowed down the collar of his coat, like an ice pick to the neck.

Fuck Krieg. Lara was my wife, her death my grief, and *I'll* find her killer.

A somber look at Lara's headstone, an etched shamrock above her words, "I'm with you, always." It was the way she ended a note left behind in the dead of night, a phrase that meant everything.

Knox could almost hear the softness of her voice. Tears froze at the corners of his eyes. He leaned against a tree, brushed a cold hand across his bearded face.

"I'm trying," he said. "Somehow, I'll get the bastard who took you away."

Knox glanced back toward his car. It idled on the cemetery lane. Exhaust spilled into the frosty air. Homicide, at forty-five is all he had left, that and the memories of her. She had told him more than once that his work had been the dark mistress in their lives, her only jealousy. That mistress, the jealousy had now become entangled in an obsession to find her killer.

His head fell back in anguish, eyes glared at the gray winter sky. "I'm sorry, Lara, I should have been there. I keep seeing you. The turn of a head in a crowd, or a fragrance in a room, a distant laugh in a café, the silhouette of a face."

Ghostlike, the illusions haunted him, it always the face of someone else.

By the time streetlights flickered on, the cold had chilled Knox to the bone. Questions of his fallibility, the meaning of God, life, death, the inequity of justice; it all tumbled through his mind as he stood in death's garden, a place that had now become part of his life.

Finally, Knox trudged to the warmth of his car. From Lara's grave he carried the tragic irony of his existence.

Detective Sergeant Harding Knox, a man who hunted killers, had become both hunter *and* victim.

The night had just begun.

One

Packard Center, a square block and forty-stories of black glass and white stone façade appeared to complement the skyline of Miami's Biscayne Bay rather than that of Minneapolis. Even so, the building comprised a suitable edifice for the one hundred sixtieth-anniversary celebration of the business conglomerate, Packard Corporation.

Quietly, Harding Knox entered the banquet room taking his measure of the place and the people in it. Reminiscent of an early 20th century ball, the room glittered with light that shown through six crystal chandeliers. Guests mingled among a broad array of circular banquet tables that bordered the parquet dance floor. Each table exuded an elegant statement; fitted with white linen, corporate monogrammed napkins, silver place settings, crystal glassware and floral centerpieces.

Knox skirted along the edge of the gathering, watched the body language, the hands and eyes of those present for clues of any threat. The assignment was to discreetly handle the objectionable gatecrasher without an invitation, a surly stockholder pissed at his earnings ratio, a disgruntled ex-employee, or a left wing, right wing someone or another opposed to the company's public policies.

A few professional acquaintances Knox knew among the lawyers, and media types who packed the expansive accommodations. The guest list, like a register for an inaugural ball included well-oiled connections that the corporation maintained across the wide spectrum of Minnesota and national politics, business, media, and social networks. Knox scanned his surroundings again, unperturbed that not much could go amiss with this crowd, evening gowns and tuxedoes the order of dress. The off-duty detail occupied the evening, kept him from a dreaded morass of his feelings.

The ballroom encompassed a quarter of Packard Center's thirty-eighth floor. Against the backdrop of pale parchment colored walls, large gilt-framed oil paintings depicted the evolution of the corporate giant's enterprises. The artwork was not some abstract cubist expressionism, or pastoral Appalachian theme, rather a style suggestive of the 1930s art-deco era. Masculine figures toiled in the 1850s timber camps of Minnesota's Saint Croix River valley, and nineteenth century flourmills towered over Saint Anthony Falls and the Minneapolis riverfront. Also portrayed were portraits of Packard enterprises in retail, agriculture, shipping and banking that found their respective spaces along the walls.

Knox was partial to the images, an element of art appreciation acquired from Lara. Her life's avocation with art and photography tragically pre-empted by a hit-and-run driver.

Without warning, the grip of anxiety, a surge of anger, emptiness and panic of never finding Lara's killer welled up from within. He stepped toward the broad windows. Thirty-eight floors below, traffic weaved along Third Avenue. A cold, clammy wave of apprehension swept over him like a tide pulling him out to sea. Slowly, the room and people in it began to fade to some distant shore.

From the windows, the sparkle of city lights from a forest of city skyscrapers presented a shimmering backdrop to the government plaza below. Knox braced himself on the sill, stared at his reflection in the glass and took a deep breath—get a hold of yourself, man.

The face that looked back was tired, worn, his mood despondent. The night Lara died, he could not protect her. Then, there was the bitterness that seethed within him at the policy restrictions that bound him from his pursuit, and at Commander Krieg who enforced those limitations. Most, he feared the hunt to find who killed Lara had become as cold as the ground she now lay in. He could not comprehend that her killer would go unfound. What burned within him was a compelling sense to seek justice for her death, or, was it vengeance he sought?

Yeah. Vengeance was an option.

A motion in the room, people clapping: the band eased into "Isn't It Romantic," a Rodgers and Hart melody, and Knox turned from the window. Jonas Packard and his wife, Caitlin, entered the room. Over six feet tall in his tailored tuxedo, handsome, and fit at seventy, Packard projected an image of the U.S. Navy Rear Admiral he had once been. Ramrod straight with thick gray hair, "The Admiral," as many referred to him, had become the shrewd corporate scion, and political power broker who influenced many things within and beyond the confines of his corporation.

Knox eased to the scintillating mood of the elegant milieu as the two celebrities crossed the dance floor, Admiral Hornblower with Grace Kelly in white diamonds.

Caitlin Packard, early-sixties, clung to her husband's arm, her styled blond hair pulled into a chignon. With a Caribbean tan, the statuesque Mrs. Packard charmed guests with her smile, unassuming manner; radiant in her shimmering white evening gown, sparkling diamond necklace, ear rings and bracelet. Some people project a presence upon entering a room. The Packard's could almost stop time. The real deal, thought Knox.

Confident that he had shed his temporary sweep of despair, Knox continued along the periphery of the gathering. A polite nod and modest smile masked a wary appraisal of those in attendance with whom he was not familiar.

Dressed in black pleated trousers, burgundy jacket, cummerbund, black-tie and patent leather shoes, not the usual attire for his line of work, he blended in. That is with the exception of a subtle bulge under the left side of his dinner jacket, a .45-caliber, ten-round Beretta. The man-stopper, rested within the constraints of a black leather shoulder holster.

Peter Shaw's Big Band, its distinctive 40s music, a subtle mix of clarinets, saxophones and piano moved into a rendition of Glenn Miller's "Moonlight Serenade." The art on the walls, music in the air and four hundred people in formal attire stood far removed from Knox's usual fare, gritty crime scenes and troubled city streets.

The tempo of the tune increased when Knox saw Jon Bass near the ballroom entrance. Before he had retired,

Bass had been the first black man promoted to manage the Homicide Unit, then to the over-all command of the Detective Division. Regrettably, a position now occupied by Karl Krieg.

For some cops, Bass's advancement had been and effort to placate the minority community. To Knox, that notion was repugnant. It had been Bass and Swede Lundgren who had mentored Knox to hunt killers. The former detective commander, now security trouble-shooter, managed the Packard estate. Bass raised his hand toward Knox and motioned him toward the hallway.

"You're a little late," chided Bass.

"I had to make a stop on the way, Skipper."

"Lara?"

"Yeah."

"Anything new on the case?"

"Nothing. Still going back over things."

Bass placed his hand on Knox's shoulder, "I wish I could be of more help. You know Lara meant a lot to me and Flo."

"Thanks, boss."

Bass nodded toward a large catered table near the service entrance to the ballroom. "Check on Swede for me. Make sure he leaves enough eats for the governor."

Knox laughed and walked toward a table of hors d'oeuvres. Swede Lundgren, a burly, silver-haired Scandinavian, hefted two hundred-fifty pounds on his six-foot-two-inch frame. Two inches taller and seventy pounds heavier than Knox, he appeared as big as a caboose in his burgundy tuxedo jacket. At fifty-eight, Swede was two weeks from retirement. The two men had been partners for twelve years. Swede unabashedly picked through the pickled sardines among the catered samplings.

"How's the bait, Swede?" Knox teased.

"Bait my ass. These are Norwegian imports."

Before Knox could reply a slight-built man, early sixties, in a rumpled tuxedo elbowed his way through the crowd.

"I've got him," said Lundgren, dabbing his mouth with a napkin, "A little early for the first cab ride of the night." He started across the room toward the figure.

"Okay," said Knox who covered Lundgren's right flank.

The man jostled through a cluster of celebrants, his glassy-eyed stare and deliberate gate edged with trouble.

A glass of champagne shattered to the floor, but caused only a casual glance. Suddenly, the interloper bolted forward, and pulled a dark object from his tuxedo waistband. Instinctively, Knox knew what it was.

Swede reached for his Glock pistol, rushed the man, and yelled, "Gun!"

Knox aimed his Beretta, the line of fire blocked by a crowd of stunned people. Everyone stopped, frozen in an instant of indecision and disbelief.

The man in the rumpled tuxedo fired—*Boom!*

"Moonlight Serenade" was displaced by the cannon-like salvo of the gunshot. A wave of panic swept through the celebrants. Screams and shouts split the air. Hysteria supplanted the chatter, muffled laughter, and tinkling of glasses. Fear etched in their faces, dignitaries fled for cover in a blur of ball gowns and tuxedos.

Swede's blood splattered across the painting of the Saint Anthony Falls. The big Scandinavian crashed to the floor.

Knox brought the sights of the Beretta to bear upon the rampaging gunman. A woman, screaming, ran through the line of fire. Hearing the shriek, the gunman turned, shot. Knox took the hit in the ribs, and the woman collapsed to the floor.

The next slug slammed into Knox with the force of a Lincoln Town Car. It hit square in the chest, the impact of both hits blew the breath from his lungs. Arms went slack, hands numb. Pain sliced through his brain as his head bounced off the edge of a table. Blunt reality struck—*I'm hit!*

Stunned, laid flat on his back, eyes struggled through a gray shrouded haze that had taken hold of his sight. The feeling in his hands faded, deadening the grip he had on the Beretta. A single thought pulsed through a disorienting fog—fight for your life, man!

Knox, half-conscious, saw the haze of an image emerge above him, a pistol in outstretched hands. Deafening shots thundered through the room. The acrid odor of cordite, gun smoke, hung in the air.

Then, the vague, sloth-like figure of the shooter pivoted. Knox fought to focus, only to see the lands and grooves at the end of a gun barrel, death on its way.

With a grimace of terror, Knox anticipated the hammer of the shooter's gun slam into the firing pin, the bullet smash into his skull.

Click! The fucking gun went click!

Adrenalin surged into every primal fiber. Knox rolled to his side, angled his .45 and fired. Two rounds exploded from the Beretta's barrel. The shooter lifted off the floor. His arms flailed as he fell back onto the debris of his own chaos. In the surreal intensity, another shape of something appeared then vanished from sight.

Nearly spent, Knox slumped back while pain pounded his ribs and sternum. Heart pulsing, each breath was an ordeal. But, he had survived.

The Beretta now firm in his grip, he searched his surroundings, trying to focus for another threat. A glance right then left, nothing moved. The shooter, a gaping hole in his head, lay dead. Close by, twisted into a tablecloth another body, it too, deadly still.

In the aftermath of madness, an edgy calm, the screams of panic turned to subdued sobs, frightened whispers.

Gun in one hand, Knox nervously searched the room for another shooter. Everyone was down, wounded, dead or playing dead to survive. The chaos settled, a voice in the back of his mind shouted, "call it in." Knox pulled out his cell phone and hit the speed dial.

"Police, do you have an emergency?"

"Packard Center, thirty-eighth floor. Shots fired. Officers down."

"We have reports, sir. We are on the way. Who are you?" asked the dispatcher, a controlled urgency in her voice.

"Sergeant Knox, Homicide."

"Sergeant, where's the shooter?"

"Dead." Computer keys clicked away in the background.

"I have a dozen victims, some DOAs. Send uniforms and EMS on the whistle."

Knox ended the call, and limped toward a .9-mm semi-auto that lay near the dead shooter. Astonished, he saw the million to one misfire that saved his life. A round had stovepiped into a vertical position, jammed in the firing chamber of the shooter's gun. No one would believe it. He captured a cell photo, cleared the weapon and slipped it into a jacket pocket.

Knox tore open his shirt. He could feel it now, the bullet. His face contorted from the ache in his torso as he plucked a mushroomed piece of lead embedded in the Kevlar fibers of his vest. Then, he reached to the inside pocket of his tuxedo. To the left of his heart his fingers edged across his badge case and discovered the bullet that had dropped him to the floor. It had smashed into his police badge—*Jesus.*

Knox slipped the case and rounds into a side pocket. Pain twisted through his body when suddenly, the post shooting tremors shuddered through his limbs. With slow, deep breaths, he had to remind himself. *You're okay, man.*

Under the painting of Saint Anthony Falls, Knox found Swede, blood splattered against the wall, eyes set wide with shock. His gun never cleared its holster. The big man was gone. Knox knelt, and gently touched the brow of his friend. "I'm sorry, Swede. I'm so sorry…"

Trails of smeared blood led to others who sought refuge behind overturned tables and chairs. Knox looked up from Swede's body.

Bass. Where's Bass?

Near the dance floor, Bass lay with a gun in one hand, the other pressed to the bloodied left side of his shirt. He uttered a grunt as Knox stumbled closer.

"Knox, you get the son-of-a-bitch?"

"Yeah, how you doing, Skipper?"

"I'll live."

Bass raised his hand, revealing a hole through the front and out the back of his shirt, just above the left kidney.

Knox took the ex-commander's Walther PPK and cleared it. "Here, put the gun in your pocket before you hurt yourself."

"Ah shit, what the hell happened?" said Bass.

Knox folded a linen tablecloth to form a compress at the exit wound, and rolled Bass onto his back. He put another napkin into Bass's hand "Press hard on the entrance."

"Knox, I can plug my own holes. Find the Packard's for me."

Legs wobbly, Knox rose to his feet. "Back-up is on the way, Skipper."

Among the debris, people cowered in corners while others pulled themselves from the tangles of gala trimmings that littered the floor. The once elegant ballroom had been transformed to a grizzly facsimile of some Middle East terrorist bombing.

Within the stunned crowd a trembling voice cried out, "Jonas."

Knox turned and saw Caitlin Packard, her husband cradled in her arms. Mrs. Packard pressed a hand onto a wound in her husband's chest. Face smeared with tears and mascara, her quaffed chignon unraveled, designer dress bloodstained, Grace Kelly of the ball peered desperately at her husband's pale face.

Knox touched the woman's shoulder. "Mrs. Packard… please."

The intrepid admiral turned tycoon wheezed heavily as he tried to speak. His tanned face now shock-white, skin clammy; frothy, red foam dribbled from a corner of his mouth. Knox, no stranger to shooting injuries, pealed away the Admiral's shirt and found a frontal chest wound.

He then turned the man slightly over where his fingers discovered the exit. Knox clamped down with his hands to seal the wounds. A stab of pain knifed through his ribs.

Huddled beside Mrs. Packard was Mayor Barbara Bergin. "Battlin' Babs" as the tabloids had labeled her. The mayor struggled to her feet, panic in her eyes. "Help us," she pleaded.

Jaw clinched in pain, Knox shouted to the mayor. "There, on the food cart, get me those plastic bags."

"Do it now, Mayor! I can't hold this long." Had it not been for the circumstances, Knox would have taken a certain pleasure in his harsh direction to Bergin.

Bergin returned from the cart, and Knox had Mrs. Packard press one of the plastic bags onto the bullet hole in the admiral's chest. He told the mayor to compress the other to the hole in his back. The simple application of sandwich bags sealed off the wounds. Packard's urgency of breathing eased, color returned to his face. Knox stood, bent over at the ache in his own chest.

"Corpsmen coming, sir," said Knox, the naval term for medic. The admiral could only reply with a profound look of gratitude in his eyes.

"Keep him elevated, the bags tight," said Knox as he looked down at Caitlin Packard. Disheveled as she was, the woman still possessed a fascinating presence.

"Thank you, Sergeant," she said the worried Mrs. Packard then returned to the care of her husband.

Sirens wailed in the streets below. Knox leaned against the bar and waited.

Moment's later, weapons drawn; uniformed officers entered the ballroom in a loose five-man wedge. An incredulous look on his face, a young sergeant had the point.

Knox held up his dented shield. "Over hear, Homicide."

The sergeant stepped cautiously across the room. Frightened celebrants crawled from hiding places, their moans and sobs no longer guarded.

"The scene is clear, bring in the medics," said Knox. He nodded at Packard. "This one's a priority. Shot through the lung."

"The shooter is over there," Knox said with another nod. "A hole in his head."

Knox pointed toward the painting of Saint Anthony Falls. "Sergeant Lundgren is there. He didn't make it".

One of the first wounded rolled off the floor was Jonas Packard as a cadre of police brass, and a gaggle of uniforms formed in the hall. Knox quickly briefed the Downtown Commander who barked out orders to set up teams, called the Forensics Bureau for evidence collection, and confirmed that Chief Ballard was en route from another engagement.

Knox relinquished his gun, that of the shooter, the miss-fired bullet and the mushroomed slugs, as well as his shield and case to the suits from Internal Affairs.

With a wince and grunt, Knox slipped from his tuxedo jacket, shirt, and light duty Kevlar vest then handed them over to the guys from IAU. A steady pain continued to throb in his head and chest as he twisted into a waiter's jacket, and walked to the elevator.

Bass lay strapped to an ambulance gurney. His shirt cut open, a bandage taped to his side and an IV stuck in his arm. He looked at Knox with a gasp. "You've been hit too?

"Yeah, Jon. Looks like tennis is out of the question for a while."

"Where'd that son-of-a-bitch come from?"

"I don't know, yet."

The ex-detective commander grunted. "The Admiral?"

"He went to Metro Medical, one through the chest. He should make it. Mrs. Packard will recover in a day spa."

"Swede?"

A medic grabbed the gurney and edged toward the elevator. The look on Bass's face searched for some affirmation that Swede was okay. Knox shook his head. Jon Bass lay back, shut his eyes and the doors slid closed.

Two

At the east window of the ballroom, Knox stared vacantly at the collage of reflections that moved across the glass, flashes raced through his mind. "Moonlight Serenade," a crescendo of bullets, the shooter with a hole through his head, dead. Mannequin-like, lifeless bodies in party clothes lay sprawled on the floor. Swede Lundgren, his throat splattered across an oil painting, would never collect his pension.

The harsh glare of halogen ceiling lights replaced the cozy glow of crystal chandeliers. Knox focused on the figures mirrored in the window. They moved quietly behind him, distorted images in a glass mirage. The wounded whimpered and moaned, and were tended to by paramedics.

Crime scene techs stalked the room, latex gloves smacked around their wrists. They made measurements, bagged and recorded evidence. Video recorders whirred, digital cameras clicked, and flashed through still frames to document the crime scene. A cadre of detectives, Knox's colleagues, interviewed witnesses, and wrote in their notebooks.

The brass huddled in muted discourse. Knox saw their reflections in the glass. Behind circumspect glances, the utterance of his name. The wheels of judgment began to turn.

An inescapable paranoia bored into Knox. He had survived two other shootings, and endured the punishing aftermath of inquiries, the unavoidable second-guessing. Administrative leave, internal affairs, threats of grand jury, federal investigations, civil suits; and, the media, shark-like, that spun events into a feeding frenzy.He endured the mind games, the anxiety of doubt-filled days and nights, while the politicians scurried to cover their ass. Like the "canoe maker" in a morgue, the system can cut apart your insides.

Although the dead still remained, Swede among them, the wounded were now nearly gone. To Knox, thoughts of the consequence of his survival persisted, potential procedure violations, firing within a crowd to take down the shooter.

He had been through this darkness before, the black kid with a gun on Queens Avenue, dead. The drug bust on Columbus Avenue South, two Somali perps went down. In the abstract, the cop disappears into the backdrop, replaced by agitators and race mongers. When the call is close, no matter how right you are, you can be wrong. Your career gone, the politicians trump all to save face.

Knox closed his eyes.

"Lara," he whispered.

"Sergeant?"

Surprised, Knox turned to see the new police chief, Thomas Ballard. He was mid-50s and a couple inches shorter than Knox's six-foot frame. He wore his reddish gray hair and mustache close-cropped.

Mayor Bergin's man, or was he? Hired from Chicago PD, the new chief had expanded community-policing programs to combat gangs, guns, and drugs. However, it was no secret. He was really Bergin's end-run around the Republicans, her crime control ticket to put a Democrat, herself, in the governor's office.

Ballard, in a navy blue suit and topcoat, owed his professional bearing to a Marine Corps pedigree, and a Loyola law degree. Knox had pegged him a little too formal, a little too Chicago, but he got things done, and went to the mat to back his officers when they were in the right.

"I hear you took a hit," said Ballard. "How are you doing?"

Bone grated against cartilage. "A little ragged, Chief."

Ballard cast a look at the bruises just visible through Knox's open jacket. "Make sure you get that taken care of tonight. Thank God you made it."

Knox squinted toward Swede's body, shrouded in a white tablecloth.

"I think God had the night off, Chief."

"Maybe so," said Ballard. "I am sorry about Sergeant Lundgren. At least you have the satisfaction of taking down the bastard that shot him."

Knox stared off beyond the chief, trying to comprehend Swede's death. "He was my partner; thirty-four years on the job, two weeks from retirement."

"Yeah, I know," said Ballard. "I lost a friend here too. Neil Wallace."

Knox frowned in surprise at the Chief's revelation. " A year ago, we...Swede and I handled his nephew's homicide."

"Damn small world," said Ballard who nodded toward the body of the shooter and placed his hand softly on Knox's shoulder. "You did more than what could be expected." Then he paused, as if trying to find the words. "You know the drill. It's likely to get rough, mandatory investigations, the media?"

"I know, Chief. I just need some time."

"It'll work out, Knox. Make your follow-up through Commander Krieg."

Knox received the chief's instruction with little enthusiasm. It was an aggravating thought, having to subject himself to Krieg's scrutiny. He turned toward the window as the chief walk away, his image reflected in the glass

On the streets below, sirens wailed, the interwoven sweeps of red and blue emergency lights sliced through the night, glanced off City Hall, off the white façade of Packard Center, and danced through the trees that bordered the Hennepin County Government Plaza. Knox rubbed the palm of his hand across his face and remembered. The shooter had only one impact wound, to the head. A sickening sense rolled in his gut—the second round.

Three

The ache in his chest and ribs competed with the dull throb at the back of his head. Eyes nearly closed from a medicated slumber, Knox squinted into the darkened room, green diodes on the bedside clock pulsed, 9:52 P.M.

His left arm in a sling, mind wrapped in fog, Knox tried to remember. He brushed his free hand across an unkempt beard, another shallow breath, painful. Swathed in a flex-bandage were his chest and ribs, otherwise everything was in place.

The haze began to clear as the pieces fell together; Packard Center, Swede and the shooter dead, Doc Payne at Hennepin General E/R, debriefing at IAU, home. When… how the hell did I get home?

Annoyed, Knox fumbled for the TV remote on the end table. A touch of the power button, and the screen blinked to life revealing Channel 7's signature program, *The Ten P.M. Journal.*

Partnered with a fifty something Ted Harmon, "The Voice of Twin City News," was thirty-six year old Cathy Conlon; Harmon had the voice, Conlon had everything else, Channel 7's embodiment of a less aged Bill O'Rielly and a youthful Megyn Kelly.

"Good evening, Ted Harmon at Packard Center with *The Ten P.M. Journal.*"

Harmon, in a navy camel hair topcoat, posed before the impressive monument anchored near the sidewalk; a long gleaming chrome affair with raised letters that spelled out, Packard Center. Behind loomed the white façade of the forty-story building bathed in lavender accent lighting. The camera angel was low, wide and dramatic.

Knox laid back and rolled his eyes. "Harmon, you putz."

"Only twenty-four hours ago," said the velvet voiced anchor, "a lone intruder entered the Packard Corporation anniversary celebration." The camera zoomed in for effect as Harmon stared into the lens. "Armed with a pistol, the intruder began shooting. Jonas Packard, the former Naval Admiral, who had taken the corporate reins of the family's Minnesota conglomerate, was injured; a bullet through a lung."

The news was a peripheral element as to why some men tuned into the *Ten P.M. Journal.* Kathleen Conlon, bright, articulate and engaging, had short red hair that fell teasingly over her brow above smiling green eyes. Most of the guys in Homicide coveted a carnal appreciation of her, a notion uncomfortably known to Knox. Kathleen was Lara's sister.

It wasn't the first time since Lara's death that Knox felt...troubled as he watched the image on the screen, the sound mute in his ears. There was Kathleen going on with life, reporting the news, and Lara was gone forever.

"The alleged gunman…" said Kathleen.

"Alleged my ass," muttered Knox.

"…described to be in his mid-sixties," Kathleen continued, "carried a semi-automatic handgun. According to police, he was shot by Minneapolis Police Sergeant Harding Knox, part of an off-duty police detail. Sergeant Knox, also shot, was later released from the Hennepin County Medical Center, Ted."

"Kathleen, local, state and national dignitaries, along with Governor Norgaard, Mayor Bergin and Hennepin County Attorney Jack Griffin were among those attending the affair. None of them sustained injuries, and praised Sergeant Knox for his courageous action. Sadly, Kathleen, there was loss of life."

"Ted, we have confirmed at least four of the nine injured died of their wounds."

Kathleen cleared her throat and took a breath for composure. Eyes noticeably moist, she looked back into the camera. Knox sensed it was about Swede. She knew him well from gatherings at Knox's home, drinks at Francine's European Grill On Main, and by the stories that Swede so often embellished to everyone's enjoyment.

"One of the dead," Kathleen stumbled with the words, "Homicide Sergeant Swede Lundgren, a thirty-four-year police veteran, just days from retirement."

Then, another gap in her presentation as she listened intently, something said into her studio earpiece.

"Ted, this just in; tragically, it has finally been confirmed that University of Minnesota Professor Neil Wallace, a distinguished PBS political commentator, and prominent civic leader is among the fatalities. Neil Wallace, a great loss to this community, Ted."

"Kathleen, with me now is Mayor Bergin." The camera closed to a full-face shot. The mayor, a mature woman of notable presence stood five-foot-ten in heels, flowing auburn hair, a Roman nose, large brown eyes and a clear, unambiguous voice.

"Mayor, we have just been informed of the death of Neil Wallace as a result of this tragedy. Your thoughts?" said Harmon, and thrust his microphone forward.

Knox remembered the chief had said Wallace, too had died. At the thought, a vague image flashed through his mind then faded. Wallace?

Mayor Bergin, the state's Democratic Party anchor gazed into the television camera, the image transmitted right into Knox's bedroom.

"Time to piss," muttered Knox.

He rolled out of bed and hobbled to the bathroom. The ache in his lower back, unlike that in the rest of his body, vanished after a pause at the porcelain throne.

Back in the bedroom, Channel 7 went to a hemorrhoid commercial as Knox squinted at the plastic amber bottle in his hand and twisted off the top. With a circumspective pause, he pondered Doc Payne's prescription. Into his palm spilled a small yellow tablet, "potentially addictive," the Doc had said. A sudden cough accompanied by the jolt in his body doubled him over. Knox opted to risk addiction.

A half glass of water for a chaser and Knox noticed that Ted Harmon had replaced both the mayor and the hemorrhoid spot on the TV. "The Voice of Twin City News" stood in the lavender light by the burnished chrome sign.

"Stay turned to Channel 7, our investigation continues."

Knox pushed the button on the remote. "Harmon, you putz." The room faded to darkness. He lay back and waited for the aches in his body and the throb in his skull to subside.

After a while, in the fog of half-sleep, Knox jittered through an unremitting flashback, Swede Lundgren, a bullet through the throat, and the ballroom shootout. Like darting through the grainy, flickered frames of an old Philip Marlow film, *The Big Sleep*, another figure blurred past the sights of Knox's gun. He struggled to sharpen the glimpse of what, or who it was.

Eyes shut, the nightmare continued. The shooter stepped from a haze, the tormenting metallic echo of a gun's hammer on the firing pin, click, click, and click.

After a while, the specter faded. Snatched from the grip of the grim reaper, Knox drifted into stillness, Percodan pumping through his veins.

Four

In the morning, Knox steadied himself against the bathroom sink, dismayed at what stared back from the mirror. The face, and dark, vacant eyes sagged like a bloodhound above a beard in bad need of a trim. His body, bruised and sore, felt as if he had gone fifteen rounds with boxer Manny Pacquiao. The Percodan, expended in sleep, left Knox afloat in a funky stew. Legs trembled under his weight. He smelled as if he had been zipped in a body bag for two days. He muttered at his image in the mirror, "Who the hell are you?"

The metal clips fluttered onto the bath rug, the cloth bandages dropped beside them. Knox hesitated in anticipation. He took a slow breath against the knife of pain, and allowed his left arm to drop slowly to his side. Cartilage grated against cartilage, but less so than before. There, to the left of his sternum an unsettling hue of black, blue, yellow, and red had coagulated within a circular four-inch bruise. A matching bruise marked his lower left ribs, both remnants of two bullets that had hurtled into him at eleven-hundred-feet per second. He said a quiet prayer of thanks to the DuPont Corporation, and the goddess of Kevlar.

With one hand, Knox showered, dried his body, trimmed his Hemingway-like beard and bandaged his chest. It was a gritty ordeal, but the gloom began to fade.

In the kitchen, wrapped in a black terrycloth robe, left arm in a sling, he sipped the first cup of coffee he had in days. The elixir of life he thought, after Crown Royal Reserve, of course.

He looked out the back window of his home. The Mississippi River flowed cold and fast past a stand of giant elms along the jagged shoreline of Nicollet Island.

The Hennepin Avenue Bridge connected the mid-river island to the skyscrapers of downtown, and to the old East European neighborhoods on the opposite shore. Down stream, the river cascaded through the spillways of Saint Anthony Falls, and through locks and dams One, and One-A.

Situated amidst the capricious flow of the Mississippi, he and Lara had transformed their piece of urban renewal amid the commercial cadence of the city. Knox shook his head, longing for her and remembering.

Ten years had past since they had restored the old house. Formerly the home of a 1880s mill manager, later a decrepit hovel for derelicts, the landmark was now on the Minnesota State Historical Register. Two quarried fireplaces bookended the old two-story limestone. On the front and back porches Knox could sit with a cigar and a drink and watch the world go by, a seldom but satisfying occurrence. Lara's irreplaceable touches, fashionable colors, and an engaging blend of eclectic furnishings provided a contented feel to their island home. Since her death, Lara's second floor studio sat silent. Nikon cameras idle, her prize black and white Eisenstaedt-like photographs hung as a warm remembrance of her talent and presence.

At the kitchen window, looking toward the river, Knox took another sip of coffee. Inexplicably, he could almost see her near the water's edge, absorbed in a city sunrise. "Lara," he said aloud.

The phone rang, intruding upon the memory of *her*.

"Hello," said Knox, his voice raw.

"Knox, its Ernie. Is this a bad time?"

"No, I…I was just—"

"I'm glad to hear you're moving around. You looked like hell when I brought you home the other day."

"So, that's how I made it."

"Yeah, listen I need to stop by in a while, okay?"

"Sure, what's up?"

"I'll talk to you amigo, when I get there, about an hour."

The call ended, Knox at least pleased with anticipation to see his friend and colleague. But, the tone of Ernesto Guzman's voice left an uneasy feeling.

At 9:00 A.M., a tan Taurus slowed to a stop in the driveway. Guzman, a middleweight Argentine expatriate with a boxing background and bachelor's degree in criminology, ambled to the front door in a dark brown suit. Know waited in the open doorway.

"Hey, *hermano*, my brother, *como estas*?"

"Fine. I'm convalescing," said Knox, attired in his robe. "Come in. I have coffee in the kitchen."

"Thanks," said Guzman. He handed an envelope to Knox. "This came for you at the office, thought I'd bring it along. Nice stationary."

Knox examined the envelope, a designer stock, not the kind you would find at Office World. The paper was light mauve, dark strands of fiber with a clean eucalyptus-like fragrance, his name beautifully scripted across the front.

Knox invited Guzman into the kitchen and slit open the envelope with an opener from the kitchen desk. The graceful sweep to each letter, and the sincerity of the words gave evidence as to its author.

Dear Sergeant Knox

My husband and I are eternally grateful for your courage to have stepped into harms way to save lives. Sergeant Lundgren gave an heroic sacrifice. His loss deeply saddens us.

May God bless you both,
Caitlin Packard

Guzman looked at Knox, a curious tone to his Latin accent. "The fragrance, it's quite appealing, hermano. Is there something you'd like to share?"

Silently, Knox glanced again at the words. For the first time in weeks, he felt a peculiar sense of calm sweep through him.

"It's just a lady's way of saying thanks," said Knox who poured the coffee.

"Nice lady. Anyway, you sure look better than a few nights ago, man. I'm glad you weren't..." Guzman nearly choked ...you know."

"Well, that makes two of us." A wince accompanied the chuckle from Knox.

"I'm sorry about Swede, my friend. Funeral is Friday. I can drive, if you want."

"Thanks, I need to be there, Ernie. But you didn't stop by just because of the funeral."

"No, I didn't," Guzman replied. "I came across something you need to know." He took a slow sip of coffee.

The hesitation caught in Knox's throat. "The shooting?"

A serious gaze shrouded Guzman's dark eyes. "Neil Wallace."

At the sound of the name, Knox felt the hammer strike a firing pin. The persistent dream that haunted his subconscious, the two shots, the surreal vagueness of a shadow falling, it now began to take an ominous shape. Knox looked into Guzman's eyes, fearing his own premonition. He took a breath, nearly audible in the stillness, not wanting to ask the question, afraid of what the answer may be.

"What about Wallace?"

"I stopped by Forensics this morning. Don Meuer had called me, said he owed you. Off the record, he wanted me to get in touch."

"Okay Ernie, you're in touch."

"Meuer did the ballistics on the slug fragments the ME removed from Wallace."

"The Bottom line," said Knox, eyes locked on Guzman.

"Harding, the shooter packed .9-mil hard balls, not .45-cals."

"The fragments in both Wallace, and the shooter were consistent with Federal .45-caliber Hydra-shocks; your load, man. I'm sorry."

Knox felt the blood rush from his head, his stomach twisted into a nauseating knot. The grim reality swept through him like the cold current of the river surging through the spillways of his being into a dark abyss. The vision that haunted him, the ghost-like shadow that fell amid the chaos behind the line of fire, behind the shooter, was no ghost at all. It was the second shot. He had killed Neil Wallace.

Knox stared vacantly out the window, Guzman's revelation an echo in the dark. "I, ah… I never saw him, Ernie, a blur, maybe; I don't know—"

"I can only guess at what you feel right now my friend. But, in case you forgot, Charles Leyland tried to kill *you*. I'm here to give you a heads up on what's coming at you, *amigo*."

Knox gave no reply.

Guzman reached across the table. "Right now, we're the only ones who know. When Meuer files his report, the brass will sit on it for a few days. Eventually there's going to be more than an internal affairs review. There'll be a grand jury investigation. The media will come after this like a *javelina* at festival."

"It's worse, Ernie. Swede and I broke bread with the Wallace family. We sent up the guy who killed his nephew."

To warm his coffee, Guzman reached for the pot. "Jesus, Knox. Whatever the case, Wallace is an accident. On that point you need to get your head straight, and be prepared to deal with the politics of all this."

Guzman took a sip then set down his cup. "There are people in this city who perceive themselves as disenfranchised; they see Wallace as their meal ticket to a hand-out, a better life, maybe. The media will spin this. Whacked by a cop, Wallace's death will be portrayed as another indiscriminant police shooting. That will be the perception no matter the real facts. The lives *you* saved will be a footnote no one will read about. Politicians are going to find distance from you like running from a plague of the Russian Flu. With every minority radical in the country turning the crank, *hermano*, you will be in the meat grinder."

"Think about it, Knox. I can reach out, get Maurice Mancel from the police federation involved. Meanwhile, my friend, you know where I'm at. Swede's funeral is Friday. I'll call you."

Five

The rural country slid by as Guzman drove the Taurus up Highway 8, fifty miles north of the Twin Cities to the little Swedish hamlet of Lindstrom, Minnesota, Swede Lundgren's hometown.

Knox sat with his arm trussed in a sling and stared through the car window, thoughts anchored in unrest. As if caught up in a torturous pinball game, his mind careened through his inability to find Lara's killer, apprehensions about his career, Swede's death, and the possibility of being indicted for killing Wallace. Adding to the strife, protestors had begun their chants, picketing Minneapolis city hall.

The night of the shootings, Knox remembered the circumspect, poker-faced headhunters from Internal Affairs. Their questioning probed for procedure violations, grilled about the endangerment of others, questions about Wallace, the shooter, and Lara's death. Did I feel that I failed Swede? The bastards.

Knox peered through his window. Emergency lights flashed among the motorcade of fifty police cars, a poignant tribute to Swede Lundgren's sacrifice. The bonded brotherhood sped through the rolling farmland, past

Wyoming and Chisago City, Minnesota then edged onto the main street of Lindstrom.

"We're here," said Guzman.

Beyond the Coffee Pot restaurant, somber faced pedestrians stopped on sidewalks as the procession of cops drove by. Finally, Guzman turned toward the Lutheran church. A bald man in bib overalls stood at the curb. He held a John Deere cap over his heart, and the hand of a little boy who gestured with an awkward salute. The tears welled up in Knox's eyes.

Guzman parked the unmarked, and the two detectives trudged toward the church along with scores of other police officers, and sheriff's deputies.

A whisper of wind through the trees, the scuff of footsteps along damp snow-edged sidewalks accompanied a reverent quiet. Inside the simple confiners of the Lutheran church, Knox and Guzman sat one row back from Swede's family. Jon Bass slid in next to them.

The subdued organ notes, a somber Swedish funereal composition, thought Knox, hung like a heavy shroud over the gathering. He listened to the creak of the old oak pews, the muffled sobs from Swede's family, hushed whispers, and the rustle of those who had packed the old place of worship.

Uniformed cops lined the isles of the church, and spilled out onto the front lawn. They stood at rest, heads bowed—duty, honor and sorrow.

Draped by an American flag, a lone bronze casket rested before the alter rail. Atop the flag, lay Swede's uniform hat. He had protected and served until death.

Present were members of the Homicide Squad and the General Investigations Division, murder and mayhem put on hold for the day. Chief Ballard, County Prosecutor Jack Griffin, Reverend Jon Odom, as well as Swede's son gave eulogies.

The voices sounded distant as Knox remembered the cases, the dark alleys, the dangers shared, and occasions never revealed when the lines blurred.

Knox felt a nudge. "You're next," Guzman said.

Beyond the casket, the austere pulpit sat on a rise, up a few steps and to the left. Knox looked out at the sea of faces. Being there for Swede, and knowing the haunting details of Swede and Wallace's death, his hands trembled. He cleared his throat.

"For the past twelve years Swede Lundgren was my mentor, partner and friend. Together, we worked homicide. 'This job is a professional calling,' Swede once told me. He was right. And when Swede went on the hunt, he was like a birddog working through an October cornfield." A few approving smiles appeared in the crowd.

"When I first partnered with Swede, he said, 'Let me tell you, Bub, we work 'em into the ground, none of this nine to five' Knox paused, stuff.'" He caught a smirk and raised eyebrow from Chief Ballard.

"Swede said, 'It's an *honorable* thing we do, because no one else stands in for a murder victim.' That attitude and dedication never waned in the time I knew Swede."

"I also knew this man to be many people, a lousy bass fisherman, a tough street cop, a man who went to a victim's funeral, a resolute investigator, a bard of the most preposterous stories, a man who loved being a policeman, and a man who adored his wife and family. He made a difference in all the lives he touched, including mine."

A tear trickled down his check, and Knox could feel the crack in his voice. The last words came hard. "Swede Lundgren is a man that I will miss each remaining day of my life." He looked down at the flag draped coffin. Guilt stabbed at him like a knife in the gut. *Swede, it should have been me.*

Knox stepped from the pulpit when his eyes, by chance, connected with those of Mayor Bergin seated near the front of the church. The benign gaze was telling. With the turn of events, he had become expendable.

Near the mayor sat a familiar woman; quite different in her appearance from the night of the shooting, the woman who had scrolled the kind note. She wore an elegant tailored black dress, private label no doubt. It went with the chic black hat. Their eyes too connected. Caitlin Packard nodded, her lips slightly parted as if to say thank you.

The internment took place in a grove of evergreens at the Chisago Lake Cemetery. Knox, Guzman and Bass stood behind the Lundgren family who sat in chairs on the brown grass under a green awning, a smell of pine in the chilled air.

The benediction by Pastor Odom preceded an order from the honor guard, "Aaaatenshun! Preeesent arms!" Two hundred uniformed police officers snapped to a salute. The honor guard's volley of shots, three sharp cracks, echoed through trees and across the field of graves, then the command, "Order arms!"

The formation dropped their salutes. Chief Ballard presented Swede's wife with the flag that had draped her husband's coffin. In separated cases, he imparted Swede's police shield, Purple Heart and Medal of Valor. On a nearby knoll stood a lone piper. Stillness broke as "Amazing Grace" pealed through the pines.

Tears came to the face of Harding Knox, and the face of many others. A cop's funeral will break your heart.

The last note played, the last good-bye said, Knox and Guzman walked away with Jon Bass. As they neared Guzman's car, Knox turned to Bass. "Who's Thomas Charles Leyland?"

Bass deferred his reply. Commander Krieg approached, followed by Darrel Edminster, Krieg's Lieutenant who ran the murder squad. The muscles in Knox's jaw tightened at their unexpected, officious appearance.

In uniform, Krieg resembled a two-hundred-and-fifty-pound goose-like figure. A black utility belt, holster and gun, handcuff case and magazine holder accentuated his girth. The gear, Knox knew, was more an appurtenance to Krieg's position than for use in real police work. Never a people person, but deferential to his superiors, Krieg projected an arrogant, often demeaning nature toward subordinates.

"Here come the clowns," muttered Guzman.

Krieg managed an obligatory smile. "Sergeant Knox, Sergeant Guzman."

The habit of addressing his personnel by rank was not out of respect, rather Krieg's way of reinforcing his own position over theirs.

Krieg turned to Bass. "Good to see you, Jon. I know how much Sergeant Lundgren meant to you."

Bass had always marked Krieg for what he was, a self-serving opportunist. "Krieg, you have no idea *what* Swede Lundgren meant to anyone."

With a nod to Knox and Guzman, Bass brushed by Krieg. "Excuse me, gentlemen. Call me later, Knox."

Bass limped off toward a dark Lincoln limo where Mrs. Packard stood chatting with Mayor Bergin.

Krieg ignored Bass's departure and turned to Knox. "Those were fine words today, Sergeant. You have my condolences regarding the loss of your partner. Lieutenant Edminster and I know that you were close."

Knox discounted the sentiment. "What do you want, Commander?"

"I'd like a word with you," said Krieg. He nodded to a discrete distance apart from Ernie Guzman.

Knox stopped a few paces short of where Krieg indicated.

"This is fine," said Knox.

"In regard to the Packard situation," said Krieg, "I've scheduled a session with Doctor Payne that concerns your physical injuries."

"Okay," said Knox, indifferently.

Krieg took a slip of paper from his breast pocket. He handed it to Knox. "You are expected on Monday. Part of the administrative leave procedure, I'm sure you know. Any problems, you are to coordinate with Lieutenant Edminster. Also, *we* need to schedule time to talk."

"I'll call you," said Knox who turned quickly, and with Guzman walked away. The commander and his protégé remained at the curb, as if waiting for a cab.

• • •

On Nicollet Island, Knox pulled up his jacket collar against the chill. The flow of the Mississippi tugged the smoke from his imported Dutch Diplomat cigar downstream toward Saint Anthony Falls.

After the funeral, Guzman and Knox had talked into the night. Alone now, Knox sat on a rock near the river, next to him an empty space. Ever since Lara's death, he could feel her presence late at night near the river's edge. Here, he still talked to her.

Tonight the feeling was no different, except for her silence. Alone, he sat in the cool air under the sparkle of lighted buildings that flickered against the dark sky. Only an errant siren that wailed in the distance, and the drum of tires over the Hennepin Avenue Bridge disturbed the night.

Inescapably, the feeling hit him. Without both Lara and Swede, he wasn't just lonely, but alone. He had shared the love of his life with Lara, and the thrill of the job with Swede. Now, both lay in cold graves. In his sleep, each night their images return. Lara's broken body lay in the intersection of Fourth and Hennepin, the man who killed her vanished into the bowels of the city. Swede, a bullet through the neck, sent reeling to the floor, the click of the hammer on Leyland's gun. It kept flooding back along with the other brutalized lifeless forms, the homicide cases he had buried long ago. Now, Neil Wallace, a vague ghost-like blur into the line of fire, hurtled Knox into a storm of more consequence.

Six

Crystals of sleet pelted its windows as the mud-splattered bus lumbered along Interstate 94 through a vestige of winter. Above the windshield the unlit legend spelled out the destination, Minneapolis. After crossing the Mississippi River, the tarnished Gopher State Coach meandered through the south side of downtown. It was an anonymous mode of transportation for a confused and bitter young man in search of a vengeful fate.

The endless metronomic thump of wheels across pavement permitted only a restless sleep. An unassuming traveler stirred under a worn blanket. He rubbed his eyes and squinted through the windows into a blurred luminescence of freeway lights. The smell of diesel fuel and body odor fouled the atmosphere. He pulled the blanket from around him and coughed as the driver announced, euphemistically, "Ladies and Gentleman, The Minneapple!"

As he awoke, the traveler, Leon Love, turned his head toward a girl of about sixteen with large, sleepy brown eyes that past his seat. She had long legs, tight black jeans and cast a nervous smile that conveyed a wary sense of Leon.

He had seen her get on the bus in Black River Falls, Wisconsin, alone. She stirred his interest, a superficial toughness, he thought, that concealed her vulnerability. But at the moment, he had another priority, the one featured in *USA Today* spread on the seat next to him.

A storm of emotions had boiled within him since the day the story broke. A single question drummed through his mind on the long night's journey. Why? The tragic event had been a headliner on the major networks, including PBS. "The Packard Corporation Shootings." Television pundits rambled on with speculation, mentioned Homicide Sergeant Harding Knox. The print media lamented the loss of life, questioned the actions of police, and offered the most telling question, "Ballistic tests…who fired the fatal shots?" For Leon it was more than just another tabloid piece that sold news.

Again, Leon picked up the paper, flicked on the reading light above the seat and scanned the paragraphs. "Five confirmed dead, four others wounded," it read. A vision of his estranged father reappeared, and he wondered who had killed him?

There were comments from politicians, Minnesota's governor, "Society morns the loss of Neil Wallace, noted educator, civil rights leader, a man for all seasons."

Love stared at the words on the printed page. "A man for all seasons," he muttered to himself.

The bus swayed as the driver nosed through a curve and entered the grimy white-tiled walls splattered with sand and brine, the Lowry Hill Tunnel.

Ignoring the distraction, Love continued through a supplement page. "A source close to the investigation has tentatively identified Thomas Charles Leyland as the alleged shooter. Former CEO of Packard Air Charter, also known as PAC Air, Leyland left his position under unusual circumstances. Representatives of the Packard Corporation have not commented...the matter under investigation."

Love sighed and closed his eyes. "Thomas Charles Leyland" he said slowly. A ripple of anger twisted through him. A photograph of the trim bearded homicide sergeant, Harding Knox, looked up from a picture. Love knew the story was not going to end on a supplement page of the newspaper.

With the swipe of his hand, Leon blurred the moisture on the window as the bus punched through the slush, exiting the north end of the tunnel. A kaleidoscope of lights, hues of amber, white, and lavender glimmered from the tall buildings, their windows lit like a cascade of stars against the early morning sky.

Interior lights clicked on, and the odd retinue of passengers stirred to life. Once past the Basilica of Saint Mary, the bus rolled down Hawthorne into the terminal. Air brakes uttered a final gasp as the bus rolled to a stop against a yellow curb.

Moments later the exit door opened to a rush of cold air that hit Leon Love like a bucket of ice water. He bristled, gathered up his bag and strode to the stark, cold terminal. His only reception was worn Naugahyde and chrome chairs, neon lights, blank faces, and a few homeless sleeping out of the weather.

The night's ride from Madison, Wisconsin had been unpleasant, but Minneapolis was the end of the line for Leon. He hunched his shoulders, pulled up the collar on his denim jacket and stepped to the street.

The orange taxi dropped Leon on Zenith Avenue near the Lake Calhoun Parkway, a comfortable, tree shaded south Minneapolis neighborhood. He stood on the sidewalk, duffle bag at his feet and looked up the steps to the 1940s retrofitted rambler. The neighboring property was a strange museum-like building coupled to a parking lot, partially secluded by trees. He trudged up the stone steps to the house. Towering evergreens occupied both sides of the front yard. The house was, as his mother had described, unpretentious, well maintained. "A place where secrets had been kept," she said with a wry smile.

Small pained windows peeked out from a stonewalled basement. There was a cozy glassed front porch, a large dormer faced the front yard from the roof. The exterior trim had a warm mahogany tone to it, the stucco a creamy tan. He slipped the key into the brass lock of the oak front door.

Once inside, the place was as if someone had just stepped out for dinner. Even after two months, the last his mother had been here, he could still smell the scent of her perfume in the air. Leon dropped the duffle bag in the foyer. Like a thief stepping through the silence of other people's lives, an experience with which he had some familiarity, he began to look into the rooms, searching for answers.

• • •

In Manitowoc, Wisconsin, a morose middle-aged man sat alone in a room. He, too, sought answers. Pictures of a uniformed naval officer in a faded album rested on his lap. A semi-auto Colt 45 sat on the coffee table next to half empty bottle of Jim Beam, and an ashtray filled with cigarette butts. Anger, nicotine, and booze fueled a desire for vengeance.

Seven

ON SUNDAY, THE morning after Swede's funeral tufts of cumulous clouds painted an early April sky. Knox drove west from Minneapolis on I-394 in search of answers.

Beyond Archie's Bait Shop, the concrete and bustle of the interstate ends, Knox nosed his Ford Explorer into the fashionable suburban village of Wayzata. He past the quaint village theater, the old Great Northern Depot tucked along the north shoreline of Lake Minnetonka, then turned toward the lake. Jon Bass was expecting him.

Along County Road 15, mansions of the city's business moguls sprawled within acreage near the water's edge. The Packard estate, old money of an earlier day, lay hidden behind an extensive evergreen hedge. Knox stopped at an imposing wrought-iron gate anchored between stone pillars. On a pedestal, two brass plates shown a dull patina, "Manor" etched in one, "Coach House" in the other. Knox hit the buzzer for the latter.

"Yes," said the familiar baritone voice through the speaker.

"I'll have a Pepsi, two cheeseburgers and a large fry."

A short pause and static preceded an incredulous response, "What?"

"Jon, it's me, Knox."

The gate opened, and Knox idled down the lane of the peninsula toward Packard House. Like majestic sentinels, rugged oaks bordered the expansive park-like landscape accented by dogwood and lilac.

Tucked into an alcove of towering ash at the end of the drive sat a long two-story, wedge-shaped Tudor style estate house. Its slate roof, green shutters, and ivy vines were evocative of another era when old money was kept well.

Knox continued beyond the portico of the manor, and rolled across the cobblestones as the drive looped to the coach house, the residence of Jon and Florida Bass. Adjacent to their downstairs kitchen was the garage. Formally stables, the garage long ago had sheltered fancy coaches, and wheel grease only to be replaced by a Lincoln Limo, the latest Jaguar sedan and convertible, polishing rags and carnauba wax.

Bass, wearing a yellow windbreaker, chino trousers, and broad smile under a golf cap waited at the garden gate. "I'll Pepsi your ass, Bub."

"Brunch at ten you said."

Bass laughed. "It's on the table, coffee, black"

Knox parked at the garden patio entrance. Evident at the base of the basket-weave fence, freshly turned soil awaited planting of the season's new annuals.

Inside, Florida Bass set out a plate of scrambled eggs, biscuits, and sausage. Amusement on her face, and a twinkle in her eye, Florida was a plucky, thin, black woman with graying hair pulled back into a bun. A Packard Corporation retiree, she had become Mrs. Packard's private secretary.

"Hello, Knox," she said. "It's so nice to see you again."

"Florida," said Knox, who gave her peck on the cheek.

The coffee sat waiting. "I've put together a brunch for you. Jon, of course, has his own diet." She nodded at the table. A bowl of applesauce, and a glass of prune juice sat next to a dish with toast and orange marmalade. She wrinkled her nose and teasingly whispered just loud enough for her husband to hear. "It's a bowel thing."

Bass stepped into the kitchen from the mudroom feigning his irritation at her disclosure. "Florida, someone put a bullet through your gizzard, you'd have a bowel thing, too. Now give me a kiss and be on your way."

Florida looked at Knox with a smile and a shrug. "You have a lot to talk about. If you'll excuse me, I have to meet with Mrs. Packard at the main house."

"Thank you," said Knox. Florida kissed her husband on the cheek and disappeared through the garden.

With the cheerful banter, a stab of remembrance cut through Knox. The lively teasing, it was the same with he and Lara.

"Have a seat, Knox." Bass pointed to the chair on the other side of the small oval table. "Dig in."

Knox pulled himself from his thoughts of Lara. He noticed an unmistakable wince as Bass pulled his chair up to the prune juice, applesauce and marmalade toast.

"That slug still got you down?" Knox asked.

Bass shook his head in disgust. "Twice in Vietnam, then thirty years on the job and I had to retire to get hit again." He took a sip of juice then looked again at Knox.

"At Swede's funeral, you asked about Leyland."

Knox put down his fork, eager to hear about the man who haunted his nights. "So, who the hell was he?"

"A man with two lives until his time ran out. About ten years ago the Admiral brought him on board to manage the company's air charter business."

"You mean PacAir near the Humphrey Air Terminal?

"Yes. He found Leyland in Fort Lauderdale, Florida, managing an airfreight operation that services the Caribbean. Leyland and the Admiral had a history, old Navy."

Knox sipped his coffee. "So what happened?"

"A year ago, there were a couple of sexual harassment allegations made against Leyland. The Admiral asked me to investigate."

"At Leyland's age, you sure it wasn't an overdose of Viagra."

"Well, chuckled Bass, "the harassment cases were settled quietly, to avoid corporate embarrassment. However, Leyland's forays into getting his johnson polished were the least of it."

Knox arched a brow. "Booze, broads and gambling, the trifecta of transgressions."

Bass waved his hand over the table. "The precursors to those is disloyalty, an equally worse corporate sin. Like the calm before a typhoon, Admiral Packard, ordered an audit."

"Just a wild guess," said Knox. "PacAir was short?"

"About five-hundred thousand, short," Bass replied.

"That's a hell-of-a-lot-a Franklins, not to mention some serious slammer time," said Knox as he finished his meal.

"Agreed. But with Packard, it was less about the money, more about betrayal."

Knox leaned back in his chair. "But, not betrayed enough to prosecute the bastard?"

"Well," said Bass. "In the business, justice comes in other forms."

"Such as?"

"The Admiral cleaved Leyland's ass from his assets."

Knox cocked his head. "The Admiral got revenge?"

"Restitution is the operative corporate terminology."

"How operative?"

"Michael Packard, the Admiral's son and CFO, and Raymond Warren, Chief Legal Counsel, took Leyland's Minneapolis and Fort Lauderdale condos, and his stock investments."

"A big hit for a man with Leyland's lifestyle."

Most of it was leveraged, but it got his attention. In the end, he got a get-out-of-jail-free card, a five-digit bank account, no job and a used Beemer."

"That's not all Leyland got, Skipper."

"How's that?"

"He got motive."

Bass pushed away from the table. "Come on, Knox. We need some atmosphere."

In a grove near the lake, a fifty-foot limestone watchtower punched through a canopy of cedars. Large metal hinges creaked as Bass pulled open the oak door. The smell of damp, metallic oil-like odors filled the air as Knox and Bass stepped into a metal-grilled cage. With the push of a button the lift shuddered and rose.

Amused. "Sometimes we make it. Sometimes we don't," said Bass.

Knox held tight to a metal rail. "Let's bet on the former."

The lift jerked upward and shuttered to a stop at the top of the tower. Bass opened the door and the two stepped onto a wrought-iron railed platform above the treetops. A breeze brushed Knox's face as a squadron of sailboats flitted through a light swell

"Hell of a view," said Knox.

Bass surveyed the lake as it spread east toward Spirit Island. "I come here sometimes, when things close in."

Yeah, thought Knox without reply. Things like the death of Neil Wallace, allegations of improper use of deadly force, a grand jury, and the prospects of a federal civil rights investigation—winds that swirled with dark karma.

After a long silence, Knox took a breath. "I'm scared, Jon. My whole life seems to be going down the shitter over the shooting."

Bass turned to Knox, a stern look on his lean, dark face. "Shit happens in a shootout, Bub. Don't take the fall for some misguided interpretations of procedure and help the system flush you down the shitter. Leyland killed Swede, shot me, and tried to kill you. *He* made the call."

Knox looked out at the lake and sighed. "There were ballistics tests, Skipper."

"What about them?"

"The bullet fragments from the second round I fired were found in Wallace. My round killed Wallace."

"Son-of-a-bitch. That is a problem," said Bass passing a hand through his gray, wiry hair. "Who else knows?"

"Guzman, and Meuer from Forensics. By now, the Chief, Krieg and IAU must have the reports. I've been through this before. The job is just not worth it anymore."

Bass looked across the water and spoke almost as if Knox were not there. "So, you think there's a fuckin' choice? Take a walk, and it goes away, an errant round in a shootout? You didn't intend to shoot Wallace, and Leyland couldn't kill you when he had the chance, so you're gonna let him do it now? You're gonna let some lecherous drunken thief come back from the grave and take your badge, take your life? You have to get junk-yard-dog-mean about this, Knox, and damn well get through it."

For more than a week, the mind-game emotions had run the gamut from profound guilt over Swede and Wallace's death, to self-pity, to anger. Perhaps the Skipper was right. Anger had sustained him in the search for Lara's killer. Maybe it was the ticket to get him through the Wallace investigation?

"I know what you're saying, Skipper. But the waiting, not knowing when or what's going to happen..."

Bass stood silent for a moment. "You take one day at a time, Bub. That's what you do." Then he turned and stepped toward the lift, but stopped.

"We each have our burdens to carry over this mess," said Bass. "I should have followed up on Leyland when we fired him, but other things needed attention, and I let it go. That's what I struggle with over this whole god damned thing. The deaths, and those who were injured that may have been prevented. It takes everyday for me to get past that."

The sanctuary that overlooked the bay, a place Bass went when things closed in, was now a place where Knox found he was not alone.

The sun peeked out through the gray sky. The wind stiffened from the west. Knox turned to follow Bass, but looked back. Across the bay, sailboats slipped across the water toward their anchorage. Knox wondered if he and Bass would ever find their own safe harbor.

Eight

After a dinner and conversation with Jon and Florida Bass, darkness fell like a fleece blanket over the western suburbs. Knox relaxed behind the wheel of his sage-green Explorer and headed back to Minneapolis. He rumbled along Wayzata's main street, past lights that glittered from the quaint community theater marquee. A bluesy country rendition, "Have A Little Faith In Me," flowed from the CD. Delbert McClinton squeezed out the lyrics through a raw honky-tonk throat. "When the road gets dark and you can no longer see—have a little faith in me..."

Although the music stabbed at the melancholy that simmered deep inside, strangely, Knox felt comfort in the words.

Unexpectedly, a call came up on his cell phone. Knox picked the cell from the passenger seat.

"Knox," he said as he watched the pedestrians passing in front of him from the theater.

"You the man looking for...?" said the voice with a deep resonance, male, black maybe, and hesitant. Knox, caught unaware, listened through a long pause.

"You lookin' for the man who run down a lady?" The words and tone slow, deliberate, not so much a question as a statement. Not any man, but *the* man, said the voice. The caller sounded as if he knew something that Knox could not ignore.

Knox swerved into the Olsen Bakery parking lot. Headlights panned across the railroad tracks and onto the Lake Minnetonka shoreline. He stopped against a parking curb with a jolt, and nearly dropped the phone.

"Yeah, I'm the man," said Knox.

In the background, Aretha Franklin cranked out, "R-E-S-P-E-C-T," on a juke. A billiard shot broke across a table amid boisterous laughter. "I maybe have somethin', 'bout that lady."

For weeks the homicide squad, Knox, and Swede had called in debts, squeezed informants, and worked every other source to find Lara's killer. Silence and frustration were the only outcome. Now, a voice, a shot from the dark, provided hope.

"I'd like to hear what you have to say."

"What I got, maybe worth something," said the voice.

"Could be, but I… I missed the name," said Knox, fishing for a handle he could put to the mysterious voice.

"Names not imp-o-tant. What I have maybe is?"

Knox knew the routine, cash in trade for information, more often bullshit than fact. Even if it were bullshit, it was the only play that now remained.

"I'd make it worth your while. Depends on what you have."

"I dunno, man."

Knox took a breath, trying to restrain the tension that tightened his throat. He needed to play this out, prevent his only lead from becoming a hang-up call.

Get control. Reel him in, Knox told himself.

"You've checked me out, didn't you?"

"Yeah, the word is you be lookin' for this guy."

He said it again. Not *a* guy, but *this* guy. Knox took another breath.

"People said you could trust me, didn't they?" Knox asked.

"Yeah, but people are thinkin' maybe you did Doctah Wallace, too."

"People who weren't there don't know the facts."

There was another long pause, the man with the voice thinking things through.

"Look," said Knox. "If you're jammed up with the cops, or need something to get you by, I can work that out. You know how this kind of thing works, right?"

"Yeah," said the caller, a hint of uncertainty in his inflection.

"You be lookin' for a blue Dodge pickup that killed the lady."

Knox closed his eyes. The caller knew. Forensics did find blue paint on Lara's coat, and headlight fragments from the scene linked to a late model Dodge truck. But, the caller could have read that in the paper. After weeks of pounding the pavement, Knox had nothing else. With this guy, he had to roll the dice.

"Okay, man. We can do this, tonight," said Knox.

"I can't be seen talkin' to no po-lice."

So, what's new? Thought Knox. No one likes to talk to cops. He glanced at his watch, thought quickly, deciding on familiar terrain within a neighborhood where the informant would feel comfortable.

"Boom Island at the Plymouth Avenue Bridge, you know the place?" Knox asked.

"Yeah, I know."

"Ten-o'clock at the lighthouse parking lot."

There was another long pause. "Okay, man. I'll be there."

"I need to know whom I'm meeting," said Knox, still probing for a name, wondering about a set up, people thinking he'd done Wallace, like the caller said.

"I'll know *you*, Mistah Knox."

The call ended. With a glimmer of hope, Knox stared out the window, the lake still in his headlights. "I'll know you, Mistah Knox."

Knox pulled off the Plymouth Avenue Bridge onto Sibley, a side street that bordered Boom Island. Cleared of decades of abandoned industrial buildings, and a stark contrast to the mid-1800s log booms and derricks, the erstwhile island formed a park with light house and a boat launch, part of the city's riverfront revitalization.

Near the dead end on Seventh and Ramsey, Knox parked in the shadows amid the neighborhood of sleepy wood framed houses. The location provided a vantage point to view the island's parking lot. He was fifteen minutes early, time to provide himself an upper hand, watch the traffic cross the Plymouth Avenue Bridge.

Knox took a set of 10x50 Nikons from his go-bag, and looked into the night toward the river. The waterfront lighthouse beacon cast a pale glow through a light fog. A lone rusted Chevy sat near the sea wall, two figures inside.

Knox sat, waited and wondered. Who is this guy? Mistah Knox and Doctah Wallace, a kind of Baton Rouge down south drawl. It may be a set up to even the score for what happened to Wallace. Whatever, he thought. I'm rolling with it.

Mischievous, youthful laughter echoed from the Chevy parked under the lights. Knox brought up the glasses, a momentary crash of beer bottles to pavement. The car engine raced as the old wreck screeched across the lot onto Plymouth Avenue and out of sight.

The sound of parkway traffic formed a backdrop to an edgy calm of the empty lot. The voice on the phone was late. Like many cold tips, Knox began to feel he held the black marble on this one, too. Waiting was the detective's curse. There were always informants that fail to show, arrests that seldom go down as planned, and the endless hours of surveillance that dulled the senses in the dreary darkness.

Knox felt the drain of anticipation as the clock wound past ten. Stay or go. Krieg's warning, "Don't let your grief get in the way of the job...there may be repercussions." Fuck Krieg, and his repercussions.

Knox let the window down, the cool damp air, low forties, kept him alert. For the tenth time, a glance at his watch told him the night was passing him by. It was now ten thirty. He sighed.

Moments later, an old gray pickup caught his attention. It drove slowly, too slowly along the Plymouth Avenue Bridge. Knox trained the Nikons on the truck. Its right signal blinked for the turn at the gate.

The pickup rolled to a stop under a light pole. In the cargo box sat a gray plywood camper with a door where once had been a tailgate.

Knox felt the beat of his heart, more rapid now. The brake lights flashed, the driver's door creaked open then slammed shut. The clunk of metal on metal resonated across the vacant landscape. A large man in a ball cap and heavy jacket strode to the sidewalk. He stopped and turned his head, assessing his surroundings. After a moment, the lighthouse beacon backlit a silhouette of the figure who plodded toward the river into the night mist. The man with the voice had arrived—alone.

Knox drove onto Plymouth Avenue, and turned through the Boom Island gate. Still wary of a set up, he parked across the lane from the pickup. He eyeballed the structure in the cargo box, took down the license number, checked his surroundings.

With a wince of pain in his ribs, Knox got out of the Explorer and held a .9-mm Beretta at ready along his right thigh. He approached the truck, searching his surroundings, tugged at a tarnished padlock and found the door of the windowless camper secure. A quick flash with a penlight revealed the truck cab, empty. About thirty yards along the walkway a hulk of a man leaned against the seawall rail. Knox approached, and the figure half turned.

Watch the hands. A caution obeyed too late for Swede only a week ago. Knox pushed the notion from his mind, the Beretta now covertly tucked in the right pocket of his jacket.

The figure leaned, empty handed, against the balustrade.

Knox paused, assessing the stillness, the movement of the river pulled a haze of fog downstream. He padded forward, hand clutching the Beretta. "You called, about a pickup truck," he said to the man in the mist.

The man straightened, arms now hung at his sides. "Mistah Knox," said the voice, an inflection thick as Louisiana gumbo.

Knox stepped closer. The illumination from the lighthouse revealed the full stature of the black man, at least six-foot-four, strong build, broad shoulders, and hands the size of a catcher's mitt.

"Thanks for meeting me," said Knox, easing into a conversation through which objectives, credibility, motivation, and perhaps a quid pro quo could be determined. For an informant, a little rapport took the edge from snitching off a killer. Ordinarily for Knox it was a basic game of finesse, verbal cat and mouse. That process now became very personal, urgency replaced finesse to find Lara's killer.

The two men leaned onto the balustrade. Cold and swift, impervious to the life and death struggles along its banks, the Mississippi ran past Boom Island, rushed down the spillways of Saint Anthony Falls, and wound its way among the bluffs of the Twin Cities.

The big man looked across the moving water, as if Knox hadn't uttered a word, their frosted breaths sent adrift with the current of the river.

"Bein' here ain't so easy, suh."

"How's that?"

"I come here to find work."

"Where from?"

"Louisiana."

"What kind of work you do?"

"Carpenter. Good at my trade, too. My cousin, he introduced me to a man who was lookin' for some help. Remodlin' old places and such?"

"Yeah, I've done that sort of thing, myself, on my own place." Knox worked the rapport, knowing he had to search for a reason for the man to give up what he had.

The man stared at the water, displayed a quiet, wary countenance, but not the manner of your garden-variety violator turned informant. Trust in cops didn't come easy where this guy had come from, which might explain the strained expression on the big man's face. Or, was it something else? Whatever the case, Knox began to help the man give up what he had.

"You are?" Knox asked, needing a personal touch to the dance of give and take.

"James is my name," said the man with a casual glance toward Knox.

Not Jim or Jimmy, but James, said with character, thought Knox. "This thing you want to tell me, James, it's been bothering you awhile?"

James let out a sigh of resignation, "The man I'm talkin' about, he gave me a job. He helped me get a place, paid me for my work. I'm savin' to bring Larise, that's my woman, up from Bogalusa. The man, he done right by me. But, he done wrong, too, Mistah Knox."

The door opened. "Who's the man, James? How'd he do you wrong?"

With a gush of frosted breath came the name, "Nichols." Like a thorn pulled from his side. "The man, his name is Dale Nichols," said James.

Maintain the momentum. "Where's he live?" The question snapped quickly.

"Monroe Street, near Logan Park and the railroad tracks." James uttered. "Dale got the pickup I told you 'bout. He called me one night, late. Said to pick him up in the mornin', so's we could finish a job. Said his truck broke down."

Finally, Knox had what he wanted. He felt a pounding impatience to wade through the maze of records and put a face, an address, to the man who had killed Lara. He envisioned himself slamming through the front door of the house on Monroe Street. He could feel his hands lock around the neck of Dale Nichols. Before the bastard could take a breath, he'd make Nichols dance the rubber chicken, like a man at the end of a gallows rope.

The ill-fated fantasy vanished as quickly as it had appeared. He'd been too long on the job for that kind of satisfaction. As a cop, he needed more.

The tone now conciliatory, "Tell me what happened, James," The big man's shoulders hunched against the cold, and he began to unravel his story.

"I picked up Dale in the mornin', a Friday. I know, cause he owed me money for the week. He been up all night, smelled real bad. He been drinkin'. Dale, he got a bad drinkin' problem. He can be unpredictable, like a bomb. Know what I mean? After we been workin' a while, I ask him bout the truck. He got real mad."

Knox watched his quarry turn and lean his back into the sea wall rail. His huge hands thrust deep into his coat pockets, he looked up at the lighthouse, a deep breath turned to frost. James was about to rid himself of his drunken benefactor.

"Dale, he come at me with a hammer, stinkin' drunk and all. 'You dumb fuckin' nigger,' he said. 'I hit a lady with the truck last night,' he said. If I told anyone, I'd be a *dead* fuckin' nigger. I grabbed the hammer from Dale and I hit him real hard with my fist, knocked him down, bad. I took what money he had, him not paying me and all, and I left him. I ain't seen him again."

The rest came easy. As James spoke, Knox logged the mental notes. Dale Nichols, alcoholic white male, thirty-six years-old, sandy hair, hangout saloon, The Old Northern Bar. Jobs worked, a description of his house and garage followed.

With what James said, Knox was certain there would be a paper trail among a labyrinth of police records. As for James, he'd just given up his meal ticket. Just the same, Knox waited for the quid pro quo. Informants aren't motivated out of a sense of civic duty. More common it's revenge, fear or greed. Everyone wants something for cooperation, the cops, and the perps.

Knox wrinkled his brow and narrowed his gaze. "What are you looking for out of this, James?"

"I dunno know no more. I thought 'bout money, maybe to bring Larise up here. But Dale, he killed that lady. He called me a fuckin' nigger, Mistah Knox. None a that just ain't right."

"You're doing the right thing now. We can work something out."

James paced back and forth a few steps then turned back toward Knox. "I can't be writtin' no statements, or testifyin' in no court."

The look on James's face said he didn't want to answer the next question.

"You got trouble in Louisiana?"

The big man brushed a hand across his face. "I can't be goin' back there. I hit a white man, like Dale. Put him in a hospital. He was goin' after Larise in a dance hall parkin' lot. I told the Bog-lusa po-lice what happened. So'd Larise. But they say witnesses told 'em different. They say they be gettin' a warrant after me. That's when I come here."

The story would not take long to verify. What mattered now was Lara's killer. From his wallet, Knox fished out a twenty and a five. He reached his hand out to James. "Take this on account. It's all I have with me. That's until I can check out what you told me."

The big man looked at the bills, tucked them into his coat pocket.

"Thank you, suh. I can use the money. By the way, you go sneekin' 'round Dale's place, you be careful. There's a big junkyard dog, too," said James. "The dog's name is Ajax, and he likes creepin' up on people."

Knox smiled and reached out to close the deal. He felt the vice-like grip of the big man's calloused hand, two strangers linked by an uncertain trust, twenty-five dollars and a skittish conscience.

Knox began to walk off when the Bogalusa carpenter called after him.

"Mistah Knox, that lady, I can tell, she meant somethin' to you."

"Yeah, James. She does."

Nine

James's epiphany at the river, revelations Knox had prayed for, commenced a paper chase for an identity and a face. A simple Google inquiry, and a listing in the Minneapolis phone directory preceded a two-hour scurry through the maze of police and sheriff's computer records. Knox pursued his quest with a hunter's instinct, and the determination of a homicide cop to move through the night to catch his wife's killer.

From the printer in the homicide unit, Knox pealed off hard copies of city, state, traffic, and vehicle records. A chance encounter with a nightshift juvenile detective resulted in a youthful offender rap sheet. At the sheriff's office, a clerk handed Knox past warrant and arrest data. Now possessing a history of Nichols's wasted life, Knox pulled into an all night stop-and-rob on Central Avenue. He bought two pounds of deli-meat, a bottle of corn syrup, and a coffee to go.

At Seventeenth Avenue and Monroe, Knox rolled to a stop near the rail yard, a neighborhood of old clapboard sided homes. The dashboard clock read 1:30 A.M. He rubbed his eyes, raw and tired from sixteen hours on the go. After a few gulps of coffee, he was good to go for another hour or so.

Knox groaned. Even the anticipation of what he had to do had not dulled the throb at the back of his head, and alternated with that in his ribs and sternum. Although he yearned for a hot shower, a shot of Crown Royal, cigar and some sleep, the night compelled him to endure. He opened the driver's window of the Explorer. A waft of fresh air flowed into his space, reviving his senses.

A streetlight provided enough illumination to digest the miserable history of Dale Allen Nichols. The rap sheets read like a train wreck in progress. Knox's gut churned as he tried to comprehend the disturbing details of the reprobate's background.

At thirty-six, Nichols's litany of arrests painted a dismal picture of the loser on a collision course with fate. Youthful drug possessions had progressed into scores of property crimes, and disorderly conduct and assaults. From the age of fifteen, both state, and county confinement systems had been second homes for Nichols. Knox read on, puzzled by the DMV data.

There was no listing for a Dodge pickup.

Nichols's driver's license history was a table of contents to the Minnesota traffic violations code. Knox searched the pages, coming to the last dated entry.

Son-of-a-bitch!

At the time he killed Lara, Nichols's license to drive was revoked! And, he had served only six months on his fifth DUI conviction, yet there were no warrants on Nichols.

Dale Allen Nichols had been a nightmare in the revolving door of the criminal justice system, a system where too often criminals become a routine acceptance, while victims become victimized again. Knox felt the pain in his body pulse with rage. His vision, Nichols dancing the rubber chicken at the end of a rope, didn't seem all that wrong.

Knox thrust back his head in despair, *Lara's life, snubbed out by this fucking loser.*

Knox unwrapped the package of meat, mixed in a few ounces of corn syrup, and one of Doctor Payne's little tickets to dreamland.

The acrid smell of creosote, a coal tar preservative for rail timbers, drifted into the neighborhood at the edge of the rail yard, and down the alley of Monroe Street. In the faint light of a shrouded half moon, Knox crept cautiously through the shadows of the ally. He stopped at Nichols's garage, the address confirmed by the police records, and description provided by James.

A ragged hedge and rusted wire fence abutted the garage. Knox unbuttoned his jacket, the .9-mm Beretta hung ready in its shoulder holster.

The garage was a blistered khaki painted structure that sat at the rear of a battered, two-story, clapboard hovel. The house appeared as unkempt and bankrupt as the life of Nichols who lived within its walls. Beyond the fence, bare branches of a large maple spread over the back yard. The decayed hulk of a faded yellow Oldsmobile squatted on flattened tires, body consumed by rust.

Next to the Olds, a snowmobile, minus its runners hunkered on a trailer with one wheel. In another corner of the yard rested the hulk of a battered Chevy panel truck. Draped with naked vines, it lay near a pile of rotted lumber. Lumps of dog feces and beer cans littered the ground near the back porch. There should be a sign, thought Knox, Landscape by Urban Gloom and Doom LLC.

Except for the far off noises of the rail yard, a lone switch engine, and boxcars that slammed into iron couplings, the night was quiet.

Through a drawn shade, second floor rear of the house revealed the flicker of a TV light. Perhaps a late night rerun, "This Old Dump."

Knox checked his watch, 1:45 A.M., and slipped on a pair of latex gloves then crept to the passageway door of the garage. Plywood covered the window. He inserted the lock-pick tines into the tumblers of the doorknob, and froze. A low, menacing growl resonated from behind. The sound told him not to move.

Ajax!

Slowly, Knox turned his head. The eighty-pound bone crusher glared through a break in the leafless hedge. Its lips quivered, lethal teeth flashed in the dull moonlight. The thought of K-9 fangs clamped to his neck compelled Knox to assess his options. Behind door number one, lose an arm or leg to Ajax the man-eater. Behind door number two, risk your career by breaking and entering without a warrant to confirm who killed your wife. Door three, leave without proof.

Knox took a breath, reached into his pocket and lobbed the two-pound blend of barbiturate-laden beef over the hedge.

From the shadows behind him, Knox heard the ravenous gulps. He quickly manipulated a set of lock-picks, and turned the handle; door number two, confirm who killed my wife.

Inside the garage, he breathed a sigh of relief having evaded the peril that still may await his exit. Within the dark surroundings, the smells of motor oil, gasoline, and rotting wood assailed his senses. Illuminated by his penlight, his breath hung frost-like in the air. In the dank shadows, Knox saw what James had described. A truck body loomed under the drape of a paint-spattered tarp.

Knox stepped carefully over the scatter of tools, past a rusted stove, car parts and stopped dead at the side of the shrouded truck. His cold fingers raised the tarp. A deep oblique dent ran across the dark blue left front fender, the impact of Lara's body. Fiber abrasions from her coat had scarfed the paint. Closer, his eye trained on the housing of the broken headlight. Imbedded in a metal seam three faint strands of red hair fluttered with the movement of his breath. In his hand the light quivered.

Transfixed by that infinitesimal part of her, Knox could still here the echo of that fateful radio call in his ear. On DuPont Avenue North, he and Swede had cleared a suicide detail, heading in for reports.

"Any squad," broadcast the dispatcher. "Pedestrian down, hit and run Fourth and Hennepin." He and Swede heard squads from the Downtown Command respond. A cold sweat came over him.

Only twenty minutes before, Knox had talked with Lara by phone. She had finished teaching her law class at the old Masonic building. It was one of those cozy winter nights, gossamer snowflakes fluttered through the still air. She wanted to walk home across the Hennepin Avenue Bridge and wait up for him.

"General Ambulance and fire/rescue en route," the dispatcher announced. Swede and Knox responded, instinctively. In the car, a dreaded silence filled the space between them. The "pedestrian down," could it be Lara?

Emergency lights pierced the evening sparkle of the Hennepin Avenue entertainment district as Knox and Lundgren rolled onto the scene. Theater and bar crowds clustered on the sidewalks, the body in the street a vicarious curiosity.

Inside Nichols's garage, the dark closed around Knox. He stood silent, body numb to the vivid slow motion re-wind of the event that wound through his thoughts.

The glitter of nightclub and theater marquis', the whirl of flashing emergency lights dappled the street, police radio chatter echoed off the buildings. Grim-faced cops, firemen and an EMS crew stood silent. Under a gray blanket, death lay crumpled in the shreds of a Kelly-green coat.

Gripped by the dread of finding what he hoped was not there, Knox rushed forward and knelt at the body. A small, bloodied hand with a torn glove protruded from under the covering. Gently, Knox reached out, the hand cold in his grasp. He trembled with frightful anticipation, wiped away the blood to find a wedding ring, *her* ring.

Slowly, Knox pulled away the blanket. Wide with terror, Lara's still eyes looked up through the bloodied trauma, her once beautiful face, nearly unrecognizable. In horror, Knox collapsed to winter's grit-soiled street and cried out her name—"Laraaaa!"

In the dank garage, that scream echoed in his ear. The image of her tore at his soul. The smell of gasoline, the shrouded hulk before him, the instrument of her death, brought him back to where he was, and what he needed to do. "Get on with it. Get out, or lose it all," he whispered.

With one last look at what ended Lara's life, Knox wrote down the serial number from the doorframe, exposed the front license plate, and noted the number. From a window on the overhead door, he brushed away a portion of dust. His work done, Knox peeked out the side door. In the moonlit rubble of the yard, a quick glance revealed Ajax in a fetal-like slumber. Near the back porch, the four-legged menace reposed amid empty beer cans and dog shit.

Knox slipped from the garage, and hustled into the night.

Ten

AT 8:00 A.M., Chief Thom Ballard entered his office on the second floor of City Hall, the 19th century rose-granite citadel of Minneapolis political power. He hung his topcoat on the corner rack, strode to the window and looked out across Fifth Street. To the right, the Packard Center, a tower of commercial enterprise, the scene of what occupied Ballard's morning. Across the broad plaza, in the towering Hennepin County Government Center, the county attorney, grand juries, and the courts meted out justice; it was where the Packard investigation would conclude. Between now and then, the public's view of Ballard's own accountability and that of the department weighed heavily upon him. The city demanded answers to the shootings, specifically, an accounting for the death of Neil Wallace. Already, protestors were in the streets to prompt those answers.

The week-old investigation had eclipsed Ballard's daily routine, police divisions doggedly worked to complete their tasks, reports and coordination routed through his office. However, the impatient court of public opinion remained suspicious of that effort. With Neil Wallace dead, a jungle telegraph of cover-up rumors rustled through the city, the unrelenting media smelled blood in the water.

Protests grew loudest among those of the inner city; a place where homicide investigations, and Ballard's community policing policy had played a roll that significantly reduced the spiral of violent crime. Liberal and minority community elements, as well as the media gave only cautious support for Ballard's pragmatic crime-fighting efforts. Now, he had been compelled to cancel leaves, place uniformed personnel on twelve-hour shifts, and heighten the alert status of special operations units.

Ballard watched the protestors on the street below, lamenting that all his careful work, building community alliances had vanished. The death of Neil Wallace accentuated the reactionary voices of discontent. The loudest, and most uninformed of those voices carried the day.

Ballard remembered a refrain from long ago. *To cry outrage is easy. To find solutions requires courage. In the end, outrage sells more papers.*

For a lifeline, to help calm the ferment of public tension, Ballard turned to Jack Griffin, the Hennepin County Attorney, and to William Flynn, the Director of the Minnesota Bureau of Criminal Apprehension (MBCA).

Already caretaker of the preliminary Packard ballistics information, Ballard hoped that the efforts of his two colleagues would buy time for further investigation, and for the city to become more composed where cooler heads could prevail.

He grasped the window ledge, thinking through the circumstances that had the potential to ignite the city. A demented gunman, and a damning ballistics report would strike the match. Not being satisfied with explanations founded in fact, the emotions of rabble-rousers, and city politics required an urgent accountability of the department.

That accountability, to avert public disorder, brought into question the destiny of homicide veteran Harding Knox, a fate that may be out of Ballard's hands. More disturbing would be ordering his personnel into lawless streets. His decision to out-source the Packard investigation, he hoped, would buy enough time to confirm facts, and avoid chaos in the city.

The phone rang. "Ballard," he said, irritated by the interruption.

"Good morning, Thom. Barbara Bergin. Is this a bad time?"

"Oh, I have a few things on my mind, Mayor."

"We probably share the same concerns. My office, say ten minutes?"

"Of course, I assume it's about my meeting yesterday."

"Yes, I'd like to hear how things went with the state, and Jack Griffin."

Ballard's footsteps echoed along the broad, marble corridor until he reached the oak and glass double doors. The gold embossed letters glistened on the glass below the seal of the city—Office of the Mayor, Barbara Bergin.

Duane Straight, the mayor's executive assistant, greeted Ballard at the door. His gender preference, Ballard knew, was other than his name implied.

"Nice of you to come right over, Chief. I'll show you in."

"Thanks, Duane. I know the way," said Ballard.

Hand outstretched, Mayor Bergin rose from behind her desk to greet the chief. A broad-shouldered, vigorous woman, in high heels she stood as tall as Ballard. Her stylish auburn hair framed a strong-featured face, dark eyebrows, tastefully applied makeup. She wore a conservative navy blue skirt, jacket and white blouse. There was a pleasant, subtle citrus-like scent about her, a trademark Neiman Marcus scarf on her shoulder. Behind the pleasant smile there was no question, Mayor Bergin's concerns were eternally political.

At the mayor's suggestion, Ballard stepped to the side chairs near the window, and turned down an invitation for coffee.

The early-morning light, deflected through the office blinds, cast the Mayor of Minneapolis in a light that took the edge off her usual intensity.

"I've spent all yesterday on the phone, Thom; the Urban League, University of Minnesota, local and national media and Minnesota Public Radio. Of course, the usual New York, and Chicago activists have chimed in. Progress on the Packard investigation is what they want. More to the point, who killed Neil Wallace?"

"I've had similar calls, some more profane than others."

"I shouldn't have to remind you," said Bergin, "of what's at stake here, and I need more disclosure to the public. In a few weeks, I go before the State Democratic Convention. I need the Party's gubernatorial endorsement. And, I have every intention of getting it. 'We have to keep the trolley on the tracks,' as my father used to say, keep the city from coming apart."

The mayor was fond of her father's political axioms. In the 1950s, Theodore Bergin had been a city councilman, state senator, and aspiring Democratic candidate for governor. The party had turned their back on him. The state was not ready for a Jewish governor. Barbara was determined to right that wrong. Cautious of political motivations, Ballard had his own axiom: *Corrupted by the power they seek, politicians come and go. Beware they don't take you with them.*

An early stint in the U.S. Marines had taught him grit and determination. Chicago PD had left him with a pragmatic approach to navigate the complexities of crime and politics. Loyola University provided an education in the rule of law, all attributes he needed to bring to bear on the Neil Wallace crises.

"Your meeting yesterday," Bergin said; "how are the county attorney and the state crime bureau prepared to help?"

"They give us time to complete a comprehensive investigation, time for facts to be viewed rationally, time for public emotions to settle," said Ballard.

"Perhaps you can explain that for me. Time is never a favorable characteristic of public emotion."

"I understand, Barbara. But truth has to be the end result of finding fact, and that is our goal, not an emotional rush to judgment. The BCA will manage the investigation with the county attorney's office in a combined task force. The findings will go to an impartial county grand jury, detached from any police department influence."

Bergin nodded. "How about momentum, Thom?" She arched an eyebrow. "Protestors are at City Hall and the Government Center, and I have the Rochester convention scheduled."

"I intend to conclude before your convention."

"That would be helpful, of course. However, the risk I take is with the razzle-dazzle of Jack Griffin. He already has the Republican gubernatorial endorsement. Assuming

I get the Democratic support, he'll be my opponent in November. At the same time, we can't afford to have the lid come off the city."

"I understand, and Jack Griffin's office is sensitive to the concerns of unrest."

"I know, but I don't like it," Bergin said. "Griffin will use that authority as a grandstand opportunity to influence the election."

"Griffin's office is unavoidable. By law, Jack is responsible to present the case before the grand jury. Ultimately, that is where this must end up."

Ballard had waltzed through the legal issues with Griffin, and Flynn the previous afternoon. Now Bergin had to come to terms with the will of law, accepting legal precedence over the vanity of politics.

"Griffin consented to bring in an independent prosecutor, Barbara. It's in his best interest. He's smart enough to know that his credibility, as well as his office is on the line. The public will smell a rat if there is any grandstanding."

"I can't afford to be that naïve. Everything is political, Thom." Bergin sighed, stared out the window for a moment then turned toward Ballard. "Okay, deferring this to a task force, I suppose is the best option. But, the moment Griffin brings this into the political arena, he'll live to regret it."

"Fine, I'll keep you informed, Barbara, but we need to schedule a press conference in this regard." said Ballard who waited for her reply.

Bergin tilted her head. "Yes, I agree about the presser, meanwhile there is the matter of Sergeant Knox?"

Ballard felt a circumspect brown-eyed gaze fall upon him. By the tone of her question about Knox, Ballard knew she was a move ahead of him on her political chessboard. Harding Knox was to become a sacrificial pawn.

"He's still on convalescent and administrative leave. What are your concerns?"

"Commander Krieg and I had a visit," said Bergin, her face void of expression. "We're old friends from the ward, my city council days. He informed me, unofficially, that bullets fired from the sergeant's gun not only killed Thomas Leyland, but Neil Wallace as well. Is that true?"

Ballard could not tolerate end runs by staff to politicians. *Krieg, that son-of-a-bitch. The mayor to governor, Krieg to... what?*

"Is that true? Are you keeping this from me?" The mayor's voice, more insistent and dismayed.

There were things you kept from politicians until the information and evidence were validated, the timing right. Experience had taught Ballard that egocentric politicians blow cases, or can destroy an operation out of arrogance, or spite.

"Barbara, Krieg was out of line with that disclosure," said Ballard, firmly. "His comment was careless, and lacked perspective."

"But, he said the confirmation came from our own lab, and you did not tell me. I had to get it second hand from one of your subordinates."

Ballard leaned toward the mayor. He felt his face tense over the impromptu leak, but proceeded calmly. "I informed you at the beginning of our inquiries that a stray bullet may be a possible issue in this matter. In the circumstance of this shooting, I want absolute corroboration from the medical examiner, and state crime lab before I arrive at any findings. If the ballistic information is irrefutable, it still doesn't explain the context of how that bullet came in contact with Wallace."

Bergin was obviously not satisfied with the answer. "You know what will happen if that information is correct?"

Ballard already knew the ballistics analysis was correct, but needed time for the state and county attorney investigations to provide context to the evidence, to counter the city's scandalmongers.

"I know precisely what will happen," said Ballard. "Any premature comment can place the city further into crisis. Your position, and your political aspirations depend on the manner in which this investigation proceeds."

"It's important, Barbara, that you maintain a posture of waiting until *all* the facts are known."

Bergin leaned back, tapping a finger on the arm of her chair. "Thom, this is still very disconcerting for me, you not telling me about the ballistics."

Ballard responded quickly. "I understand, but we need to get ahead of the curve on this entire situation. That's why, after my meetings from yesterday, we schedule a press conference. I would suggest at 11:00 A.M., today. I recommend that you make the opening remarks. Update the public on our course of action with the state and the county attorney's office. Our interest is objectivity in determining fact. We discuss the process, but not the particulars of the investigation."

Bergin rose from her chair. "I'm not at all pleased with any of this. You should have come to me sooner about the ballistics details." There was a sharp impatience to her tone. "However, your suggested course with the state and Griffin's office is sensible. It's just so damn unpredictable, the media with these kinds of things. We need to be on the same page, Thom. *Both* of our careers depend on it."

The later comment was a sober reminder of who pulled the strings of power in the "Granite Citadel." Ballard let it pass, opting for a diplomatic withdrawal. "As I've outlined, a collective approach is in the best interest for all concerned."

Bergin stepped toward the window. "I trust your judgment on that. Please, make the arrangements. And, make certain I'm in the loop on any further developments."

As if confiding to herself, the mayor spoke again. There was a sober, calculating tone to her voice. "In the end there may be measures vis-à-vis Sergeant Knox that may have to be considered. Give that some thought, Thom."

Eleven

COFFEE HELPED SWEEP away the cobwebs from six hours of sleep, and the early morning foray into the junkyard life of Dale Allen Nichols. Knox dressed in crew socks, blue jeans and a sweatshirt. He rocked back in the chair of his den and erased the media messages from his phone recorder. On his desk rested the *StarTribune*. Speculation had increased community unrest about the Packard Center shootout. In spite of the mayor's task force endorsement, anxious segments of the public perceived the police investigation as a cover up; editorials eagerly fanned the flames of impatience. Dr. Neil Wallace dead, and the department had been less than candid about the investigation, and the actions of Sergeant Knox.

Knox scanned further articles and began to grasp that his career could end.

The phone rang.

"Knox, Ray Noonan here. I got your message."

Years ago, Lieutenant Noonan had supervised Knox in the hard-hitting Street Crimes Unit. Noonan had been in uniform for twenty-nine-years, and now headed the Traffic Unit, the unit now delegated to find Lara's hit-and-run killer.

"Thanks for returning the call, Ray," said Knox restraining his skepticism as to how Traffic could be anymore successful than Homicide at resolving his wife's death. However, Noonan was now the only one to whom Knox could turn.

"What's up?" said the veteran patrol lieutenant.

Knox sighed. "I think I found the guy who killed my wife."

Knox could feel the pause in Noonan's response, a delay that said Krieg would be somewhere in the loop, and that Noonan needed to evaluate that option.

"Okay, Knox. What have you got?"

"Last night, I received a call from a guy that said a mutt named Nichols admitted to running Lara down."

"You know Commander Krieg called me, Knox. He's concerned about your involvement, or rather your non-involvement in this."

"That's why I have to reach out to you."

"Your caller legit, or you think he's jerking you off?"

"What I've got pans out. I need you to work it through."

"You got a name and DOB on the guy?

"Yeah, this asshole's rap sheet that goes back to his days in diapers."

"All right, one step at a time, tell me what you have."

Knox laid out the details. Conveniently left out were the face-to-face with James at the river, and the nocturnal B & E at Nichols's garage, information that would jeopardize the investigation, deny justice he sought for Lara—for himself.

"Your alphabetical and lien registrations," said Noonan, "They show that Nichols owns a Dodge?"

"No. They show he has an old Oldsmobile and a Chevy truck. But, don't go sour on me, LT." Knox couldn't tell Noonan that he had the plate number on the Dodge, and had learned that it listed to a woman named Sandra Jean Jablonski. That information, because of how he obtained it, would void the investigation, letting Nichols walk and end Knox's career. He needed to guide Noonan to that discovery.

"I need corroboration, Knox. You know the drill."

"That's where you come in. I need three favors, and I need to trust you," said Knox, who now had to rely on their former friendship.

"I'm listening."

"Do a house-to-house in Nichols's neighborhood regarding the Dodge. Check the jail visitor records for an ex-wife, girlfriend, or any visitors who may have a Dodge pickup registered to them. Check—"

"I think we know what to check, Knox. Homicide isn't the only place where police work is done in this department."

"I don't mean to imply anything, but the only lead I have hangs on what I've just learned from my source."

"Look, Knox, I'm here to make this work, so let's not piss each other off, okay?"

"I know. It's just that—"

"It's about your wife," said Noonan, a note of sympathy in his voice. "I understand."

"Thanks LT, but I need you to handle this yourself. I need you to locate the truck. If the probable cause links back to Nichols, I'll need you to write the search warrant. Can I trust you to make that happen?"

"We're short of personnel because of the demonstrations around the court house. But, okay, you've got the house-to-house for the neighbors to confirm what we're looking for, and I'll throw myself in for the warrant. That's two favors.

"I need to be there, Ray, when the warrant goes down, when you hook up the son-of-a-bitch that killed my wife."

"That's the one, Knox, the one I'm gonna have a problem with. You're too close to this, and I can't risk something going wrong, something we both may regret."

"Ray, I need to know that it's done. It's my wife."

There was a moment of silence.

"That's the favor I gotta think about," said Noonan

"And, Krieg?" Knox said, apprehensively."

"I'd say the urgency of this demands my undivided attention," said Noonan. "Before that truck disappears, I need to set up a team, coordinate field operations, write a warrant and find a judge. I don't see any telephone time in there. Do you?"

"Thanks, Ray. I owe you for this."

"You're damn straight. Just stay loose.'

"Okay. I'll fax you what I have on Nichols."

"Fine, I'll call when we get something."

Slumped in an Adirondack chair on the back porch, Knox rubbed a hand across his bearded face. Thoughts of the Dodge truck floated through his mind. What is Sandra Jablonski's connection to Dale Nichols? What does she know about Lara's death? Noonan has to find her.

Knox breathed in the spring air, and closed his tired eyes.

Nichols has no clue. The endgame is coming, and so am I.

Twelve

The dais of the Minneapolis City Council Chambers formed the official setting to the 11:00 A.M. press conference. The large city seal hung on the chamber's wall, a backdrop to the proceedings. Attired in tan business suit and customary designer silk scarf, Mayor Bergin stood composed at the podium. Jack Griffin stood to her right, Ballard to her left. Director Flynn of the state crime bureau took a politically deferred position behind the mayor. Amid the camera lights and assemblage of reporters, the sober expression on Bergin's face corresponded to the theater of her surroundings. In command of the occasion, Bergin waited for the rustle of reporters to subside, for the flash of photo stills to end.

"Thank all of you for being here this morning," Bergin began. "In the wake of the tragic Packard Center incident, members of the Minneapolis Police Department have performed in a tireless manner. It has been a daunting task, the scope of which requires us to seek the assistance of the Minnesota Bureau of Criminal Apprehension, as well as the Hennepin County Attorney's Office. This has been an especially difficult ordeal for the families and friends of those who were lost or injured in this tragedy. Therefore, I have authorized this task force configuration to bring about a factual and complete resolution to the events."

Channel 7's Ted Harman interrupted. "Mayor, is this in response to allegations that the police department is lagging in its progress?"

Bergin gave Harman a polite nod, acquaintances from years on the political scene. "Thank you for asking, Ted, and I am aware of that concern. However, I know that the work of Chief Ballard, and the department has been extremely professional. In spite of that, we have asked for help to reassure the public of a judicious, factual and impartial disposition to this matter."

Ballard read the non-verbal feedback of the press, knowing that a curve ball question lurked somewhere within the crowd.

The mayor recognized a young, fresh-faced woman from the Minnesota Daily, the University's paper. Unexpectedly, the woman sidestepped the mayor, going instead to her political nemesis, Jack Griffin.

"Mr. Griffin," said fresh-face, "assuming that Mayor Bergin may represent the Democratic Party in November, how will the involvement of your office in this 'so called' task force impact the gubernatorial elections?"

Griffin stood six foot two, was ruggedly handsome with a charming smile and slow deliberate way of speaking. He stepped to the podium beside the mayor. It was the first time Ballard had ever seen the two of them together.

Cameras flashed from around the room, note pads, recorders at the ready; a fortuitous campaign opportunity.

Politics aside, Griffin and Bergin's physical characteristics complemented one another rather well. Yet, Ballard couldn't help but notice the mayor's discomfort, Griffin being physically in her political space. She cast an awkward smile of acknowledgement at Griffin as she relinquished her momentary command of the spotlight.

"Ladies and gentlemen," said Griffin, "the issue at hand this morning is not about politics. It is about community, about providing answers, and a resolution to the city's tragedy. It is also about the judicial application of the rule of law. In that context, it is my responsibility to provide the legal process required under the law that affords closure to this terrible circumstance."

Then, Griffin placed his hand on the mayor's forearm. "Mayor Bergin, you and the people of Minneapolis can count on me."

A strained smile creased Bergin's lips. Another place, another time, thought Ballard, and Bergin would have cold-cocked Jack Griffin right in the jaw. BCA Director Flynn took the podium. Ballard counted Flynn, the recently retired chief of the Minneapolis FBI field office, and now head of the state crime bureau, as a friend. Flynn had a penchant for the game of poker, and a reserved, calculating nature that he brought to his philosophy in fighting crime.

To Director Flynn, it was about cause and effect. You cause as much grief as required to the criminal element that, in effect, puts as many of them in jail as possible. The Irish poker player explained the BCA's task force responsibilities, and returned to his position. He played his hand. No one was going to prompt more from the ex-fed.

Ballard had insisted on a narrow focus for the press conference, to describe the configuration and objective of the task force. A response to specific questions about Neil Wallace would only add to the speculation that fermented the boiling turmoil within the city. Explain the process and get off the stage. Linger too long and risk your objective.

At the back of the room Ballard saw Bernie Floyd, an edgy political reporter from the *Star Tribune*. Floyd leaned casually against the wall. He was always in search of *the* story—a Pulitzer Prize. His pieces, provocative, his reputation tenacious, often unorthodox, his sources somehow well placed. At a press conference, reporters often deferred to his instinctive ability to ask *the* critical question.

In blue jeans, rumpled shirt, and tan sport coat, Floyd raised a hand, and shouted the curve ball Ballard had dreaded.

"Chief Ballard, I have been told, by a reliable source, that the bullet that killed Neil Wallace was fired by Sergeant Harding Knox of the Minneapolis Police Department. Can you please confirm that?"

The question, like a ninety-five mile an hour fastball hurtled toward Ballard who stood behind the podium. The forum had lingered too long.

Heads in the room swiveled from Floyd to Ballard. Again, cameras flashed while everyone waited for Ballard's counter swing. Floyd had just lit the match to a riot. Steely-eyed, Ballard leaned forward to quell the unrest.

"Bernie, I'm the only reliable source for this incident, and I have disclosed nothing to you about any corroborative details in regard to the shootings. Right now, there is no factual component with reference to your statement."

"Then, are you denying the information, Chief?"

"What I'm saying is that this is not a drive-by-fast-food investigation. Give me three innuendoes, two rumors, one reliable source, a bag of questionable facts, and a chocolate shake to go."

"That's very good, Chief," said Floyd with a smirk on his face. However, the information I have is attributed to one of your own administrators," Bernie checked his notes. "Bullet fragments taken from Wallace are consistent with bullets fired from the gun of Sergeant Knox." That sounds awfully specific to me."

"Bernie, I don't know your source, or the context in which the comment is alleged. But, in this case, a ballistic analysis will take extensive time to support any conclusive finding. In the meanwhile, your speculation is completely irresponsible."

Before things could proceed with Bernie Floyd's line of questioning, Mayor Bergin stepped forward to conclude the presser. She thanked Bill Flynn, and Jack Griffin for their cooperation to find a timely resolution to the Packard affair.

The conference concluded. Bergin and Griffin stepped into the hallway behind the council chambers. Out of the corner of his eye, Ballard saw Mayor Bergin step into Jack Griffin's personal space. Ballard moved quickly toward them, expecting a confrontation that would do no one any good.

Bergin seized Griffin by the arm. "Jack," she reproached under her breath. "We had an agreement, no politics, I don't know what the hell you were trying to do in there, putting your hand on my arm like that, using me as your shill," Bergin took another breath, "but, if you try to use me like that again, I'll break your balls." With that, she stormed off in a huff.

Bernie Floyd stood in the shadows, eyes on the story fingers on the keys of his iPad.

Outside, protestors crowded the sidewalks of city hall.

• • •

Waiting for word from Bud Noonan, Knox turned on the 6:00 P.M. news. Ted Harmon reported on the morning press conference, and Knox saw his career plunge down the crapper.

He listened to Harmon's commentary until the sound faded in his ears. The department, the state, and county attorney would be coming at him. He felt sick, slammed the kitchen door and he stepped out onto the back porch. He sucked in a deep breath then lumbered down to the river.

It was nearly an hour before Knox returned to the house. He reached for a bottle of Makers Mark, interrupted by the chirp of his cell phone.

"Knox," he said, half-expecting Noonan.

"Hello, Sergeant," said the monotone voice. "In the news again. Handy with a gun aren't you? But, allowed your partner to get killed. And, what about your wife… Lara, wasn't it?"

"Who the hell is this?"

"Someone who shares a loss, not unlike you."

A pause and the phone went dead.

• • •

BEYOND THE GLASS of the metal-framed telephone kiosk, traffic rustled by on its way along the boulevard past the urban tree-lined Lake Calhoun. Leon Love, late of the Dane County, Wisconsin jail, hung the receiver back on its hook. A twisted smile crossed his lips. He'd just tapped into the life of Harding Knox. A sneer still on his face, he turned and walked along the lake toward the Zenith Avenue bungalow. Tomorrow, a new chapter to his life would be enriched.

Thirteen

Knox leaned on the porch rail at the rear of his island home, a Dutch Diplomat cigar between his fingers. A half-empty glass of Crown Royal rested near the rail post, ice melted. The sun tilted west over the city skyline, it was 7:00 P.M.

"Where the hell are Noonan and the warrant?"

The sudden chirp caused Knox to reach into the pocket of his leather jacket. The message screen on his cell displayed Noonan's number.

"Knox?"

"Give me something good, LT."

"I've got the warrant. A half an hour, Logan Park."

"I'll be there."

Knox grabbed his go-bag. Noonan had come through. Into the early evening traffic, Knox maneuvered his Explorer onto East Hennepin. A snarl of cars and buses slowed his progress at 1st Avenue, and again at University.

Blood racing, muscles taut, Knox gripped the wheel and raced through a yellow at 7th Street. Logan Park, the end game with Dale Allen Nichols, lay ahead.

At 13th Avenue and Jefferson, Knox braked to the curb. Old clapboard and stucco two-story houses bordered the park, their weathered front porches, and cracked sidewalks testament to age and neglect. On the B-ball court a basketball *swooshed* through a chain net. Three weasel-eyed gangbangers crouched crow-like on the back of a park bench. They drew hard on cigarettes, ball caps twisted to the right, a sign of their street gang affiliation—Logan Park Disciples.

The ball fell silent as the "Disciples" paused to glare at the po-lice rides that had curbed in their hood. Knox could read their thoughts. *Shit goin' down, man.*

Six months earlier, the park had been a crime scene. The body of eighteen-year old Martin Luther Wallace had brought Knox and Professor Neil Wallace together. In a disagreement over a basketball score, the gangsta, Sly Jackson, had murdered the nephew of the noted community leader.

A relentless crackdown on the gang led Knox and Swede Lundgren to grab Sly from the projects of south Chicago, Illinois.

Knox felt the punk-eyed stare as he past by Sly's former bros, poster boys for retroactive birth control.

Noonan, in uniform and flak-vest, leaned over the hood of his white unmarked Crown Vic. A world-class police weight lifter, his subordinates referred to the LT as "No Neck." His ham-hock-like arms formed a powerful accouterment to a beer barrel chest. At fifty-four, head shaved, standing five-foot-nine, No Neck was an intimidating powerhouse. But, no one ever called him by the moniker to his face. His radio call sign was 9902. Commander, Traffic Unit was Noonan's job.

As Knox approached, Noonan straightened up from the diagram spread across the hood of his car. "Glad you could make it."

While introducing Knox to the police entry team, Noonan acknowledged the presence of a twenty-one-year-old baby-faced young man from animal control. Ten to fifteen years younger than the others, he appeared anxious, a Remington tranquilizer rifle held at his side. "My first raid," said Remington.

"Here's the deal, gentlemen," said no neck. "Special Ops Units are on stand-by for the protestors. So, we are taking down the guy that probably killed the wife of Sergeant Knox."

Knox saw the look of reckoning on the faces of the others.

"The perp is Dale Allen Nichols," said Noonan, who pulled mug shots of their target from a manila packet and passed them out. "I don't imagine you need one of these," he said to Knox.

"Nichols is a hot tempered, five-foot-eight drunk," said No Neck. "He keeps a shotgun in his second floor bedroom. The physical evidence is a late model blue Dodge pickup parked inside the garage at the alley." Noonan pointed to the landscape photo of Nichols's house and neighborhood. "Somewhere on the premises is a harlequin mastiff pit bull. The pooch'll take your balls off in the blink of an eye, name's Ajax. That's where you come in," said Noonan with a nod to young Remington. "You get the dog."

The animal wrangler acknowledged with a nervous gulp.

Knox made no comment. The raid had to be Noonan's gig. He would define the objective, make the plan and execute it. However, plans can go to hell the moment the first cop plows through the front door. Still, you had to have a plan.

Noonan pointed to the designated positions on his diagram. He would wield a metal ram to the front door, accompanied by a uniform officer, and the dog wrangler with the tranqgun. Another uniform would enter the back of the house along with the plainclothes officer already there.

"Where do you want me?" Knox asked

"Here," Noonan's finger ardently pressed on the diagram, a garage across the alley from Nichols's property.

"What about the truck?" Knox asked.

"Funny thing about that truck, we saw it through some dust on the garage window. A tarp lifted just enough to expose the front license plate. Awfully careless for a guy trying to hide evidence."

Knox avoided the observation, and moved quickly to the next obvious question. "Who's the registered owner?"

"The R/O," Noonan said, "is Nichols's ex-wife. She's the one who told me about the shotgun and the dog. Her name is Sandra Jean Jablonski. Her name was on Nichols's jail visitor log."

Knox caught a discerning glance from Noonan.

"Jablonski hustles tables at Little Jax, northeast. She has a kid by Nichols, suspected I came to her because of the truck. Said she signed for the truck so Nichols could work to pay child support. You know how that goes. Nichols got the truck, and Jablonski got screwed."

Noonan looked at Knox. "The day after your wife was killed, Nichols called Jablonski. Said he fucked up the truck, had to put it up. Nichols's helper, a black guy she didn't know, had run off and left him. Said it would be awhile until he could get his shit together. But Jablonski said Nichols never could get his shit together. Said he's a menace like his dog, and both ought to be put down."

Knox nodded at Noonan. “I’d like to accommodate her.”

“Not today you’re not,” replied No Neck, a stern note of caution in his tone. “Due to the obvious sensitive nature of this Op,” Noonan continued, “Sergeant Knox is to take no direct action concerning the arrest of Nichols, or the seizure of evidence. He is here strictly as a professional courtesy, to observe and advise.”

The lieutenant’s gaze struck Knox with clear meaning.

“Anything further?” Lieutenant Noonan asked.

“Nope,” mocked a uniformed officer. “We’ve got a dangerous dog and a drunk with a shotgun, what could go wrong?”

As dusk took hold, Knox concealed himself behind a box elder tree in the alley, his assigned position. He watched the plainclothes cop and his uniformed partner approach Nichols’s garage. They peered through the window. Knox heard a static squelch of a radio key in his earpiece. “The package is here.”

Guns drawn, the two cops at the garage paused at the chicken wire fence, searching for the pit bull.

In a low crouch, both officers edged through the backyard, past the junk van, snowmobile, piles of wood, the Oldsmobile with flattened tires, and the dog shit.

The two men mounted the rear porch and positioned themselves at each side of the screen door. Knox felt the blood race through his veins. The moment before entry, the feeling is always the same: a desperate anticipation, trying to perceive the unpredictable that lay behind a bolted door.

Ajax barked, sensing the presence of the officers.

Knox strained to hear the entry signal in his earpiece.

There was the command, "9902, go, go, go."

No Neck behind the ram, the front door crashed open. "Police, search warrant! Police, search warrant!" Cops from the alley burst through the back door.

Knox felt his heart pound like a jackhammer, emotions juxtaposed to the stern warnings from Commander Krieg, reemphasized moments earlier by Lieutenant Noonan, "Take no direct action."

From across the alley, Knox heard the menacing bark—Ajax gone berserk.

Nichols's voice bellowed, "Get'em Ajax. Get the muthafuckers."

Another voice called out, "Shoot the dog!"

"Get out of the way," yelled another. Ominous growls and barks were punctuated by the crash of furniture, and breaking glass. The boom of a shotgun, the crack of a pistol resounded from the house into the neighborhood. Knox pulled his Beretta, darted across the alley, and leaped the rickety back fence into Nichols's yard.

As Knox reached the rusted Chevy van, Remington, the dog wrangler, wailing in pain, burst through the back door, the jaws of Ajax clinched vice-like to his ass.

"Shoot the fucker!" Remington screamed.

The plan had gone to hell. No Neck bulled his way onto the porch, pivoted on the plug of a dog turd, and went down with a crash.

"Son-of-a-bitch! Son-of-a-bitch!" Noonan shouted amid the pandemonium.

Remington tumbled down the porch steps, Ajax jerking at his buttocks; the dog's hindquarters peppered by buckshot, spackled with blood.

Remington, in mortal desperation screamed, “Shoot. God damn it, shoot.”

Knox crouched, and aimed. One shot cracked through the tumult. A piercing yelp followed. Ajax and Remington went down, the dead dog’s jaws parted from Remington’s bloodied backside.

With officers in chase, Nichols bolted through the back door, scrambled over Noonan, and leapt off the porch toward Knox.

Knox hefted a trashcan lid, hauled it back, and swung it square into the face of the bastard that had killed his wife. Nichols sailed off his feet, blood spurting from his nose and mouth. He dropped like a sack of garbage onto a scatter of Ajax’s feces.

Knox holstered his gun, rolled Nichols onto his stomach, pulled back his arms.

“Cuffs!”

One of the uniforms handed over a set of Peerless. With demented pleasure, Knox listened to the ratchets tighten around the wrists of his quarry. The dirtbag was his.

Nichols groaned, twisted in pain. “You muthafuckers!”

Through the resonance of a broken nasal passage, epithets were all that Knox heard amidst the glisten of blood and snot that Nichols spat into the dirt. Knox glared. This was as close as he could get to the revenge he really wanted. A long easy breath, and a roll of his broad shoulders released the tension.

Noonan’s voice crackled in Knox’s earpiece.

“9902.”

“9902 go,” said the dispatcher, impassively.

"Send HCMC, Forensics, and the Watch Commander from Two's. Our location on Monroe, shots fired, no officers injured. One animal control is down with serious K-9 injuries. We are code-4, one in custody. No other cars needed."

The dispatcher acknowledged, sending the paramedics from the Hennepin County Medical Center, Forensics, and the 2nd Precinct's Watch Commander. "Understand your scene is secure with one in custody. Other cars going can cancel."

Noonan grumbled, "That's 10-4."

Knox felt the lieutenant's steady hand on his shoulder.

"You okay?" Noonan asked.

"I had to move, LT. I heard the shotgun, the dog, the animal control kid."

The lieutenant sighed and brushed a hand across his baldhead. "Well, the kid won't be able to shit for a month. You just put a slug up the ass of the pit bull from hell, and I've gotta explain to my wife why I smell like dog crap."

"And, look at that," said No Neck. "We got Arco Aluminum stenciled across the forehead of our suspect who at least has a broken nose and jaw. The bottom line is *you're* not even supposed to be here. You see the predicament, Knox? You and me assigned to permanent latrine patrol in Loring Park. "Jesus," Noonan exclaimed. "How'd this get so fucked up?"

Like a pack of feral cats in search of a bag of kibbles, the news crews arrived on location for a juicy morsel. A forest of transmitter dishes rose into the sky as half the neighborhood assembled for the show.

The backyard of Dale Allen Nichols looked like the set of a low budget fright film, *"Ajax Cemetery."* The story would be a 10:00 P.M. news headliner.

The young lacerated animal control officer, who likely contemplated a career change, departed in an ambulance with emergency lights flashing.

A uniformed officer accompanied Nichols in an EMS rig that sat in the alley, its rear doors open. The blink of warning lights flashed a surreal amber glow across the scene.

Nichols lay cuffed to a yellow metal gurney, cervical collar around his neck, an IV stuck in his arm, an ice pack taped to his head. The demented drunk reeked of beer, cigarettes, and excrement, the latter of his own making.

Elmer Fud-like, while cameras rolled, Nichols ranted through a broken nose and jaw about police brutality, and demanded a lawyer.

In the aftermath, the adrenaline rush faded. Knox struggled with the pain that returned to his chest, each breath an ordeal. The throb in his head added to his misery. A medic re-wrapped his ribs and sternum, a Tylenol taken for effect.

From the garage, behind yellow crime scene ribbons, forensic investigators gathered evidence. The Watch Commander stepped before the reporters while Knox vanished into the crowd. The arrest, while sweet retribution, was only half the job.

• • •

Darkness had fallen across Nicollet Island by the time Knox parked in his driveway, arms and head rested on the steering wheel, the events of the past week tumbled through his mind. At the Packard Center shootout, had he done enough to cover Swede's back? Then came the phone call in the middle of the night that led to James at the river. The Nichols bust on Monroe, Remington, from animal control, chewed to bits, Ajax blown to pit-bull hell, and, finally, Nichols cuffed in the dirt. He heaved a sigh, and pushed a hand through the tangle of matted salt-and-pepper hair.

The job was still not done, not until Nichols was on the bus to Oak Park Heights Prison. Knox had to place the dirtbag behind the wheel on the night he ran Lara down.

Knox backed out of the drive, and drove north past the dreary wrecking yards, and north side saloons. Once over the Broadway Bridge he drove onto Aldrich. The neighborhood was a little foreboding for a cop in plainclothes without backup, working on a case he did not belong.

He strained to see the house numbers through the dim streetlights. Half way down the Aldrich Avenue alley, he coasted up to an old sway-backed garage. A faded gray Ford F-150 with a wood camper box sat in the dark. He had found James LaBeau.

Knox drove back onto Aldrich, eyeballed the yard then parked at the curb down the street. The second floor of the old clapboard was dark. He climbed the stairs to the front porch and stepped into the shadows. A faint glow ebbed through the shear curtains of the front parlor window, the room empty.

Two weathered mailboxes hung near the front door, "M. Lloyd, #1." On the other, "J. LaBeau, #2." He stood to the side of the door, reached across and raised his left hand toward the doorbell.

"Wutch you want?" Demanded the voice from the dark.

Knox turned and reached for his Beretta.

A stub of an old woman shuffled into the light at the bottom of the porch steps. Knox heaved a sigh of relief at the sight of the leather-faced woman with large-framed glasses. Under an old gray cardigan, her housedress drooped nearly to her ankles.

"Police, Ma'am."

"You don't look like no po-lice," she said as she hobbled up the steps.

Knox stepped toward her, and held out his shield. In black orthopedic shoes, she clumped up the steps. She leaned close. Her eyes squinted in the dim light, examining the authenticity of the gold and silver badge.

"Sergeant Knox, Homicide," he said.

"Ain't nobody kilt here. Now, wutch you doin' sneakin' 'round my house?"

"I might ask you the same thing, it is a little late for a lady to be out."

"That's my business. Now, what's your business bein' here?"

"James LaBeau. He lives upstairs."

"How you know that?"

"I'm the po-lice, Mrs. Lloyd."

The woman let out a chuckle. "Oh, you know my name, too?" A sly smile slipped across her face. "Or, maybe you can read a mailbox."

Knox laughed. "You got me there, Ma'am."

"Yes, suh, I do. Now, what you want with Mistuh James? He in trouble?

"No Ma'am. A woman died and James may have seen—"

Her eyes peered up through her thick glasses as she studied Knox's face.

"James ain't kilt no woman.

"No, Mrs. Lloyd, but he's a very important witness."

The door to #2 creaked open. Knox turned to see the hulk of James LaBeau framed by a light in the doorway.

"I heard voices, Mrs. Lloyd, said the big black man."

"Mistuh Knox, what...how'd you find me?"

"He the hom-cide po-lice, James," said Mrs. Lloyd. "You ain't kilt no one, have you, boy?"

"No. Ma'am."

Knox thanked the old woman as she turned the key to her door and hobbled inside, no doubt an ear kept to the window.

James leveled his gaze at Knox. "You come here about Nichols?"

"That's right," said Knox. "And, about Bogalusa."

"You come to get me, then, about that thing down home?"

"I called Bogalusa."

The big carpenter stood silent.

"Forget the warrant. The guy you beat up in Bogalusa is doing a nickel in Angola State. No one's looking for you, James."

"You ain't just sayin' that?"

"It's official. You're free as a fart in the wind."

Like atlas relieved from the weight of the world, James slid into a chair on the porch, shoulders slackened. His arms, like tree trunks, rested on bent knees

Knox leaned against a pillar beside him.

James stared into the emptiness of the darkened yard. "A thousand times I wanted to make that same call. But, a black man down south in trouble with the po-lice, well—"

A deep sigh preceded that *I owe you look* that Knox saw in James's eyes, in his conscience.

"What you need me for about Nichols?"

"I put Nichols in jail tonight, James. We found the truck."

"That's good. Then why you need me?"

"I need you to put Nichols behind the wheel. I need you to give a statement about what Nichols had told you the night he killed…killed the lady."

Knox gave the big man a hard look. "I can take you in James, as a material witness in a death investigation." It was bullshit, but an edge that Knox felt he needed. "I want to trust you, and I don't trust many people. I think you're a good man, and no one should be calling you what Nichols did."

"Nichols, he ain't never gonna call nobody that again. And, I feel real bad about that lady. He gonna answer for that, too."

"Tomorrow morning, I need you to see Lieutenant Noonan. He's a friend of mine at the police department, head of the Traffic Unit. He'll take a statement from you; how Nichols told you that he killed the woman on Hennepin Avenue. You can put him there, James; behind the wheel of that truck."

James took the business card Knox offered, studied it for a moment. "Okay. I'll see your lieu-tenant in the mornin'."

"When you're done, call me. I know someone who needs a good carpenter."

James' eyes narrowed. "Why you doin' that for me, you bein' a po-lice-man?"

Knox stood up. "Sometimes people need a break, James. Don't let me down. Don't make me come after you."

With James, Knox knew he had crossed the threshold, ignored the rules that say never trust an informant. Never get caught up in their personal lives; have their problems become your problems. Don't be their priest, rabbi, or even worse, their lover. Stick and carrot, keep them motivated by whatever means reasonable, but keep them on edge, guessing about where or when you're coming, and why.

Exhausted, Knox drove back to Nicollet Island. His hunt for Nichols over, but the nagging question of conviction still remained unresolved. James LaBeau was the link that could put Nichols behind the wheel of the truck that killed Lara. Tomorrow would determine if Knox had rolled snake eyes.

The Explorer's headlights fanned across the circular drive. Knox pressed the opener and the garage door rumbled up. Lara's yellow Mustang, ghost-like, sat in the shadows as if it were waiting for her. Through the windshield he stared. The permanence of her absence was like a bullet through the heart.

Nichol's arrest had merely masked his anguish. Knox felt the pain of both battered mind and body. Everything twisted and strained in the torment of her loss. Coupled with the Packard shootings, uncertainty remained his only future. Before time, and career ran out, Nichols had to be convicted.

Knox pulled inside, the garage door rolled noisily along its runners back into place. He plodded into the house, wanting to find solitude from the anxiety of his world. Instead, there was only a haunting silence. He stood alone, wrapped in loneliness, perplexed as to what to do next.

Within the stillness, *her* absence lingered like a dark shroud that shut everything out from his life. The warm, familiar surroundings closed around him. Three fingers of bourbon into a glass and he went to the porch that overlooked the river, a space less confining. In the night air, he slumped into one of the Adirondack chairs.

In his weariness, the lights from the skyscrapers didn't sparkle as before. He took a sip of bourbon, and another, allowed the aggravations, the grief, his anger at God, at himself to flow forth. Tears ran down his face. Of all the people in the city he had protected, he had not protected *her*. Finally, his eyes, too tired to cry, closed.

Fourteen

AT 8:30 A.M. Leon slid into the rear seat of a Twin Cities Taxi waiting at the curb. "Saint Paul, North Star Bank," he said to the driver.

"Okay," the cabbie grunted and headed to Lake Street then east toward Saint Paul. Immaterial to Leon, the Lake Street bars and restaurants, used car lots, second hand furniture stores, liquor emporiums, and shopping malls past unnoticed by the windows of the cab. Held between his fingers, Leon rubbed the surface of a brass key.

Visions floated through his mind, his recent bitter past. The ominous slam of jail cell doors, days of monotonous routine, the struggle for survival, voices of despair that yelled in the night. In his hand, the smooth, cold brass key was a means of deliverance from the recent discontent in his life. Mom, killed by a wetback in a farm truck, and his back up plan gunned down by a Minneapolis cop.

Across the East Lake Street Bridge and over the Mississippi River, the cab sped toward I-94. Leon touched the inside breast pocket of his sport coat for the letter, his assurance from Rico, the attorney, that affairs would be concluded at the bank.

The cab swerved off the interstate into downtown Saint Paul. The early-morning gridlock snarled the narrow streets. Cars inched through the commercial center of the capital city, a contrast of early twentieth century brick buildings and modern skyscrapers. Ahead, Leon's destination emerged, his pulse quickened.

The tall concrete and glass bank loomed above the riverfront bluff. At its pinnacle, a golden North Star gleamed in the morning sun. It was a star that pulled Leon toward his destiny. With anticipation of the legacy he anticipated, expectations beat against the crawl of traffic. Leon stopped the cab, paid his fare and walked the two blocks to the golden North Star, to Alonso Rico, and payday.

The glass and chrome doors revolved with a *whoosh* as Leon pushed into the cavernous entry of the skyscraper bank. He sauntered across a glistening Botticino marble floor, a muted cream-colored stone with brown veins. A comely woman in a white blouse sat at the information desk, eyeglasses perched on the lower bridge of her nose. She raised her head.

"May I help you?" Asked the information lady with an automatic customer-service-smile.

Two weeks out of stir, a sudden flicker of anxiety, Leon took a breath, about to cash in on his future. "I'm looking for a Mr. Alonzo Rico. My name is Leon Love."

She pointed to a mahogany and glass enclosed waiting area. "Please, have a seat, sir. Mr. Rico will be along shortly."

"Thank you."

The woman nodded without comment. Leon turned, and with a slow stride crossed the lobby. From above and behind the teller's windows, he felt the eyes of security cameras follow. Their gaze held you in their control like the CCTV monitors of the Dane County Jail.

In the waiting area, Leon sank into the cushions of a leather couch, and browsed through pamphlets advertising the bank's various services.

After fifteen minutes the swarthy little attorney, Rico, in his early sixties shuffled out from a warren of glass-walled offices. A large worn, leather briefcase thumped against his right thigh. Short bowed legs and Italian lifts conveyed a heavy bull-like frame. Across his large balled pate lay thin strands of dark, oily hair.

With a slight smile, "Hello, kid," said Rico as he approached. "It's been awhile." The distinctive graveled voice accented a tough façade that gave way to an amiable manner. He appeared, as Leon remembered, more like a mobbed up wise guy than a shrewd Twin Cities attorney.

"You have my condolences about the passing of your mother," said Rico. "She was an ardent woman in her own right, and, of course, your father."

"Thank you, sir," said Leon with deference to the man who had once brokered Leon's ten-year sexual assault charge into a six-month misdemeanor.

"You have my letter concerning your mother's estate, as well as the mutual interests of your father in your regard?"

"Yes. I have the letter and the key."

Rico motioned with the sweep of his left arm. "Let's have a seat at the desk and get down to business. I'll show you the significance of that key in your hand."

Leon retrieved the letter from his breast pocket. He didn't know what mutual interests had brought Rico and his father together over the years, interests that the attorney had never divulged. All Leon knew was that his father had sent Rico to Madison, Wisconsin to thwart his prison sentence to a substantially reduced jail stretch.

It had been a case concocted, insisted Leon, by his girlfriend, Wanda Rippie, and a Madison PD dick, Walt Meyers. Then, upon the death of Leon's mother, Rico handled the estate. Now, it was time to settle the estates. Rico placed the documents on the desk and began.

After the meeting at the bank, Leon found himself on Saint Paul's Jackson Street. A green neon sign flickered in a narrow window tucked into a granite wall, *Bar & Grill.* He pushed open an iron strap-hinged door. Daylight pierced the confines of the downtown watering hole.

The cool, grainy smell of draft beer struck his senses as Leon slid onto a stool, his eyes adjusting to the dim light. Except for a few late morning boozers, the oak tables and leather booths sat nearly empty.

The usual neon beer signs hung along the wall over the booths, Budweiser, Leinenkugle, Stroh's, Miller and Pig's Eye, the latter a local fermentation. Roy Orbison cried out the melody to "Blue Bayou" from the Wurlitzer in the far corner of the room.

In a tight red sweater, a well-endowed forty-something blond sat at the other end of the bar. She pulled a slow drag from a narrow cigarillo, nursed her drink and flirted with the bartender. Behind the bar, an array of liquor bottles glimmered in the mirror on glass shelves. Leon put a large manila document folder on the bar, the one given to him by Rico. Inside the folder, the papers addressed his take of his mother's erstwhile estate, and his father's confidential arrangements. It also contained the key to a safe deposit box.

Finally, the bottle slider turned his attention from the red sweater.

"What'll it be, sir?"

"A Bud."

A beer slid into Leon's hand. He took a long drink, savored the taste and glanced at the newspaper on the stool next to him.

Opened to the City Section, the *Saint Paul Pioneer Press* headlined, "Saint Paul Attorney Investigated."

Leon picked up the paper, and gaped. Alonzo Rico stared defiantly from a small grainy photo that bore a resemblance to a 1930s gangster.

"Circumstances" said the article, "alleged by the Minnesota Attorney General that the familiar Saint Paul Attorney is suspected of unlawfully diverting client's funds. Investigators believe that Mr. Rico had moved money from various escrow accounts, as in a "shell game," to leverage real estate investments."

Leon wondered if the Hiawatha Trust, the *mutual interest* Rico disclosed as being shared with his father, maybe connected to the allegations of fraud.

The news piece finished, Leon's recollection regressed to the safe deposit box, and to Rico. In the box, he counted $65,000. Leon had expected much more. It was all the cash left from his mother and father's combined estate. "There were expenses," said Rico.

But, the house near Lake Calhoun was worth thousands more, deeded to Leon from the entity called Hiawatha

Trust. Rico insisted that Leon not discuss the money, the deed, as well as the trust, with anyone. Rico's caution about the transaction appeared peculiar. When pressed, the attorney advised that it was to protect Leon's interests, and the memory of his father. Suspicions sharpened after reading the disclosure in the newspaper. Leon grappled with the idea that the little Guiney may somehow have swindled him out of more than what he received. Equally puzzling was the comment about protecting the public memory of his father. Was it that, or perhaps it was Rico himself that required protection? Through the array of liquor bottles behind the bar, Leon peered at his reflection in the mirror.

Fuckin' lawyers.

Fifteen

Recent rains, and warm weather had transformed Lakewood cemetery from its bleak winter setting into a flourishing carpet of green grass, trees burgeoning with buds. The drive along the cemetery lane was still as painful as it was familiar. Shafts of sunlight gently filtered through a veil of early morning mist. Knox stopped his SUV near the ash tree that sheltered Lara's headstone its surface glistened with dew.

Alone, Knox stepped toward the grave, the sting of winter replaced by a fresh scent of spring, a rebirth of life with the change of season. Knox looked stoically at the grave and heaved a sigh. Slowly, he bent down and placed a bouquet of roses with sprigs of baby's breath at the base of Lara's marker. He sat on the grass, leaned back against the stone, knowing *her* life would never bloom again.

"Hello Lara," he spoke softly. "I brought news."

Knox brought his knees up, cradled his head in his hands, the anger and weariness faded away to a calm he had not known in a long while. He could almost feel her arms close around him; hear a whisper of comfort in his ear. He wanted her to understand that he had not let her down, that he had found her killer. Most of all, he wanted forgiveness because he had failed to protect her.

Alone with Lara, Knox sat, lost among the monuments of the marble orchard. Finally, he looked upward. Tears filled his eyes. Then came the words.

"I got him."

• • •

A PROMISE FULFILLED, Knox left the cemetery and headed to his fitness for duty exam at the Hennepin County Medical Center.

In the examination room, Doc Payne turned from the backlighted X-ray charts. The look on the Doc's face was serious, not what Knox was expecting.

"I'm not pleased with the results of these charts," said the Doc. The night of the shooting, you sustained a bruised sternum and left lung, two cracked ribs and a minor concussion. In fact, I'll bet you still hurt like hell."

Knox sat on the examining table, ridged, with his shirt off. "Yeah, I get headaches, and it's difficult to take a breath at times. But I had things to do."

Doc Payne drew near, hands on his hips, smock open, stethoscope draped around his neck, "Things to do? Can you tell me where shooting dogs, and smashing a perp with a trash can lid fall within the parameters of convalescence?"

Knox looked up sheepishly. "It was only one dog."

"Skip the humor, Knox. I know why you were there which makes this all the more difficult. I'm responsible to help get you on your feet. As a cop you are responsible to follow my guidelines to get back on the job. Those are the rules."

"So, what are you telling me?"

"I'm extending your medical leave another week. The shape you're in now, you'll end up further injuring yourself, or maybe getting someone else hurt."

"I'll behave, promise," said Knox. He stuffed a bottle of Tylenol Codeine III, and Doc Payne's report into his jacket pocket, pushed through the back doors of the Hennepin County Medical Center and walked to his SUV.

"Recommendation, extended medical leave," the Doc's report said. That, and he still had heard no word from James LaBeau. Unabated, the clock ticked off the hours to get Nichols charged, or set him loose.

As he got behind the wheel of the Explorer, his cell rang.

Determined to capture the voice of the asshole so interested in his personal affairs, he was prepared. He hit the record button on his cell.

"Knox," he said with anticipation.

"Its me," said Noonan.

"What have you got, LT?"

"You owe a few favors, buddy. Your friends in the lab worked all night on the Nichols collar," said Noonan. "The preliminary results indicate hair samples, and fibers taken from the truck are consistent with your wife's hair. The coat fibers, abrasions and blood are also a match. Also, the vehicle parts from the hit and run scene fit Nichols's Dodge. In short, Nichol's truck killed Lara."

Knox was silent, relieved that one more nail had been hammered into Nichols's coffin.

"You there, Knox?"

"Yeah, I'm here, Bud."

"Some neighbors," Noonan continued, "have seen Nichols drive the truck. But, your CI, LaBeau is the ringer."

"Did he show for the statement?"

"At 8:00 A.M. He put Nichols right behind the eight ball. Now we can put the asshole on that bus to Oak Park. I'm headed to the county attorney's."

Knox breathed a sigh of relief. James had come through.

At city hall, a small group of protesters walked the block; "No cover-up. Justice for Dr. Wallace," they chanted. Knox ducked into the 5th Street entrance. The echo of footsteps accompanied detectives, and uniformed cops as they went about their duties. Room 108, was behind a plane oak and glass door. The plaque on the wall said Criminal Investigations. Inside, a large oak framed Plexiglas window overlooked the waiting area. Shelly, an attractive blue-eyed blond, acted as receptionist and gatekeeper to the office.

Shelly greeted Knox with her usual pleasant smile as she buzzed him through the security door. He stopped, wondered about the man behind the voice.

"Has anyone called for me, Shell," Knox asked, "a male asking about my wife, Swede, or any of my cases?"

Shelly's brow furrowed in recollection. "Yes, about the Sly Jackson conviction, the one you and Swede worked. Said he had the information you needed, and had to call you, quick. I gave him your cell number. It really sounded urgent."

"Shell, do me a favor, if anyone asks for my number again, take a name, get their number, then call me."

"Okay, sorry, Knox."

"Not a problem, I've just had some screwball calls lately."

Inside the warren of cubicles, the close knit, twelve-man, homicide unit was busy, especially in the absence of Knox, and Swede Lundgren. In the past four months, the small squad continued work on a growing number of homicides.

Knox acknowledged a few greetings of encouragement that seemed almost obligatory as detectives continued about their routines.

In Knox and Lundgren's workstation, Knox found Herb Wesel who busied himself with Knox and Lundgren's outstanding files.

"Hey, Herb," said Knox. Has anyone called for me, inquiries about my wife, Swede or our cases?"

"Knox. Good to see you. But no, we've had orders. Don't discuss anything about you or Swede, especially with the newsies. If the guys heard something, I'd know."

"Thanks, man," said Knox noting something uneasy in the mood of the office.

He left Homicide and headed down the rabbit run toward the office of Commander Krieg. His gut told him that the inevitable rumors had surfaced. Rumors that suggested he'd fucked up on the Packard shooting. People would now begin to distance themselves from him.

With a warm Latin smile, Ernesto Guzman approached. "Hey, amigo, you finally climbed out of the bat cave."

Knox chuckled. "I think I should have stayed in the cave." He nodded back in the direction of the other offices. "The reception seems a little strained."

"There're a few things in the wind, the Packard deal, the usual stories about who shot whom beginning to surface. Some of the guys are a little anxious not knowing where it's all going to fall. No one knows what to say."

"Yeah, well it's not a pot of gold on my end, either."

"I guess loosing the pot of gold is what's bothering the union. Because of the Packard shooting, there's a move among some community groups to stop the department's involvement in off duty details."

"Jesus," said Knox, guarding the tempo of his voice. "I already have a grand jury breathing down my neck. Now it's my fault that the off duty income is threatened, the SUVs, boats and summer cabins in the Land of Lakes all going down the shitter?"

"Hey, man," said Guzman, the Latin's face sober. "Easy, there's something else in the wind. The chief met with the city attorney, reviewing the suspension and transfer clauses in the union contract. You've seen the demonstrations at city hall and the government center, accusations about a cover-up. The national news media, and a couple of the usual race mongers from Chicago and New York are all here stirring the pot, making headlines. The chief is canceling leaves, and met with the county attorney and the BCA chief. This morning I saw Krieg with the chief. Watch your back on this one, *hermano.*"

"Thanks. But I still have some unfinished business."

"Lara?"

"Yeah, and Krieg wants to see me."

Guzman cracked a smile. "By the way, nice collar on Monroe last night. Heard you put out some trash. I would have liked to have been there."

As Knox approached Krieg's office, Barbara Koch, the division's secretarial supervisor, looked up from her desk. Knox had known her long before Krieg came to command the division. Secretaries like Barb typed the correspondence, and overheard the constant flow of rumors that filtered through the department's bureaucracy. Barb often knew the score before the game began.

"Hello kiddo," said Knox. "Is Krieg in?"

The look in Barb's eyes said Knox was behind by several points.

"He's waiting for you, Knox."

The plaque on the wall next to the door read "Commander Krieg." As his shoulders stiffened, Knox knocked and entered the spacious corner office. He anticipated the topics of discussion, the Nichol's arrest, and the Packard shooting. He remembered the words of Jon Bass, "Shit happens in a shootout over which you have no control. It's *you* who *must* survive."

Knox had seen the careers of cops collapse after a shooting, the result of a system that strived for political correctness. Some officers failed in their struggle to cope with events, lost their families, fell into a bottle, abused drugs, or committed suicide, options Knox vowed were non-starters. He would survive.

The unease smoldered to animosity as Knox stood in front of Krieg's desk, waiting to be acknowledged. Finally, Krieg looked up from his yellow legal pad.

"Sergeant Knox, have a seat."

Knox drew up a chair only to look into the cool gray eyes behind the steel-framed glasses. A hollow smile, and forced congeniality, re-enforced the perception of Krieg's pretentious character. Knox slid Doctor Payne's report across the desk.

Krieg took a moment, panning the report's contents while Knox quietly recalled their history: the 2nd Precinct over twenty years earlier. He had been a uniformed training officer, assigned to the probationary rooky, Karl Krieg. The assessment, "Not Recommended for Retention," too analytical, too tentative in decisive street action, lacks constructive people skills. A lieutenant, who became Krieg's mentor, over ruled the assessment that resulted in Krieg's retention. Over the years, Karl Krieg emerged as an austere, manipulative bureaucrat rising to command status.

Springs squeaked under the strain of his weight as the commander eased forward, and looked up from Payne's report. "I wanted to see you this morning about a number of issues."

At that moment, Knox pulled the cell from his coat pocket.

"Excuse me," said Knox. "I need to take this."

Krieg acquiesced with a wave of his hand.

Lieutenant Noonan's secretary came on the phone. "Sergeant Knox, Lieutenant Noonan asked me to inform you that the complaint has been issued against Mr. Nichols, and the lieutenant is on his way to the jail to serve the warrant."

"Thank you," said Knox. "That's very encouraging." He ended the call and placed the phone back in his pocket.

Satisfaction eased his apprehension about the Nichols case. Both James, and Noonan had come through.

"Okay, Karl. What's on your mind?"

Krieg's ordinarily pallid complexion took on a reddened hue that edged up from the collar of his white shirt. Placed subservient to a phone call, and called by his first name instead of his rank, had tweaked Krieg's well-known penchant for deference by his subordinates. He rocked back in his chair, eyes locked in an unsettling stare, lips pursed with tension.

"I hope that you understand a few things," said Knox, attempting to appease a complicated ego in the man that sat across from him. "It's been a lousy month, the Packard situation, Swede's death, and finding my wife's killer."

"Precisely the reasons you are here, Sergeant."

Knox stared into the stoic face across the desk. There was a heightened tenor to Krieg's voice. The tension was palpable, all bad vibes.

"So then, what's coming down on me?" Knox asked,

"In disregard of my orders, Sergeant, you have directly involved yourself in your wife's death investigation, maimed the suspect in that matter, and shot his dog."

Knox leaned forward as he held back the urge to knock the Krieg from his chair.

"Let's go back a little further, Karl. My partner died in the past week-and-a-half, I was shot, knocked unconscious, and now a grand jury will try to bag my ass for surviving a shootout."

"As far as my wife is concerned, Karl, no one turned anything on her killer. Not until a CI came to me."

"That was for Traffic to work out, Knox."

"Not until I could cultivate some trust with the guy could I hand him over to Bud Noonan."

Krieg glanced at his legal pad. A shaky hand jotted a note then his eyes peered over the top of his glasses, his voice gathering momentum. "Which brings me to your part in the arrest on Monroe. Was I not clear with those instructions, to take no action? "

Krieg flashed to a righteous glare. "Right to the edge, Sergeant, that's where you always go. And this time your presence on Monroe is one that can be perceived as a cop out for revenge, compromising the entire case against who killed your wife."

Knox snapped back. "There would be no case if I hadn't worked the informant. As far as the arrest is concerned, my position was across the alley, away from anything that was supposed to happen. I was content to let it go down without my involvement."

"But, you did get involved," said Krieg. "That is, after all, your nature to push the limit of your instructions."

"Listen, Karl. Shit happens in field operations. The perp bailed off the back porch, and sent his pit bull to tear a new asshole in the animal control kid. It was the kid or the dog. That was the choice. I killed the dog and let Nichols live, in spite of the fact *he* killed *my* wife."

"Regardless of the exigent circumstances, you were not supposed to be there. Another officer could have dealt with the animal. In that regard, I spoke to Lieutenant Noonan, and to his superiors about his lack of judgment regarding your presence."

"So, you intend to take action against Noonan, too? What next?"

“The Packard shooting,” said Krieg.

“What about it?” Knox asked as he gazed into the steady glare of Krieg’s eyes.

“The Packard affair has been handed over in large part to a state and county attorney’s task force, with us assisting. They’ll—“

“I know. I watch the news,” said Knox. “The night it happened, I gave Internal Affairs all the information I had. They have my reports, and I don’t have anything to add. All I need, Karl, is to get back on cases again.”

“Let me cut to the chase, Knox. Based on you’re medical report from Dr. Payne, you are relieved of *any* police activity for another week. Following that, you are to be reassigned indefinitely to uniformed operations in the 2nd Precinct.”

Knox felt the blood drain from his face. The bolt of pain, like a hot poker, shot to his brain. His stomach wrenched to a knot. It had taken ten years to make homicide, the goal of his career, followed by twelve more years of dedication, hunting killers, doing God’s work as Swede had said.

Uniform Division, Second Precinct!

The words hit Knox like a sucker punch to the gut. He tried to catch a breath as a demand for an explanation slowly formed.

“What do you mean—?”

Another call interrupted Knox’s response. He fumbled for his cell, using the distraction to struggle for composure.

“Yeah,” Knox said, bluntly.

“It’s Noonan. You sitting down?”

“Yeah,” repeated Knox.

Krieg sat Buddha-like in his chair across the desk, face flushed, jaw tight.

"Nichols is in the wind," said Noonan.

"What?"

"Jail fucked up. I walked the case through the complaint process. Before I got the warrant to jail, Nichols was released."

Suddenly, the abysmal order of banishment to the uniformed division was lost to a greater urgency.

"What the hell happened?"

"Another guy, same name, similar spelling and age got mixed into the paper process. Our guy got released by mistake."

Without a flinch, Knox held his gaze on Krieg.

"Okay," he said flatly. I'll get back to you." Knox ended the call and placed the phone back in his pocket.

"Did you hear what I said, Sergeant?" Krieg's voice trailed off, his face twisted to a quizzical stare.

"I heard," said Knox, evaluating the steps to track down Nichols.

"Look," said Krieg, "I know this isn't easy."

Knox rolled his shoulders to relieve the tension. The all too familiar pain channeled to what now seized the moment, getting Dale Allen Nichols.

"Is that all?" Knox asked.

"Listen, Knox, in spite of our…well, I just want to—"

"Don't waste your breath, Karl. I have to be somewhere."

Sixteen

By late morning Knox slid into the alley off Monroe and eyeballed Nichols's backyard. With a .9-mm in hand, he left his SUV and stalked down the alley to Nichols's garage. Turning the corner, he did a quick peek through the window of the overhead garage door. He pushed through the passageway door and scanned the dimness through his gun sights, no sign of life.

Knox crept by the derelict Chevy van, snowmobile and trailer, piles of discarded boards, remnants of Nichols's loser life. Eyes trained on the rear windows, he surveyed the house then mounted the porch. The storm door was still knocked off its hinges, the inner door closed.

A look through dingy windows into a rear bedroom revealed piles of debris, no sign of Nichols. Knox turned the door handle, and quietly pushed his way into the kitchen.

The stench of rotted food, feces and urine nearly over powered his senses. He closed his mouth, and took in shallow breaths through his nose. Beyond the muzzle of the .9-mm was a sink filled with dirty dishes, fast food cartons. From an accumulation of black plastic yard bags, the putrid smell of garbage permeated the air.

Covered with white plaster dust, the entire lower floor sat in various stages of failed remodeling efforts. Four by eight sheets of wallboard lie stacked against a bare stud wall along side of the staircase. In a corner of the lower parlor, power tools littered the floor near a table saw.

One step at a time, Knox approached the stairway to the second floor then stopped. Thoughts about falling into a dark hole of his own making, "a cop-out for revenge," as Krieg had said slipped through his mind.

Fuck it. This time there would be no mistakes.

Knox would take Nichols in. That was the job. But, given the slightest excuse, he would take Nichols out, too. There would be no screw up in paper work, no get-out-of-jail free card, just two .9-mm's in the ten-ring, and a trip to the morgue.

Mouth dry as sand, heartbeat and breath-rate steady, Knox began to ascend the stairway. The carpeted treads were putrid, caked with dirt, urine stains, and plaster. Controlled, determined, hands held firm the Beretta's grips, finger pressed lightly against the trigger guard.

At the halfway point, a sound like a bottle hit the floor. Knox paused, cautious about giving away his own position, resisting the urge to call Nichols out.

At the top landing, Knox pressed against the gritty green wall. He took in a breath and heard a grunt, feet stumbling, something scraped across the bare wood floor. He edged toward an open door, straining to interpret the sounds.

Another breath, he would roll around the doorjamb, shout for Nichols. At the sign of any threat, he would blow the dirtbag into eternity.

It's all in how you write the report.

A long silence sent a nervous chill through Knox. Then another grunt came from inside the room. Knox imagined Nichols holding a scattergun, waiting around the corner. Time to crawl down the rabbit hole. Whatever happens... happens.

Another breath, gun ready, Knox spun into the room.

"Nichols!"

The drunk wheeled atop a teetering wood stool. The stool tumbled. The rope around Nichols's neck snapped, like the tension of a piano wire. Feet lashed out, and Nichols danced the rubber chicken, then limbs and body fell slack.

Knox lowered the .9-mm.

"Don't let me hold you up," Knox muttered.

Astonished yet resigned to what had happened, Knox leaned against the wall. The adrenaline, and his own death wish ebbed from his body.

The rope bit into the flesh of Nichols's neck. Head tilted left, while a swollen acne-scarred face turned waxen purple, and lips parted, the tongue protruded between the teeth. Lara's killer twisted in space as the rope, tied to a joist through a hole in the ceiling, searched for the memory of its own coil.

Next to the toppled stool laid an empty bottle of Wild Turkey. To his last breath, Nichols struggled against the death of his own making. Knox wondered if it had been as horrifying for Lara.

On the nightstand, Knox found a scribbled note—pathetic.

I killed a lady and can't do no more time. Somebody take care of my kid and old lady. This is the only way.

Good-bye, Dale

Without regret, Knox cast a despondent gaze upon the wretched remains of Nichols, eyes stricken with the finality of death. Then in disgust, he turned away.

In the alley, two cars screeched to a stop, footsteps, running. Lieutenant Noonan, and Ernesto Guzman vaulted up the steps of the porch, guns drawn. Knox stepped into the sunlight, broad shoulders sagged, arms heavy at his sides.

The two men stopped, eyes locked on Knox in a long silence.

"You didn't —" Guzman, couldn't finish the question.

"You're late." Knox said. "He's hanging out, upstairs."

The two men rushed inside the house. Knox trudged toward the alley. Behind, Nichols hung at the end of a rope. The need for retribution had sustained life for Knox, provided a counter balance to loss and loneliness.

The endgame. Done.

Seventeen

Jon Bass, in the red windbreaker and yellow trousers looked like an entry in the Senior Master's tournament. Unlike other golfers, the sixty-something duffer carried a semi-auto pistol in his golf bag. Cap in hand, head bowed, he stood next to Lara's grave. Knox smiled to himself as he slowed to a stop on the cemetery lane.

The ex-detective commander craned his neck then returned his gaze to the Verde granite marker as Knox approached.

"I didn't think Lakewood Cemetery was on your tour card, Jon.

"I was on the links at Hiawatha, thought I'd stop and pay my respects."

The two friends shook hands. "Thanks for being here," said Knox.

For a quiet moment, they stood beside one another.

Bass broke the silence. "Is this the end? I mean with Nichols?"

"How'd you know?" said Knox. "You have a crystal ball in your golf bag?"

"Nope. Gotta cell phone in my pocket. What about my question? Are you going to find some closure in all of this?"

Knox continued to stare at the tombstone. "All I see is Lara lying dead in the icy slush on Hennepin Avenue. Killed by a piece of garbage that had no redeeming value to his pathetic life." Knox sighed. "How do I close that, Jon? I just came here to let her know it's done, he's gone."

"Somehow, I think she knows," said Bass. "And, Nichols?"

"What about him?"

"Hung himself this morning, right?"

"Yeah, tied a rope to a ceiling joist."

"Tough on the neck. Did you watch him do it?" Bass asked.

Knox didn't reply.

"I know what you and Lara meant to each other. Hell, Nichols did you a favor, taking a dance like that. Had you killed him, consider the headlines, Revenge—Homicide Cop Blows Away Wife's Killer.

"Make no mistake Knox, the bastard freed the both of you, justice for her soul, relief for yours. Now, let it go. If you don't, the bitterness will rot your insides until you're no good to yourself—or to *her* memory."

"I know what you are saying, Jon. Someday maybe I'll get there. For now revenge is as good as it gets, letting go is too much to ask."

"Time to leave," said Bass, a final nod to Lara's grave. "The two of you have things to talk about."

Knox felt a gentle touch on his shoulder, and his mentor slipped off among the towering trees.

• • •

ABOVE SAINT ANTHONY Falls on the Stone Arch Bridge, Knox took a drag from a cigar. Tendrils of spray drifted up from the cataract amid the night air. A faint, soulful rhapsody from a base sax crawled through the open French doors of Francine's European Grill, and crept across the cobblestones of East Main.

Memories, the nights at Francine's were the best; Lara and him, Ernie Guzman and his wife, Jon and Florida Bass, Swede and his wife as well. But events of the past few weeks had turned all those occasions to dust; nothing would be the same.

As if drifting back into a dreadful dream, the memories were suddenly replaced by the vision of Nichols as he twisted and died at the end of a rope. The awful specter accompanied by the image of Lara, dead on Hennepin Avenue. And, there was Swede, gone in a gunfight. Knox didn't have any trouble rationalizing—an eye for an eye. Perhaps, with Nichols gone, like Bass had suggested, light would finally cut through the fog of chasing hope through darkness.

Knox stared down river. He had made only two life commitments, one to Lara the other to his job. She was gone, but the death of her killer left him with only a hollow sense of satisfaction. The useless bastard was dead, but that would not bring Lara back from the grave. The anger continued to roil within him.

Reflex, rather than a conscious effort compelled him to answer the annoying summons from his cell phone.

"Knox," he said gruffly.

"Listen, Sergeant," said the condescending voice. "Did you find your revenge on Monroe?"

The voice pulled Knox from his thoughts.

"Who is this?"

"I know your grief, and like you, I know how grief is resolved."

"Say that again," said Knox.

"Sorry about your wife. It's tough to loose someone you care about, isn't it?"

The same voice as before, sly, patronizing. Knox paged through the Rolodex of his memory for a connection, incidents, convicts and informants, nothing. He listened.

"You were there, weren't you Sergeant?"

"Where?" Knox asked, tossing aside his cigar.

"Hung himself, the man that killed your wife. Died before your eyes, I'd bet. Revenge was it? Satisfaction?"

"Listen," said Knox, "I don't know what your preoccupation is with me, but you may regret ever calling this number."

A clever chuckle accompanied Leon's retort. "Oh, that's hard, but that's what they call you isn't it? Hard Knox?"

"Cute," said Knox. "So, what's this about, you and me?"

"It's about vengeance, Sergeant."

With that, the caller was gone. Knox strained to see the callback number. No Data.

Knox stuffed the phone into his pocket, and scanned his surroundings. A new threat had crept into his life, and it pissed him off.

Instinct, or was it a little paranoia, compelled Knox to look into the darkness as he shook the chill from his shoulders. He walked toward Francine's and climbed the steps from the street to the bar. His mind searched for connections to the voice on the cell.

• • •

LEON LOVE LEANED on the girder of the bridge trestle down the street from the favorite haunt of Harding Knox. He tossed a throwaway cell into the river below. A smile slithered across his face. "I know where you are," he uttered.

Leon relished the enjoyment of lurking in anonymity, to stir the wounds that bled inside the soul of Harding Knox. And now, he'd move against the Packard Corporation that deprived him of his entitlement to a good life.

Forty minutes later, Leon found himself cloaked in the shadows of Lyndale Park. He tapped an address into his IPad then made a note. Home—Helen Troyer, executive assistant-—Jonas Packard.

Eighteen

CHIEF BALLARD SCANNED the column of the *StarTribune* on his office desk. The group photo of the news conference dominated the front page, accompanied by the headline, "Mayor Endorses Task Force." However, the subtitle gave Jack Griffin the final authority, "County Attorney to Determine Fate." The headline put the mayor in a leadership position, but the subtitle placed her subservient to her political adversary, something Ballard knew Bergin would find disconcerting.

Bernie Floyd wasted no time fanning the flames of controversy. "Minneapolis Police…shootout investigation outsourced. In question, noted homicide detective…the death of celebrated community leader. Early reports link Knox to the death of Thomas Leyland, dismissed director of Packard Air. Task force grinds on in secret…Mayor… Packard Corporation…authorities avoid comment…case under investigation."

Floyd's article referred to the mayor as avoiding questions specific to the investigation, but addressed her confidence in the task force. The piece eulogized Wallace, and implored the community for patience and understanding.

"No," said Mayor Bergin, "there is no controversy between me and Jack Griffin concerning this terrible matter. I am grateful for his support, and told him so."

Really, thought Ballard, recalling that the mayor's parting comment to Griffin had more to do with busting his testicles than sharing a moment of Kum Bi Ya. A quite knock at the door diverted his attention from the paper.

Mary Cohan peered over the top of designer red cheaters perched near the end of her nose. "Sorry to disturb you, Chief," she said. Then with a raise of an eyebrow, and an utterance just above a whisper, "Commander Krieg is here."

"Please, show him in, Mary. Then you may close the door."

A stoic remnant of the previous administration, Krieg stepped in, and shot a casual glance over his shoulder. The office door closed, not the most congenial omen.

"Good morning, Karl, is that for me?" Ballard motioned for a report file in Krieg's hand.

"A complaint for IAU," said Krieg, "Sergeant Knox, for violating orders."

"About his wife's death investigation, the events on Monroe?" Ballard asked.

"Yes, he was instructed to avoid involvement—"

Ballard reached for the envelope in Krieg's hand. "I'll take it, Karl. Lieutenant Noonan has informed me of the particulars."

Ballard placed the folder in a drawer, depending on its contents it would eventually disappear.

"I assume Knox took the transfer news pretty hard," said Ballard.

"Yes. It won't be an easy transition for him."

"Have a seat, Karl."

The paunchy six foot two commander took a chair in front of the chief's desk. The gray suit, corresponding mop of unruly hair, gopher-like jowls that creased into a double chin seemed to mirror his personality. Not a people person or field commander material; instead, Krieg's prowess lie in bureaucratic abilities. He was a man more suited to formulating, and administrating policy than acting on it.

In the months Ballard had been chief, he had struggled to develop an appreciation of Krieg, intentions that had not progressed well. Perhaps bad chemistry, he initially thought. As the significance of other matters evolved, he simply put the issue aside. However, Ballard had to reckon with Bernie Floyd's disclosures concerning the Packard shootings, as well as Krieg's association with the mayor.

"Have you seen the morning paper?"

"Yes," said Krieg. "Floyd's usual unnamed sources."

"I'm working on that, Karl. The sources, I mean."

"Recently, you met with Mayor Bergin, correct?"

The question posed, the inquisitor knowing the answer.

Krieg's face slackened. He leaned back, took a breath as if contemplating the solution to a riddle.

"The mayor and I go back a long way, Chief. I campaigned for her in her old council district, and for mayor. We speak on occasion. Is there some problem?"

"The problem, Karl, is the Packard investigation."

"Well, the Mayor and I have talked, although not specifically to discuss that issue."

"Then what?" Ballard asked, noting a hedge in Krieg's response.

"Recent crime activity in her old district, certain cases."

"And, you informed her about the Packard ballistic tests, correct?"

The blood drained from Krieg's face, he licked his lips. "I ah…I…may have inadvertently let something drop."

"Well, Karl, the mayor has told me about your impromptu disclosures. Moreover, Bernie Floyd certainly hasn't overlooked that inadvertence. He told me, in front of a press conference no less; that the ballistic report on Knox came from one of my administrators. You were *the* administrator in charge of the case, Karl."

"Chief, I never talked to Floyd. In fact, my standing orders are that no one is to speak to the media about the investigation."

"Who else was with you and the mayor at the time of your disclosure?"

"No one. We were in her office."

"And the door was open?"

"I… Ah… I don't recall, possibly," said Krieg.

"Is it possible that Floyd's source may be in the mayor's office?"

Krieg swallowed hard without reply.

Ballard, not content with the silence, "In the event you missed the memo, Karl, wolves are at the door in regard to the Packard case. I have pulled in favors that I may not be able to repay with the state crime bureau and the county attorney. After Floyd's *StarTribune* revelations, my phone and the mayor's have lit up like Christmas trees."

Krieg gripped the arms of the chair, eyes cast down at a personnel file atop the chief's desk, his file. He had no response.

Ballard lowered his gaze. "I don't have time to chase this leak to ground, but understand this, Karl; any disclosures concerning this case will come through my office, not yours, not the mayor's. I will make them. Are we clear?"

"Of course, absolutely, Chief."

• • •

Near Leon's house on Zenith Avenue, a brisk breeze rustled across the greens of the Minnekata Golf Course. Leon Love jogged along the east tree line and surveyed the backyards of unsuspecting homes nestled near the fairways.

Leon had thought about the plunder that lay behind bay windows and French doors. Burglary had been an avocation that had augmented his days at the University of Wisconsin.

Leon's attraction to crime wasn't about the actual act of theft, although, on occasion it did prove profitable. The lure was in the thrill of invading someone's home, the challenge of getting away with it. And, he did get away with it, until his relationship with Wanda Rippie proved to be as thrilling, and as dangerous as doing burglaries.

The relationship, and booze, pills, and sexual kicks came with a price tag, a negotiated six months in the Dane County Jail. He pushed the thought aside and exited the path near West 39th Street. Once on Zenith Avenue he jogged to his inherited digs, did some stretches and went into the house.

The bathroom was adjacent to the spacious master bedroom. After his morning jog, the hot moist shower chased the chill from Leon's body. He stroked his soapy palms across the ribbed scars on his abdomen and right thigh, reminders of an encounter with a jailhouse shank. He let the warm water flow over his body, hard from hours of confinement exercise. Survival behind bars meant keeping fit.

He bore other scars that haunted him, the death of his mother, decapitated in a car accident, while Leon languished in the Dane County Jail.

Behind the wheel of a produce truck that struck her was a migrant worker, a miserable irony given that political science professor, Lucile Love, brought academic credibility to advocating migrant rights. She railed against corporate greed, its control over political institutions, and the globalization of economies, the wealthy that ignored the needs of impoverished people, and the modern world that subjugated the third world. God, she was hell on wheels, Leon remembered.

On news of her death, Leon's father drifted back onto the scene. He arranged the funeral, a number of university progressives and social activists attended. In handcuffs, shuffling between two jail deputies, Leon made the service, his motherly meal ticket interred, the consequence of blowing a stop sign without a seat belt.

The last time he had seen his estranged father was at his mother's internment. Dad's parting words. "I've arranged for you to come to Minneapolis. I'll take care of things, and you."

Leon took comfort in his old man's intentions. It was as if he would be bank rolled, just where his mother had left off. Social academics, he had come to learn, were so naïve, so easy to manipulate.

Back in his plane, dad flew off forever, later to be gunned down in a corporate tower of avarice that Lucile Love so despised.

Water from the shower pulsed onto his body. Tears fell from his eyes, and deep inside Leon was afraid to admit that what he really wanted was someone to care about him. The old man was his last chance.

"I just needed…somebody," Leon moaned.

Eyes closed, he pushed away at the past, allowed the warmth of the water to sweep across his face, to wash away the haunting thoughts, the anger. His hands glided through the soap, down his body. Touching himself, he eased the pain.

Nineteen

Mrs. Cohan looked up from her morning cup of rose hip tea to see Knox come through the office door.

"I'd like to see the Chief," said Knox, an edge to his tone.

Ballard called out from his inner office. "The Chief is in, Sergeant Knox."

In dark pleated trousers, blue oxford shirt, regimental stripped tie and leather braces, the chief stepped into Mrs. Cohan's office. He held a folder of papers in his hand.

"I'd like to speak with you, Chief. It's about—"

"I know what it's about. Please, come in." Ballard motioned Knox to his office with a sweep of his arm and closed the door.

On the office wall loomed mementos of Ballard's past, a Loyola Juris Doctorate diploma, plaques of the FBI National Academy and Executive Forum, Chicago PD, the anchor, globe and eagle of the United State Marine Corps.

An array of family photos sat on a credenza behind the Chief's chair. Mrs. Ballard was the new provost at Saint Katherine' College in Saint Paul where their two daughters attended school. The items provided an interesting glimpse into the background of the man Knox had come to see. The office was as squared away as the image Thom Ballard projected.

"Please, have a seat, Knox."

"Thank you, sir," said Knox, noting the contemplative expression that grasped the features of Ballard's face. The order for Knox's transfer originated above Krieg's pay grade, and the explanation had to have come from Ballard.

"I'm here about the transfer," said Knox somewhat defiantly. "I've spent over twenty years on the department, more than half my career has been in Homicide. You've read my record."

"Why?" Ballard asked, his voice more akin to a shrink than a police chief. "Why homicide?"

"It's about fit, suitability, Chief; knowing that I make a difference each day with what I do. You can understand that."

Ballard, circumspect in his reply, "Some may say that sounds self-serving."

"As self-serving as it is to be the chief of police?" Knox replied.

Ballard smiled and nodded as if to say touché.

"Of any assignment, Knox, homicide is quite an emotional challenge. At best, most cops burn out after a while then move on."

"I know where you're trying to go with this, Chief. I'm not looking to move on, to explore other options. I need to get back in the game I came from. It's what I do, what I'm about." A thought of Lara and Swede swept through his mind, both gone. "Homicide is what I have left."

Ballard leaned forward, voice quiet. "I understand, Knox. Your record, your recent history has become compulsory reading for me over the past two weeks."

"Then you know enough to understand why I'm here."

"I know this sounds callous, but there is a larger picture that I have to consider. The department, and the city have incurred substantial scrutiny in light of Neil Wallace's death. I've had to re-assign personnel, cancel leaves, and place Special Ops on alert to handle the unrest."

"You mean I've become politically disposable before all the facts become known." Knox let the sarcasm linger.

"I know how you may feel," said Ballard, an empathetic nod, hands apart.

"I don't think you do, Chief."

"Sergeant Knox." said Ballard, "In the past, you've been through two other shootings, and a grand jury hearing. Recently, your wife and partner were killed, and you're staring into the jaws of another grand jury; it's time to take a break."

The cool, bureaucratic numbness in Ballard's reply accompanied that featureless look too often viewed in the eyes of Karl Krieg.

"So that's it?"

"It is, Knox. I hoped for another way, but there isn't one."

Knox walked out, and closed the door behind him.

No other way.

• • •

The Nicollet Inn, off Main Street Park, sat at the east end of Nicollet Island. The old limestone building had operated since the 1890s in various forms of millwork and manufacturing before falling into disrepair. By the late 1970s, it had been transformed to one of the city's more discreet, refined dining and hotel scenes. Chief Thom Ballard found the Inn convenient, away from prying eyes for a meeting with Jack Griffin.

The breeze blowing down river brushed his face, lights on the old lampposts had flickered on, and cast the street in a soft evening glow. Ballard entered the dining room off Merriam Street, took a table near a window, ordered a dry martini and waited.

About the time the olive had slid to the bottom of his glass, Ballard saw Jack Griffin crossing the remnant span of the old steel Broadway Bridge. Now an antique feature of the island, the bridge spanned the spillway to the NSP power plant.

In his early fifties, Griffin retained an athletic, purposeful stride, reminiscent of his former days on a rugby pitch. A gust of wind caught the tails of his topcoat, and a boutique shopping bag carried in his hand.

Ballard waved when Griffin entered the dining room.

"Sorry I'm late, Thom. Wife's birthday," Griffin said as he sat down. "I had to pick up a last minute gift."

"My regards," said Ballard with a glance at the bag.

The waiter appeared. Ballard ordered tomato soup, a baguette and dirty martini. Griffin ordered the same.

"Thanks for meeting me," said Ballard. "I thought this would be a less conspicuous venue to talk, off the record, of course."

Griffin hesitated with his response. "I heard that Harding Knox has been reassigned to uniform duties," said Griffin. "Anything to that?"

"You have a bug in my office, Jack?"

"No, but some people have got a bug up their ass about the transfer, if it's true."

The waiter delivered the martinis. "It's true," said Ballard.

"I understand the circumstances, Thom, but there are people in this town, like myself, who are indebted to Knox for a number of things."

"I've seen his record, Jack, and can understand why."

"A few years ago," Griffin paused over his drink "two muggers pulled my wife into a dark alley. One of them, a woman, slashed Diane's neck in the process of taking her purse. For added effect, the male slug kicked her in the ribs, and the side of her head."

Griffin brushed aside his Martini.

"Diane," emotion caught in Griffin's throat, "had been shopping for a gift for *my* birthday. There wasn't a fucking shred of evidence as to who the suspects were."

The waiter appeared with dinner. "My tab," said Ballard. "Please, continue, Jack. I had no idea."

"A month later Knox shot a woman during a methamphetamine buy that went bad. Ernie Guzman was involved as well."

"I read about it in Knox's file. The woman sliced at his face with a meat cleaver, but there was no mention of your wife's case."

"There wouldn't have been. In those days, Knox and Guzman were assigned to narcotics and vice. A real dynamic duo, they solved murders, broke up fencing operations, took down drug and burglary rings, armed robbers and—"

"And, street muggers," added Ballard.

"Exactly. Then, as U.S. Attorney, I had handled their federal cases. They took an interest in my wife's situation, worked some sources. A few days after the drug incident a box appeared on my office desk. Inside I found my wife's purse, some personal ID. There was a note and two business cards, one from Knox and the other Guzman's. The note said, 'Mr. Griffin, your wife can sleep easy.'"

There was never any direct evidence connecting the drug dealers to my wife's situation, just the purse, and Knox and Guzman's street sources. But after you've been in this business a while, even without clear evidence, you know."

Ballard felt the prosecutor's contemplative gaze as Griffin sipped his drink.

"My point is, Thom, you may be compelled to exile Knox. But don't put him where you can't get him back. Someday you may need him."

"I'll take it under advisement, counselor."

"Please do. And, now, you want to know about the grand jury?"

Just then, Ballard glimpsed the image of a figure hurry pass the window. His curiosity trumped the question Griffin had posed. "Hold that thought, Jack."

A puzzled look registered on Griffin's face.

Ballard left the dining room, and padded into the nearly vacant bar. A young couple sat in the muted light at a corner table of the stylish early 1900s décor. Two men dressed in business attire paid their waiter and left. From his vantage point, Ballard could see through the space between bottles in a wine rack.

Duane Straight saddled onto a stool near the end of the bar next to the prominent political reporter, Bernie Floyd. Floyd pressed his hand onto Duane's thigh.

Floyd went wide-eyed, at Ballard's approach. The word "Extra" flashed through Ballard's mind while Floyd suppressed a hand-caught-in-Duane's-cookie-jar smile. Duane turned his head with a flash of total surprise.

Floyd had the reputation of having a stable of confidential sources from the back halls of the state capitol to the city council chambers of both Saint Paul, and Minneapolis. He cultivated those who had scores to settle, dirt to peddle, and scandals to expose. As a result, he was both lauded and reviled depending on whose ox was being gored. In the process, he sold a hell-of-a-lot of newspapers.

"Hello Bernie," said Ballard. "Taking a little dictation from our boy, Duane?"

Floyd replied with feigned indignation. "I resent the implication?"

"I wasn't implying."

Ballard slapped Duane on the back, and slid a twenty-dollar bill toward the bartender. "Whatever these characters are drinking," said Ballard. "And, don't forget the little umbrellas."

Upon his return to the table, Ballard couldn't conceal his mischievous smile

"What's up?" Griffin asked. "You run into the Marx Brothers at the bar?"

"More like Bernie Floyd with his hand on the thigh of the mayor's executive assistant. Quite stimulating."

Griffin, chuckled. "Jesus. I'd give a hundred votes to see the expression on Barbara Bergin's face when she finds out."

"Give me a few days. I'll let you know."

The two men finished their meal, and Ballard walked Griffin back to the bridge.

Griffin paused in mid-span. "In response to your grand jury question, I've selected outside counsel to present the case. There is, however, a matter of evidence that we need to obtain."

Ballard leaned against the bridge railing, "Video recordings of the shootings?"

"You've heard."

"My liaison people keep me in the loop," said Ballard.

"Naturally we have obtained witness photos and videos," said Griffin, "but Packard's Chief Counsel, Ray Warren, has ignored our efforts get the actual corporate recordings. I have to pursue the issue. To disregard the existence of those videos, and have them surface later would be a disaster for my office."

Dark water swirled below the bridge. "There may be no winners in this, Jack. We don't know what's been recorded, or how the contents may be perceived."

"Think of it, Counselor, "a flock of litigant vultures descending onto Packard's holdings. Then, they'll circle to pick the lint from the city's pockets. You can almost begin to appreciate Ray Warren's position, protecting the company."

"I know," said Griffin. "But the credibility of my office compels me to go after the recordings, whatever the case."

The credibility of Griffin getting into the governor's office was also in play. A prospect Ballard knew all too well. In any case, Griffin was right. To ignore the existence of the videos was out of the question, regardless of the consequences.

"So, where are you with Warren?

"I'm sure he's examining options. I talked with him, supplemented that with a formal letter. That was days ago. We can subpoena the damn things, but first I need to confirm the videos exist, and where they are before they disappear."

Ballard sighed. "You're the county prosecutor, Jack. Go straight to Packard."

"Listen, I know that sounds logical, but the corporation has gross revenues that exceed those of the state of Minnesota. That's a lot of power, and Ray Warren orchestrates the threat management process that protects that power."

The wind rustled through the giant elms, and the old brick facades of the riverfront buildings. Ballard saw that peculiar, crafty-eyed-lawyer look cast by Griffin. It begged the question that Ballard had to ask.

"So, how are you going to get the recordings?"

"I'm not," said Griffin. "I'd like you to get them for me."

Twenty

By 8:00 A.M., Ballard finished reading the *Bullet*, the department's encapsulated digest of mayhem in the city. He shoved his cup of coffee to the side of the desk, contemplating his move to out flank Ray Warren, and obtain the Packard shooting video.

Mayor Bergin unexpectedly entered the office. "Good morning."

"Mayor, I hadn't expected you." Ballard motioned her to a side chair near his desk. Bergin's tone of voice indicated that the trials of the day had not yet trampled upon her surprising cheerfulness.

"I hope that I'm not interrupting anything, but I wanted to see what progress has been made with the Packard situation."

The encounter with Duane, and Bernie Floyd from the previous night was still fresh in Ballard's mind. As well, the mayor was sensitive to Ballard's relationship with Griffin. The disclosure of both matters was about to darken Bergin's morning. For the moment, Ballard decided to set aside the Duane Straight matter.

"Yesterday, I spoke with the medical examiner, and Bill Flynn at BCA. And, last night I met with Jack Griffin."

"Griffin?" said Bergin. "Really?"

"Everything is moving forward," said Ballard. "Jack is appointing an outside prosecutor for the grand jury. It provides the process, and his office, with more of an objective buffer in light of public opinion. But, there may be one glitch."

"Glitches I don't need, Thom."

"An issue of direct evidence," said Ballard.

"I need to take you into confidence on this, Barbara," Ballard used her first name to reinforce the seriousness of what he had to tell her. "There may be a corporate video of the Packard shootings."

The mayor wrinkled her brow in surprise. "My God, that could be.... Her hopeful tone checked by her instinctive caution. "Unpredictable."

"I agree. We really don't know what's on the recordings."

"I assume Griffin will go after them?" Bergin asked.

"First we have to prove they exist. There are indications that Packard's chief counsel is circling the wagons, assessing their corporate liabilities.

"Well, I'll call Jonas Packard and get this ironed out," Bergin said.

"I appreciate that, but involving your office in a criminal investigation may not be a prudent move given your future political intentions."

Bergin thought for a moment. "Then, you have an alternative?

"I've received a call, exploring an option," Ballard replied.

"Okay," said Bergin, a note of caution to her acceptance. We need to ensure that option protects the city from any risk. Make certain that you keep me informed."

Bergin stood and turned toward the door. "There *is* one more thing, Barbara."

"Yes, what is it?"

Ballard studied the mayor a moment, thinking of the loop she wanted to be kept in, or was it a noose that was to be fitted around the neck of Duane Straight.

"At the Nicollet Inn last night, while I met with Jack Griffin, I saw two other individuals of interest in the political scheme of things."

The mayor cocked her head, a slight smile on her face as if Ballard was about to divulge some torrid tidbit. "Go on."

"One of those individuals was your executive assistant, Duane Straight."

"Oh?"

"The other was Bernie Floyd."

The smile dropped like a stone from Bergin's face.

"Barbara, in addition to having a hand on Duane's thigh, I'd say Bernie probably has an ear into your office, and your campaign."

A scowl swept across the Bergin's face. Her fingers bit into the back of the chair she now stood behind. "Duane, that son-of-a-bitch." The words were uttered as if Bergin was about to expel some spittle of vile phlegm.

Ballard maintained an apolitical position with Bergin, but having a snake like Duane in your midst was intolerable. "Is there anything I can do?"

The Mayor's reply was icy. "Thank you, Thom. I'll handle it." Bergin stalked from the office, leaving Ballard to speculate about the fate of Duane Straight.

• • •

The Walker Museum, one of the city's cultural centers of art, sat tucked into the southwest corner of downtown. Contemporary, some would say eccentric exhibits from around the world, eventually found their way to the Walker where satisfaction of eclectic tastes brought financial sustenance to the institution.

Ballard parked at the far edge of the sculpture garden, scanned the area for signs of anyone familiar. Finding no one, he strolled along the walkway past the imaginative larger-than-life representations of the sculpture garden. A contemporary bronze nude emerged from a large block of stone. A wood horse of weathered sticks, "Woodrow," stood amidst a stand of poplars. "The Spider," a tripod formation of balanced steel beams moved about in the wind. Then Ballard paused a moment at the garden's centerpiece, Oldenburg and van Bruggen's gigantic white spoon. Its long handle arched to the daub of an island amidst a small pond where a huge black-stemmed cherry rested within the ladle of the spoon. Bizarre but there was a strange appeal to the garden's landmark. Chicago had a one-hundred-sixty-ton untitled Picasso, while Minneapolis possessed a giant spoon and cherry. Ballard shrugged.

About thirty yards along the pathway, a large, rusted metal sculpture, a snowplow-like blade sunk its jagged, spiked teeth into the earth. Nearby, a large man sat on a wood bench. Ballard recognized him from the call he had received.

"I'll be by the plow blade, east of the spoon," the caller had said. "Look for me wearing a plaid golf cap."

Ballard almost asked if there was a secret password, but thought better of it.

The intermediary had wrestler-like shoulders rounded long ago by the sands of time. He stood, and both regarded one another for a moment.

"We spoke on the phone this morning," said Ballard.

Round Shoulders extended his hand, "Pleasure to meet you, Chief."

"The spoon and cherry thing were pretty good clues," jested Ballard, "the plow blade more of a challenge."

Ballard glanced around the nearly vacant grounds. "Rather empty after 6:00 P.M."

"That's the point."

"Then you don't mind that we get right to it; the point I mean."

Round Shoulders looked beyond Ballard, across the open lawn toward the distant hedge maze. "Off the record, correct?"

"That is the condition, yes," said Ballard.

The source exhibited a calm resignation to his disclosure. "Four video CDs," he said. "Raymond Warren, Packard's chief counsel has them off site in a safe deposit vault at Saint Anthony Federal on the Nicollet Mall."

"Then Warren is trying to protect the company?" said Ballard.

Round shoulders gazed at Ballard a moment. "I'm not authorized to provide any background, just point you in the right direction."

"I'm open for suggestions," said Ballard.

The demeanor of the source remained composed, demonstrating his experience with such discussions. "This has to be handled carefully, and quickly, Chief. Follow along, it's not complicated."

Ballard listened intently as the plan was unfolded to him, being a patient listener was part of the trade. He had only a few questions, but wondered, as cops do, about the intent of his source. Perhaps there was the nature of intra-corporate scheming to consider, a board of directors maneuvering against its president. However, Ballard's sense was that it was more personal. "Just one more question."

Round Shoulders chuckled, "Why am I doing this?"

"I had to ask. Comes with the job, you know?

"Enjoy the evening, Chief," was the enigmatic response.

A tug at his cap, Round Shoulders turned to start down the walk. "I'm going this way," he said with a nod toward the cedar hedge. "Remember, we were never here."

Ballard called after the man. "Thank you, Commander Bass."

There was no response.

Twenty-one

Just after dawn, Leon drove to suburban Wayzata then west on County Road 15 to the entrance of Packard House. He eyeballed the location, making mental notes of the terrain. Monitored by security cameras, an iron gate rested between two stone pillars at the estate entrance. A placard gave notice that the property was alarmed. A twelve-foot hedge of cedars blocked access to the peninsula. Leon opted for a boat rental.

The sixteen-foot aluminum boat, ubiquitous among the fishing craft that plied the fourteen-thousand-acre lake, idled to a slow drift parallel to Packard Point. Leon dropped anchor and cast a line, but he wasn't there to fish.

The visor of his ball cap pulled low on his forehead, Leon jigged the rod held between his hands. He scanned the water's edge, studied the landscape with a predatory gaze. A prominent feature, a stone tower loomed above the treetops toward the east side of the peninsula. On a knoll, set back from the lake, the estate house appeared through a line of huge trees. At the shoreline, of particular interest, a stone boathouse sat at the water's edge, doors open to reveal two large craft. Leon entered a note in his iPad, his repository of information about other homes, other people.

With a sudden gust of wind, Leon felt the boat move. He hauled up the anchor, having lost purchase of the sandy lake bottom. It banged against the side of the metal hull, the dull metallic bang breaking the morning silence. He turned to start the motor, and slipped away. As the boat turned into the wind, Leon caught sight of a man in a window of the boathouse lodge, a set of field glasses trained in his direction.

Within its one hundred forty miles of shoreline, Lake Minnetonka meandered through the western suburbs of Minneapolis. The lake, and its islands had been a resort and fishing destination since the 1860s. Eventually, the area evolved to provide secluded acreage for scores of fashionable estates, Packard House with its three-season boathouse among them.

A flagstone walk wandered through the pink azaleas and the west logia of the estate house, then descended to the stone boathouse. Inside, cradled above the water on motorized hoists, sat a twenty-two-foot center console fishing boat, and a gleaming twenty-six-foot lake cruiser. Electric overhead doors kept out the weather. Above the boat-well was a three-season recreation lodge with fireplace and veranda.

Jonas Packard sat in a chair, a blanket over his lap, legs rested on a footstool. The glow of an early morning sun cast long shadows from the tree line across the water. It had been three weeks since the ballroom shootings. With the help of Jon Bass, Jonas Packard was able to venture beyond the manner house, noticeably on the mend from the wound in his chest.

Packard, warmed by the fire in the fireplace, sipped his tea; the shootings still fresh in his mind, a murdered policeman, another nearly so, Jon Bass, among others, shot. Innocent people gunned down before his eyes. Unbelievably, all of it carried out by the hands of the once trusted Tom Leyland. Some on the board of directors were skeptical of Packard's judgment in hiring Leyland. Presently, Ray Warren, Chief Counsel, evaluated corporate cover, attempting to deflect some of the blame on the police to diminish the impact of lawsuits. Jonas Packard was not about running for cover. He glanced at Bass.

"I take it your meeting with Chief Ballard was successful, Jon?"

Bass turned to acknowledge the question, preoccupied with a fishing boat in the bay.

"Everything is in motion, sir." His gaze returned to the lake.

"Good," said Packard. "I appreciate Ray's motivation to protect the company, less so the motives of some board members, but that's for another day. The thing is, Jon, Harding Knox took a bullet likely meant for me, saved my life. To let him hang out to dry over this shooting affair is, well, dishonorable."

Bass didn't respond, a set of field glasses pressed to his eyes.

"Something wrong, Jon?'

"No sir. Just a small boat on the sand flats, two o'clock, 100 meters out."

"I'm sure he'll move along, Jon. There's never been good fishing there."

"Exactly, sir."

Twenty-two

Transferred to the Uniformed Division, Knox gazed at the stranger who stared back from the reflection in the mirror. Beard shaved, regulations, he rubbed a hand across smooth, chilled skin. He peered into a beardless face that he had not seen since his assignment to vice and narcotics, then homicide, more than a decade and a half ago.

The trace of a horizontal scar, about an inch long, ran along his left cheekbone. The scar, a souvenir retained from a drug bust that went bad. Knox rubbed his finger along the faint line, remembering. On occasion, the event still played out in his nightmares.

It had been a cold January night on Columbus Avenue South, a buy-bust on a small meth operation. In a dingy second floor flat, without warning, a woman cranked up on methamphetamine, charged out of the darkness from behind a beaded curtain. Knox turned, a meat cleaver thrust toward his face. He put a .45 round, point-blank, into the woman's chest. The blade lanced his cheek. Ernie Guzman pumped two rounds into the clown that pulled a shotgun from under the kitchen table. A third doper lived to shit his pants. Not suspecting they were cops, the intended play was to rip-off Knox and Guzman.

The incident, Knox remembered, helped to settle a score for then, US Attorney Jack Griffin. The dirt-bags who had beaten, and robbed Griffin's wife lay dead.

The deceased and wounded were Somalis. The woman whirling the meat cleaver was white. Protests poured forth regarding the deaths, Knox and Guzman cleared of any wrongful action. Knox mused that nothing had changed over the years, cops and shootings interlocked in a hyperbole of race and politics. This time, a grand jury was to decide his fate for the death of Neil Wallace.

Knox slipped a light blue uniform shirt over the Kevlar vest. On each upper shirtsleeve, department shoulder patches and sergeant chevrons sported a knife-edged crease. The Navy blue trousers filled out the remainder of the figure in the mirror. He slung his gun belt over his shoulder then, one last glance in the mirror.

Unexpectedly, Knox felt pleased with the image he saw. Younger in appearance than the forty-five years his mind refused to accept, but his body knew better. Bike rides along the river and exercise helped to heal the job's physical wounds, but the anger and anxiety still welled within him about the transfer. He had grown accustomed to the independence, creativeness, and lack of restriction that went with the responsibility of detectives. Uniformed Division was like the other side of the moon; structure, regulations, precinct assignments, confined geography.

• • •

The telemetry dishes of Channel 7, like a cluster of giant mushrooms, covered the roof of the Premiere Media Center at 11th Street and Nicollet.

For a half hour, Leon Love sat in the parking lot shadows, an occasional glance through his binoculars. Across the street, surveillance cameras directed their gaze into the lot of the electronic metro media merchant, but not at him. He sighed as he slurped on the straw of his cherry soda. Patience.

Soon, Kathleen Conlon, the red haired driver of a tan Audi roadster, would roll out from behind the chain-linked fence, away from the gaze of security cameras. As co-anchor on the 10:00 P.M. nightly news, Leon knew her face and schedule. He acquired a fascination for her, that certain look, an impish glance into the camera at the end of a story. His hobby, compulsion actually, was computer research, a study of backgrounds and habits of those in whom he found an interest. However, his allure to Conlon led him to a surprising association. Conlon was the sister-in-law of Sergeant Harding Knox. A notation had gone into Leon's iPad.

Now, he sat in the dark, watching, waiting. With the object of his fascination not being aware of his presence, or his intentions, he felt the race of his pulse. It was all part of his game.

At 11:55, the tan Audi Cabriolet edged out of Channel 7's parking lot into night. Leon turned the key and the Camaro's electronic ignition sparked to life. He rumbled out of the lot, and slid onto Nicollet Avenue to shadow the Audi.

The eye-catching news anchor handled the Audi with the spunk that resembled her TV persona. She maneuvered through the downtown streets, and wound her way south along the meandering tree lined Lake of the Isles. Conlon slipped through a curve then glided into a turn near Thomas Avenue South. Leon dropped back, keeping the taillights in sight as the Audi darted into an alley. Leon doused his headlights. A touch of a toggle switch shut off the rear lights, but not the controlled excitement that surged within.

Brake lights flashed in a garage near the far end of the alley and Leon coasted to a stop. He shut off the ignition and interior light then stalked into the shadows, heart pounding with anticipation. He watched Conlon push through her back gate having no idea that *he* would invade *her* life.

Concealed in the dark, Leon crept forward and watched Conlon tromp up the steps to a broad deck. She put a key in the door and let herself in.

At the edge of white pickets of the back yard fence, Leon found cover behind a shrub. A lamplight brightened a sitting room at the back of the house. Leon crept onto the deck, knowing Conlon could not see out with the light on, but he could see in. She dropped her coat on a chair and picked up a cat, a big fuckin' cat, Leon noted. She was alone, and he watched, catching a glimpse of her as she past from room to room. Leon moved position when a light went on in what Leon found was Conlon's bedroom.

Through a space at the bottom of the blinds he watched Conlon slip from her clothes. He swallowed from the elation of seeing her perfect naked body, breasts and pubis. In the dark at her window, he opened his pants and masturbated. The thrill of wanting her, the excitement of her not knowing that he was even there fulfilled his rapture.

It was all part of the game, like getting high, the feeling Leon retained as he slipped back to the Camaro and idled down the alley. A picture of plans he had for Kathleen Conlon formed in his mind. Before he headed home, he had to make a call.

Leon parked near Lake Harriet and tapped in the public number.

"Minneapolis Police, Second Precinct," said the voice in a routine, institutional response.

"Sergeant Knox, please."

"Just moment," said the voice.

Leon waited. Like invading an occupied house in the middle of the night, he felt a rush pulse through him.

"Sergeant Knox, can I help you."

"First night on the job, Sergeant?" said Leon, with mock sincerity. "Congratulations on your new position."

There was a pause on the line. Leon savored the tension. He had inserted himself into the life of Harding Knox. And, like twisting the blade of a knife, he intended to make him bleed a little at a time.

Knox, now familiar with the voice that taunted him, wanted to reach through the phone to grab the asshole by the throat.

"Listen," said Knox, "You want the crisis hot line."

"Very cleaver, Sergeant, but I'm not the one in crisis. It must be difficult to cope with your own downfall, reduced to obscurity behind a desk."

"Listen pal, if you keep calling me, you'll be the one reduced to obscurity. Find yourself another hobby, before I make you mine."

"That's where I have been to night, Sergeant, exercising my hobby."

Leon ended the call; gratified that Knox had no idea why he had become the subject of Leon's interest, or, even who the hell Leon was. Laughing, Leon put the disposable phone in his pocket and drove off to the Why Fi Café, a Lake Street eatery and geek hangout. He had a late appointment with a contact that had something to share, for a price. Sergeant Knox would be fare for another day.

Twenty-three

ACROSS THE BROAD pavestone plaza from Minneapolis City Hall, traffic rustled unobstructed under the Hennepin County Government Center that straddled Sixth-Street. Two halves of the building joined by exposed steel girders and glass reached twenty-six stories into the city skyline. A giant open atrium, chimney-like, rose through the county court side of the building. In the 1970s, the distinguished architectural innovation fostered a decidedly tragic notoriety when a couple despondent souls had leapt from the interior cantilevered balconies. Their plunge, reached terminal velocity twenty stories below in the mezzanine reflection pool.

After the usual committee meetings, project bid assessments, and another body; the balconies became glassed in, the waters of the reflection pool stilled.

It had been two months, but seemed like yesterday, since the Packard Center shootings. Knox had settled into the monotony of his new position, seemingly anonymous to the rest of the world, as intended by the prevailing politics of the city. His anonymity was about to change, a witness chair awaited in the chambers of the grand jury.

Knox stood on the 21st floor of the Government Center. He stared through the balcony glass, his turn in front of the grand jury about to commence. He remembered the stories Swede had told him about those despondent souls who had plummeted to the pool below. He could, after the last couple of months, empathize with that state of mind; but that's not want he was about, not what Lara would have imagined of him.

At 9:00 A.M., he turned from the glass. Through the door, just across the hallway his fate awaited.

Maurice Mancel, the Police Federation attorney, approached. He possessed a hawk-like gaze through alert brown eyes. A bantam stature at five-foot-seven complemented his appearance as that of a bird of prey. His reputation was that of an ardent advocate for his clients.

An ex-cop, and William Mitchell Law School graduate, part of Mancel's practice was devoted to representing cops who had the misfortune to be at odds with the system.

Mancel's voice, hurried, "Knox, I'm glad I caught you. I just found out that the entire shooting is on a corporate video. The grand jury has it, and I assume they will show it to you."

Of course, Knox thought. It had to be the reason the lid was shut tight on the case—me on video, a Minneapolis police sergeant, gunning down Neil Wallace. His heartbeat quickened.

"Look, Knox, regardless of the video, you know what will be required of your testimony," said Mancel. "You're the one who must put everything in context. You were there, not the prosecutor, not the jury."

"I know, Maurice. It still doesn't change the fact that I'm the one on trial, the one who risks an indictment for killing Wallace."

Mancel pointed toward the jury room. "Then damn it, go in there and set the record straight."

Just then, a bailiff called out, "Sergeant Knox."

The grand jury was situated in an impersonal auxiliary courtroom with a light oak paneled accent wall, and commercial oatmeal gray carpet. The room was the size of a small condo with high ceilings, and lights that cast a harsh, indifferent glow.

Uncertain of his fate, Knox paced to a simple soft back office chair. It sat behind a plain table at the front of the room. He stood, and waited.

Ed Farber, the talented criminal prosecutor who Jack Griffin had brought in from Dakota County, would handle the proceedings.

Three legal pads lay on an oak laminated table in front of Farber. Paper evidence bags with exhibit tags sat near the table on the floor. In front of the jurors was a small diorama of the Packard ballroom. A fifty-five inch LED screen and DVD player occupied a table to Farber's right.

Farber, a thin, angular man, had wispy blond hair. His face pinched in concentration added to the age of a man not more than his mid-thirties. "Please, have a seat," said Farber.

Knox took the witness chair, his eyes scanning the stoic faces of twenty-five expressionless strangers in whose judgment his future rested. The prosecutor paged through his legal pad.

Like decapitated scarecrows, three mannequins stood at the front of the room, each fixed to a metal pole mounted to circular floor stand. On the first mannequin, Knox immediately recognized his tuxedo jacket and shirt fitted over a Kevlar vest.

On the second, a black tuxedo jacket hung over a blood stained shirt. The third mannequin had two small bloodstains, one center of the chest, the other in the upper center back. Knox forced his gaze back to the prosecutor.

Farber stood, his head quickly bobbed up from the review of his notes. "Good morning, Sergeant Knox. We appreciate your attendance today. As you know, this grand jury has been empanelled to investigate the circumstances of the shootings at the Packard Center in Minneapolis, mid-March of this year."

"Yes, I understand," said Knox with a measured response.

"To assist the jury in assessing what happened, you will be asked a series of questions, and asked to comment on exhibits associated with that event. Do you understand, sir?"

"Yes," said Knox, cognizant his responses should be brief.

"You have the right," continued Farber, "against self incrimination under the Fifth Amendment of the Constitution. If you chose to waive that right, you are compelled to answer truthfully the questions put to you, and will not have counsel present to cross-examine, or to challenge any of the exhibits."

At what amounted to being given a Miranda warning reserved for criminals, Farber paused, as if to drag out the drama. Knox hoped that his irritation at receiving the admonition did not register on his face.

"If represented by counsel," Farber droned on, "I shall permit you to consult with him, or her, outside the confines of the grand jury room. However, you are not to delay or impede this process."

Farber's tone was flat, anchored in years of focused procedure, and an idiosyncratic demeanor. With stooped shoulders and brisk speech, he had an awkward way of looking out of the corner of his eye, head slightly turned when addressing Knox.

The witness oath followed. Right hand raised, Knox repeated it, controlling his apprehension, a cop perhaps transformed to political scapegoat over the death of Neil Wallace.

In the sterile atmosphere of the jury room the detached analysis of violence and mayhem had begun, moments of chaos repackaged into an orderly, clinical process. For Knox, that night in the ballroom was devoid of process, procedure, and clinical assessment. That night was about a split second decision, life or death.

To remain silent, to take the 5th, was to convey a perception of hiding something, tantamount to guilt, and, he had nothing to hide. "I am ready to proceed."

Very well, Sergeant." Farber continued through a Q&A of Knox's professional history, uniformed officer, five years in vice and narcotics, and twelve years as a homicide sergeant.

Curiously, Farber made no mention of two previous shooting incidents, where Knox had been justified in the shooting of two assailants. Farber's cadence of oratory was banal as the jury sat pokerfaced until it was time to cut to the chase.

"So, tell, me, Sergeant," said Farber, "how is it that you came to be at Packard Center the night of the shootings?"

Some members of the jury put pens to note pads, others rocked back in their chairs, eyes narrowed in speculation. Knox hesitated, a flash of reflection; Lara's grave on that terrible night, then he commenced his account.

What followed was a two-hour barrage of questions and answers. Knox replied, succinct, on point. Farber established the chain of events. Then at Farber's request, Knox positioned figures on the ballroom diorama, the location of Swede Lundgren, Jon Bass, the Packard's, and where Knox took down Thomas Leyland. Farber avoided questions concerning the bullet that killed Neil Wallace. Knox knew, Farber was setting the stage; the question would come, like death itself.

At Noon, the jury broke for lunch. Knox, feeling spent, sat back in his chair and watched them file out.

The preliminary round complete, Knox stepped into the hall, as Mancel ushered him away from prying eyes and ears. With a whisper, he asked, "How is it going in there?"

"It's like standing in front of a shotgun with no place to run."

"Remember, Knox, it was Leyland who tried to kill *you*."

"Yeah, I remember, Maurice. Every night when I close my eyes."

"There was no choice, Knox. What happened to Wallace was a tragic accident."

"That's what I keep telling myself, Maurice, but I feel like my neck has already been measured for the noose. What bothers me is I don't know where Farber is headed?"

Knox sighed, "I gotta hit the men's room."

At 2:00 P.M., Knox resumed his seat as the jury filed in. To his surprise, Samantha DeAngelo entered the room, and took a chair at the prosecutor's table. At forty, with a supple figure and short bobbed raven hair, dark eyes and almond complexion, she was naturally attractive.

Long ago, she had been a prior chapter to Knox's life. Now only a professional relationship existed. He made the arrests; she on occasion prosecuted his cases. His gaze lingered, and caught her eye. A matter of self-conscious reflex, both averted their look, Knox to his water glass, DeAngelo to Farber.

An Assistant Hennepin County Attorney, Samantha DeAngelo consulted quietly with Farber. While they talked, Knox felt his history with DeAngelo ebb into mind.

They had been two independent souls racing along career paths when their personal desires collided. The impact lasted longer than expected, then burned out as abruptly as it started. Had it not been for Lara, Knox sometimes wondered...Sam?

DeAngelo was not present when Knox had given his previous testimony. Her poise with Farber, and familiarity with the proceedings gave an indication to Knox that she was handling second seat in the hearing, perhaps Jack Griffin's hand in the game.

Farber stood. His voice exuded more authority, an octave stronger than before the recess. Knox had the feeling that the presence of DeAngelo may have had an influence. Evidently, Farber had a vain streak, but after all, he was an attorney.

"Sergeant Knox, when was it that you first observed Professor Wallace?"

"I did not see him."

"Did you observe him post shooting?"

"I did not. My attention was to the shooter, my own wounds, and to others."

"Was there another shooter?"

"No, there was only Thomas Leyland."

Farber now headed toward the meat of his examination.

"What type of weapon did you carry on the night of the shooting, Sergeant?"

"A .45-caliber Beretta. It's a semi-automatic pistol."

"A large caliber. Can you explain?"

"The .45-caliber round is a slow moving projectile, about 950 feet per second. It has more blunt force stopping power, and less collateral potential than higher velocity rounds."

Farber began to pace between the prosecutor's table and Knox seated in the witness chair. "You use what is known as a Hydra-Shock bullet, correct?"

"Yes," said Knox.

"For the benefit of the jury, please describe that type of bullet."

"The tip of the bullet," said Knox, "is cupped in such a manner that at impact it breaks apart, causes sufficient damage to enhance its stopping effect."

Farber reached to the witness table, picked up an ammo magazine and placed it in front of Knox. "Sergeant, please describe to the jury this exhibit."

"It is a .45 magazine, inscribed with my initials.

Farber grasped a brown evidence box and set it on the witness table. "Sergeant, I'd like you to open box and describe the contents."

Knox didn't need to be told what was inside. Slowly, he slipped the clasp, held the object in his hands, and read the serial number. A red plastic strap had been zipped through the slide and firing chamber to disable the gun.

"It's my Beretta pistol."

"Is that the weapon, type of bullets, and magazine that were used by you on the night of the Packard Center shootings?"

"Yes," said Knox.

Farber picked up the magazine, and Beretta from the witness table. With both in hand, he passed among the jurors like a circus barker with two kewpie dolls. A movement of bodies, a murmur of voices rustled through the room.

Farber returned to the prosecutor's table, and examined his notes. DeAngelo consulted with him in whispered tones. In the momentary silence, Knox sat in the witness chair. He struggled against the pressure that pulsed in his skull.

There was a slight tremor in his hand as he took a drink from the water glass on the table. He had stared death in the eye on more than one occasion, and had killed to stay alive. What possibly could Farber know of that experience? What could these people know of that terror, to sit and render judgment against him?

The long minutes past, Knox could feel the circumspect glace of one or another of the jurors assessing him. He turned his eyes from theirs to the exhibits that pulled him back to that night, wanting Swede and Wallace to be alive, wanting the aftermath of that ordeal to go away.

The murmured whispers of Farber and De Angelo ceased as Farber looked at the wall clock. It was 5:00 P.M.

The discomfort of the daylong testimony registered in the faces of the jury. Farber, too, got the picture, thanked the jury and adjourned for the weekend.

Knox allowed the jury members to file out first. His brain on fire from the headache, he then headed toward the door.

"Sergeant Knox," Farber called out.

Knox stopped, took a patient breath then turned toward the attorney, "Yes, what is it, counselor?"

Farber stood at the prosecutor's table, a legal pad in hand. Knox's eyes followed the departure of Sam DeAngelo. In a navy blue suit and white blouse, she slipped out through a side door, and did not look back. Knox felt a twinge of disappointment. Her exit left him with no glance of acknowledgement.

"Sergeant," said Farber, "I know this is difficult. Please understand that I bear you no malice concerning this hearing. I hope in time that you will come to accept that."

"Mr. Farber, are you trying to tell me something?"

The prosecutor cast a blank look at Knox, his reply as enigmatic as Ed Farber himself.

"Good evening, Sergeant."

Twenty-four

On the 39th floor of Packard Center, Helen Troyer, Admiral Jonas Packard's executive assistant, stepped from her mahogany appointed, glass walled office. A glance at her gold Movado watch showed 8:00 P.M. Her occasional twelve-hour workdays endured through compensation of a six-figure salary.

Mrs. Troyer, as everyone respectfully addressed her, was a woman who possessed extraordinary competence, composed forbearance, and an ability to instill those qualities in others. She could walk into administrative disarray and walk out with I's dotted, T's crossed, and all her people on the same page. At fifty-four, she exhibited a stylish appearance, wore fashionable clothes, and had great legs. A seemingly ageless face graced her theater-like poise. Most important, she was the Admiral's confidant who possessed an adjunct power that most appreciated, some resented, but few confronted. She was keeper of the confidential stratagem in which Jonas Packard's corporate, and political world evolved. On occasion, she would gleam a smile while over-hearing a muffled reference to her unofficial moniker—"Helen of Troy."

Mrs. Troyer paid little attention to the maintenance man or the whir of his vacuum as she locked the office and strode toward the bank of elevators. A constant companion, she carried an Apple laptop in a chic black custom leather bag. The strap cut into the shoulder line of her smart Bill Blass business jacket. Without losing grasp of her matching purse, she punched the elevator button for the executive level garage. The elevator reached the 39th floor, preceded by a gush of air that pushed through the open space of the shaft. Once inside, and as the car dropped to its destination, Mrs. Troyer uttered a sigh of relief after an exhausting day. Then, conscious of her lack of privacy, she rolled her eyes, and waved a weary hand at the security camera notched into the corner of the descending car.

A feeling of release came once she reached her champagne colored Infiniti G coupe. Buckled inside, Helen turned the ignition, and the 330 horsepower G purred to life.

Troyer sped down the vacant aisles, breezed by garage pillars and zoomed out of the ramp onto Marquette Avenue; kind of like running the S turns at Le Mans. Well, it was fun to pretend. The G was her liberation from a demanding business environment, placating egos, dousing administrative brush fires, the rearrangement of the Admiral's schedule. Helen's car, the solitude of her home, and the love of her husband, Bill, were the comforts in her life, her refuge.

Married for thirty years, she and Bill were perfect soul mates. Bill, intelligent, ebullient and her hunk, was still remarkable in bed. A smile brightened her face; so was she.

Life's only regret was no children. Their compensation was having each other, and good friends.

Helen Troyer's Infiniti purred south on Hennepin Avenue through evening traffic then turned through the light onto Lake Street. A chef salad and a bottle of Snapple had been her office dinner nearly two hours ago. A warm shower, soft, clean sheets, and a good book were minutes away. South of 38th Street, she turned into the driveway off Highway of the Kings. The dignified white two-story colonial was characteristic of those that lined the street, and overlooked the charming Lyndale Park.

The garage door opened with a touch of a button on her visor. The G coasted inside to a stop, the engine now still. Mrs. Troyer touched the button once again, and rested her head back as the garage door slid down its rails. Odd, she thought without much interest, the automatic garage lights were out. Bill could fix it tomorrow, when he returned from Montana.

Helen grabbed the straps of her purse, laptop, and keys then slipped out of the car. Aided by the interior light, she fumbled with the key fob, the door key from the garage to the house. Inexplicably, her body tensed, something was terribly wrong.

A figure stepped from the dark. Her mouth opened only to have her scream stifled to a rasp by the hand around her neck. The laptop and purse tumbled to the floor. A sick, weak feeling overtook her. Her knees began to buckle.

Instinctively, the fingers of her left hand searched franticly for the alarm button on the key fob. But another hand grabbed her wrist, slammed it on the rim of the open car door. A blast of pain shot up her arm. The keys went flying.

Her eyes, wide with horror, stared into a black ski mask stitched with garish red lips, and green reptilian eyes.

The figure pressed her against the car, the head in the horrid mask bent toward her right ear. She could feel the hot, moist breath, and the sickening cigarette smell.

"Listen, sweetheart. Don't fuck with me and you won't get hurt."

Helen, with a trembling nod, acknowledged. The hand loosened from her neck.

"I'll give you anything you want," she pleaded. "My car, I have money, credit cards, you can have it all."

His face came close, she turned away not wanting to look, not wanting to see the terrifying specter that had just become her worst nightmare. A hand grabbed her chin, and slowly turned her head into his gaze. In the awful dim light, strange eyes, like piercing gold orbs, glared at her from behind the green stitching of the black mask.

The man pulled her out of her shoes, dragged her to the back of the garage, nylons tearing on the cement floor. From a shelf, he grabbed a furniture-packing blanket; it fluttered open as it hit the floor. Helen Troyer crumpled down on top of it.

"I'm not here for your fuckin' money, lady." The man kneeled and spread her legs.

"No. Please, don't hurt me like that."

Helen's heart pounded as she feebly grasped for the persuasive skills to survive.

"We don't have to do this here," she said, her voice desperate.

"This is good enough for me, Mrs. Troyer."

She gasped. "How do you know my name?'

The man in the mask reached under Helen's tailored skirt, gripped the top of her panties then tore at her hose.

The black mask bent closer, his hand firmly grasped the mound between her legs. "I know everything about you," the voice whispered, "Especially, where you work."

"Please, don't. You must have a sister, a mother."

The man's laugh accompanied the terrifying glint of a knife. The blade sliced through her blouse and bra. Helen Troyer had run out of options. Her evening meal erupted from her mouth. There was a quick, blunt blow to the side of her face. She soiled herself, and her night of horror went to black.

Vomit and urine had not been on the evening agenda. The quick punch to Helen's jaw did little to calm Leon's frustration. He got up unable to consummate further humiliation upon his victim. He looked at the unconscious wretch spread on the floor.

"My mother is dead, bitch."

Twenty-five

THE SECOND PRECINCT Station, with its Art Deco façade' emblematic of the 1930s Depression Era, was a large brick and mortar building that anchored the commercial block of 19th Street and Central Avenue Northeast. An ethnic melting pot for 61,000 people, crime was no stranger to the nineteen neighborhoods of the 2nd.

Across the lobby from the front door of the station, Harding Knox sat behind a broad elevated reception desk. A bank of telephones, communication equipment, and operations manuals sat within easy reach. Clipboards that hung on the walls held the latest department advisories and roll call information. The desk could be a place of ultimate boredom, or controlled disorder. It all depended on the time of day, day of the week, or the latest tempest in the city.

Twenty-two years before, the 2nd Precinct is where Knox began his career. Now, circumstances of that career had brought him back.

It was 8:00 A.M. when Ernie Guzman walked into the lobby. Knox looked up from reports, "Hey, man. You lost?"

"No, still on the job from last night," said Guzman. "Jan Lescoe and I got called out at ten-o'clock."

"That must have put a crimp in Jan's beauty sleep." Knox buzzed Guzman through to a chair beside him at the desk.

"Helen Troyer," said Guzman, "that name ring any bells?"

Knox shrugged, "No."

"She was attacked at her house on Highway of the King's."

Knox, still puzzled, "Pretty up-scale neighborhood, so—"

"She's Jonas Packard's executive assistant."

"Jesus, what the hell happened?

"All we know is that the Packard Center security camera has Troyer in the elevator at her office at 8:03 P.M. The garage camera has her car pulling onto 6th Street at 8:08."

"So, what the hell happened?" Knox asked.

"About 9:45 uniforms arrived on scene for a silent house alarm. They broke in after they saw Troyer lying on the kitchen floor unconscious, the passageway door to the kitchen from the garage was standing open."

The phone rang. Knox answered, referred the caller to communications and looked back at Guzman. "So, Mrs. Troyer is on the floor. She's unresponsive in a locked house, and the silent alarm has gone off, right?"

"I know," said Guzman. "Sounds like the butler did it the pantry with a candle stick, but worse. Troyer's blouse and bra were cut apart, under pants and hose pulled down, knees and hands all scuffed up. She'd vomited, bladder and bowels let loose, and the perp broke her jaw."

"That's rough," said Knox. "I'd pass on the butler and candle stick. I suppose the newsies will be all over this by noon today."

"I think we're safe, at least for a while," said Guzman. "The guys handled the location follow-up by cell phone, keeping everything off the air."

"What have you got at the scene to go on?"

"Not a damn thing, no latent prints, no neighbor witnesses, no security video. Not much hope for fiber and fluid traces, either. Her purse and laptop are missing. Maybe the perp will try her credit cards. Or, we'll get lucky if he tries the computer."

Guzman sat back in his chair. "I called Bass. He's pissed as hell, knew Troyer really well. He came in, worried about a compromise to the company computer system. They're checking now. I said if anything turns up, we'd like to know."

"You did a rape kit exam?" Knox asked.

"You forget, hermano, I do sex and family violence."

"I hope you don't take that home with you."

"Cute," replied Guzman, "But, yeah. They did the exam at the hospital, and X-rays. Forensics has the exam kit and her clothes at the lab. We'll see what happens. As for Mrs. Troyer, she won't be telling us anything for a while. She's sedated with a broken jaw. Consume' through a straw will be her meal of choice for the next month."

"That's a bad break," said Knox with a scowl.

"That's really lame, Knox. "How's the grand jury going?"

"I'll be called in again. Maurice confirmed they have a corporate video recording. Who knows what that will show?"

Guzman paused. "Regardless of the press conferences, the bosses have a lid slapped on this tighter than a gnat's ass stretched over a rain barrel. The newsies continue to speculate about a cover-up, the same old bullshit that riles up the minority community. The word is, you leak you get suspended."

"I just don't know about Wallace, Ernie, how he was hit?"

"Keep the faith, amigo."

Knox gave Guzman a pat on the arm, "Thanks, my friend."

• • •

HEADLIGHTS FROM THE Audi roadster panned down the alley and settled on the garage. The door rose and Kathy Conlon pulled inside. There had been something in the wind about a burglary at the house of Jonas Packard's executive assistant the previous night. But, she couldn't chase it to ground by news time, and Knox was mum about the matter. She grabbed her gym bag, and headed to the house and Atlas, her cat.

At the back gate to the yard, house keys in her hand, Kathy continued to scan the shadows as she mounted the rear deck, the dimness of the alley light providing the barest of illumination. Her house key posed a difficult fit in the deadbolt and door lock.

Oh, the problems of home ownership, she lamented. While at CBS in New York, all she had to do was call the building super. Another twist of the key and door came open. She stepped inside.

Atlas, Kathy's giant Himalayan cat, was not there to greet her, odd she thought. She dropped her bag on the floor and closed the door. A sense of eerie silence gripped her. She was not alone.

Before her fingers could reach the light switch, a figure blitzed her from the darkness. He pounded her against the door with the force of his body. Her eyes, widened and fell upon the black ski mask of her attacker, fluorescent green stitching around the eyes, and a lurid red mouth gaped back at her. His hand gripped her neck as he put his head to her ear.

Kathy gasped, struggled to control her emotions. Through her nose she managed a breath, nurturing a surge of adrenalin, anger to foster survival. She broadened her stance, placing one foot against the base of the door.

The man began to say something, "Listen sweat—"

Kathy lunged, a right knee upward. The desperate thrust hit its mark, leaving the attacker's statement incomplete; the grip on her neck was abandoned for the groin. Kathy pivoted away then shot a kick to the man's knee. He grunted with pain, and crumpled to the floor.

She whirled again, thrusting a kick to the side of the head. The man parried, grabbed the door handle as she backed away for another strike. He pulled open the door, and hobbled onto the deck toward the railing. Over he went. A flurry of epithets preceded a deck chair that Kathy hurled toward the masked invader.

Leon Love evaded the flying chair. He crashed through the back gate, hobbled along the alley and limped a block to his car. For his efforts all he had to show was sore gonads and a crumpled knee. Leon's fantasy encounter with Kathy Conlon had turned to a painful reality.

"Fuckin' bitch!"

An incessant ringing brought Knox out of a fitful slumber. He looked at the clock, 12:19 A.M. it said. He brushed a hand across his face. "Yeah, what is it?"

"Harding, it's Kathy. I've just been attacked."

"Who? What?"

"Harding, wake up, damn it. I've been attacked. It's Kathy. I'm at home."

"Okay. Okay. Are you hurt? Are you safe?"

"I'm just a little shook up but I'm fine. The guy is gone."

"You call the police?"

"Jesus Christ, Knox, you are the police. Who else am I going to call?"

"Right, thanks for the reminder. You still have your Sig .380?"

"Yes."

"Then lock yourself in the bedroom with your cell and the gun."

"I did and I am. I mean I'm in the bedroom with the gun."

"Okay, communications will call when the 3rd Precinct guys get on scene."

"Good, Atlas is loose somewhere. Maybe they can find him."

Knox rolled his eyes at her sudden shift in priority.

"I'm on the way, kid."

Twenty-six

MONDAY AT 10:00 A.M., Knox waited outside the jury room and thought about his sister-in-law, Kathy Conlon, and the perp who got away. The forensics tech arrived late due to other calls, not leaving until after 2:00 A.M., Sunday. The perp had left no defining characteristics behind except fresh scratches around the lock that explained Kathy's difficulty with her key. A lock-pick had likely been used on the door, a covert forced entry.

Unlike the Troyer incident, Knox retained some degree of satisfaction. Kathy had put a hurt on her assailant. Knox stayed the night, and after breakfast he called Guzman to compare notes. The two amusingly concluded that, at least in Kathy's case, they were looking for a perp in a ski mask who walked with a limp, and had acquired a falsetto pitch to his voice. There was little else to go on.

The door opened and the bailiff called for Knox. The jurors occupied the same crescent formation of chairs as on Friday. It was a racial mix but mostly white. Since the Packard shooting, the TV media had sold a lot of airtime, and sales were up in the print news. You didn't need a magnifying glass to find the bias, and rush to judgment between the lines, Wallace, another black man shot by a cop. Knox wondered how that stigma would sway the grand jury's decision. To complicate matters, Neil Wallace was not just any black man.

Knox could feel the jury's gaze as he crossed the floor to the witness chair. Six men in their late sixties, like retirees from an MBA class, sat in a group. Two of them were minorities. Several women, a variety of ages, two black, were intermingled among some mid-level management types. Four blue-collar workers in blue jeans and Pendleton shirts sat impatiently in the back row. By their appearance, a couple of college students, and two Latinos rounded out the assembly. Behind the façade of impassive faces, Knox wondered what they were thinking.

Ed Farber wasted no time as he rose to his feet, a legal pad in hand. "Good morning, Sergeant. I'd like to remind you that you are still under oath."

"I understand," said Knox. He glanced at DeAngelo. She sat at the prosecutor's table in a gray business suite. A long, delicate finger searched along the lines of legal notes.

Farber rambled through a review of the previous session's testimony, recalling developments up to the actual shooting, positions of the principal figures. Then he turned to Knox.

"Sergeant, tell us the events as Mr. Leyland became present."

Knox scanned the jury. The moments flashed through his mind as he proceeded to unravel the disorder when people ran in terror.

Swede Lundgren killed with a single shot to the throat, and a woman grazed by a bullet that also struck Knox in the chest. Even in the witness chair, he could still feel the impact. Another shot had dropped him, the back of his head glanced off the edge of a table. He toppled to the floor, cloudy semi-conscious moments followed. The fatal sound of gunshots thundered in his ears. Finally, a sense of focus and sensation began to return. Leyland stood over him, finger on the trigger, the .9-mm Browning ready to fire. Knox waited for the bullet. Instead, the dull click of the misfire, a sound that continued to echo in Knox's nightmares.

The impassiveness had faded from the faces of the jurors. Knox paused, poured some water from a decanter into a glass. He took a sip. Farber uttered a stoic summons.

"Please continue, Sergeant."

Knox moved on, and described that Leyland had already demonstrated the intent, means and opportunity to kill. There was no time to assess the misfire of Leyland's gun. Instinct, the will to survive, and training dictated the only option. Under the strain, all peripheral senses vanished. Knox peered up through a narrow adrenalin induced tunnel. The only image in focus was Thomas Charles Leyland. Two shots and Leyland went down.

Silence, hung like a muslin cloud, over the jury. Knox took another sip of water. The sound of throats nervously being cleared echoed in the room.

Knox tried to read the reaction to his account in the jury's faces, a futile effort given the deliberations, and unpredictable verdicts that juries render.

Farber took a breath. "Thank you Sergeant, is there anything further you would like to say before we proceed?"

Knox thought about the question, and down what dark ravine Farber would lead him? Would he now bring up the other shooting incidents?

"I have nothing further."

"Sergeant Knox," said Farber. "There are three mannequins to your right. Please approach them and identify the first."

Knox walked to the mannequin on the pole that held his jacket and shirt. He described the hole through the left front of the tuxedo jacket, another in the left breast pocket. He identified his Kevlar vest; exhibit P-3, and the impact area of Leyland's .9-mm slug to the corresponding holes in the tuxedo.

"And exhibit P-4," said Farber who pointed to the exhibit table.

DeAngelo handed the object to Knox. A fresh, clean fragrance wafted from her presence, dark eyes accented by tiny crow's feet, her raven hair projected a warm sheen under the harsh lights. His fingers brushed hers as he took the badge case and badge from her grasp. Their eyes met. For an instant, she held his gaze, an almost imperceptible nod of acknowledgement.

"Sergeant?' said Farber, expecting a reply.

"It's a mushroomed bullet, my police shield case with a hole in the leather facing. The case was in the breast pocket of my tuxedo jacket."

"And, exhibit P-5?" said Farber.

Knox heaved a sigh, "My police shield from the wallet case. There's a dent in the left quarter, the impact from Leyland's bullet."

Farber passed the exhibits before the jurors then directed Knox to the second mannequin. "For the record, Sergeant, please tell us what you see."

Painstakingly, Knox scanned the front of the shirt and jacket for evidence a bullet hole. The narrow stares of judgment bore down on him. There was only blood. His heart sank.

Farber had him, an indictment for Wallace's death.

"Sergeant," said Farber, his voice insistent. "Whose jacket and shirt is that?"

"It belongs to Thomas Charles Leyland, "said Knox, the sound of his voice hollow. No evidence of a second round. He felt sick, and paused to take a breath.

"How many times, Sergeant, did you shoot at Mr. Leyland?"

"Twice," Knox affirmed.

Farber stepped toward Knox. With that goofy sideway stare, he extended a pair of latex gloves. "Please put these on, sir."

"Leyland was hit with one shot under the chin, is that correct Sergeant?"

Knox twisted into the latex fingers, pulse pounding at his temples, like OJ Simpson in LA. "Yes, under the chin," he replied.

The front of Leyland's blood soaked shirt and tuxedo jacket draped the mannequin. Again, the sequence snapped through Knox's mind. It all came down to the second shot, the one that downed Neil Wallace, the one that could lead to a possible indictment of manslaughter, or worse.

"Open the jacket, Sergeant," Farber uttered, calmly.

Knox reached out and pulled back the left side of Leyland's tux. He stopped, waiting for his mind to process what he saw.

"Again, for the record, please describe for the jury what you see," said Farber.

"There's…Knox paused, began again. "There's a hole in the lower left side of the shirt," said Knox. He cast a confused glance at Farber who returned a knowing nod.

"Continue, Sergeant."

Knox then proceeded to describe the spatter of stippling, gunpowder residue, near the entrance of a bullet hole, common in close quarters shooting engagements. The trajectory of the shot continued through the shirt at an upward angle. A small amount of blood indicated a flesh wound to the outer rib cage. The side flap of the jacket, toward the back, had an exit hole. Clearly, the second shot had struck Leyland.

"Thank you, Sergeant, you may take your chair," said Farber.

Farber turned to the jury, his voice sober. "A Packard Corporation video that recorded these events was introduced into evidence earlier in these hearings through Mr. Jon Bass. We will now view that video, the scenes of which are quite unsettling. People are wounded, some die. It is a tragic, but key element of evidence that will have a significant impact in your deliberations."

Jury members cast a cautious glance at one another. Lights in the room grew dim. The fifty-five inch LED screen flashed into a high definition, and the jury was transported into an otherworldly exposure of glittering chandeliers, hundreds of impeccably clothed members of the uber-privileged holding glasses of champagne, and mingled within an exquisite ballroom setting. Amid the chatter and the clink of champagne glasses, the melody of Glenn Miller's 1940 standards flowed from a tuxedo-clad orchestra.

To Knox, the spectacle played out like a depiction of the last night on the Titanic, the ending of which was no less heartbreaking.

The jurors gazed at the screen, faces gripped in suspense. Through one scene and another, the festivities progressed. Then, nearly unnoticed, a man entered the picture, upper right corner of the screen. His pace was quick, direct. He headed toward the dignitary's table where Admiral and Mrs. Packard had gathered, unaware. Near by stood Mayor Bergin, and Governor Norgaard.

Knox turned his head from the screen, knowing the details of the first shot. He heard Swede's voice—"Gun!"

The fatal shot cracked, followed by the sounds of a terrified crowd. Knox looked back to the screen. Swede clutched at his throat, fell against the wall and bled to death on the floor. Leyland came at Knox, both men, guns pointed at one another, a woman in the line of fire. Knox hesitated, Leyland shot through the woman, the bullet striking Knox who fell back. Leyland fired again. Knox went down, lost to moments of semi-consciousness while gunshots thundered in the background.

The indiscriminant chaos continued. Leyland fired, bodies dropped, including Jonas Packard. A trumpeter in the band, a woman from North Oaks, Minnesota, a lobbyist from D.C., a businessman from Duluth, a Packard Corp staffer, dead.

Women in the jury sobbed. Narrow, angry eyes flashed from the faces of the blue-collar guys. The young collegians sat with mouths agape; somber, shocked expressions predominate among the others.

Knox took a deep breath, eyes fixed upon the screen. Gun pointed, Leyland closed in. Click, click, and click, the misfire. Knox rolled to his side, elevated his Beretta—*boom, boom!*

A collective gasp surged from the jury.

Farber froze the video, reversed, then forward frame by frame. Leyland, shot in the head, rose upward. Arms opened like a preacher in a gaze toward the hear-after. The sides of the tuxedo jacket flung open, and the second shot went up through the left side of Leyland's shirt, and out the back of his jacket. His Browning semi-auto dropped to the floor. Rewind and forward again.

Inexplicably, Wallace darted behind Leyland, struck by the second shot as it past through Leyland's out-flung jacket. Neil Wallace, a champion of the city, a bullet in his back, fell dead.

It was over.

After the video, DeAngelo cast a glance at Knox as she left the jury room. Her assurance, thought Knox, that the uncertainty in his life had now been resolved. Finally, he had answers to his nightmares, and the anxiety he had endured. Witnessed in high-definition, the reality even more tragic—the verdict, pending.

Dismissed from further testimony, Knox walked into the hallway without a word. Maurice Mancel walked him to the elevator. When the doors opened, out stepped the widow, Sheila Wallace. Inescapable was the surprise that filled her angry eyes at the sight of Knox. Early fifties, she was a proud, erect woman with striking facial features in a fashionable black dress.

Silence. Knox froze.

A stabbing look of disdain was cast from those dark eyes. "Pardon me," she said.

At the touch of Mancel's hand on his shoulder, Knox stepped aside.

The cold disregard cast by the widow Wallace chilled the air, the encounter a sudden jolt. A burst of recall flashed through his mind. Knox and Swede at graveside, the Wallace nephew buried after being brought down in a gang killing. After months of Knox and Swede on the hunt, Samantha DeAngelo secured the verdict at trial. The murderer, Sly Jackson, went away, twenty-five to life. Embraced with gratitude, the two detectives had broke bread at the Wallace table. Now, Sheila Wallace would learn the truth of how Knox had killed her husband.

Knox stepped into the elevator with Mancel.

"I need a drink, Maurice. You can buy."

Twenty-seven

THROUGH THE TREES, dappled sunlight graced the tony East Lake Calhoun neighborhood of south Minneapolis. To Leon Love the balmy June day felt fresh and clean. Dog walkers, couples arm in arm enjoying a stroll, part of a welcomed change in season. Leon idled the Navy blue Camaro around a corner to Irving Avenue South. Three boys clattered by on skateboards racing home for dinner. A block from the lake the elegant two-story Victorian clapboard crowned a rise on a corner lot above the street. A glance at his iPad showed that Leon had the correct address.

With gingerbread trim and fresh paint, the house set a stylish pace within the well-established, tree-lined neighborhood. Across the broad pillared porch, a glow of lights shone from inside the house. It was the home of the Packard Corporation's chief legal counsel, Raymond Warren. In addition to the house and Packard stock, Ray Warren owned a ski condo in Jackson Hole, Wyoming, and a vacation villa in the Virgin Islands.

Then there was the family, Leon's real interest; two kids in college, and Mrs. Warren, who occupied her time on various charitable boards. More importantly, Rachel, the Warren's seventeen-year-old daughter, still lived at home.

Leon assessed the hour and pedestrian traffic, street access and egress from the neighborhood. He made another turn around the block, spotted a pathway that emerged through the trees, and saw her. Rachel appeared from the path, crossed Irving Avenue, and sauntered to her house.

Tall and agile, Rachel played squash at Bryn Mawr Academy. She was an alluring girl with long, tan legs, athletic stride, and a firm little ass. Her dark hair tied in a ponytail exposed a pretty face. Leon had pictures, of course. Rachel, in a modest bikini, caroused at the beach with friends, youthful figure and pert breasts. Leon knew she was worth the time he had spent to find her. The Camaro in gear, he glided past, she on the sidewalk, unaware. The anticipation rippled through him.

Leon turned toward home, and a bag of ice. His unfortunate encounter with Kathy Conlon lingered, the latent throb in his knee a reminder. Regrettably, martial arts were among the attributes he failed to notice in *her* dossier. Rachel Warren would be different.

• • •

KATHY CONLON HAD ended her noon report on WCCM. News of Helen Troyer's attack had finally made the media. Knox had watched the presentation as he finished ironing a uniform shirt. He knew he would incur Kathy's wrath for not telling her about the incident. But she knew that

Knox maintained a separation of powers between his job and hers.

There was a crunch of tires, the sound of a car in the driveway. Perhaps Guzman or Mancel had news of the grand jury deliberations?

Knox opened the front door, astonished. It was not Guzman or Mancel. All he could manage was, "Mrs. Packard".

Early sixties with blond hair swept back in a bun, she stood before him in tan linen slacks, jacket and floral print blouse. Her makeup was flawless, a fashion shot from *Vogue* magazine. Her champagne-colored Jag sat in the drive.

Bewildered, Knox stood in front of her, unshaven, in blue jeans, sweatshirt and moccasins. All he needed was a six-pack of beer, and a tattoo of a naked lady on his arm.

"I apologize for intruding," Mrs. Packard said, uncertainty in her voice. "Is it Sergeant, or is it Mr. Knox? I…I don't know which is proper under the circumstances."

"Its just Knox, Mrs. Packard. You caught me on my cleaning day," he said with an awkward shrug. "Please come in, the back porch, I have coffee."

"That would be fine. With milk if it's not any trouble."

Knox brought coffee and milk to the table on the veranda-like porch. Mrs. Packard stood, purse in hand, looking up from the island at the city.

"This view must be extraordinary in the evening," she said, "the skyline lit like a Christmas tree."

Knox realized why she was standing. It was not because of the view. He glanced at the chair she was to sit in and brushed it clean.

"Thank you," she said with a polite smile.

Knox poured. "It's nice to see you, Mrs. Packard. I hear from Jon Bass that Mr. Packard is progressing well." It was polite, small talk, leaving Knox to wonder that a woman of Mrs. Packard's stature wasn't there to survey the eccentricities of Nicollet Island.

She set her cup down. A kindness resided in her eyes. She hesitated before she spoke, as if trying to find the words.

"I...I came here to see you... Knox. I have my husband back because of you. I needed to thank you personally for that. We shall always be in your debt, and remain deeply saddened at the loss of Sergeant Lundgren."

Knox felt the touch of her hand as she reached across the small table. He felt awkward, uncertain how to respond. She withdrew and he looked at her. "I was just trying to stay alive, Mrs. Packard, like everyone else that night. But, I appreciate your sincerity. It makes getting through the consequences a little easier."

"Yes," she said, "there are so many consequences in life." Her voice trailed off, eyes drifted toward the view of the city.

"Is there something else?" said Knox, the likes of Mrs. Packard not usually having police sergeants on their just-stopped-by-to-say-hello list.

"Yes. There is something, rather someone else. Helen Troyer."

Knox recalled his conversation with Ernie Guzman. "I heard about her situation. Were you close?"

"I talk with her nearly every day. I sat with her this morning, and can say that Helen will survive her physical injuries. I am more concerned about the psychological issues. Not only does she experience that horrible attack each time her eyes close, she perceives that she betrayed the confidence of my husband and the company."

Knox leaned forward in his chair. "I'm afraid I don't understand… the part about Helen betraying your husband and the company?"

"The animal that attacked her," said Mrs. Packard, "not only destroyed her spirit, he took her link to the corporation, her laptop computer, and the information it contained."

Knox looked into Mrs. Packard's troubled eyes. "It's common in situations like Mrs. Troyer has undergone, that victims will find fault with themselves for a whole host of reasons; for not being more careful, too naïve, not fighting back, even betraying a trust."

Knox thought a moment. The Troyer case, however terrible, was a crime out of his reach. It was Guzman's case, the Sexual Assault Unit. Yet, he could not resist probing further. "I assume the information on that computer was sensitive?"

"Yes. Helen often took work home."

"Have those files been compromised, Mrs. Packard?"

There was a deep sigh. "Regrettably, yes."

In his mind, Knox began to question the motive for the attack. Was it a random sexual assault, or something else? "So, whoever had the laptop, had her checkbook, notebook, appointment schedule, credit cards, and whatever else she had with her."

"Yes."

"From that, someone figured out her password and entered the files. Is that possible?"

"Yes, that's what Jonas, my husband, has told me that the police suspect."

"What about the files?" Knox said.

"I don't know the particulars, but a lot of the executive information was deleted. The company is working through Helen's backups to reconstruct everything."

With that, the Troyer assault did not appear to be that random. Perhaps it was more about the company than Helen Troyer. But Knox held his suspicions to himself. He no longer had any authority into that venue of police work.

"You must tell Mrs. Troyer," said Knox, "that she did her job. She backed up the files. She didn't betray anyone. What happened was completely out of her control. The police *will* find who did this."

"They will try, I'm sure." the sound of Mrs. Packard's voice unconvincing. "Helen is family to my husband and me. What happened to her cannot go unpunished."

Mrs. Packard's brow creased with concern for her friend. "I know a good deal about you, Sergeant. I know that you get things done. In that regard, I have come to you so that I may help Helen. No one knows I am here, and I'm really not familiar with the police protocol for such things, but I would like you to work on her case."

"Mrs. Packard, I've been reassigned to a desk in the uniformed division," said Knox. "I don't have the position or the authority to do what you're asking, as much as I would like to. But, I know the detectives on Mrs. Troyer's case. They will do their best to fine who attacked her."

Mrs. Packard gazed back across the table, the kindness in her eyes now replaced by determination, and a formality in her tone.

"Sergeant, their best may not be good enough."

Twenty-eight

KNOX STEPPED FROM the shower and dried himself. Mid-shift in the 2nd Precinct was a few hours away. The phone rang. In a huff, he tramped through the bedroom to the nightstand and picked up on the fourth ring. "Yes?"

"Knox, it's Mancel. Turn on your TV. Call me later."

Mancel hung up. Knox stood, a dead phone in his hand.

It took a moment to register, the grand jury verdict.

Knox checked the time, slipped into a robe and turned on "Noon Report," and Ted Harmon the voice of twin city news.

"From the Hennepin County Government Center there is breaking news. The grand jury has just returned findings in the Packard Center shootings."

At the government center, Hennepin County Attorney Jack Griffin stood at the podium, wearing a dark blue pin-stripe suit. Mayor Bergin stepped into the frame, breathing rushed, seemingly late for the photo-op. Chief Ballard in uniform and MBCA Director, Flynn stood in the background along with the anonymous appearing Ed Farber, the special prosecutor.

Knox tried to read the faces, but all wore politically correct blanks. He pondered why Mancel had hung up. Did he know the outcome? Surely, he would have said. Then again, jury verdicts were often a crapshoot.

"Ladies and gentlemen," said Griffin looking into the cameras. "After more than two months of exhaustive investigation by the Hennepin County Grand Jury, a finding has been reached in the Packard Center shootings."

Griffin's poker face presented no tells.

"Jesus, Griffin." Knox muttered. "What the hell is the verdict?"

"It is the finding of the grand jury that Thomas Charles Leyland had been dismissed from employment at the Packard Corporation on March 15th of this year. Subsequently, Mr. Leyland entered a Packard Corporation celebration, shot and killed four individuals, and wounded seven others before being mortally wounded by Detective Sergeant Harding Knox of the Minneapolis Police Department."

Knox, burned with impatience, "Griffin…the verdict?"

"Given the gravity of the case to the community…" Griffin went on to summarize the process of the hearing, the viewing of video recordings, the need for an independent council, and thanked investigators. "A debt of gratitude is owed to all of those who participated in this arduous endeavor."

Griffin paused, again. "It is the finding of this jury, that with the exception of Professor Neil Wallace, Thomas Charles Leyland acted alone in causing all other deaths and injuries in this terrible tragedy."

Knox held his breath, "Wallace, what about Wallace?"

"Clearly, the evidence shows that the death of Professor Neil Wallace was unintentional, the result of a errant, mortal round that had first struck Mr. Leyland in an effort to halt this carnage." Griffin looked firmly into the cameras. "Therefore, in connection with the loss of Professor Wallace, no indictment will follow."

An avalanche of reporter's questions fell upon Griffin. The tumult suggested that a far different verdict was expected.

Griffin held up his hand, like a traffic cop in a busy intersection. "I have no further comments about the deliberations in this case. It is by the very nature of a grand jury being able to examine evidence without outside influence that it is able to discover the facts. These proceedings are now closed."

Relieved, Knox switched off the TV. Griffin had not mentioned his name in connection with Wallace's death. Regardless, the verdict would gain little acceptance among the conspiracy theorists in the media, and the public. There were still those who looked for a scapegoat, and would label the process a cover-up. Attempts to impose a federal case review, coupled with a flood of nuisance civil suits, were certain to follow.

Knox breathed a deep sigh. For the moment at least, he could value one small victory. The phone rang, again.

"Well," said Mancel, "it's over."

"Maurice," said Knox, still trying to comprehend the findings. "You knew there was no indictment."

"Knox, take it easy. Griffin called me a few minutes before he went on TV. He sends his regards. I thought I would let you savor the moment."

"Thanks, but you could have spared me the drama."

The attorney laughed, "Stay safe Knox."

"I work a desk, Maurice, what could happen?"

• • •

By 7:00 P.M., a dozen personal threats, and crackpot remarks about the grand jury decision were fielded at the 2nd Precinct desk, calls threatening justice for Professor Wallace. Guzman and Bass had sent along their congratulatory remarks. Noticeably absent were any messages from Krieg, or Chief Ballard, not that Knox was expecting any.

By 10:00 P.M., radio calls in the 2nd had fallen into a usual Monday night routine. Through the closed circuit television at the desk, Knox noticed a disheveled black man, about sixty, stumble up the front steps to the station.

The man pushed through the front door. Unsteady on his feet, he wore a pair of rumpled brown trousers and a dark blue suit coat over a dull tan shirt.

Weathered face, wrinkled and unshaven, eyes bloodshot, Knox could smell booze on the man's breath as he stopped about three feet from the desk.

"Can I help you," Knox said.

The words slurred out from a liquored tongue. "You're Serr-geant Knox?"

"Yes, what can I do for you?'

"I'm here fffor Pro-fessor Wa-Wallace."

The man sounded more intoxicated and confused than threatening. But Knox saw the weighted right pocket in the brown tattered suit. The right hand reached into the pocket. Knox instinctively dropped a hand toward his Beretta.

"Wait just a—"

The drunk pulled out a snub-nosed revolver.

Knox yelled, "Gun," and maneuvered down from the desk. Two officers rapidly approached from a rear hallway.

Inexplicably, the revolver's cylinder tumbled from the drunk's gun to the floor. It rolled harmlessly across the room to rest against the baseboard of a wall.

Bewildered as a child with a broken toy, the drunk stared at the empty gun frame in his hand then staggered back, looking for the absent cylinder.

"Ah shhhit," said the boozy gunsel.

Knox stepped behind the man and grabbed the inert gun then ratcheted the cuffs gently onto wiry old wrists.

"Come on old-timer, I think we have a room for you."

"Ah shhhit."

Twenty-nine

At 9:30 P.M., Leon peered out from his forested hide above the parkway at West 33rd Street and Irving. Rachel Warren paused at the crosswalk near Thomas Beach. Her stride exhibited a spry, youthful independence as she moved in and out of the shadows cast by dim streetlights. Her dark hair tied in a ponytail bobbed teasingly as she sauntered through the light beams of a passing car. Black spandex pants caressed her tight, athletic loins. Young, aloof and innocent, Rachael hurried toward a wooded pathway, vulnerable to the night. Like a ghost cloaked in darkness, Leon watched and waited.

Rachael walked quickly up the path, past the House of Transcendental Meditation, a place with closed curtains where strange people often entered and departed like monks at a monastery.

Late again, she hurried along the short cut home, a scary, confining stone walkway that rose from the parkway to West 33rd. The darkened greenway was thick with ash, hawthorns and underbrush that crowded out the light of a half-moon. A fragrance of blooming lilac loomed in the air.

A dull light glimmered from the windows of old gabbled houses.

Half way up the footpath apprehension gripped Rachael's senses. A furtive glance back, she half expected the Headless Horseman of Sleepy Hollow to gallop out of the gloomy shadows. Up the path in the distance the comforting glow of the West 33rd streetlight relieved her anxiety.

From the thicket, as quick as the strike of a snake, a hand grabbed her ponytail. A powerful figure wrenched her to the ground amidst the dark wooded greenway. Another hand clasped her mouth. Her shock so complete she didn't utter a sound. Eyes filled with terror, she struggled for a breath.

"Listen, Sweetheart," said the low, menacing voice. "Cooperate and you won't get hurt. Understand?"

Panic gripped every part of her being. She choked, unable to muster a response.

In the faint light, she stared into the horror of a mask, hideous red lips, and lizard-like green eyes. Then, a cold steel edge skimmed along her skin; cut through her blouse, slipped between her breasts, and sliced apart her bra. Her clothing cleaved open like a breast of roasted chicken, she felt the cool air rush at her body.

A hand clamped down over her head, and pushed her face to one side. She closed her eyes, unable to comprehend how this could happen. Her attacker said something she didn't understand, something about her father, revenge. Then she felt a tongue lick her breasts, suck at her nipples, the blade of a knife prick her belly. Death felt near.

Leon sliced open the spandex pants, exposing Rachel's dark pubis. He felt her wither in his grasp. He had complete control. Buried in rapt obsession he copulated his prey with a deep, fulfilling sigh.

Somewhere out in the night a screen door slammed. Transformed, like a carnivore in a forest, Leon hunkered over his kill. He peered warily into the darkness, searching for a threat to his conquest. After a moment, there was silence.

Satisfied with his seclusion, Leon rose to his knees and spread the legs of his quarry. Spasms trembled through his body as he thrust himself into her. He let her squirm as he throbbed and shuddered with a climax. His need fulfilled, he lay supine atop Rachael, inhaled the scent of her hair at the nape of her neck. It mixed with the fragrance of lilacs, the smell of the earth.

After a few moments, Leon straightened, took a breath. Rachel stirred, and tried to cry out. Leon sent a fist to the side of her face, and her body went limp.

He pulled off his mask and once more licked the silk-like freshness of her youth, soft and moist. He tasted her salty perspiration, the electricity of her fear.

Desire and revenge fulfilled, thoughts of flight crept into Leon's mind. He smeared Rachel's body with leaves and moist soil, rolled his conquest, unconscious, onto her stomach. She being of no further use, Leon evaluated his escape, peered through the underbrush and stepped into the night.

• • •

Sirens echoed through the urban landscape from across Lake Calhoun, police responding to the plight of Rachel Warren.

From the seclusion of his back porch Leon could hear the noise, but was not concerned. He knew most crime was never solved, and this case would be no exception. He believed that he had come to know how not to leave anything behind, how not to get caught. And, he knew he left nothing behind with Rachel Warren, even of himself.

Like the computer, and personal effects taken from Helen Troyer, Leon would not leave anything for the police. He would destroy it, part of the rules of not getting caught.

Leon lit a marijuana cigarette and held it to the corner of his souvenir, Rachael's black hair ribbon. He watched the heat dance through the black silk, destroying his memento, but not the memory of his encounter. Rachel would never walk down that path again. Each time she closed her eyes, she would remember. More to the point so would her father.

The last ember of ribbon turned to ash, Leon's thoughts floated in a haze of cannabis. He grabbed a cell, and tapped in the number for the 2nd Precinct.

• • •

Leon was amused to hear the familiar voice.

"Sergeant Knox, 2nd Precinct."

"You beat the system, Sergeant, the grand jury. But, do you ever wonder?" The voice paused then faded to almost a whisper. "I mean about people who avoid being accountable, and bam. Hit by a shit storm out of nowhere, they never know its coming or why. You ever wonder?"

Again, the call came in on the general public line to the station. The voice that kept coming at Knox from out of the blue was back. Tonight, it sounded heavy, maybe stoned, thought Knox. The words "No Data" printed out on the communications board. Knox covered the receiver and mouthed the word "trace" to Lieutenant Miller, the watch commander who sat next to him at the desk.

"Yeah, I wonder," said Knox, acknowledging the caller in an effort to extend the conversation. "What are you trying to tell me?"

"One day a person has an unsuspecting, comfortable life. The next day, they never come home. Like your wife killed by a drunk. Remember?"

"I remember," he said wanting to tear the throat from the caller.

"Or," said the voice, "it could happen to someone simply out for a walk."

"Walking where?" said Knox.

"Have a good shift."

The phone went dead. Knox looked expectantly at Miller.

"Sorry," said the LT. "Not enough time."

"That the guy you told me about, the guy making the goofy calls?"

"That's the one," said Knox, thinking of an earlier radio call. "There was a girl down in the 3rd tonight wasn't there, near Lake Calhoun? Some sort of an assault?"

"I'll check it out," said Miller.

"Thanks," said Knox, wondering about what the caller said, accountability, someone out for a walk, a shit storm to come out of nowhere. He wondered…who?

Thirty

LEON SLEPT LATE, the encounter with Rachael Warren on playback in a dream. By 11:00 A.M., he was busy in the garage. Plastic sheeting covered his work area as he packed a mixture of ammonium nitrate and diesel fuel into commercial grade cardboard tubes. Later, a safety fuse and explosive booster would be coupled to a throwaway cell, and he would be in business, the bomb business.

Leon mused of his plan, and smiled, remembering the lessons of "Jessie the Bomber," his erstwhile cellmate at the Dane County, Wisconsin, jail. With the necessary stolen material and a favorable weather report, he was ready.

Leon chuckled. The results will be a blast.

It was 1:30 A.M. when Leon skirted along the north shore of Lake Minnetonka in his Camaro. A heavy fog floated on the lake; a quarter-moon peeked out from dark clouds.

Headlights, interior and rear lights shut off, Leon coasted into the graveled lot of the Shoreline Marina, a small Lake Minnetonka boat rental and repair operation. He concealed the Camaro behind a thirty-foot sailboat. Among others, the boat sat in its storage crib, masts collapsed, blue tarp over the hull.

Beyond the parking lot and chain link fence, three docks, long wood-like fingers on pontoons, disappeared into fog at the water's edge. In the mist, a variety of boats floated at their moorings.

From the trunk of his car, Leon hefted out a flat bar, and a backpack filled with enough nitrate to blow a small house to smithereens. In a separate bag he carried the fuse arrangements. The contents of both bundles were carefully water sealed.

Explosives on his back, a penlight in hand, Leon squeezed around the far side of the chain link fence near a giant willow tree. He knew the marina had only an old local alarm and video surveillance, having rented a boat from Shoreline weeks before.

At the rear of the building, Leon disabled the local alarm with a pull of the wires from the alarm box. After he pried through the back door with the flat bar, then grabbed his actual objective, the boatyard video surveillance disks from the office. Then he rifled the cash register, rental records, and bashed the outer casing of the old safe. On the way out, he grabbed the petty cash from a desk drawer, enhancing the appearance of a random burglary. As adrenalin pulsed through his veins, Leon fled into the fog. The smell of dead fish, lake water, and vengeance was the air.

Midway down the dock an eighteen-foot Boston Whaler with a one-fifty Evinrude bobbed in the water. Leon found a key attached to a float fob under the seat. In a moment, with a half tank of gas, he was underway. The stout little Whaler sliced through the fog as Leon monitored his GPS. After a mile, the peninsula loomed out of the mist, and Leon cut the throttle. The momentum carried him to his mark.

Quickly, he tied the boat to a couple of cleats, unloaded the explosive packages onto a ledge and slipped into the water. It took only a moment to duck under the closed doors that shielded the two big boats from the weather. A tiny beam of Leon's penlight pierced the darkness to illuminate the twenty-eight foot Cabrio cruiser.

The weight of the sleek, lavish vessel hung above the water on a huge lift. Suspended next to it, a twenty-two foot center-console fishing boat.

Leon cut the fuel lines to each boat, carefully tucked the nitrate charges near the engine blocks then attached his detonation devices and cell phones. Soon the cavernous building filled with the smell of gasoline, and Leon slipped back into the water.

When he shoved off the compulsion to open the throttle and make a quick get away was nearly overwhelming. However, he could not afford to miss his heading, or alert anyone to the sound of his motor.

His mind raced.Did he set everything correctly? It was too late to worry now. A half-mile to go, he settled the marina's surveillance disks into the water, and edged the throttle forward.

At the dock, Leon's pulse raced as he secured the Whaler and replaced the key under the seat. He grabbed the cortex bags, left the flat bar at the marina's rear door, and made his way out of the boatyard.

"Have to get away." He looked at his watch, and fading fog then ran toward the chain link fence, slipped past the willow tree and hustled to the car. He tossed the empty bags into the trunk, and trembled with the anticipation of escape. Then, unable to resist the compulsion to glimpse the affects of his labor, Leon looked toward the bay, and he dialed the bombs.

In a millisecond, a tremendous explosion echoed across the broad bay. The shock wave shook the windows of Shoreline Marina. Lanyards of sailboats that rocked at anchor rattled like wind chimes against the forest of metal masts.

A glow of the fireball from Admiral Packard's boathouse rose through the fog like the plume of an atom bomb.

Astonished, Leon froze in place.

"Hoo-llly shhhit."

Thirty-one

In his expansive office suite, Jonas Packard peered through the lens of a brass telescope. He looked east toward Saint Paul when his secretary knocked, and announced the mayor's arrival.

Politics and business had intersected the careers of Packard and Bergin for over a dozen years. Packard turned from the looking glass. "Barbara, thank you for coming over."

"I hope I'm not interrupting your view, Jonas."

"No, but it is amazing. On a bright day, I can see the state capital building through this lens. Clear, unambiguous, unlike the lens of politics one could say."

Bergin stepped toward the broad office windows, the cityscape below. She turned to her host. "Yes, I suppose. However, there are days when both lenses can be obscured by the turn of events."

"Quit right, please have a seat, Barbara, I've ordered lunch."

Packard showed the mayor to a table near the window, place settings for two. The table was of an oriental-modern style, clean, lines, dark wood, as were the furnishings throughout the suite.

In a frame on one office wall hung an exquisite Samurai sword. In another, a black-penned ink of a mounted oriental warrior at full gallop, lance extended. The office was otherwise quite Spartan, with the exception of two orderly bookcases that contained volumes on history, politics, business, and family photos. Plaques, commemorating Jonas Packard's Far East and Pacific naval commands hung center place above the credenza behind his desk.

The desk had an in-basket and out-basket side; neat, squared away like Packard, himself. Absent were the usual photo-op reproductions with political and sports figures.

Bergin leaned forward across the table, her tone, sympathetic. "How are you doing, Jonas? I mean since the shooting, and that awful explosion?"

"Thoughtful of you to ask. The explosion scared the hell out of us. Like a sixteen-inch naval gun had gone off in the yard, it blew us out of bed, glass all over the place. We lost the boats, the entire boathouse, and all the windows on the west side of the house blown out. But, Caitlin and I survived. That's the most important thing."

A knock at the office door and a man in a white chef's uniform entered, followed by an assistant pushing covered food carts.

"Good afternoon, sir, Madam Mayor," said the chef in a heavy East European accent. "Your lunch has arrived."

Packard did the introductions, and the chef soon departed the room with his culinary assistant.

"Bernkastel Auslese," said Packard, "a nice compliment to the Chilean sea bass. The hollandaise asparagus and seasoned string potatoes preceded desert, a raspberry-chocolate mousse."

The mayor placed her napkin across her lap. "Regular fare?" she asked Packard.

The admiral raised his glass to his guest. "To success, Madam, and a full life."

"And, what of success and life, Jonas?"

Packard came abruptly to the point as they ate. "Barbara, someone is targeting my company, and endangering the lives of those close to me."

Bergin sipped her wine. "You know that Chief Ballard has assembled a task force for that investigation."

"I'm aware, but without success. My executive assistant, Helen Troyer, was brutally attacked in her home, and my executive files compromised. Rachel Warren, the daughter of my chief legal counsel, raped and beaten. Thank God, both Helen and Rachel survive, but to endure what kind of emotional trauma, I can't imagine. These are human beings, Barbara, who have been turned into tragic exclamation points meant to intimidate my company. To what purpose, I have no idea."

"And, my boathouse explodes, spread hell and gone across Lake Minnetonka."

"Jonas, please believe me, the joint task force is doing all it can."

"So, Jon Bass and Chief Ballard have informed me."

"Then, what do you suggest, Jonas?"

"Barbara, a task force is good at gathering and analyzing information. What's needed is an open field runner with solid instincts who will take the necessary risks." Packard pointed to the etching on the wall. "Someone like that Samurai warrior astride that horse."

Bergin's sigh was audible. "Jonas, I can't afford a risk taking Samurai, especially if you're about to suggest, Harding Knox." She dabbed a napkin at the corner of her mouth.

"With all due respect, Jonas, regardless of the grand jury findings there still exists a perception that Knox is responsible for Neil Wallace's death. A proposal to put him back in the public eye, would be quite...difficult."

"Barbara, this corporation and I do difficult every day. We manage perception, that's part of how we stay in business."

"Perhaps, Jonas, but the politics of running this city is clouded with complexity. In the minds of certain community segments, the death of Neil Wallace remains cloaked in suspicion. Politically, those perceptions, however misguided, must be managed. For the foreseeable future part of that containment is placing Sergeant Knox out of public view."

"Let me be blunt, Barbara. Your political issues are not so much managing the city as it is attaining the governor's office. I suggest that you're capable of managing certain perceptions, vis- a-vis Sergeant Knox, in order to achieve both ends."

Bergin finished her sea bass. "Your meaning, Jonas?"

"The political criticism you may receive is insignificant compared to finding who is responsible for hurting my company, and my people. Keep in mind that long-term endorsements sustain political ambitions. If I find some accommodation on the one hand, perhaps I can help influence progress on the other, or not."

"Jonas, I'm beginning to feel uncomfortable with your suggestion. What is it? I approve the transfer of Sergeant Knox to the task force in exchange for your political support?"

"I'm suggesting that we are both faced with certain objectives. One may not necessarily be exclusive of the other." Packard leaned into the table. "Neither of us have time to dance too much longer with these issues. I hope you understand."

"I see," said Bergin who glanced at her watch.

Packard sensed the faint. After all, she was a woman, and politician, accustomed to having options, used to dictating her own rules, while not being subjected to those of others. To Jonas Packard, political animals, even Barbara Bergin, were pawns in the larger game. In the end, the Barbara Bergin's of the world were pragmatists to their own self-serving nature.

Bergin paused, and both rose from the table.

"I will take your proposal under advisement, Jonas."

The mayor hesitated at the door and turned.

"The sea bass was excellent. Sorry, to miss desert."

Thirty-two

ON THE TWENTY-FOURTH floor of the Hennepin County Government Center, Leon Love skulked in the shadows of an office renovation. He was not done with Kathy Conlon. She looked up from a note pad into the TV camera to file her report on a county commission meeting.

WCCM's captivating news anchor still stirred Leon's fantasies, aspirations of a forced conquest not diminished. The next time he'd be ready for any of her Kung Fu bullshit. A sly smile crept across his face, anticipating the encounter.

Following the feed to the studio, Conlon and the cameraman entered an elevator along with others. Leon discreetly followed. With each stop, he edged his way across the back of the car as people got off, and others got on. Closer, as a whisper of his clothes brushed against hers, Leon felt an electric quiver pulse through him. He inhaled her delicate, clean scent of perfume. It was as if only he and Kathleen were hurtling through a chasm of the building together.

His pulse quickened, and perspiration dampened his forehead. When the elevator stopped at the mezzanine, the doors opened and Conlon made her exit. She took a few steps, and looked back, eyes narrowed with a questioning expression.

The doors closed.

• • •

Off duty, Knox sat in a side booth at the Gavel Bar and Grill, a local pub-like watering hole on 7th Street, a block from the government center. The bar catered to prosecutors, defense attorneys, judges, and politicians who worked the warrens of the county, and city legal systems. The Gavel provided an off-the-record atmosphere where a plea bargain could be brokered, political influence wielded, where rumors flourished amid booze, beer, a good story, and an occasional crude joke. A select element of city and county detectives, Knox among them, found acceptance amid the more notable clientele.

Wearing a Navy blue mock turtleneck, blue jeans and boat shoes, Knox nursed a bottle of Leinie's beer. In a shoulder holster under a comfortably worn sport coat rested his back-up Beretta. He watched the front door, and waited.

Just after 2:00 P.M., Kathleen Conlon entered the nearly empty bar. A burst of June sunlight followed her silhouette into the setting. A tan linen skirt and jacket, matching shoes, and white blouse complimented her appealing figure. Two suits, alone at the bar, gave her an admiring look.

"Hello Harding," Kathleen said as she swept into the booth.

"You look a bit rushed," said Knox. "What can I get you?"

"Please, nothing stronger than a Perrier."

Knox ordered from the waitress and turned to Conlon. "Thanks for meeting me."

"Oh, that's fine." She paused a moment, glanced back at the entrance to the bar.

"Something wrong, kid?"

"No, it's just that...I don't know how to explain it."

Knox took a sip of his beer. "Explain what?"

"I was in an elevator at the government center. After a few floors, I felt this presence... someone looking at me."

Knox smiled. "You're among the most known faces on television. It's not unusual to be recognized."

"It wasn't that, more like someone watching, creepy."

"Do you think someone was following you, someone from the break-in?"

"No. I got off the elevator and looked back. The doors closed. There was nothing, only that weird feeling. I took an escalator to the street and came here."

"Has anything happened since the break-in?"

"No," Conlon said. "I've have locks like Fort Knox, automatic yard lights, carry pepper spray in my purse, keep 911 on speed dial, and went back to martial arts classes. Hell, I'm the most combat ready news anchor in the Twin Cities."

Knox laughed. "That's not altogether a bad thing."

"I'm okay, really, Harding. When you called you asked about Lara's things."

Knox sipped his beer. "I think it's time. I've made a decision—"

Kathleen reached across the table, placed her hand softly on Knox's forearm. "I know, time to move her things out of the house."

"Yes," Knox replied, his distant gaze cast toward Conlon. "We were in love, Kathy. Ten years was all Lara and I had. I walked into her office one day, looked at her for the first time, and knew she was the one. How the hell does that happen?"

Tears welled up in Kathy's eyes. "It's called magic, Harding."

Knox sighed. "The kind of magic I can't hold in my arms anymore."

"I know. I know how strongly she felt about you." Kathy, pursed her lips, and gave Knox a teasing wink. "You were the best she ever had."

There was a momentary pause then laughter. The suits at the bar turned to look at the gaiety coming from the booth.

"Well," Kathy said, with a shrug and still laughing, "You know how girls talk. That's what Lara said."

For some reason, Knox felt embarrassed by the comment.

"My god, Harding, you're blushing."

The laughter continued over Perrier and beer until Kathleen caught her breath. "Harding, of course I will help."

"I'd be grateful, Kathy.

"Tonight, after I do the 10:00 o'clock news," said Conlon, "I can come over. We can start in the morning."

Knox finished his beer, "Great, use your key and take the master bedroom. I haven't slept there since...in a long time. I get off about 3:00 A.M. and will see you in the morning."

"Done," Kathleen looked at her watch. "I must be going."

They stood. Knox put his arm around his sister-in-law, and gave her a peck on the cheek. "You're the best, kid."

"I know." She said, and scurried toward the door.

The two suits cast a curious glance at Knox, then at the young TV anchor, shrugged and ordered another round.

Knox discreetly followed Kathleen toward Nicollet until he was satisfied she was safe. Back to 3rd Avenue, he crossed the paving stone government plaza. The Packard Center climbed skyward to his left. The government center rose from the plaza on his right. The distinctive rose-granite city hall lay ahead.

Resentment still pulled at him, marked as both savior, and killer in one building, dismissed from his position in another, and thrown before a grand jury in the third. Lara and Swede gone, indefinitely strapped to a desk job, his professional compass, his passion, and meaning of life remained unsettled.

As he past the 4th Street entrance to city hall, Knox picked the cell phone from his pocket on the second ring and hit the record button, anxious to capture the anonymous voice that kept pulling his chain.

"Knox," he said, the greeting brusque.

"Sergeant Knox?"

He heard the unmistakable voice of the chief's secretary. Knox could swear that she kept a pint of Irish Mist tucked in her desk, a kiss of the shamrocks to bless the lilt in her voice.

"Sorry, Mrs. Cohan, I was expecting someone else.

"So I gather. I'm calling for Chief Ballard."

"About?"

"I think he will tell you himself, Knox. I'm just the messenger, you know."

"I'm at the 4th Street entrance now."

"Hold on, please." There was a brief silence.

"Come right up, the Chief is waiting."

Ballard came around the broad oak desk, an historic remnant of his predecessors. He wore a double-breasted Navy blue blazer with regimental stripe tie.

"Have a seat, Knox. I'm glad you were close by."

Knox, guarded and uncertain, shook Ballard's extended hand, the chief's grip firm, his demeanor reserved.

"I'm sure that you are aware of recent events," said Ballard. He paused to take a seat behind his desk, "The two assaults in Minneapolis we feel are tied to the Packard Corporation, and the explosion at the Packard residence on Lake Minnetonka."

Unsure of Ballard's intentions, "Yes, I see the news."

"A decision has been made," said Ballard, "to reassign you to a task force investigating those incidents."

Knox leaned back in his chair. A sting of bitterness spiced his response. "I was under the impression that I had been designated persona-non-grata around here."

"Situations change, Knox, and assignments with them."

For a long moment, Knox cast a steely gaze at Ballard.

"You knew, didn't you?'

"About?" Ballard replied.

"That I was in the clear about Wallace."

"I did," said Ballard, firmly. "Not at first, but soon after."

So, explain why I get sacked then sweat out a grand jury?"

A sober expression crossed Ballard's face. "I understand your anger, Knox. Although you don't agree, the process was necessary to avoid *any* perception of a cover-up, to defend the department's integrity, sustain public safety, and to clear *you*."

"And, the politicians wanted me out of sight," Knox retorted.

"I don't deny that," Ballard replied.

"That's part of the ugly picture of this business. Each of us has to work our way through those circumstance as best we can."

The chief raised his hand. "Believe me, Knox, sit in my chair any day of the week, and the picture becomes more complex. Caught in the midst of any screwball political kerfuffle, I just don't get transferred, I get fired, period."

Knox didn't respond.

"What I'm offering you," said Ballard "is an opportunity to move on. You can go back to a desk in the 2nd, or help find the bastard that hurt these people."

Ballard unclasped a folder in front of him, and pushed a couple eight by ten photos across the desk.

Knox picked them up. He stared at the face of a woman in her late fifties, eyes sandwiched shut, black and blue, jaw in a brace, hair matted, cuts and bruises across her face; a woman devoid of spirit. He was no stranger to pictures like this, nor was he a stranger to his own personal anger at those who perpetrated such things.

He remembered Mrs. Packard, the plea for help she had made on the porch at the back of his home. The woman in the picture had to be her friend, Helen Troyer.

In the second photo, Ballard explained, "That's seventeen-year-old Rachel Warren. She is the daughter of Jonas Packard's chief counsel. Raped and beaten in the woods near Lake Calhoun. That's how she ended up. Look at the face, Knox."

Like Helen Troyer, blackened eyes stared back from the photo, face disfigured, a broken jaw. Rachel had become a cowering, beaten figure. Knox remembered the call from the phantom voice. "You could just be out for a walk, and shit happens."

Knox studied the photos, weighed his dead-end options, and loathed the morose moods he had sunk to. He pondered the improbable connections, the Packard Corporation, a rapist with explosives, his sister-in-law's assault, and a voice with no identity. Suddenly, his inner compass had changed direction. The latent passions began to simmer. His gaze returned to Ballard.

"When do I start?"

Thirty-three

A SWEEP OF headlights cut across the loop of the front drive. Kathleen Conlon's Audi sport coupe came to a stop a little after 11:30 P.M.

There was a look of surprise on her face as Knox opened the front door. "Harding, I thought you were at work."

"I have the night off, transferred to another assignment."

The comment spiked Kathy's curiosity. "Transferred, to?"

"Not tonight, kid." said Knox.

"Harding, is there something I should know?"

"Remember? In this house, your reporter's hat remains at the front door. Besides, we have work in the morning, and you need some sleep."

"You're right," she huffed. "It's been a long news day."

Knox checked the locks on the doors, and poured another Crown Royal while Conlon trudged up to the master bedroom. His body clock still on nights, Knox went to Lara's studio next to his second floor den. Photography, her hobby, had permitted a creative oasis away from her demanding legal services job.

A half hour had past when Knox finished paging through the black and white stills of city streets, the homeless women and children who lived in shelters, some that were Lara's clients. Knox remembered her enthusiasm, as much a social worker as she was a legal aid litigator. Often, she put people back on their feet toward a better future.

On the ledge of the window sat a framed black and white of Knox and Lara together, she in his arms, he looking fondly at her. He picked up the picture, longing to hold her again. He turned out the light.

From the darkness of the studio, Knox looked out across the street at the shadows cast by the street-lit landscape. The vague outline of a hooded figure stood in a scrub of woods. The figure, motionless, appeared to watch the house. Could it be the man with the voice on the phone?

Knox grabbed his Beretta, went down the stairway through the darkened house, and slipped out the back door.

Past the woodpile and rock retaining wall, Knox scurried by the rear of the garage. In the shadow of a hedge of the side yard, he paused.

In a dim luminescence sixty feet away, the figure stood half hidden by a box elder tree. Knox scrambled along the hedge when the hooded figure turned and bolted along West Island Avenue. In close pursuit, gun in hand, Knox closed within five yards. As Knox and the hoodie neared the Burlington Northern Rail trestle, both grunted and gasped like racehorses headed into the final stretch.

"Police," Knox shouted.

Even faster, the hoodie was spurred on by the warning. Onto the bridge over the swift flowing Mississippi, rusted lamps high in the girders bathed the pursued and pursuer in a faint glow. Then the strain of a two block all out sprint began to take its toll. Lungs burned, the legs tightened, sensory perception narrowed. Knox woefully watched the runner pull away when a piercing light shattered the night. The trestle began to tremble.

A mammoth rail engine bore down, coal cars rumbling in tow. The hooded runner became a distant silhouette in the engine's light. At the last moment, Knox leapt to a girder and hung on for life.

When the train past, the figure gone, Knox stepped back onto the trestle disgusted that his body could not do what his mind wanted. Huffing like a tired bull, stiff-legged, he limped to the end of the bridge then trudged to West Island Avenue. Exhausted, he climbed the steps to the front porch.

Boooom!

Parked at the edge of a lot above the West River Parkway, the Camaro sat concealed within a number of other cars. His lungs about to burst, Leon Love stumbled through a clump of trees to the car. He had not anticipated Knox being home, or the arrival of Kathleen Conlon, but it was a gift not to be wasted. He waited, just long enough for Knox to return to his house then punched in the last four digits of the burner cell.

At the sound of the blast, Leon grinned at his accomplishment, Knox and his house blown to smithereens. For a long moment, Leon watched the flames rise through the trees, and glistened at the waters edge of Nicollet Island.

Leon drove slowly from his parking lot hide, lamenting the likely loss of Kathleen Conlon, his latest sensual obsession. "Fuck it, man," he muttered. "It's all on Knox."

Amid the flames, Knox crashed through the front door. Kathy, in black shorty pajamas, caked with dust and trembling, collapsed in his arms. The Audi car keys were a quick grab off the entry table. Knox hustled Kathy and a coat to her car and backed it to the street. The wail of sirens began to fill the night.

Police cars, followed by fire trucks from station 11 arrived quickly, but the explosion and flames had done their work. Two officers made their approach to Knox who could see their eyes focus on the Beretta in his holster. "Sergeant Knox," he said. "Minneapolis PD."

The uniforms relaxed their demeanor. "Everyone out?" said the senior officer.

"We're out," said Knox looking beyond the two men.

The back wall of the house was blown in, the garage roof caved onto his SUV and Lara's Mustang. Flames and smoke rose into the air. The covered walkway to the house had burned to the ground, the house, his and Lara's treasure, a total loss.

"What happened, a gas leak?" Asked the younger officer.

Knox didn't respond at first then rattled off instructions.

"Check the 2nd Avenue, and townhouse lots across the river. I chased a male in a dark hoodie across the BN Bridge."

"Male, white, black...?" The officer asked.

"Maybe white," said Knox. "Also, have your watch commander get forensics, and arson units to the scene, as well as the 710 car, the on-call detective."

"You think someone blew the place up?"

Knox looked at the officer, "Just call it in."

The officer nodded and walked off, talking into the mike of his handy-talkie.

By 12:30 A.M., against the backdrop of flashing emergency lights, smoke-like fingers wafted among the tree limbs then vanished into the night sky. The sparse, eccentric island residents gathered in yards wearing bathrobes and slippers. A few holding beers, stood in the street. Others on porches watched the extraordinary commotion of the island night.

Wrapped in her coat, Conlon walked from her car. Knox put his arm around her. The senior officer cast a curious gaze at Conlon.

"Say, aren't you—"

"Yes, I am."

Knox interrupted. "Ms. Conlon is my sister-in-law."

"Okay, right," said the officer, and glanced at his partner.

A few minutes later, a hand touched Knox on his shoulder. It was Chief Ballard.

"You need anything more," said Ballard, "I'm here."

Knox looked at the Chief, surprised at his presence.

"Thanks, Chief. Can you look after Ms. Conlon for a moment?

Knox, lost in thought, went in search for a link to the runner he had chased. At the back of the house, smoke and flames began to dissipate. He kneeled down to study a V-like detonation pattern where the gas main had been. In pieces, blown into the back yard, was the back porch. Knox thought of the Packard explosion, the photos of the women Ballard had shown him. Now, someone had slipped through the night to blow his island home to kingdom come. In the background lurked the taunting voice on the phone. Determination burned within him to find how the pieces fit.

The job just got personal, again.

Thirty-four

IN SEARCH OF a connection, Ballard listened intently to the voice of Jon Bass on the phone. Someone had targeted Admiral Packard, his corporation, and two people connected to the company. Knox, too, appeared to be in the cross hairs. Revenge for killing Leyland, or Wallace would be motive enough. The question remained who, on behalf of which man would seize upon such a vindictive course of action? Bass was in the best position to conduct a cursory check into Leland's affairs.

"Leyland and the Admiral go back to the close of the Vietnam War," said Bass. "The Admiral had been shot down. Leyland flew cover, and directed the rescue. When Packard sacked him for embezzlement, Leyland was not the same man as he was during the war. In his twisted mind-set, even though he was a thief, it was he who felt betrayed. The rest is where we're at now."

"Is there anyone else in Leyland's background who could have a motive for coming after Packard?" Ballard asked.

"I know Leyland's ex-wife is dead. But, he had a son. I'll know more in a few days. By the way, the transfer of Knox from the 2nd was a good move."

Ballard smiled. "Yes, I don't suppose your boss had any influence with that decision?"

"I'll get back to you, Chief."

The non-response made Ballard all the more curious about a quid pro quo between the admiral, and the mayor's change of direction, allowing the reassignment of Knox to detectives. Then again, everything was political. Minneapolis was no exception.

• • •

JANICE LESCOE, THE forty-year-old lieutenant who supervised the Sex Crimes and Family Violence Unit, looked up from her chair in the briefing room.

Knox offered a polite smile. "Morning, Janice."

"Morning, Knox. How are you?"

"Peachy, someone blew up my house."

Knox took a seat across the table from her. Their relationship, although he worked homicide, had been relaxed but professional. A lateral career transfer from the Uniform Division, Lescoe had supervised the Sex and Family Violence Unit for three years. Her brow was creased, and a revealing cigarette odor on her clothes equated stress.

Just then, Krieg stepped into the room. His presence addressed the question of Lescoe's tension. Krieg had that effect on subordinates. "Glad you could make it, Sergeant. Sorry about your house," he said, easing himself into a chair.

"Thanks for you concern. It's been a swell weekend."

Without response, Krieg transitioned coolly to the subject at hand. "The Chief has seen fit to reassign you to our task force, Knox. The Lieutenant's team has the lead on two sexual assaults. We feel those incidents may connect with explosions at your home, as well as Jonas Packard's. Somehow, you may figure into the why, and who is behind these events."

"Somehow, I had that suspicion," said Knox.

"Yes, I'm sure," said Krieg. "There are some ground rules in regard to your tenure, Knox. Under Lieutenant Lescoe, you will do backgrounds, work the case peripherals, and route everything through *her* to *me*. Any questions?"

"Sounds plain enough, you're in charge, and I work for Janice."

"Very well. Lieutenant Lescoe will provide you with the necessary details. Keep me briefed people." Then Krieg stood and left the room.

Knox looked at the briefing room wall; photographs, lines, and symbols interspersed with notes. It was a graphic presentation to known facts and evidence, to timelines of the crimes, all links to visually map the investigation. Knox was no stranger to the process, having applied it in many homicide cases.

"You can see," said Lescoe, "that ATF, Minneapolis, and Hennepin County bomb squads are pursing the explosives links. A team from homicide, the county and state" she continued, "will have access to the injured, and deceased families from the Packard Center shootings. White Collar Crime is working the computer compromise at the Packard Corporation. Forensics is coordinating the physical evidence. Ernesto Guzman is handling the sexual assaults."

"That's where you come in, Knox," added Lescoe. "You're with Guzman, on a tight leash. We need to keep you in sight, safe, and on the team."

Knox looked at Lescoe, "Put me wherever you want, Janice. I just want the bastard that blew up my house."

"Remember, Knox, you're tethered to Guzman. In regard to your house, the bomb units have found remnants of a safety fuse, cortex material, and trace elements of ammonium nitrate, fertilizer concentrate."

Knox examined the bomb scene photographs on the board. "So, what you're saying is cow shit blew up my house?"

"I'm glad you can find some humor in that, Knox."

"How's the Packard bombing tie in?"

"The sheriff's divers pulled part of a boat hull from Lake Minnetonka. Embedded in it was a portion of a miniature cell phone computer board. The bomb techs are looking for a similar find at your place."

"The evidence from both locations will be sent to the ATF lab in Maryland," said Lescoe. "Optimistically, we're hoping to find characteristics, signature aspects, among the samples that link both scenes. Unfortunately, the results could take a couple months, and won't tell us *who* made the bombs."

"This asshole is on a mission, Jan. We don't have months."

"That's why you're here," said Lescoe.

"Anything on the Wallace family?" Knox asked.

"The state investigators are working that angle."

"How did that work out?"

"Not well," Lescoe replied. "A wolf-pack of lawyers crept out of the woodwork for a shot at the corporate and city pockets. The family is keeping their civil suit options open. However, their attorneys assured us that their clients have no motivation that concerns the Packard incidents, or the bombings."

"Oh, I guess we can take that to the bank, and Mrs. Wallace?"

Ernie Guzman entered the room, set a case folder on the table. "Mrs. Wallace, remains the grieving widow with two daughters at the U of M, and a dead husband worth at least an eight figure lawsuit, and a pile of life insurance benefits."

Knox starred at the maze of information arrayed on the board, processing what Lescoe and Guzman had said. In Sheila Wallace's eyes, he remembered the gaze of vengeance the day he saw her walking from the elevator.

After seeing the grand jury evidence, he wondered if she still possessed her hatred of him. On the other hand, sponsoring rapes, corporate sabotage, and bombings were a little out of her league.

"What about Thomas Leyland?" Knox asked.

"The Chief's office is handling that," said Lescoe, "Stay tuned for further information in that regard."

Politics, thought Knox.

Guzman stepped to the marker board and summarized the assaults on Warren, Troyer and Kathleen Conlon. "These have similar M/O's—brutal, blitz attacks at night."

"The suspect," said Guzman, "appears to have stalked the victims, knew their habits. During the attacks, he wore a distinctive ski mask, luminous red lips and green eyes. I can assure you the design had the intended shock factor. There's a verbal signature to the attacks, as well."

"How so"? Knox asked.

"On Troyer, the perp said, 'listen Helen—.' On the Warren attack it was 'listen sweetheart—.' The perp that attacked your sister-in-law used the same phrase, 'listen sweat—,' but was interrupted when Kathleen kneed his *cojones*."

Knox smiled. "Physical evidence?"

"*Perplejo*, perplexing," said Guzman. "We know perps usually bring something to a crime scene, take something away, or leave something behind in the form of physical evidence."

A frown crossed Guzman's face. "In these incidents, we have nothing. A combat knife dropped at the Conlon scene had no prints. You can buy it through any gun shop, magazine or from any surplus store."

"The Troyer woman?"

"No sexual assault," said Guzman. "She vomited and soiled her pants as the perp beat the hell out of her. He took her laptop and personal affects. Somehow, he found a computer password and deleted some executive records the night of the assault. That's an indication he has a hard-on for the corporation, and that Troyer may have just been a surrogate victim to get at the company. None of Troyer's personal items have been used since her attack."

"And the Warren girl?"

"He took a black hair ribbon from Rachel Warren," said Guzman. "Maybe it turns up as a trophy. Fingernail scrapings from each victim, we have nada."

"At present," said Lescoe, "we have no direct or indirect evidence. There are no witnesses, latent prints, definable shoe impressions, fiber or hair."

"Okay," said Knox. "This dirtbag raped the Warren girl. There must be semen samples."

Lescoe responded with dismay. "Rachael's body was contaminated with dirt and leaves, then showered by the mother before the first officers arrived on scene. Vaginal walls were swollen and torn. At the hospital, vaginal swabs and rape kit were done. It'll take a few more days before we get the results."

"And, this mutt will hit again," said Knox.

• • •

LESCOE DEPARTED THE briefing room, leaving Guzman to help Knox gain a better understanding of the cases. In shirt-sleeves, Knox and Guzman pored through each of the files, the tedious, analytical process of investigation that no one ever sees, or can appreciate. Over five hours, they clarified connections among the reports, diagrams, and photographs when Knox felt the walls close in. Guzman complained of eyestrain, stale air and lousy coffee. Exhausted, both detectives stood and stretched.

"Who and why?" said Knox as he stared at the collated piles on the ten-foot table.

Guzman, rubbed his eyes, again, "What'd you say?"

"Who, Ernie. Remember, if you can identify and connect *who* the victims are, you can sometimes find *why*, the motive. If you find the motive, you may find the perp."

"Okay, then. All of our victims have an association with the Packard Corporation in one form or another. Troyer is Packard's executive secretary. Rachel Warren, the daughter of Packard's chief legal counsel. You shot Leyland, and are perceived to have shot Wallace, and Conlon is associated with you. So, if you're looking for motive, we look at Wallace or Leyland, both of whom are dead."

"So, we consider someone who wants to avenge their deaths," said Knox.

"Yeah, consider is a good word, until we have evidence."

Across the table, Knox's cell vibrated, an incoming call.

"Hello, Sergeant." Knox knew, instinctively, the voice on the phone somehow figured into the mosaic of the case, a wild card not yet connected to the files that lay on the table before he and Guzman. For now, the man behind the vexing messages remained as elusive as was his motive for the calls.

Knox tapped the record button on his cell and held a finger to his lips, a sign to Guzman for silence, and pointed to the cell.

"I haven't heard from you in a while," said Knox.

"I called the 2nd Precinct. They said you were no longer there. I was concerned."

"Why?" Knox asked, playing for enough conversation for a voiceprint. "Why are you so concerned?"

"The explosion at your home, all those fire trucks. Is Ms. Conlon all right? She's been missing from her anchor spot."

"You're assuming she was there."

"Listen, Sergeant. She was there, the wrong people... wrong place, that sort of thing."

"Tell me about that, the people...places," said Knox.

"You mean your dead wife, and those people killed at the Packard Center, the wrong people, wrong place, wrong time."

"So, tell me about Packard Center, or are you just some prankster who jerks off playing on the phone?"

"Listen Sergeant, I'm no prankster. You should know that by now. Don't you find that curious?"

"You know what they say about curiosity?" said Knox.

A taunting laugh echoed in Knox's ear. "I'm the kind of cat you'll find has nine lives, Sergeant."

"Not when you blow up my house, asshole."

"Goodbye, Harding Knox."

Knox looked at the cell in his hand. No Data.

Guzman, with a puzzled expression, shrugged. "What...?"

"I need you to hear something, Ernie."

Guzman sat down at the table, the cell on speaker. As the recording ended, Guzman turned to Knox, a puzzled expression on his face. "So, who the hell was that?"

"That's our perp, Ernie. Tomorrow, we'll begin to hunt him down."

Thirty-five

KNOX STOPPED THE Ford Taurus near the footpath at 33rd and Irving, the location of Rachel Warren's attack. It was 9:30 P.M. Shadows of the trees shrouded the pathway under a single streetlight when Knox and Guzman stepped from the car. Guzman wanted to check a couple of unanswered responses to a previous neighborhood canvas. Knox needed to get a feel for the crime scene.

On the footpath, Guzman pointed to where the Warren rape occurred. Knox stepped off the path. His penlight pierced the darkness into the tangle of bushes and vines. A piece of crime scene tape still clung to a twisted branch. Knox sank to his knees, took a deep breath, closed his eyes and allowed the flicker of photos, the descriptions in reports to fill his thoughts, to *feel* a sense of *whom* it was that he and Guzman were hunting. He could almost hear the voice, "Listen, sweetheart—"

The voice on the briefing room call, "Listen, Sergeant——"

• • •

Leon Love watched the mansion from the tree line. Nestled on a flat wooded promontory on the southwest edge of the city, the moneyed Kenwood neighborhood provided seclusion, sanctuary, and exclusiveness to its residence. At 9:30 P.M., Leon Love stepped from the dark to trample the Kenwood illusion.

At night, from the back of the house, there was an impressive view of the Minneapolis city lights. The house, and the people in it, had been among Leon's research projects. It was the home of Michael Packard, the Admiral's son and chief financial officer, CFO, of the Packard Corporation. Michael, and his wife Sara were at the Walker Art Center for an art foundation charity.

Pilfered from a Packard Center laundry truck, Leon wore a security uniform, ball cap, and blue blazer with the Packard Security crest sewn onto the left breast pocket. He watched as the real security patrol drove away from the sprawling two story executive mansion on Waverley Curve.

Leon gave a tug at his ball cap, low over his forehead, enough to show a glimpse of the security emblem, yet conceal his face from closed circuit monitors. He walked calmly up the marble steps of the front entry. From his source, he knew where to find a computer to wage further retribution on the corporation. Home alone was Alexandra Packard, in whom Leon would find added satisfaction in popping her cherry. With a gloved finger, he tapped the doorbell.

The Westminster-like chime preceded the pace of approaching feet. The face of fifteen-year-old Alexandra Packard peered out through the side window of the door.

"Security," said Leon.

"You were just here." was the nervous, youthful reply.

"I forgot to check a sensor, the one in the den."

Leon's pulse quickened as he heard four beeps, Alexandra entering the code that disabled the alarm. A dead bolt in the door slid back. Leon bent down, stuffed the hat in his pocket and pulled on the ski mask. The door handle turned, he bolted forward.

The impact of Leon against the door knocked Alex across the foyer. He kicked the door closed and pounced on Alex like a leopard onto its prey. His hand clasped her throat, and stifled a brief attempt to scream. He leaned looked into her eyes.

"Listen, Alex, tell me who is in the house."

Her eyes widened. She gasped. Leon relaxed his grip.

"No one, I swear. Please don't hurt me."

Still wary, Leon rolled Alex onto her stomach, duct taped her mouth and flex-strapped her wrists and ankles.

The excitement pulsed through him as he dragged Alex down the tiled hall to the den. A set of French doors looked out to a patio, and garden. In the dim mahogany-paneled office, a faint, blue glow emanated from a CPU light. Leon rumbled quickly through the desk drawers, and found the codebook.

Quickly, he went about his work to drive a stake into the heart of the Packard Corporation. The password discovered, he inserted a flash drive into a USB port then hit enter. He glanced to the hallway, Alex moaned and twisted in her bindings. The tell-tail ribbon of green crept across the entry box on the computer screen. Leon hit done, and inserted another flash-drive. The tension of milliseconds dragged on. From the foyer, Leon heard the sound of a door open, and a scream.

Done, Leon grabbed both flash drives and lunged toward the French doors, his escape.

The hand of Michael Packard grabbed Leon's blazer collar. Leon whirled, put an elbow into Packard's head, a fist into his gut. The CFO crashed to the floor next to the large mahogany desk. Screams echoed from the hall.

Leon burst through the French doors in a shower of glass and splintered wood. An old man in a suit wielded a baseball bat, and rushed across the patio. Leon hit the old fart with a cross body block. The bat went high over his head. The bald man went down amid the broken glass.

Chaos left in his wake, Leon stumbled through the tangle of the urban wood. Thorny branches clawed at his face like the boney fingers of some unrelenting witch.

Heart pounding, he stopped at Summit Place and peered into the neighborhood. His clothing sweat soaked, the ski mask and cap grasped tightly in hand, he dashed across the street.

On Groveland, at the edge of a greenway, the sound of sirens filled the air. In the parking lot at Lowry Hill, Leon's car waited precariously within reach. A sudden flash of emergency lights painted the darkened treetops. Police cruisers sped by into Kenwood, one, two and a third. Leon made his break.

The Camaro was backed into the shadows at a west side condo lot. Leon bolted from the trees, and hit the door opener on his key fob.

Heart still racing, he slid into the seat, turned the ignition, and the Chevy's mill thundered to life. Two figures stepped from a darkened pathway as Leon slipped into first gear, swerved, then bounced off a curb.

A glance through the Chevy's dark windows, the figures bolted out of the way. Leon turned his lights on, and sped away.

"A fuckin' dickhead and a dog," he muttered.

Thirty-six

THE SEQUENCE OF Rachael Warren's attack continued to play through his mind as Knox trudged up the pathway toward the Taurus.

"Knox!" shouted Guzman.

"Yeah, what is it?"

"Five's caught a call in Kenwood, Michael Packard's home. It may be our guy."

• • •

KNOX AND GUZMAN parked behind the department's forensic van. Five police cruisers crowded Waverly Curve, and a K-9 unit on Summit Place. Officers engaged in a neighborhood canvas, knocked on doors, and checked yards and bushes with flashlights. The nighttime din of traffic on the distant interstate filled the background.

Guzman nodded toward the ambulance leaving the driveway of the prominent executive town home. "That's not a good sign."

"Yeah, let's see what we have," said Knox.

A 5th Precinct uniformed sergeant stood next to his car as Knox and Guzman approached, their shields displayed.

"I was about to call detectives," the sergeant said.

"What have you got?" said Knox.

"Fifteen-year-old girl disables the alarm, answers the front door. The perp, dressed in security garb blitzed his way in, bound the girl. The father and company arrive. The Perp assaults dad in the den then crashes through the French doors into the woods. By the way, the perp wore a ski mask; red lips, green eyes. You guys interested?"

"Yeah." Said Guzman. "We'll take it. What's the deal with the ambulance?"

"Ellis Saeks, Michael Packard's father-in-law. They were with the Packard's, Walker Art Center. They came home early, and Mr. Saeks tried to take out the perp with a ball bat."

"Looks like the old man struck out," said Guzman.

"Concussion, dislocated shoulder; full of piss and vinegar for seventy-two. He wants another swing at the asshole who hit him"

"Tell Saeks," said Knox, "that we're the designated hitters."

The sergeant escorted Knox and Guzman inside the Packard mansion. Alexandra sat on a leather half-moon sofa in the great room at the back of the estate house. Through tall floor to ceiling windows, city lights glittered, as if painted on a huge glass canvas.

A phone to his ear, Michael Packard paced the room, a blue ice bag held to the side of his head.

"Look, we've had a break in. I can't deal with that now," Packard exclaimed. "Get someone from IT. Okay?"

Packard, a beefier, forty-five-year-old cookie-cutter image of his father, the Admiral, acknowledged Guzman and Knox with a nod and spoke again into the phone. "I'll call back. Some detectives are here

"I apologize for the distraction, gentlemen," said Packard. "I'm afraid there's been an IT issue at our company."

"I see. Right now," said Knox, "we'd like to focus on what happened here."

Packard put an arm around Alexandra. "Thank God, my daughter is alright. Her sister, Kate, is with my parents."

Near the den, camera flashes punctuated the movement and muffled conversation of the forensic team.

Packard, Alexandra in tow, motioned Knox and Guzman to the bar. He poured a scotch and soda. "Anything to drink, gentlemen?" He shrugged, awkwardly, "Of course not, just trying to be hospitable."

Guzman walked Alexandra back to the great room. Packard took a sip from his drink as Knox allowed the clearly upset executive to vent.

"This is not a random burglary, Sergeant," said Packard. "My father's executive assistant is beaten and robbed, his boathouse blown up, and the executive records system crashed. Even with an alarm and extra security patrol, whoever came into our home, and attacked my daughter is trying to hurt our family, and destroy our corporation."

"I understand, Mr. Packard," said Knox. "My partner and I are part of a unit assigned to those cases. Right now, I need you to tell me what happened here."

Anticipating the customary allegation of police inaction, Knox took out his notebook, and moved quickly to the follow-up questions, taking notes as Michael Packard spoke.

"You have an exterior video security system, we'd like the disks to evaluate who broke in, "said Knox.

"Of course, Sergeant. It's an auto-feed to Packard Security. I can arrange for you to have the recordings."

"Thank you, Mr. Packard. Now start from the beginning, tell me what happened."

Packard filled in the evening incidentals, a night at the Walker, arriving home early, seeing his daughter trust up in the foyer, the intruder in the den, the shouts and screams.

"And, the intruder burst through doors of the den after he struck you?" Knox asked.

"Yes, my father-in-law, Ellis Saeks, came around to the patio with a baseball bat from the front closet."

"Tell me about that, Mr. Saeks and the bat."

"The guy that hit me wore a ski mask, red lips, greens eyes as I recall. He had on a blue blazer with gray trousers, like our security people. Ellis, swung the bat at the man, but went down when the guy threw a block into him. I picked my self up and went to Ellis lying in glass just outside the den. He was delirious, bleeding from the side of his head, couldn't move his shoulder. My wife and mother-in-law were screaming, and called police and an ambulance."

"Now, the computer, the call you took as we came in?"

Packard sighed and sank onto a stool at the bar. He took another sip of scotch. "I'm the CFO for Packard Corporation. Alexandra, my daughter, said the guy that broke in went to my computer. Just when you arrived, my people informed me that our finance computers crashed. Everything is down. IT is working on it."

After a half hour, satisfied he had obtained what he could, Knox put his notebook in his pocket when the cell on the bar chimed to a catchy little tune, from the Broadway play, *Cabaret*'. With a self-conscious shrug, Michael Packard picked up the phone to the tune of "Money, Money, Money."

"That's not a problem, Joel," said Packard. "No, we are all fine, thank you."

Knox listened. Then, a sudden change in Packard's tone from appreciative and accommodating to shock.

"Joel," said Packard. "That's just not possible!"

There was a further pause "Okay, do what you can," said Packard then hung up.

"Your IT people?" asked Knox.

"Yes. And I can't believe what they are telling me."

"And, what's that?" asked Knox

"The prompt that zapped our system, our IT people said it came from my computer's address. The computer in the den."

"Who ever broke into your house had access to your system? Where are your passwords?" Knox asked. "Who'd have a major grudge against your company to access to your computer system?"

"Sergeant, in the course of business a corporation can piss off a lot of people, but I have no idea who could be doing this. As for my password, it's in a codebook, upper right drawer of my desk. Regrettably, I failed to lock the desk tonight. We were late for the Walker."

Packard poured another scotch and soda.

Knox walked to the den, the forensics team finishing their detail. The lead tech cast a look at Knox and shrugged. It was not a good sign, the physical evidence slim, or none. There was no codebook.

"Take the computer," said Knox.

• • •

KNOX AND PACKARD watched the forensics team pack up when Guzman stepped into the room.

"Knox I need a minute." Packard excused himself and walked to his daughter in the great room.

"It's our guy," Guzman said. Alex described the same mask that Helen Troyer and Rachel Warren had seen. His opening remark was, 'Listen Alex—'" He knew her name, man."

"How does he know, Ernie? How does he know about any of the victims?"

"There's one more thing?"

"What's that?"

"His eyes, she said they were golden brown, and had what she described as exploding stars around the pupils."

Beyond the French doors, the glow of light cast the broad shadow of Jon Bass. He stepped across the broken glass and wood splinters. "So, we've got more trouble," he said as he entered the broken doorway. Dressed in a windbreaker, tan trousers and golf cap, his face held a sober expression. Hands in his pockets, he assessed the damage, and looked at Knox.

"Scene secure?"

"Yeah, Jon."

"Michael's wife called me," said Bass. She's at the hospital with Saeks."

Knox shook Bass's hand. "I haven't heard from you in a while."

"I've been out of town. Heard your house blew up, now this."

Michael Packard entered the hallway. "I thought I heard your voice, Jon."

"Your dad sent me, Kate's in the car. How's Alexandra?"

"We're both fine. Thanks."

"Michael," said Bass, "would you mind getting Kate while I talk with Sergeant Knox?"

Bass's tone was more instruction than request, an indication, thought Knox, that Bass occupied a position of more significance in the realm of Admiral Packard's world than a simple estate manager, and so-called security consultant.

Knox and Guzman briefed Bass on break-in, as well as the phone calls Knox had received.

"The son-of-a-bitch has got some kind of itch to scratch. Rape, assaults, explosives, baited phone calls, home invasions, computer sabotage. A lot of resentment there," said Bass.

"Yeah, I get that," said Knox.

"We keep coming back to Leyland," said Guzman, "but he's dead. For some reason the Chief's office is running the background on him which keeps us in the dark."

"I'm running the background," said Bass.

"Oh, *you* are?" said Knox. The sarcasm was sharp.

"I had my instructions. Anything I found went directly to the Admiral, then to Chief Ballard. An hour ago, I concluded that part of the deal. Now, I'm telling you."

"Like telling me about the ballroom videos?"

"Knox, there were legitimate reasons for not disclosing that to anyone until the proper time. You know that, now."

"Well, Jon, you think *now* is a proper time to tell us about Leyland?"

"Yeah, it's time," said Bass, a cautionary tenor to his voice. "I just flew in from Wisconsin tonight. Thomas Leyland has a son, Charles, no middle name, goes by Chuck, and he may be headed this way. He was third officer on a Great Lakes ship, the *Michigan Conveyer*. After the shooting, Chuck took leave to attend his father's funeral."

"Did he return to the ship?" Guzman asked.

"He made the *Conveyor* in Thunder Bay, Ontario. Over time, Chuck became isolated, and argued with shipmates. Last week at port in Detroit, the captain called him on his change in attitude. Chuck said he was having problems adjusting to his father's death. The skipper relieved him until he could get his head straight."

"So, Chuck Leyland may have a score to settle?" Knox asked.

"I confirmed that he left his home in Manitowoc, Wisconsin. A loner, he gave a neighbor three-hundred-dollars to look after his place, said a lawyer would get in touch if he did not show up again. No lawyer in town knows him."

Knox took a breath. "Bank accounts, credit cards?"

"He cashed out his bank accounts a few days ago. Credit cards went dormant until a gas charge in Manitowoc, and another in Eau Claire, Wisconsin surfaced."

"Sounds like Chuck's next port-of-call may be Minneapolis," said Knox.

"I'd bank on it," said Bass. "The guy is in the wind behind the wheel of a blue Ford F-150 pickup." Bass pulled a sheaf of papers from the breast pocket of his jacket. "Here's the low-down on Chuck. You watch your back, Harding."

"The eyes?" Guzman asked.

"What about them?"

"What is the color of Chuck Leyland's eyes?"

Bass thought for a moment. "His DL says Hazel. One last thing, fellas; this spring Packard Corporation had a couple farm silos explode over in Wisconsin."

"That's too coincidental," said Knox.

"Yeah, I thought so." Bass replied.

Back on Waverly Curve, the face of the 5th Precinct sergeant looked grim. "Sorry guys," he said as Knox and Guzman approached. "We don't have much for you. The K-9s picked up a positive track from the den. It went east through the woods. The scent went to the parking lot of the Lowry Hill Condos, then nothing. You'll get the reports."

"The guys find any clothing, a hat mask, small code book?" Guzman asked.

"Like I said, fellas. Nothing."

The police cruisers made their slow departure from the scene amid a sound of communication acknowledgements.

The two detectives padded to their car when a small, wiry man in a tan windbreaker approached. Wisps of reddish-white hair poked out from under a tartan tam. A black Scottie strained at the leash held tightly in the man's right hand.

"A little excitement tonight, officers?" The man asked.

"Do you live in the neighborhood?" Guzman asked.

The man chuckled. "No, sir, Baron's Hough," the brogue thick as a haggis stew.

"That somewhere in New Jersey, huh?" Guzman joked.

"New Jersey—no! Scotland, man! I'm here on a visit to my daughter."

The man walked closer, the terrier sniffing at the shoes of the two detectives.

"The name is Gordon Pendleton, gentlemen." His face brightened with a smile. "If it doesn't take you away from your duties, I do have a bit of a complaint?"

"And what would that be Mr. Pendleton?" Knox asked, expecting one of those ubiquitous traffic ticket protests.

"Well, you see, I was walking Shamus, here. We stepped off the pathway into the car park at the condominiums, just nearby. All of a sudden, this dark Chevrolet Camaro, fancy wheels, came rushing at us. There were no lights at first. The car swerved and struck the curb. I couldn't see the driver, windows being so dark. Then the lights came on, and the car sped away. Bugger nearly killed us, he did."

Guzman cast a glance at the Scotsman. "About what time was that, sir?"

"Around the time Shamus and I heard police sirens, and saw the emergency lights. We saw all the commotion here, so, we thought we'd walk by, take a look."

"Mr. Pendleton," said Knox, "I don't suppose you got a license number of that Camaro, did you?"

"Aye, sir. I did, here on ma hand."

Thirty-seven

AT NOON, KNOX and Guzman breezed into the briefing room, a sheaf of printouts in hand. Lescoe and Commander Krieg glanced up from reports. Krieg wore his customary glum expression, and slid the paper work aside. "With everything that went on last night, I hope you two have something of substance that I can give the Chief."

"We have a license number, and a name," said Knox.

"Fine, but help me out here," said Krieg. "Lieutenant Lescoe tells me we have a home invasion at Michael Packard's in Kenwood, a corporate computer crash, and an unidentified masked man that matches the other assaults. Then, we have a witness from Scotland walking his Scottie who gets a license number to a Chevy Camaro owned by a Hispanic male from Mesa, Arizona."

Krieg threw up his hands. "Am I missing anything, here?"

"No, that pretty much nails it," said Knox.

Guzman chimed in. "Mr. Pendleton, our witness, was nearly struck by the Camaro as it sped away from the Lowry Hill Condos. It was right after the home invasion, and the Camaro was initially running without lights."

"So, how does a man from Scotland know the difference between a Camaro and a Camry?" Krieg asked.

Knox pulled out a chair and sat down. "Mr. Pendleton is a car buff, watches *Wheeler and Dealers* on the telly."

"It's a British automotive program," said Lescoe. "It's televised here in the states—"

"Okay, people," Krieg interrupted, "please pull this together," "You're telling me that our big leads are a phantom Camaro, a Scotsman with a Scottie, and a British car show?"

"Listen," said Knox. "Pendleton wrote the license number on his hand. It's an Arizona tag flagged for resale.

The Camaro's registered owner is Enrique Mendoza. At five-foot-six and a hundred-forty-pounds he's not the man I chased across the bridge the night my house blew up."

"Commander," said Guzman, "Arizona DMV and the Saguaro Auto Auction show the Camaro was sold to Devin Riley's Lake Street Auto, Minneapolis."

"Okay," said Krieg. "See Riley. Find out who has that car."

"That's not all," said Knox. "We may have another player."

"Yesterday we had no players," said Krieg. "Now we have two?"

"Leyland, the ballroom shooter, has a son, Chuck," said Knox. "He left Wisconsin a few days ago, and is in the wind."

"Are there anymore surprises, Sergeant?"

"That's it for now," said Knox.

"Good. Keep working through it. When you get a little more lipstick on this pig, give me a squeal," said Krieg who left the room.

The uncharacteristic feint at humor lingered, but not long. Knox rolled his eyes. Within an hour he and Guzman had a BOLO, be on the look out, for Chuck and his truck that was sent to Minnesota, and Wisconsin agencies. Along with dossier on Chuck, a note went into the file—follow-up.

A records check turned nothing of interest on the background check for Riley's auto business. About 2:00 P.M., Knox and Guzman curbed the Taurus on the 600 block of East Lake Street.

Riley's was a small operation sandwiched among the modest Lake Street businesses. About thirty late model used cars lined the street frontage. Sale banners fluttered in the breeze. A big label dealership, it was not.

Behind the windows of the showroom hunkered the specialty of the business, eight gleaming American muscle cars.

Devin Riley, a genial sixty-something Mickey Rooney look-alike, stepped out from the side of a red Cadillac CTS.

In no-wrinkle slacks, Caribbean print shirt and a short brimmed straw fedora; Riley looked more like a South Beach cigar salesman than a Lake Street wheels hustler. "Can I help you, detectives? I'm Devin Riley,"

"Busted before we laid the tin on you," said Guzman.

Riley laughed. "I've been around, fellas. Two guys in there 40s, a standard issue police unmarked, telltale bulge under the left shoulder of the sport coat. You aren't here to pick out a couple mid-life crises convertibles."

Knox hoped Riley could remember cars as well as he could read people, and handed Riley his business card. "Actually, we're here about a 2002 Chevy Camaro, Navy blue, mag wheels."

"I remember. Nice piece of work...picked it up at an Arizona auction in January, sold it for cash in May. Riley paused, a sly smile danced across his face. "You know, you guys do that pretty well."

"What's that?" Guzman asked.

"You seemed surprised that I knew about the car, looked at each other with that expression cops have."

"What expression is that, Mr. Riley?"

"The Dragnet thing, you know? When Sergeant Joe Friday and Frank White look at one another, when they find the zinger, the hook to the case?"

Knox laughed. "Okay, Mr. Riley you've got us. We're looking for the zinger, and it may be that Arizona Chevy."

"And we need the facts, man. Just the facts," Guzman spoofed.

"There you go. That's it," laughed Riley. "Let's find the paper work."

At 3:00 P.M., Knox waited in the Taurus, parked in the shade of a boulevard elm on Nicollet Avenue South near 43rd Street. Old brick front stores serviced the comfortable, but aging residential neighborhood.

Knox called Lescoe on his cell. "Janice, we're eyeballing a UPS store on Nicollet South. By the way, the guy at the car lot, Riley, said fifteen percent off for Lieutenants on any Lexus in the lot."

"Right," chided Lescoe. Let's try to stay on task here, Knox"

"Okay. The sales contract says the R/O is a twenty-five year old guy named Leon, no middle name, Love."

"Knox, are you pulling my chain again? We're looking for a sexual assault suspect and the guy's handle is Leon Love?"

"Yeah, like in *Love*, handles."

"Not funny, Knox, what else do you have?"

"Well, on the sale papers, our subject used this Nicollet Avenue UPS mail drop for an address. He had a Madison, Wisconsin address on a Wisconsin driver's license for ID. Get this. He paid $11K for the Camaro and another $1,500 for insurance. That's all in cash, a lot of walking around money."

"There's one more thing, Jan. Riley said that Love had strange eyes, a burst of brown and gold in the iris around the pupil. Alexandra Packard told us the same thing."

"So far, I like where this is going, Knox. Where's Guzman?"

"I'm here, Janice. Our subject's UPS mailbox is number 69. How's that grab you?"

"Guzman! What am I dealing with here, the Two Stooges?"

"Stooge who?" Guzman feigned a puzzled response.

"Never mind," Lescoe snapped. "What's the UPS setup?"

"PC on a warrant for the box to get a physical address is a stretch," said Guzman. "Besides, if this is our guy, we'd have to leave a receipt and tip our hand."

"Okay," said Lescoe. "Options."

"If we run surveillance for the Camaro to show, we could be here for a week. If it does show, we tail it to the perp's crib. Then what? All we have is a vague reasonable suspicion, no leverage for an interview, and no PC for an arrest."

Lescoe had no immediate response.

"Janice, this is Knox. The AZ plates expire in June. Run a Minnesota alpha, and insurance vehicle registration on Love. Minnesota plates must be mailed to a physical address. Also, run Minnesota and Wisconsin DLs, state crime bureau and NCIC checks."

"Anything else, Knox?"

"A couple more things; run the surveillance possibilities by Krieg. Eventually, we have to consider that option. Finally, I need the phone number for Madison Wisconsin PD, the detective unit. Call me back when you have that."

"Knox, you have your own cell phone, and digital terminal. How about you and your partner run all that down yourselves, and call *me* back when *you have it?*"

"I love the sound of your voice when you get edgy, Janice."

"That's not edgy, Knox. It's bitchy." Lescoe hung up.

Knox and Guzman ran the paper work to be printed back at their office, and waited. They watched the UPS lot, hoping to get lucky.

At nearly 5:00 P.M., Guzman returned to the office. Getting lucky was something for Saturday night after dinner, with an attractive woman and a seductive bottle of cabernet. It was not for two cops doing surveillance at a UPS shop for a Camaro that wouldn't show.

In the briefing room, Lescoe and Krieg sat amidst state crime bureau, DMV, NCIC, DL and Wisconsin DCI reports on Leon Love. Guzman casually entered, anticipating the obvious question.

"Where is Sergeant Knox?" Commander Krieg asked.

Guzman shrugged, "Gone to Wisconsin."

Thirty-eight

KNOX DROVE ALONG Highway 8 through the bucolic east Minnesota farm country, a route often traveled to Swede Lundgren's home for afternoons filled with fishing on the Saint Croix. This time, he was casting a line for Leon Love.

Knox was not confident that Guzman's explanation of why, and where he had gone would be received well by Lescoe and Krieg. After all, he was off his leash. But, you have to keep moving when the lead gets hot, or a case dies.

Eager to meet the man who awaited him, Knox crossed the Saint Croix River gorge at the Taylors Falls Bridge. North along the Wisconsin Highway 87, he slowed at a stone obelisk with a hand-hewn sign, "River Haven."

A turn to the left, and the Taurus crept along a sandy drive, the land forested by lofty conifers. A soft breeze whispered through the trees. The clean scent of pine wafted through the open car window. A final bend opened to a clearing occupied by a lodge-like home and small barn with stone foundations. A man in a red and black-checkered lumberjack shirt, and blue jeans stood at the railing of the front porch, ax in hand, a Longhaired German Pointer at his side. Knox slowed to a stop at the backwoods Valhalla.

The sergeant at Madison, Wisconsin PD had said retired detective Walter Meyers had been their man on Leon Love.

Meyers stepped from the porch. Knox slipped from the car, introduced himself and held out his credentials. Meyers gave them the onceover, and grasped Knox in a vice-like handshake. In his sixties, bald, and broad shouldered with a barrel chest, the double bladed ax, and a cord of wood stacked near the house provided an explanation for Meyers's physical condition, not the mold of a typical police retiree.

"Glad you could make it," said Meyers. "Don't get many visitors, lately. Retired, people forget who you are, kids off with their own families, wife gone, too. So, I'm kind of on my own, except for Max." The pointer waged its tail as Meyers patted its head.

"It's really a beautiful here," said Knox, who could tell by the old detectives' rambling that he welcomed the company.

"Yup, Trudy and I spent fifteen years putting this together, long weekends, vacations," Meyers paused, head bowed, "Damned if she didn't die after I retired."

"I'm very sorry to hear that, sir."

"Call me Walt."

"Okay, Walt," said Knox, still troubled by his own loss. At least the new assignment had somewhat restored a meaning to who, and what he was. Walt, on the other hand, lived alone in the wilderness. More than anything else, the loneliness, 'people forget who you are,' he said, had probably influenced Meyers's reluctance to discuss Leon Love over the phone. What he wanted, and maybe needed was the company.

Inside the house, a large stone hearth formed the centerpiece of the great room. Log beams crossed the ceiling. Knox casually assessed the living area, log walls, gleaming wood floors, Oriental rug, leather chairs, sofa, broad windows, bright, clean, nothing out of place.

"I promised I would take care of things, just the way she left it," said Meyers.

Knox felt embarrassed, caught in the appraisal of his host's home. On the granite kitchen counter sat fillets of bass, and cold Leinenkugle beers in a tub of ice.

"I told you I'd make the trip worthwhile," said Meyers, handing Knox a beer. "Dinner will be ready in a few shakes."

As Meyers prepared the bass, corn on the cob and boiled potatoes, he and Knox exchanged small talk about their mutual police experiences. While they ate, Knox tried to move the conversation toward the purpose of his trip. Instead, Walt rambled about fishing, his volunteer duties with the Sheriff's office, filling in at the American Legion Post in Saint Croix Falls, and choir at the Lutheran church.

Knox listened. Walt Meyers, retired cop, coping with his loss, filling the voids of life as if trying to convince himself that he still had a place in the world, a sense of belonging, of value. Knox wondered if he was looking into the glass of a distant mirror. He shrugged off the chill of that notion to finish a morsel of grilled bass.

They finished dinner, washed and dried the last plate.

"Leon Love," Meyers finally said, and disappeared into the master bedroom beyond the hearth. He returned with a three-ring binder the thickness of a small telephone directory.

"This book," said Meyers, "is about Leon Love."

"What was your interest in Leon, Walt?"

"Where do you want to start?"

For the next hour and a half, Meyers revealed the litany of arrests and releases he had encountered with Leon Love. It was a biography of a self-absorbed young man. Considered not intelligent but resourceful, not ingenious but cunning, not amiable but manipulative. Over time, Leon had dabbled in various courses at UW, Madison. His recreation, outside of drugs and alcohol, was to hang out in country western, rhythm and blues joints where he ate barbecue, and hustled young women. But the influence of drugs and alcohol caused him to anger easily with vengeful results.

Knox followed the narrative, scribbled notes as Meyers disclosed Leon's penchant to use his mother to bankroll his easy life, to bail him out of trouble.

Then, for a moment, Knox stopped writing, stunned by Meyers's revelation about Leon's father, the unique estrangement with Lucile Love, Leon's mother. Meyers continued while Knox tried to grasp Leon's possible motivations for the assaults and bombings, the computer sabotage, trying to foresee Leon's intended end game.

"Are you sure about the father, Walt?"

"Oh, yes. Lucy would call me from time to time. When I would arrive at her home, she already had a few cocktails. She was lonely, tired, wanted someone to talk to, and worried about what would happen to Leon. I put him jail on his last beef. It was then she opened up, told me the whole story. You've heard it before, a single parent, absorbed with a career, a crusader for the underprivileged who now held herself responsible for her own son's foray into crime."

"I've heard the same violin played many times, Walt."

"Anyway, Knox, she was crying when she told me about Leon's old man, a flyer among other things. He dropped in and out of their lives like an old song you can't forget, an old love she could never have. Leon was the secret bastard son, the guilt for which the father paid the freight.

Lawyer fees, school fees, occasional outings, expensive gifts were all on account. And, Lucy's estranged lover would take her for clandestine weekends, sometimes to a house in Minneapolis."

"Do you think Lucy would talk with me?"

"Not unless you have a shovel and an Ouija board."

"She's dead?" Knox asked, disappointed.

"She is," said Meyers, a hint of empathy in his voice. "Two months before Leon's jail release, Lucy drove back from an immigration support meeting. She skidded through a stop sign in a rural area near Stoughton, Wisconsin. T-boned by a farm truck and not wearing a seat belt, she died at the scene. The irony is an immigrant farm hand was driving the truck. The truck belonged to Agra-Pac Farms."

Knox gaped in surprise at Meyers.

"What's a matter, Knox, look's like you swallowed a cat?"

"Agra-Pac Farms, as in a subsidiary of the Packard Corporation?"

"Correct," said Meyers. "And within a week of Leon Love's release, two of Agra-Pac's silos near Stoughton exploded in the middle of the night."

"Walt, the more you tell me about this mutt, the more I like him for our cases. But, how did Leon get clipped in Madison?"

"I caught the Wanda Rippie case," Meyers said. "She was Leon's last of dysfunctional girlfriends. She was a pharmaceuticalized, bipolar psychology major at UW, Madison, and she satisfied all of Leon's sensual desires."

Meyers uttered a chuckle tinted with irony. "One Friday night, Wanda said no. Spurred on by a few joints and jiggers of Wild Turkey, Leon took exception. In the course of forcing his advances on Wanda, he used her for a punching bag. Unfortunately, Wanda is the only daughter of a wealthy Lake Geneva, Wisconsin attorney, Tom Rippie, who insisted that Leon be locked up for ten to twenty."

"We know that didn't happen."

"And I'll tell you why," said Meyers. "Leon languished in jail for a while when, once again, this Guiney attorney from Saint Paul shows up, Alonzo Rico."

"I know Rico," said Knox. "He's a gutter snipe who handles criminal defense work for a bunch of low-lives."

"Well," said Meyers, "Leon's old man paid the freight, and Rico got the kid off with six months in county jail on a misdemeanor."

Meyers popped a cap on another Leinie and explained the background on the extraordinary plea bargain Rico engineered. Knox gasped with disbelief. Walt highlighted other crimes in which Leon was suspect; failed surveillance operations, reluctant victims and informants, the lack of supporting evidence all resulted in the lack of arrests and prosecution. Knox was left with a deep sigh of frustration.

"Walt, if I get the chance, I want to get Love in the box, see what he'll say."

"Don't hold your breath. He'll sit in a chair as if you were wasting *his* time. He has this superior 'fuck you' kind of smirk on his face. Makes you want to reach across the table and punch his lights out. Know what I mean?"

"Yeah, I know precisely what you mean."

"The other thing that'll piss you off, Knox, is his stare; dead, emotionless, like he's looking right through you, gives you a hell-of-a-chill. There are times, even way up here, that I look over my shoulder, wondering if he's somewhere close by."

"The eyes," said Knox, remembering the Packard home invasion. "What about the eyes?"

"Strange, I guess you could say," said Meyers who wrinkled his brow in recollection. "They were hazel with gold and brown flecks, like a star burst."

"Jesus, one of our victims said exactly that."

"If you want background, Knox, I can tell you what records Madison PD, Dane County and UW have on this scumbag. You may also want records on Leon's cellmate while he was in county lock up. An explosives background, the guy is doing federal time, Oxford, Wisconsin. It should provide an interesting link in your case."

"I'll run it down," said Knox. "But let me ask you, after all this time, you're retired, live up here in this pristine wilderness, in this wonderful home, why do you hang on to this stuff?"

"Some day Leon is gonna show up on my turf. It keeps me primed to pull the trigger."

Knox wanted to stay, help keep the loneliness from Walt's front door, but he was still on the job, and Leon Love had just become more than just a person of interest.

"Walt, what you told me is really significant. I don't mean to be rude, but I need to get back to Minneapolis, tonight."

At the car, Meyers shook hands with Knox. "If you get this prick, I'll give you an all expense paid vacation at Walt Meyers's River Haven Resort. Free beer and all the fish you can eat."

"Keep the griddle warm, and the beer cold, Walt. I'll be back."

As Knox drove off, a quick glance in the rear view mirror revealed a silhouette in the glimmer of a porch light. Alone among the whispering pines with his dog, Walt Meyers leaned against a veranda post of his log home, thumbs hooked in his belt. "I'll be back," whispered Knox.

Headlights cut through the night as the Taurus crossed the Saint Croix River Bridge. Knox pulled into the state park on the Minnesota side of the flow. His mind whirled at Meyers's disclosures, and picked up his phone.

"Janice?"

"Knox, where the hell are you?

"I'm back in Minnesota. Did I catch you at a bad time?"

"Damn it. It's 11:00 P.M., I am in bed, so—"

"Janice, have Krieg and Ernie in briefing, 8:00 A.M."

"What did you find out in Wisconsin?"

"See you at eight."

• • •

AT PRECISELY 8:00 A.M., Knox pushed through the briefing room door, satchel in hand. Along with the smell of fresh brewed coffee, expectations hung heavy in the air.

Lieutenant Lescoe and Ernie Guzman flanked Commander Krieg. Chief Ballard looked up from the table.

"Good morning, Knox," said Krieg. "You were out of town?"

Knox took the question for what it was, disapproval for venturing beyond the scope of instructions, beyond his tether.

Knox directed his reply to Chief Ballard. "I was doing some background work, Chief, handling peripherals."

"Well, it's your meeting," said Ballard, "I'm anxious to hear what *peripherals* you've uncovered. The staff has brought me up to speed on your person of interest, Leon Love. Is that right?"

Knox stood at the opposite end of the table from the Chief. He took a yellow legal pad from his satchel.

"I met with retired Madison, Wisconsin PD detective, Walt Meyers who spent several years, periodically, investigating the exploits of Leon Love."

Knox described the string of Leon's arrests, and subsequent releases. Through no fault of Meyer's, assault victims failed to come forward for fear of intimidation by Leon, or being ignored by the system. They subsequently left UW. An ex-girlfriend had informed police about property crimes, but circumstantial evidence frustratingly failed to support prosecution. Leon also foiled surveillance operations that ran out of time and money. In other scrapes, Leon's mother, driven by guilt over the emotional neglect of her son, paid restitution to keep him out of jail.

"It was all part of Leon's learning curve," added Knox, "his aptitude for cunning manipulation to avoid accountability."

Krieg asked about the six month Wisconsin jail term Leon had served.

"I was getting to that," said Knox. "Ultimately, Meyers bagged Leon for the sexual assault, and battery of his ex-girlfriend, Wanda Rippie. Compliance with the word 'no' was not in Leon's lexicon."

"On that case," Knox said, "Leon faced 5-10 on a sex offender beef. Enter the esteemed Saint Paul attorney of questionable note, Alonso Rico. He finds that Wanda had been shagging her psychology professor, tennis coach and a campus cop while titillating Leon's loins."

Guzman moaned. "Can anyone say plea bargain?"

"Plea bargain," said Knox. "The cop, professor and coach quietly resigned, saving UW's face. The Rippie's, to save embarrassment, shuffled whacky Wanda into a rehab center at an undisclosed location. Leon does a misdemeanor stretch in county, and has his sexual offender record expunged.

"And, we get the dirt bag in Minneapolis." said Guzman.

"Think of it as criminals without boarders," said Knox.

A frown of impatience creased Ballard's face. "This is all interesting, Knox, but how does Love link to our cases?"

"There are more *peripherals*, Chief. Leon had a cellmate at the Dane County, Wisconsin jail. His name is Jessie James Poon, serving time on an explosives, theft and bank burglary rap. I checked. Poon is at Oxford Federal in Wisconsin."

"Jesse James Poon," said Ballard with a slight pause. "Who the hell would give a kid a name like that?'

"I think Vlad the Impaler was already taken," said Knox. "Poon, an ex-army explosives guy, knocked off a National Guard Armory, and a bank, a neo-Nazi thing."

Ballard rolled his eyes. "Right. So, Love is in jail with Jessie James, where is the connection to Packard, and to you, Knox? Where's the motive?"

"More peripherals, Chief. The first being Leon's mother, Professor Lucile Love, Ph.D., migrant worker civil rights activist, and tenured political science professor at the University of Wisconsin. She was Leon's primary bankroll."

Lescoe, jotting notes, "Is she still at UW?"

"She's departed, actually," Knox replied, "in her car when she blew a rural stop sign, and was broadsided by a farm truck. No seat belt. She died at the scene. The owner of the farm truck is a corporation called Agra-Pac."

"As in Packard Corporation?" Guzman asked.

"Ernie, you are so good with clues," quipped Knox.

Krieg, ever skeptical, said, "So your theory is that Leon Love is going after the Packard Corporation because their farm truck killed his mother?"

"The civil case in regard to Lucile's death was tossed out of court. Packard's legal and finance staff, Raymond Warren and Michael Packard, dismissed any effort to recover the slightest amount of compensation, even though it was alleged the truck driver's legal status was in question. Then, within a week of Leon's release, two Agra-Pac silos blew up in the middle of the night. Fertilizer bombs were the source of the explosions."

"Now, you have my attention," said Ballard.

Knox took a breath before proceeding. "Years ago, at the University of Minnesota, Leon's mother had an affair upon concluding her Ph.D. studies. A little on the fringe-side, strangely attractive, she became the desire of an otherwise scholarly, and handsome bi-racial assistant professor, a case of opposite attractions. Leon Love is the progeny of that relationship."

Ballard, his voice wary, "And, the father is?"

Knox paused, as would a trial attorney before delivering the final line of a closing argument, "University of Minnesota professor, Neil Wallace."

There was a collective gasp within the room. "Sergeant, you're quite certain of the credibility of your information?" Ballard asked.

"From Lucile Love's lips to the ears of Walt Myers, Chief."

"And," said Ballard, "an errant round from your gun killed Neil Wallace, the father of Leon Love."

Ballard thought for a moment. "Okay, people. The details about Lucile Love, and Neil Wallace are not to leave this room. The public fallout vis-a-vis Wallace's death, and the department would be substantial. Take every effort to clearly establishing all links to Leon Love, and our cases."

For a moment, the room fell silent; the elements of motive, intent, ability, means, and execution fluttered through Knox's mind... *facts and evidence.*

Ballard broke the stillness. "There was a computer compromise to the finance operations for the Packard Corporation. What's going on with that?"

"We think it occurred during the Packard home invasion," said Lescoe, "a thumb-drive was used to transmit the virus from Michael Packard's computer to corporate. We have people on it.

Ballard had one more question. "The last item on my list, Knox, is someone named Chuck Leyland. I understand you are aware of him."

"We are," said Knox. "A BOLO is out on him, and his truck."

With a nod to Krieg, the chief stood. “You have a lot of circumstantial information on your plate, Commander. Corroborate your findings. Stay focused. I don’t want this Wallace-Love connection to rest on the word of a dead professor. It applies to establishing motive. Let’s quietly get a DNA confirmation, and keep me informed.” He stopped at the doorway.

“Sergeant Knox,” said Ballard, “good work. Keep this Chuck Leyland character on your radar, and watch your back.”

Thirty-nine

Mayor Bergin conferred at her desk with her executive assistant, the replacement to the erstwhile Rodney Straight, who was now pushing papers at a remote water treatment plant north of the city. Ballard walked in, unannounced.

"Hello, Chief. This is unexpected," said Bergin, trademark Niemen Marcus scarf draped her left shoulder.

"May we have a moment," said Ballard, knowing he was taking a risk with what he was about to disclose to Bergin.

"Call me when you want," said the assistant who left the room, and closed the door.

"Barbara, we have a person of interest in the Packard cases."

"Thom, that's wonderful news. How did this happen?"

"I'll spare you the details, but some good work by Sergeants Knox and Guzman led us to where we are now."

"Excuse me, Thom, but my understanding was that the activities of Sergeant Knox were to be restricted, *managed*, out of the public eye?"

"They have been. Knox has been working in tandem with Sergeant Guzman, and both have provided the direction we have at the moment." It wasn't entirely true, but Ballard didn't have the time to massage' the Mayor's ego.

The pensive expression on Bergin's face subsided. "Okay, then where are we, Thom? Who is it that you're looking at?"

"Remember, you told me you to keep you in the loop?"

"Yes, of course I remember."

"Well, I'm doing that now, Barbara, but you must understand what I'm about to tell you is in the strictest of confidence."

The Wallace revelation a shock, Ballard watched the mayor's jaw drop and her eyes widen. Speechless, she gasped and slipped back in her chair. Ballard knew, amid her astonishment whirled the calculus of political impact.

Forty

Somewhere in the distance, a commercial lawn mower hummed among the mausoleums and tombstones. The noise jarred the tranquility of the morning. Like the mechanical whine of an early morning weed trimmer, it disturbed Knox's sojourn to Lara's grave. He leaned back against her marker, the grass soft to the touch. Giant oaks and elms cast umbrellas of shade on a green, park-like carpet that rolled across the cemetery grounds.

Knox craned his neck to gaze at the bouquet of baby's breath and three red roses; one rose for Lara, one for him and the other for their life together. Lara's grave was his only place to find solace, to be alone with *her* and with his thoughts.

"There has been progress on the Packard cases," Knox told her. "It began with the simplest of things, a man walking a dog, a Scottie named Shamus no less?" Knox reminisced about the revelations of Walt Meyers in his lodge on the Saint Croix. He told her how Meyers and Swede would have enjoyed one another's company, had Swede lived. He made no mention of their home being blow to bits.

At the grave, Knox thought about the case elements he and Guzman had pulled together on Friday. Monday, the surveillance on Leon Love would begin. He worried about how things would go down, always the unknown to fathom, the case always with him, like the mistress Lara had been resigned to accept.

The phone in Knox's jacket pocket came to life with a beep.

"Have I caught you at a bad time, Sergeant?"

It was the goddamned voice again, Leon's voice. Even at Lara's grave, the son-of-a-bitch had found him. However, now Knox had put a form to the vexing phantom—a name and a face.

"Bad time?" Knox asked. He sat up and stopped himself before he nearly said *Leon*. He fumbled for the record button. "Listen, ah—"

"I'm listening, Sergeant. You have something to say, or are you just trying to coax a name from me?"

"You seem to know all about *me*," said Knox. "I think it's time to share?

"I'm not the sharing type."

Knox couldn't resist pushing a button. "Were your mother and father the sharing type?"

Silence. Finally, "You know nothing about my mother, my father."

"I told you to find a hobby."

There was a pause then the voice pushed back. "You *are* my hobby, Knox, sitting by that grave. Pathetic. Say hello to your wife for me."

The phone went dead. A shot of adrenalin pierced through Knox like a hot poker His hand slid inside the open breast of his windbreaker. The Beretta pulled from its holster, Knox scanned the landscape.

Leon. He's here.

From somewhere in the cemetery, Leon was watching. At the top of a nearby hill, Knox settled his eyes on the figure of a lone gardener. The man wore a broad brimmed straw hat, bulky tan jacket and brown trousers. He raked leaves at the front of a Victorian-appearing mausoleum. Bent over a rake, his movements were too agile, too fluid for an old laborer. Besides, what gardener works on Sunday? Knox rose from his position. The gardener glanced toward Knox then furtively stepped into the shadows and out of sight.

Past trees and monuments, about forty yards, Knox jogged toward the mausoleum. Anger rose. With each step, his pulse quickened. A stumble on a tree root caused him to take his eyes off target. He cursed the misstep, approached the crypt and burst around the corner, gun on point.

Nothing. A rake lay where the figure, Leon, had been. Frustration rose as Knox rattled the vault's locked gate then surveyed the remainder of the grounds. The "gardener" had gone.

Forty-one

It was Monday morning when Knox walked into Lescoe's office. She sat glumly behind her desk. It was the same look on Ballard's face, just before Knox was exiled to a desk in the 2nd.

Lescoe sighed, pursed her lips. "There's no easy way to tell you this, Knox. So, I'm just going to say it. We're pulling you off the surveillance."

"What the hell is going on, Janice?"

"It's apparent that Love has you as a target. And now, we have Chuck Leyland rattling around somewhere hunting your ass in a pickup truck. Besides, the decision was made above my pay grade."

"And you want me to go home and stare at my fish tank?"

"Knox, you don't have a home, or a fish tank."

"Right. I live in a loft, and I need to go after this guy."

Lescoe's eyes were heavy, tired, her face fatigued. "And we need you to go to Oxford Federal Corrections to interview Jessie Poon."

"I'm looking for a plan B here, Janice.

"There is none, Knox. You go to Oxford, or go back to the desk in the 2nd."

Knox pushed a hand through his salt and pepper hair. The look on Lescoe's face said the issue was non-negotiable. "Okay, then it's Jesse James. When do I leave?"

"Now." Lescoe pushed a manila folder across to Knox. "Here's the background on Poon, and the number for the U.S. Attorney who prosecuted him."

"Get Poon to roll," said Knox, "and we have a shot at Leon."

"That's the deal, Knox."

"I'll need a credit card."

"I'll need receipts," said Lescoe.

Knox took the file and card, started toward the door then stopped.

"Is there something else, Knox?"

"He called again, yesterday."

Lescoe arched her brow in surprise, "Leon Love?"

"I was at the cemetery. He saw me at Lara's grave."

"He saw you? Did you see him?"

"Near a mausoleum, a grounds keeper. I think it was Love."

"Did you go after him?"

"Yeah. If I'd caught him, he'd be in the morgue."

"Precisely my point, Knox, being out there as a target does not help our case. Ernie Guzman will handle the field ops. You get the backgrounds, and handle the liaison with the county attorney's office."

"This does not make me happy, Janice."

"Knox, you should know by now, I'm not about happiness."

"Neither am I. Who's the prosecutor?"

"Samantha DeAngelo, I think you're acquainted."

"I'll be in Wisconsin."

• • •

KNOX HEADED EAST on I-94. Ancient history, and the dark eyes of Samantha DeAngelo ebbed into his thoughts. Yeah, they were acquainted. He had been genuinely surprised to see her as second chair at the grand jury.

Before Lara, Samantha had been the torrid affair in his life. Over the years, the job, time and Lara ended the matter. With Lara, there was no reason to think otherwise. Some dormant passion may have lingered for Sam, but he never allowed himself to go there, the past too complicated, too distant. The occasional professional obligations he had with DeAngelo were just that, professional. However, she would now become an unavoidable fixture in his life. For whatever reason the thought of Sam, and what could have been, felt awkward. Lara was still very much a part of him.

Knox pulled off I-94 at Black River Falls, Wisconsin. He parked in the lot of the Bull Moose Bar and Lounge; a north woodsy affair, paneled walls, salad buffet with the head of its namesake mounted on the wall. A waitress showed Knox to a table and a menu. He ordered a Bull Moose burger and fries, Bull Moose coleslaw, pickle, and a Pepsi.

He opened the Jessie Poon folder and dialed the number for Oxford. The associate warden took the call. Informed of the nature of Knox's business, the warden set an interview with Poon for 3:00 P.M.

Over lunch, Knox perused Poon's folder. Left on his own much of his formative years, Jessie was the son of an over the road trucker, and a mother who supervised a big box garden center. High school was simply a blur before Jesse found a vocation in the U.S. Army Engineers. He had discovered a talent for blowing things up.

Somewhere along the line, distorted loyalties evolved. Discharge from the Wisconsin National Guard, Jessie became a member of the Badger Brigade, a paramilitary separatist group on the Fed's radar. Now Jessie Poon was serving a negotiated stretch of ten to fifteen for bank burglary, unlawful possession of explosives, weapons, and theft of a LAWS rocket launcher. Nice Hardware. Bad judgment.

Bill paid and waitress tipped, Knox grabbed a receipt and hit the road for Oxford, a couple of more hours east.

Wisconsin Highway 82 was a déjà vu mix of Midwest rural roadways. Farms, forests, church steeples, and silos comprised the rolling landscape that slipped by. Willie Nelson, Roy Orbison, Garth Brooks and Delbert McClinton came along for the ride on local country western radio.

Cut from a pine forest, northwest of Oxford, Knox found the sprawling federal prison that occupied nearly an entire section of Adams County, Wisconsin.

Electrified concertina fences encircled ten concrete block barracks-like confinement buildings. Knox parked at the reception center, a modest granite faced structure that looked more like a bank branch office than a gateway for medium custody federal criminals.

At the desk, Knox secured his Beretta and cuffs in a lock box, had his satchel inspected, and followed his escort across the compound to the main building. In a barren interview room reserved for law enforcement, Knox took a seat at a table secured to the floor. After a few moments, a metal door opened. Two uniformed guards escorted Jessie James Poon into the room.

Knox looked at a six foot two, muscled up two hundred and thirty pound frame in a prison jump suit. Head shaved, the tattoo of a badger was inked on the back of his skull. Another tattoo of a finned bomb, and crossed lightening bolts with a laurel wreath of the Army EOD graced his right bicep.

From his size, Knox knew no one ever survived addressing Jesse by an obviously imprudent jailhouse handle, Poon Tang.

"Have a seat," said Knox.

The guards shackled Jessie's cuffed hands to a metal ring of the table then struck an alert stance near the wall.

Poon straddled his chair, head back with an impertinent glance cast down his nose. Poon's body English conveyed the message; fuck you and the horse you rode in on.

Knox leaned into Jessie's space. "I'm a detective from Minneapolis. I'm here to talk with you about your stay at the Dane County, Wisconsin jail."

"Minneapolis, Dane County, how's that work?"

"You shared a cell with a guy I'm interested in."

"So?"

Knox didn't want to spend the remainder of the day playing twenty questions with a tattooed, bungled gun thief sporting the name of a 19th century bank robber. It was time to bring Jessie up to speed on a proposal that may have a more positive impact on his future.

"Before Dane County, Jessie, you did a couple tours in Afghanistan. At some rock hovel in the mountains your EOD team took a rocket hit. Wounded, you hauled your injured buddies to safety, maintained a field of fire, called in an air strike and took out the bad guys—purple heart, bronze star. Pretty damned impressive."

Jessie sighed with false bravado, "That's history, man."

"You made staff sergeant then something went sideways, right?"

Jessie gave a shrug with no response.

"Long story short, Jesse, you end up in Oxford on a ten to twenty. Oh, I missed your reduction in sentence, down to ten to twenty, and time in a medium prison facility in your home state rather than some super-max shit hole in Illinois. Cooperation with the U.S. Attorney?"

Jessie Poon gave no response.

"But what the fuck kind of a deal is that," groused Knox, "for an Army hero with a bronze star and a purple heart?"

The tough guy stare began to fade, and the shoulders began to sag.

"I'm working a bomb case, Jessie. You help me and I can express my earnest appreciation to the U.S. Attorney."

Jessie stared at Knox. "What the fuck you want, man?"

"A guy named Leon Love."

• • •

It was 6:00 P.M. when Knox found his way to a small main street restaurant in rural Oxford. He had covered a lot of territory for the day and decided to spend the night in town, head back to Minneapolis in the morning. He tapped Lescoe's number on the contact list of his cell.

"Knox, can't you ever call me during business hours?" said Lescoe.

"Caught you at a bad time?"

"Dinner with a friend. Is this about Oxford?"

"Jeeze, Janice. I'm sorry. I didn't know you had a friend."

"Sorry, Bill," she said to someone in the background, "but, I need to take this."

"Knox, I'm beginning to understand why a certain commander is so preoccupied with parking you on a desk in obscurity. Now, what have you got?"

"Okay, Poon spent a month with Leon in Dane County. All Leon did was bitch about the Rippie deal, and rant about the Packard Corporation killing his mother. Then, Leon told Poon that his old man was a big shot professor who was taken out in a shooting."

"I'm still listening, Knox."

"Leon kept asking Poon about his experiences in Afghanistan, about explosives. To pass the time Poon told him how different compounds are mixed to make bombs. Love said he'd like to nail the asshole that took out his old man, too fuck up the company that killed his mother. It was all general bullshit between two guys in stir. When Poon left Dane County for Oxford, Leon grabbed his arm, gave Poon a strange smile. '"Things will go boom in the night,'" he said.

"A little cryptic, Knox."

"Well, don't compose my atta-boy memo yet."

There was a pause, Lescoe acknowledging a waiter. "Okay," she said. "What's the catch?"

"At this point, Poon is willing to fill in all the blanks with specifics. But he wants a reduction on his federal time in exchange for a video statement, and testifying against Leon."

"Yeah, and I want a Lexus for Christmas," said Lescoe.

"Guzman and I know a guy named Riley on Lake Street, has this car lot—"

"Knox, you're off the reservation, again."

"It was just a thought, Janice. Anyway, an assistant U.S. Attorney, John Norrey, handled Poon's case. I filled him in on our situation. Norrey said they had already cut Jessie a deal on the federal cases when he rolled on his back woods militia bros."

"So, that's it?"

"I pitched him some options. He'll call in a few days. Right now, I'm hungry and tired, Janice. And, you're steak must be cold."

"So is my date, buster."

"Buster? I thought *his* name was, Bill?"

"See you tomorrow, Knox."

Forty-two

Headed west on Highway 82, Knox had the rising sun and Oxford, Wisconsin in the rear view mirror. Jesse Poon marked a questionable hand in the prosecution game as long as the US Attorney held the deciding card. Samantha DeAngelo would have to assess that angle.

A turn off Highway 82, and the concrete ribbon of Interstate 94 stretched all the way to Minneapolis. The miles went by, and the means of how to nail Leon Love would not leave Knox's thoughts.

Through the chronology of events, Knox tried to tie the threads of cases to Leon's vexing phone calls, the connections to Leon's motivation. Lucile Love's death, and that of Neil Wallace explained the motivation for the Packard incidents, and the bombings. Then, there were the associated cases, the attacks on Kathleen Conlon, Rachel Warren, Helen Troyer, and Michael Packard's home invasion. The linkage seemed apparent, yet proof beyond a reasonable doubt was out of reach. Like some religious prayer, a refrain Knox learned long ago from Jon Bass kept repeating itself in his mind; *passions and protests don't make cases, facts and evidence do.*

• • •

At 1:30 P.M., dressed in khaki trousers and a long sleeved plaid shirt, Jonas Packard stood at the garden gate of the coach house. He leaned on a gnarled shillelagh, Jon Bass at his side. Knox rolled to a stop on the cobblestone drive. Packard made the first overture, and stepped to Knox's Taurus.

"Sergeant Knox," he said extending his hand. "Jon said you were coming by. Finally, I can extend my personal gratitude for everything you've done, saving my life primarily." He chuckled.

"Thank you, sir. I see you're doing well, my regards to your lovely wife."

"I shall pass that along. I'll be one my way. I know you and Jon have things to discuss." A few steps away, the Admiral turned with a crafty smile on his face, and a wave of his cane.

"By the way, Sergeant Knox, my wife spoke of her visit with you. I'm glad things have evolved in the right direction."

Knox thought the comment odd, but remembered Mrs. Packard's request, wanting him on Helen Troyer's case. The answer to the mystery of Knox's sudden reassignment had just been revealed.

Packard stepped off with a resolute stride toward the manor house. Bass ushered Knox to the patio, surrounded by a plethora of irises and roses. Iced tea, and oatmeal-raisin cookies sat under the umbrella of the wrought iron table.

Bass poured the tea, "What's up?"

"Like I said on the phone, Jon, I need to talk about the Packard case, clear a link to someone you may find surprising."

"Oh? Well then, you go first," said Bass.

Knox described the ground thus far covered in the investigation, referring to the key suspect only as "the person of interest." When Knox revealed that the person was Leon Love, the bastard son of Neil Wallace, Bass choked on his tea.

"We suspect," said Knox, "that Leon had motive against Packard for his mother's death, the Agra-Pac truck accident in Wisconsin, and his father was killed at Packard Center, by me."

"So that's the connection," said Bass. "The state and county in Wisconsin knew ammonia nitrate explosive were used on the Agra-Pac silos at Stoughton, but there was no evidence to connect Leon, or anyone else."

"Right, and right now I seem to be lost in the trees, Jon. I guess I'm looking for some validation to what I see."

"And, what is it that you think you see?"

Knox dabbed at the corner of his mouth with a napkin. "Kathleen Conlon, my sister-in-law, is the first assault victim. The shots I fired, that killed Charles Leyland, also killed Neil Wallace. Leon tries to get to me through Kathleen. She's family and an easier target. That's were Leon had been hit, his family, his mother and father taken from him."

"Helen Troyer," Bass added, "the gatekeeper for Jonas Packard, becomes a proxy victim, the Admiral's right hand. Ray Warren, Rachel's father, the corporation's chief council, denied a settlement in the death of Leon's mother. Your suspect rapes his daughter, another oblique act of revenge."

Bass leaned back, tea in hand. "Michael Packard heads corporate finance. Take out the money, and you take down the company. To sweeten his idea of retribution, Leon blows up the Lake Minnetonka boathouse, and your home on Nicollet Island.

"You see, Knox, your on the right track, everything is connected. However cunning he thinks he may be, he's also gutless. He never comes right at you. His vengeance is achieved from a distance. Like poking needles into a voodoo doll, he destroys by wounding things that are meaningful to others."

"End game, Jon. What the hell is Leon's end game?"

"Blowing up the boathouse, and your place, may be as close as he can come to that. Everyone has taken precautions, and as a result Leon will become more frustrated. He's likely to become more unpredictable. I don't think Leon Love even knows what to do next."

"What about Chuck Leyland, the shooter's son?"

"Unlike Love," said Bass, "he's the ghost in this game, maybe more dangerous."

Knox's cell phone vibrated in his pocket. "Give me a minute, Jon."

"Is this Sergeant Knox, Minneapolis PD?" said the caller with a tone of authority.

"Yes. Who is this?"

"Sheriff Kline, Polk County, Wisconsin. Sergeant, are you familiar with a man named Walt Meyers?"

Forty-three

Headed back to Minneapolis, Knox drove through the lakeside village of Wayzata and called Guzman.

"Ernie, where are you at?"

"In the surveillance van, target location."

"I'll see you there."

Thirty minutes later, Knox rolled to a stop in the parking lot of the Bakken Museum, an eclectic repository of electrical magnetism studies. In a huff, he climbed into the van.

Guzman turned from the window. "Hey, what's up?"

"Walt Meyers is dead."

Guzman looked at Knox in disbelief. "Oh, Jesus."

"The Polk County, Wisconsin Sheriff just called me," said Knox. "Sunday night, Walt came home from the Legion Post. What the S/O pieced together is that Walt opened his front door, flicked on the light switch, and the house exploded."

Knox took a breath to contain his bitterness at the turn of events. "The interior propane gas line to the house was disconnected. In the debris, Deputies found the light switch that was near the front door. It was in the 'on' position.

Walt lay in the yard with head injuries, a broken neck, and torso trauma. The porch roof landed on him. His dog was blown out the kitchen window. Poor bugger had his throat slit. Although the place was burned up, Walt's casebook on Leon was nowhere to be found.

"It had to have been, Leon, Knox."

"I'd bet on it. Walt had a premonition Leon would show up some day. I guess he was right."

"When did you begin surveillance, Ernie?"

"There were four of us. We started at 10:00 A.M. Monday. But at 7:00 Monday night, he went to Barry's Rhythm and Blues Joint on Lake Street, barbecue ribs and country western music. We put him to bed at 11:30 and called it half past midnight, with no garbage for us to grab."

"However," Guzman added, "we may have another problem."

"What now?"

"Monday afternoon we tailed Love to the downtown public library. Erhardt from VAT, Violent Apprehension Team, went in. She found Love doing computer research."

"Let me guess," said Knox, "Explosives 101."

"No. He was looking at us, Knox: you, me, Lescoe and Assistant County Attorney DeAngelo. Oh yeah, your sister-in-law remains on his top ten list, as well."

"What the hell is with the library?

"There's no link to him," said Guzman. "He can obtain everything reported about us in the press, print what he wants then hit delete."

"I don't understand. This clown has a library card?"

"No," said Guzman. "None. He probably flashed a phony guest pass, and the clerk neglected to verify.

• • •

At the office, Knox brushed by Janice Lescoe without saying a word, the death of Walt Meyers heavy on his mind. He headed to a cubicle arranged for him in the Sex Crimes Unit.

Lescoe approached. "Knox, we need to talk."

Knox tossed his satchel on the desk and turned. "Not now, Janice. Walt Meyers's house blew up. He's dead. I have to make some calls."

Lescoe hesitated a moment, "Oh God. Leon Love?"

Knox didn't reply, and reached for the phone on his desk.

When he reached Sheriff Kline, Knox further explained the background on Love. A fax with Leon's photo and record would be sent. Once the information was received, Kline would initiate a check of hotels, restaurants and gas stations near Saint Croix Falls on the Wisconsin, and the Minnesota side of the river.

The Wisconsin DCI, and state fire marshal were still working the scene at Meyers's home, but Kline was not optimistic. The extent of the damage and the work of the fire department had severely diminished the discovery of crucial evidence.

Walt Meyers had said that Leon had taken computer and criminology courses at UW. And, Meyers was the only cop to put Leon behind bars. Coupled with the tutorials of Jesse James Poon, thought Knox, the circumstantial combination added up to murder. Leon had exacted his revenge.

• • •

At 3:40 P.M., Knox leaned quietly against the office threshold of forty-year-old Samantha DeAngelo, supervising assistant county attorney. He held a box that contained his property released from the grand jury hearings; one .45-caliber Beretta with shoulder holster, police shield and case with a bullet impression, one Kevlar vest, and one tuxedo jacket and shirt vented with two bullet holes.

DeAngelo turned from atop a wood step stool, her reach steadied on a law book, upper shelf. At five-foot-five, the white blouse and black slacks caressed her in all the right places. Knox could still not help but notice.

"Hello, Sam."

DeAngelo nearly tumbled from the stool. Knox rushed forward to steady her, his hand on her lower back as she stepped to the floor. "I'll get that for you."

"Thanks, I was doing fine until you startled me," said DeAngelo, feigning her annoyance."

DeAngelo took the book from his hand. "It's good to see you, Harding. I like the new look, no beard."

He smiled. "Thanks, but I need to see you about something."

Knox took a chair. DeAngelo sat at her desk, her official comfort zone. Hands folded in her unruffled supervising prosecutor posture.

She nodded toward the box Knox had placed on the adjacent chair. "You have questions about the grand jury."

"Another time, I caught a piece of the Packard case, Sam."

"Yes, I heard. You must be pleased to be back on casework."

"The beneficiary of some unsolicited influence peddling. But, I'll take the job."

"The work suits you. Are you presenting something, or is this for discussion?"

"Discussion."

Knox provided his summary of the Conlon, Warren and Troyer attacks, the computer sabotage, and bombings. DeAngelo listened, scribbled notes across her legal pad as details fell into place. She interrupted only to explore a legal point or two. Rules of criminal procedure, admissibility of evidence, capability of witnesses and victims: corroboration and trial tactics were her business.

Then, Knox dropped the bomb, the Leon Love, Neil Wallace relationship.

DeAngelo looked as if she'd been slapped with a wet subpoena.

"Jesus, Knox. The political...social...family implications —"

"You might say I'm a little ambivalent about all that, Sam. In the end Leon Love is just another dirtbag criminal."

DeAngelo wrinkled her brow, put down her pen. "You're pursuing a DNA track? It will help with the Wallace-Love connection, exploring motive. It seems your assault cases are weak on evidence, coupled with the victim's inability to make an ID. I'm afraid, Knox, everything else is vague suspicion."

"I know. We're using surveillance to snag Love's DNA, and maybe get lucky if he goes for another victim."

"You said Love was busted for a sex crime in Wisconsin."

"He was, but his attorney got him a six month gig in the county jail, misdemeanor second degree assault. In the deal, the DNA was destroyed and the sexual offender tag was set aside."

DeAngelo sighed, "There must have been a lot in the weeds on that case"

"A ton of weeds, Sam."

"So, what about Love's ex-cell mat, Jessie James... Poon? Is that a real name?"

"Yeah. Comes with a wall poster, and skinhead tattoos. He's in federal lock-up, ex-national guard doing a negotiated ten to twenty for explosives, weapons possession, and bank burglary. He'll do a video statement, and testify about Leon's interest in bomb components, but wants a reduction in his federal time."

DeAngelo rolled her eyes in skepticism. "A skinhead white supremacist? He really sounds credible. What did the feds say?"

"An assistant US attorney in Chicago kicked it up the food chain. They've given Poon as much as they are willing to give. The Poon deal is dead. The USA said don't bother calling back."

"Swell," said DeAngelo, a sigh of exasperation. "Without direct or trace evidence, or witness corroboration, all you have, Harding, is reasonable suspicion to continue your investigation."

"I'm just running out the laundry on the line, Sam, to see what's there."

"You need a few more clothes pins, Harding, substantiated facts and evidence. Anything else?"

"Just one item. Love did some research at the public library."

"What's the relevance?"

"The relevance is you, Sam, among others."

"What?" A subtle unease shaped her response.

"Leon spent some time reviewing news articles. You were a featured subject."

"Why me?"

"I don't know. Perhaps, he found your involvement in my grand jury hearing interesting. All I'm suggesting is that you need to take some precautions in your life."

A hint of tension wrinkled DeAngelo's brow. "Harding, you know I've prosecuted some pretty hard core cases. Threats come with the territory, and so do the precautions I take."

"Sam, don't dismiss Leon Love. Our so-called reasonable suspicion indicates that he blows things up, and likely killed our source, Walt Meyers."

DeAngelo sighed and pushed back from her desk. "Okay, Harding, I appreciate your concern. I'll speak with our people."

"If you need me, Sam; I mean if this clown comes anywhere near you, here's my card. Call me, anytime, twenty-four-seven."

For a moment, Knox saw the prosecutorial presence in DeAngelo's eyes shift to the softness of gratitude, or was it something else.

"Still the white knight, Knox?"

"Yeah, the armor's a little tarnished, but if you need me..."

An awkward feeling held Knox for just an instant. Perhaps it was the way she looked at him, or the way her voice, yielding, came at him. "I...ah, I'll get the photos of Leon to you."

Knox was at the door when Sam's voice stopped him.

"Harding, I'm still very sorry about your loss of Lara."

"Thanks. I saw you at the funeral, got your card, and I...ah—"

"Go get the dirtbag, Knox."

• • •

At 5:15 P.M., Knox stepped into Violent Crimes, surprised to see Lescoe and Commander Krieg still present. Dour expressions cloaked both faces.

Krieg looked over the rim of glasses perched low on his nose. "We've lost surveillance support from the VAT Unit. As of Saturday, available personnel are re-assigned to street duty for the Aquatennial festival."

Blindsided, Knox slumped to the edge of Lescoe's desk.

The Minneapolis Aquatennial was the city's summer commercial celebration. The block parties, food and sports festivities, parades, museum tours, and political rallies were all designed to celebrate the city's heritage and stimulate business. Augmented by a large police presence, it was both a blessing and a curse to the cops who raked in the overtime while contending with assorted incidents of disorderly conduct, gang dust-ups and an occasional shooting.

"Damn it," Knox cursed. "We're after an asshole who blows up homes, rapes and beats women, is trying to take down a corporation, maybe killed an ex-cop, and now we're told to take a hiatus?"

"Knox, you know the situation," said Krieg, "civic and political interests versus police priorities. We scale back, make adjustments then move forward."

"Right, Karl, has anyone told the Packard's, the Warren family, or Mrs. Troyer to scale back, make adjustments then move forward?"

"That's enough, Knox," Krieg demanded. "For the moment, we fall back, pull what we have together, and get back up to speed after the Aquatennial."

"Commander, it's early in the process," said Lescoe. "We do have foundation for our suspicions, and we need to get this guy."

A long pause followed Lescoe's plea. Krieg taped his pen on a desktop then looked at her. "You have until Friday, Lieutenant. Get me something that I can take to the Chief by Friday."

"We have one more thing," said Knox. "We know where Leon eats."

• • •

THURSDAY, AT 4:00 P.M., Knox sat in the back of an unpretentious van in the parking lot of the Bakken Museum. He peered through the van's window at Leon's crib, a retrofit 40s Rambler huddled in the trees about fifty yards away. Knox mused about the Bakken's eccentric collection of electricity studies. A thought kept repeating itself: Leon Love strapped to a chair, testicles wired to a twelve-volt battery, and Knox holding the switch.

With time to get the DNA slipping away, Knox remained out of sight in the van. He'd give the word when Leon and his Camaro hit the street. Lescoe and Guzman were mobile, while the two VAT officers, Stephanie Erhardt and Dave Dunbar rounded out the detail. Knox would anchor, while two units would run parallel, as well as one in front and to the rear of Leon Love. They would switch positions as needed so as not to alert the target. That was the plan.

After an agonizing three-hour wait, the Navy blue Camaro backed from Leon's garage. Knox alerted the team by radio-cell. The target was on the move.

Within minutes, frenzied cell transmissions filled the air. Erhardt caught a red light behind a car at Lake Street and the West Parkway. Leon, unchecked, headed east in traffic. The plan was going to hell.

Lescoe made a right turn on red from the Calhoun yacht basin, ending up two cars behind Leon's Camaro. Like a chess game on wheels, the team jockeyed positions for advantage. Leon went east then south on side streets, left and right again. Suddenly, Leon was in the wind; he had shaken the tail.

While others combed the side streets, Knox parked a half block east of Barry's Rib Joint. He watched as the Camaro edged from a side street and stopped at the curb. Leon got out and glanced along the storefronts. Then he strode into Barry's, the best barbecue rhythm and blues bar in town. Knox alerted the team.

A bluesy tempo spilled from surround-sound speakers, a Walter Merchant piece, "Whiskey Blues." All part of Berry's ambiance, neon beer signs hung along the wall, peanuts shells, and sawdust covered the floor. From the grill, award winning smoked barbecue permeated the atmosphere. To the crowd it was an edgy, blue jean happening place for urban affluent wannabes.

The Latin forty-something Guzman shuffled in with a three-day beard, shaggy hair, jeans, dark blue silk shirt, boat shoes and designer smoked shades. Erhardt, twelve years younger, blond and curvy with a surly manner, nuzzled up to him as if they were some hip May-September thing.

It wasn't long. Guzman and Erhardt spotted Leon alone at a tall table near the rear of the place, a plate of ribs, cob of corn, biscuit and a beer in front of him. He ogled the female patrons. The duo watched their target from a table across the joint.

After about a half hour, and three failed hits on female customers, Leon finished his meal, laid some cash on the table, then made his way toward the restrooms. A red exit sign glowed in the hallway. Leon did not return.

Mark Korpi's, "Slap You Silly," finished its last musical note when Guzman tapped the waitress on her shoulder. Her eyes widened to the sight of a police shield.

"Hi. We're the clean plate police," said Guzman. "We'll take everything on the table."

Outside the back door, Leon lit a cigarette, and headed for the Camaro as Officer Dunbar called it in. Guzman and Erhardt seized, tagged and bagged the remnants of Leon's dinner. The DNA evidence was placed it in Guzman's trunk destined for the property room, and the state lab in Saint Paul.

The surveillance detail shadowed Love to a couple south Minneapolis bistros where he struck out in his attempt to score on anything in a skirt, or tight pants. He then idled along the near south side through the tree-shrouded Chain of Lakes. Streetlights glittered in the humid July night, an inviting setting for late evening strollers, and a loveless predator on the prowl.

By 10:45 P.M., the team shadowed Leon through the Lake Harriet neighborhoods, coordinating their change in surveillance positions. The intermittent squelch from encrypted cell traffic heightened the tension. Knox felt his pulse quicken. Instinctively, he had a premonition where Leon was going.

The Camaro turned off the west parkway onto South Forty-Fourth Street when Knox cut his lights, parked and waited.

A flash of taillights glowed as the Camaro slowed in front of Kathy Conlon's bungalow. Knox looked at his watch. 11:00 P.M., Conlon would still be at WCCM.

Still blacked out, Knox looped around the corner. Taillights of the Camaro blinked again as Leon made a left into the alley. Knox told the team to hold their positions. His pulse pounded, anticipating that Leon would do something fortuitously stupid. At Conlon's garage, another flash of taillights, and the new back yard security lights illuminated the alley. The Camaro accelerated then rumbled off toward Lake Hiawatha.

Knox signaled the team to go mobile again, resigned that it would have to be another time, another place before Leon would be his. Knox called Conlon, informed her of Leon's drive-by and told her to stay at his loft for the night.

At 1:00 A.M., an hour after the lights went out at Leon's crib, the team met at the Calhoun yacht basin.

Lescoe pulled into the lot, red eyed and weary. She got out of her car and leaned back against a fender. “I had a call from Commander Krieg, tonight,” said Lescoe. “I filled him in on the DNA seizure. He expressed his appreciation, and reminded us we that we have one more night.

Forty-four

His Friday night fantasies blighted, Leon pulled away from the Lake Street's Hide-A-Way Bar, and went west on the boulevard of broken dreams. Someone waited for him in a computer junky hangout, someone waiting for a payday.

A purple neon sign scrolled out the words *Why-Fi Café*. Affixed to a brass rail, a green curtain obscured the lower portion of the front window.

Leon drove into the rear parking lot off Lake and eased into a spot next to a red late model VW ragtop. The car belonged to, Nikki Rothman, an eighteen-year-old waitress that had fired Leon's passions, and he wanted her, simply for the sport of it. He took a newspaper from the Camaro and tucked it under his arm.

Close behind two chatty young females, Leon entered the café and paused to survey the crowd of techno-media players. Clientele clustered around tables, typed on laptops and iPads, quietly conversed with one another, or chatted on cell phones. Gregor Duchak, a man in his early thirties, sat at a corner table. He wore, blue jeans and a wrinkled linen sport coat. The bows of tortoise shell horned rimmed glasses sat tucked into a tangle of reddish, blond hair that hung over his ears.

Gregor looked up from his laptop. "You're late." The nervous tenor in Gregor's voice bore an east European accent.

"I was checking out the strip," said Leon and took a seat. He set the folded *Star Tribune* on the table.

Gregor leaned toward Leon with a cautious whisper, "I saw the news." His voice still low, "The house on Kenwood. Was that you? Was that about our arrangement?"

"You ask too many questions, Gregor."

"So you say, Leon. But, I must look after my own interests."

"You're being paid for your interests, the passwords, the end game program."

"Then, you have something for me?" said Gregor. "Half upon completing the initial portion project. That was our arrangement."

Leon slid the newspaper across to Gregor. "There's a finance article in here that will interest you."

With a nod and sly smile Gregor pulled the paper to him. Like a poker player checking his cards, he thumbed the pages until he saw an envelope.

"It's all there, Gregor. The first half," said Leon.

Nikky, the waitress, strode up. As on other nights, she wore a low cut black leather blouse, tight fitting pants, black nail polish eye makeup, and long raven hair to the shoulder. Leon had repeatedly tried to lure Nikky's attentions, to partake in the smoldering sexuality that he knew must lurk beneath that mysterious Gothic getup.

"Do you want to order something?" she asked. Her cheerless attitude matched her dark ensemble.

Leon held her in a lured stare as she took an order of a Pepsi-Cola, turkey wrap and onion rings from Gregor.

Nikky turned to Leon. "How about you? Or, are you just drooling tonight?"

"Listen sweetheart," said Leon, undressing her with his eyes. "I really like the leather. I'll just have a Pepsi. I won't be staying long."

"That's my good fortune, *sweetheart*," said Nikky.

Leon swallowed, and watched her stride off.

• • •

"We wait," replied Knox over the radio. The surveillance team had parked in line of sight of the Why-Fi.

A call from Knox's cell broke the stillness in the van.

"Sergeant Knox, this is Sheriff Kline, Polk County, sorry to bother you so late."

"No problem, Sheriff. Go ahead." Knox listened intently for several minutes then hung up. Lescoe looked on from the passenger's seat.

"Polk County?" Janice asked.

"Yeah. Leon was at a gas station, Saint Croix Falls, the night Walt Meyers's place blew up."

"Jesus, Knox we need to nail this asshole. When we move, I'll take Dunbar and stay on the guy Leon is with, see where he goes. The rest of you remain with Leon."

"Leon is leaving," reported Dunbar from his position.

Lescoe bailed from the van. "Later, at the yacht basin."

Leon followed a previous routine, prowling the Chain of Lakes Parkway. Knox and the surveillance team vexingly jockeyed through side streets to keep pace. Finally, along the East side of Lake Calhoun, Leon stopped at a secluded pathway, the scene of Rachel Warren's rape. The team froze with anticipation, the perp returning to the scene of the crime. Disappointed, the team watched as Leon moved on, eventually rolling into his crib at 11:50 P.M., and lights out.

At 12:30 A.M., Lescoe drove slowly into the yacht basin lot, Dunbar close behind her. With slumped shoulders, she got out of her car. She turned to Knox, eyes imbedded with dark circles, fatigue in her voice.

"Gregor Marcus Duchak, white male, thirty-two, drives a gray Saab. He lives at 34th and East Medicine Lake Drive, suburban Plymouth, a few parking tickets, no warrants or criminal history. I'll background him more tomorrow, or is it tomorrow, already."

"We need to go again," Knox said. "Leon prowled the Chain of Lakes again, stopped at the Warren assault scene. Last night he cased Kathleen Conlon's house."

Lescoe shook her head, working Love plus the backlog of pending cases had taken its toll on everyone. "The VAT officers are now released, Knox. Ten A.M., in the briefing room. We re-group, suspend further activity as ordered." Then Lescoe got in her car.

Knox watched the tail lights disappear into the night and turned to Guzman.

"Give it a rest, Knox."

Forty-five

On Saturday night, Barry's Joint was jumping. University kids, office workers and young singles mingled to a dreamy Bonnie Raitt piece, "Do I ever cross your mind?"

Leon recognized the waitress from Friday. Tonight, she seemed different, or rather indifferent as she placed a beer on Leon's table.

He tried to strike up a conversation. "Rough night, huh?"

She walked away, dismissively.

Leon took a pull on the bottle of Bud, eyes narrowed in scorn.

Another night of strikeouts, not a bitch in the crowd could be had to ride in Leon's Chevy, smoke a joint by the lake, or fuck the night through at his Calhoun hideaway. The want to possess a woman became stronger the longer he listened to the throb of music, and watched the parade of female ass pass by. The frustration clawed at his gut. He knew where he had to go.

Obscured in the shadows of the boulevard trees, Leon slouched in the driver's seat of the Camaro. The scroll of the purple neon sign, *Why Fi Café*, blinked out at 1:15 A.M. Nikky Rothman, Leon's Gothic fantasy, ambled across the café parking lot. The dim light caught the shape of her long legs fitted into those tight, black leather pants. An air of independence in her gait was reminiscent of Rachel Warren. Nikky slid into her red VW, started the engine, and dropped the convertible top.

Into sparse night traffic, Nikky turned west on Lake Street. Her long black hair flowed fetchingly from the open car. Leon glided along behind, careful to keep a blue Camry between him and Nikky's VW to mask his presence. A light haze made the night air feel moist and heavy. South on the West Parkway, the Camry turned off. Leon sped up to keep Nikky in view.

The VW circled the urban Lake Harriet, bound by parks, walking trails, and cozy traditional neighborhoods. Finally, the car slowed, then turned into a secluded parking lot.

Leon idled by, cut his lights, and glided onto a pathway isolated from the road. The pulse in his temples throbbed with anticipation.

Ski mask in hand, knife in his pocket, Leon made his way along the edge of the woods. Gregor, his computer virus source, was right. Nikky, after a busy night, would find a spot among the city lakes, pull off and have a joint or two before going home.

"No one else," said Gregor in his Hungarian accent, "just Nikky alone in the night with a joint."

Leon prowled to the side of the clearing. He watched. Nikky, in silhouette in the dim light reclined against the front of her car, legs apart, like one of those garage girlie posters. Head tilted to the night sky, her black hair fell back from her shoulders. She pulled long on a joint held between her lips.

Captured by the seduction, Leon crouched in the bushes. He drew in the cannabis smoke as wafted toward him, swallowed hard; primed to jump the loins of the sultry, gothic bitch.

Another toke on the joint, and Leon watched Nikky close her eyes and exhale. He could feel the dream-like sensation take hold of her. He'd been there. Done that, and now he was going to do her.

The body blow knocked Nikky to the ground. Gravel cut into the fair skin of her hands and face. Her scream muffled in the palm of a gloved hand that gripped her mouth. Her attacker breathed into her right ear. "Listen sweetheart," said the throaty, threatening voice. "Cooperate and you won't get hurt." He grabbed her hair and pulled her to her feet, a knife under her chin.

"Walk," said the man.

In the murky light, Nikky stumbled to the trees, landing on her back. Her eyes widened in terror as she gapped into the hideous lizard-like green eyes and red clown lips of the ski mask. Her heart beat as if it were to burst.

The dark figure pinned her to the ground. Her breathing panicked. She choked as a hand seized her throat.

It was then the blade of a knife glistened in the faint light. With one thrust, it sliced through her blouse and bra, the dull side skimmed along her skin. A bare hand fondled her breasts. There were only moments to live.

A sudden crunch of tires on gravel, she heard a car moving fast, saw the sweep of headlights through the trees. Nikky kicked and clawed at her attacker.

"Help! Help me!" Nikky screamed.

The man clutched a hand to her mouth and lowered his face to hers. Behind the lizard-green shapes were the golden hazel eyes, and the sound of a voice, a voice from the café.

"Listen, Nikky, I know who you are," her attacker whispered. "I can find you." Then, like a ghost, he vanished.

Nikky rose and stumbled toward the headlights, clutching at her clothes, her hands and face bloodied. The next moment she saw a badge.

"Police officer," a man said. "Where did he go?"

Stunned but lucid enough, Nikky sobbed as Knox caught her in his arms.

Knox quickly sat her in his car, put his jacket around her then pushed her hair from the side of her mascara-smeared face. She had a superficial cut to her neck; hands and face scraped from gravel abrasions.

"He had a knife," Nikky sobbed. "He went there." Nikky pointed into the woods.

In Knox's mind, two bickering voices called out. Each contended for the next move. "Stay with the victim. Call it in." The other beckoned, "Get Leon Love."

The decision was determined by the slam of a car door that echoed through the trees. Knox called in the detail on his handheld radio, and added a BOLO for Leon Love and his car; probable cause, aggravated CSC, armed criminal sexual conduct.

Knox turned the blue Camry onto the parkway. Nikky sat buckled into the passenger seat. To his right, a dark movement, the Camaro running without lights. Knox hit the accelerator.

At a "Y" in the parkway, the Camaro had vanished. Right and Leon would head for his crib. Knox turned left assessing Leon would avoid the natural instinct of a thug who would run for home.

At 1:40 A.M. Knox strained to see through the night as he sped along the parkway. Traffic was absent in the old established neighborhoods south and east of Lake Harriet. Knox searched intersecting streets for a sign of Camaro taillights.

A 3rd Precinct car radioed he had arrived to secure the assault location for forensics and impound Nikky's car.

"I have the vic," acknowledged Knox.

Nikky Rothman safe, the crime scene secure, and a BOLO out for the Camaro, Knox called for units to sit on Leon's home. Although, Nikky's injuries were superficial, he had already stretched protocol and could not delay any longer getting her medical attention. For the moment, Leon had slipped away, but precinct cars, like nighthawks, would lie in wait on shadowed streets to take him down.

At West 43rd Street and Kings Highway, Knox stopped the car at a bus stop. He peered through the windshield.

"You're safe, Nikky," he said. "I'll find who did this to you."

With cold assertion, she said. "I know who he is."

"The man who attacked you?" Knox asked, his voice calm, compassionate.

"Yes, he is Gregor's friend from the café."

Knox listened with restrained expectancy.

"He wore a ski mask. It had green shapes around the eyes and red lips. But I know his eyes. They are strange, hazel-gold with, like starbursts, you know? I know his voice, too."

"What's his name, Nikky, the man with the starburst eyes?"

"Leon. He made passes at me at the Café."

"Tonight, how did he hurt you?" said Knox.

"He knocked me down," she began to whimper. "He cut my clothes."

Knox handed her a tissue. "It's all right. You can tell me the rest."

"He dragged me to the trees. I cut my hands and face on the gravel. He took a knife and put it to my throat, cut open my blouse and bra. He grabbed my breasts. That's when I heard your car, saw the lights. He was on top of me then. I could smell his breath, see his eyes, and hear his voice."

"What did he say to you?"

"He said like, 'Listen Sweetheart,' the same thing he called me at the cafe. Then he said my name. He said he could find me again."

"Nikky," said Knox as he looked into her eyes, "I'll find him. Bank on it."

The words were hardly said when Leon's Camaro cruised through the intersection in front of Knox. It took a moment to register, his mind not comprehending the good fortune of what he had seen.

Knox grabbed his radio. "The dark blue Camaro BOLO," he said, "Lincoln-Union-King-969, is north on Kings Highway from 43rd."

Cars from the 5th Precinct acknowledged for an intercept. Knox made a left and headed north.

The Camaro made a jog onto DuPont Avenue as Knox saw headlights approach from the rear. Squads 520 and 510, without emergency lights, blew by— *whoosh*, *whoosh*.

Moments later the intersection at DuPont and 32nd Street South ignited like the Fourth of July. A burst of emergency lights swept eerily through the trees, painted the fronts of sleepy houses. With resolute vigilance, Knox braked behind the cruisers.

Hands behind his head, Leon Love crouched on his knees illuminated in police spotlights. The dash cam reruns would be classic.

Crouched behind open car doors, guns drawn, officers had Leon framed in their sights. Knox approached the officers of squad 510.

"Hey Sergeant, you want the honors?" asked the driver.

"Yeah, I'll take it."

Commands, voiced through a police loudspeaker, echoed across the intersection into the night. "Driver, stay on your knees. Keep fingers laced behind your head. Do not look back."

Knox walked slowly up behind Leon, a burst of exhilaration coursed through him. He squeezed Leon's interlaced fingers and watched him flinch, and flinch again as the handcuff ratchets clicked tight on the right, then left wrist.

Leon turned his head. "You," he gasped.

Knox bent closer.

"Listen sweetheart, you're under arrest."

Forty-six

Although Nikky said there was no sexual penetration, Knox had to make sure. Also, injuries would be photographed, and fingernail scrapings done. At the Hennepin County Medical Center, Knox waited with Nikky in a closed exam room.

"I know you're eighteen, Nikky, but I think it would be a good idea if I broke the news to your parents. It's my job."

"Shit. Do they have to know I was smoking a joint, because I was, you know?

"Yeah, well, I'll skim by that little detail."

Covered in a hospital smock, lying on the gurney, Nikky smiled a nodded. She took Knox firmly by the hand. Through clinched teeth she uttered, "Thanks for getting that fucker."

"That's my job, too, kid," said Knox.

On the fourth ring, Rothman, a Twin Cities automotive mogul, answered.

"Mr. Rothman?" Knox asked.

"Yes. Who is this?" The sleepy voice sounded puzzled yet business-like.

"This is Sergeant Knox, Minneapolis Police Department. I'm sorry to bother you at this hour, sir. Your daughter, Nikky, was assaulted early this morning—"

"Oh God! Is she all right?"

Knox discussed with Rothman a summary of events that included the arrest of Nikky's attacker, and where she was at.

Rothman thanked Knox. However, the expression of gratitude sounded flat, like an informal handshake after the sale of a Chevy. Curious he thought. There seemed to be a tone of concern, yet premonition in Rothman's voice. Apparently, raising Nikky had been a difficult endeavor for the business executive, and his wife.

Knox put the thought aside and moved on. "In these circumstances, sir, there are resources that are available to Nikky, as well as the family."

"That won't be necessary, Sergeant. We'll be at the hospital, directly."

Parked on 3rd Avenue at city hall, Knox tossed the department ID placard on the dash. The call to Rothman's was an unappreciated conclusion to the night, but it came with the territory. Still, Nikky was safe and that's what mattered. Across 3rd, the Hennepin County Jail complex loomed surreal in the glow of the sodium vapor lights. Leon Love sat in a holding cell in the confines of the one square-block building.

Knox locked the car door and stopped. He knew that he had strayed off his leash again, bagged Love, though the surveillance detail had been suspended. The irony was he didn't collar Leon for the bombings, computer sabotage, assaults, or murder.

Sometimes you take what you can get, and use the leverage, screw the repercussions.

Leon had beat the hell out of Helen Troyer, raped Rachel Warren and took a knife to Nikky Rothman, surrogate victims in Leon's demented fantasy of retribution. Nikky, least of all, was just a tool through which Leon could act out his frustrations.

Anger rose within him the more Knox thought about the beatings, rapes, bombings, and the chicken-shit phone calls. Then there was the murder of Walt Meyers. He crossed the street toward the jail.

Leon sat chained to a table bolted to the floor in a small steel-walled room. A neon light mounted behind a metal grill in the ceiling added to the stark institutional setting where Knox hoped Leon would be confined for an indefinite future.

It was 3:45 A.M., when from behind a small one-way window Knox watched as the gravity of events seemed to have no impact on his prisoner. He activated the video and voice recorder. Leon sat there, just like Walt Meyers had said. The son-of-a-bitch had an air of defiance about him, head cocked toward the ceiling, an insolent smirk on his face.

Knox entered the room. The door and latch, steel on steel, slammed shut with an intimidating finality. Leon didn't flinch.

"Hello, Sergeant Knox," the acknowledgement, predatory.

Knox stepped around the table opposite Leon and pulled a case file from his brief case. He let it drop to the table with a thud. For effect, Leon's name and date of birth were written above seven case numbers.

Leon glanced at the file, his insolent façade, unyielding.

Knox fixed his quarry with a sober stare. Leon's eyes, as his victims described were bizarre. Hazel-like orbs fragmented with strikes of gold bursts surrounded cold, black pupils.

Leon possessed what could pass for dark, handsome, Latin features being the offspring of Lucy Love, his white mother, and Neil Wallace, his biracial father. Features he used, said Walt Meyers, to manipulate his way through life. There was also a palpable aura of menace about him, like a serpent poised to strike.

"We have a lot to talk about, Leon." Knox, at first, avoided a direct question, even though Leon was technically under arrest. What he needed was a hook, some *res gestae* statement as the lawyers called it, one spontaneous utterance where Leon would put himself behind the eight ball.

"Tell me what *we* have to talk about, Sergeant?"

"Those scratches on your face for starters. Then we can move on," Knox said with a glance toward the file. "This book is about you. Perhaps you would like to see the photos."

"Yeah, well… I'm not interested in your family photo album. Old flicks of your dead wife in there, huh?"

The attitude and smirk accompanied a cold, sociopathic glare that Walt Meyers had mentioned; a gaze that bored through you as if calculating your own insignificance.

Knox had seen that dead-eyed look before, other assholes that were just plain evil. Leon conveyed the same quality, a total absence of conscience.

"Well, Leon, there's a waitress at the Why Fi Café," Knox said, calmly. "You let your dick, and that goofy mask over ride your judgment."

The only response was a sneer, and a sick chortle.

Knox opened the book to a photo fold of Lucile Love and Neil Wallace. "I'd like to start with your dead mother, and your so-called father."

Leon stared at the pictures, took a deep breath then lurched forward. The bolted chain snapped against the table. Hands locked in cuffs clawed at Knox, eyes filled with rage.

"You motherfucker! You don't understand! I win!"

Knox sent Leon back into his chair with a fist to the head.

"The fuckin' game is over," Leon raged. "Now get my lawyer."

Sunlight had crept through the slats in the venetian blinds. At 6:15 A.M., Knox sat like a man in a vast empty warehouse. Within the banks of vacant cubicles of the Investigations Division, he finished editing the last page of his report, the arrest of Leon Love. Stale and bitter was the taste of his third cup of coffee.

Knox wondered what to expect of the call he was about to make. He'd been operating on his own, against orders in a suspended investigation.

A sleepy, confused voice answered the phone.

"Yes, who is this?" said Janice Lescoe.

"It's Knox, Janice, sorry to bother you."

"Just a minute, Bill," she said to a voice in the background.

"Bill?" said Knox, unable to resist a jab. "That the same guy from the restaurant last week?"

"Listen, Knox, it's after 6:00 A.M. It's Sunday morning. If you're feeling lonely, and need someone to talk with there's a hotline for people like you."

Knox chuckled at her rebuke then paused.

"We've got forty-eight hours, Janice."

"Is this some kind of riddle, Knox? Forty-eight hours for what?"

"To charge Leon Love with kidnapping, and aggravated sexual assault."

"What?"

"Follow the honey, Janice. Leon went after the Why Fi waitress tonight."

There was a loud groan in the background. Knox could only imagine, Bill struck by a flying elbow as Janice vaulted from bed phone in hand.

"I put Leon Love in jail this morning," said Knox. "Sunday doesn't count on the charging clock, so that gives us forty-eight hours after the stroke of midnight tonight to get him charged or he walks."

"Jesus, Knox, we... you…better have a righteous collar on this arrest."

Knox briefed Lescoe, an early morning drive-by at the Why Fi Café, a chance encounter he said.

"You know the conflicts of interest in all of this, Knox?"

"Janice, the arrest was about an attack on a defenseless waitress, nothing else."

"Are there any admissions?" asked Lescoe, a tremble of hope in her voice.

"Like Walt Meyers said, Jan, Leon Love is a stone-cold asshole. The only thing he admitted was demanding a lawyer.

"I don't know how Krieg will take this when we present the case to him?"

"We aren't. I've been on this for fourteen hours. My report is on your desk."

"Fourteen hours, and Leon's arrest was just a chance encounter? That better be a good report, Knox. I'll be at the office in an hour."

"What about Bill, LT?"

"Get some sleep, Knox. I'll call you. By the way, nice job—I think."

Minneapolis had just begun to stir with a 6:40 Sunday morning yawn as Knox, feeling weary, stepped off the curb at City Hall. Impulse caused him to turn at the sound of a car's sudden acceleration. Instinct compelled him to jump back toward his rented Camry. A flash of gray, a shaggy-haired driver behind the wheel was all he saw. The impact hurled Knox into the air. He landed on the street. Eyes stared into the pores of asphalt. His left side numb, breathing labored, somewhere, something must be broken. Consciousness ebbed to fuzzy gray.

"Lara," he said, then darkness.

Forty-seven

As if emerging from a long dream, a light appeared beyond closed and tired eyelids. Knox felt a needle, stabbed into his left forearm. A wave of dull pain throbbed through his left side. The ache in the back of his head, like the night of the shooting, had returned. Groggy and hurt, he lay on his back and slowly opened his eyes. Bedside, a large figure loomed in the haze.

Oh, Jesus...it can't be.

"Krieg?"

"Hello, Knox," said the commander. "You've had quite an ordeal."

"No shit. Where am I? What are...what are you doing here?"

"You're in a recovery ward at Hennepin County Medical Center. You've been sedated for a couple days, a mild concussion and soft tissue injuries."

"Jesus, I hurt...all over."

"Sunday morning, you went to your car, and were hit by a gray Toyota."

"I'm trying to follow, but I'm a little hazy," Knox said.

"Male, white, shaggy blond hair, sunglasses, a gray shirt and a ball cap," said Krieg. "Does that ring a bell?"

"Right now all my bells are ringing," Knox said.

Krieg moved closer to Knox's bed. "We have everything on CCTV. The car that hit you had been stolen from the Mall of America a couple of days ago. It had license plates stolen from the same place. Both the car and plates are unaccounted for."

Knox took a sip of ice water from a cup on a nearby tray, both hands shaking. "Okay, I'm trying to work with you, but the meds... stolen car, plates, Sunday morning. I put Leon Love in jail Sunday morning."

"He's still there. Knox, I viewed the video a half dozen times of the car that hit you. There was no other traffic. The driver accelerated straight for you."

Knox took a breath, gathered his thoughts. He looked at Krieg, and winced at the sharp pain that rippled through his right side and leg. He took another sip of water.

"If it wasn't Love, Karl—" Knox caught himself. It was the first time he had called Krieg by his first name with any degree of respect.

"I'm ahead of you, there," said Krieg. "I re-sent the BOLO on Chuck Leyland. No one has heard from him since he went missing from Manitowoc, Wisconsin. With Leon Love locked up, my bet is Chuck Leyland drove the car that hit you."

"What about the Love case, Karl?"

Krieg backed away from the bed. "You were out there again, Knox, at the edge of that envelope, taking down Love."

"Sometimes that's the only way."

"Within reason, I'm trying to accept that," said Krieg. "Love's arraignment is at 1:00 P.M. this afternoon. Lescoe and DeAngelo will see you tomorrow. Guzman is in Saint Paul at the state crime lab, and I'm headed back to the office."

Krieg stopped at the door. "By the way, you're back on convalescent leave."

A rush of nausea swept through Knox "Swell, I think I'm gonna hurl."

A good night's sleep helped clear the cobwebs of his drug-induced recuperation. He strained against the pain of moving his limbs. His entire right side was a contusion-like rainbow, a palate of black, blue, red and orange. Now that Leon was locked up, Chuck Leyland had just gone to the top of the hit list.

After lunch, Knox pushed the empty cup of applesauce to the edge of the meal tray, leaned back on his pillow and closed his eyes. Soon, a vision of him and Lara, their evening strolls to the river after dinner, filled his mind. He carried a glass of Drambuie and a cigar. Her Irish eyes held a glint of tranquility, red hair fluttered in a tangle around her face. The dream so real, he strained against the dread of losing the image of her, the love of her, fought against fearing that both would vanish.

Then, in some distant corner of the illusion, Lara flickered out of sight to the sound of footsteps. Knox opened his eyes. Janice Lescoe, and Samantha DeAngelo paced toward his bed.

"Sorry. Did we wake you?" said DeAngelo.

"No, It's a habit to sleep with my eyes closed. Can I offer you some apple sauce?"

"Thanks," said DeAngelo, "but I'm sort of sauced out."

"You look good, Knox, considering." Lescoe said.

"Gee, thanks, Janice. Does that mean we're going steady?"

Lescoe hardened her features in faint irritation, and extended her hand toward the hospital bed. "Just tell me where it hurts."

DeAngelo interrupted the banter, "Love has been arraigned, criminal sexual conduct in the second degree, CSC 2, with a weapon," she said. "We added kidnapping for a kicker. The bad news is Judge Brunn only authorized $100,000 bail."

"He'll make it," said Lescoe. "Ten percent, with his house as collateral, and he's back on the street."

Knox winced as he pushed up in bed. "Did you hit Leon's house, Janice?"

"Yeah, we did. The evidence in the Rothman case, *Listen Sweetheart*, gave us links to the other incidents. We did the warrant with our bomb squad, ATF and the county. The garage smelled like a bleach factory. Swabs for nitrates of the basement, garage, and the car were negative. We took the place apart; no computers, no explosives evidence, no storage rental evidence, and nothing relating to the Warren and Troyer attacks, or the Packard's. Keepsakes from the assaults, the Troyer ID and computer, gone."

"Son-of-a-bitch," said Knox, and leaned toward Lescoe.

"Are you okay?" She asked. "Can I get you anything?"

"Give me a second, Jan. Sometimes I have to vomit."

Lescoe took two steps back from the bed. "But you don't have to vomit...now?"

"I think I'm good, Janice. Did you do a line-up?"

"Yes, Samantha and I were there."

DeAngelo shuddered. "You were right, Knox, about the eyes. Strange, almost captivating. At the arraignment, I caught him staring at me. It was spooky, intimidating, like he didn't give a shit, like I was next on his list."

"You could be, Sam. Watch yourself."

"I will. Thank you for caring."

Knox cleared his throat, turned to Lescoe. "What about the line-up. Did you use the five blue-eyed dwarfs I recommended?"

"Sorry, Knox, they had the day off with Snow White. So, we went with the regulation six subjects about the same height and weight, all of who had hazel eyes. We had them wear a ski mask, walk up to the window and utter that familiar refrain, "Listen sweetheart, cooperate and you won't get hurt."

"Yeah," said Knox. "And, they always get hurt."

"Well, we got lucky," said Lescoe. "Nikky Rothman nailed Leon Love dead-bang on voice and eye recognition.

"There is no doubt the defense will challenge the line-up in court. The relevance of voice and eye recognition is unusual, but I'll argue the precedence for it, besides Nikky identified him from the restaurant," said DeAngelo. In addition, we have the DNA from the fingernail scrapings pending at the BCA lab in Saint Paul.

"You'll do fine, Sam. What about the other victims?"

"Mrs. Troyer, and Rachel Warren are still in rough emotional shape," said DeAngelo. Their circumstances were quite different from Nikky's. You weren't there to rescue them. We struck out with both. Michael Packard's daughter, you remember, the home invasion? She locked on Love as soon as he appeared at the window. She started shaking. Unfortunately, she could only say the eyes *look* like those of her assailant's. The voice *sounds* the same. She was too tentative, I think too frightened."

Knox let out a sigh, heavy with disgust.

"Don't get discouraged," said DeAngelo. "Thanks to you we have an arrest that's reasonably contemporaneous to the time of the crime. Also, Nikky's ID is supported by physical evidence, the mask, and knife were in his car. The Camaro tire tracks are in the mud are near the crime scene, it all comes together."

"Nikky is our best victim," DeAngelo continued. "Her case is fresh, she's motivated, and her memory is sharp."

Knox chuckled. "That's not motivation and memory, Sam. It's called pissed off and payback."

"But, we have another problem," said Lescoe. "Leon's arrest was at 0214 in the morning.

"Yeah, that's about the time I hooked him up."

"Well, near that time Packard Center's computers crashed. They have an off site backup, but there is a delay when the main system goes down. They're still trying to put humpty-dumpty back together again, but some data may be lost."

"Jesus, Jan." said Knox, and grimaced as much from the pain in his body, as from trying to remember. "We inventoried a blackberry, lap top computer, and an iPad from Leon's car."

"All were fried right down to their precious little hard-drives. Our lab and the state are looking at everything. Packard Corp is trying to find a link from their end."

Knox sighed and looked out the hospital window. "Packard's computers ran a pretty complex world of commerce, a world that Leon Love wanted to destroy. At jail he said something in addition to wanting an attorney. I'm trying to remember."

"It's in your report," said DeAngelo. "His closing remark, 'You don't understand,' he said. 'I win.'"

The words came rushing back. "Yeah, that's it," said Knox. "The moment we took down Leon Love, he somehow hit a computer key and took down the Packard Corporation."

Forty-eight

Knox had not been the most congenial patient during a week on medication and physical therapy. Medical confinement did not suit his temperament. A nurse stood by as he grimaced and slipped into a shirt. A metal cane leaned motionless against the side of the hospital bed.

"You're gonna need a hand with that walking stick, Bub," said a familiar voice. Knox looked and saw Jon Bass in the doorway. He wore his customary yellow windbreaker and plaid golf cap. Guzman stood close by, a grin on his face.

"You guys miss your tee time?" Knox asked.

"Yeah," said Bass. "Our golf cart is double parked, outside."

• • •

Bass and Guzman drove Knox to Nicolette Island. It had been two weeks since Knox had been there, over a month since Leon Love blew the place apart. Still, shreds of yellow crime scene tape clung to the trees and shrubs.

The roof had buckled into the interior. Tentacles of black smoke stained the stones of the 19th century landmark. A burned and gutted shell, the scene was sadly reminiscent of antebellum Atlanta, burned to cinders.

Knox leaned on his cane, head bowed. The loss of Lara, his home, and life seemed to tumble from his being.

In one respect, he had his revenge, seeing Dale Nichols hang himself. And, if not for the other crimes he had committed, Leon Love was going down for the attack on Nikky Rothman.

You take what you can get, for now.

Bass and Guzman stood within arms length. Knox turned to them. "Some asshole underwriter at the insurance company said that the *alleged* bombing circumstances pose a problem for them. It could be considered an act of war, therefore excluded from coverage. They're still reviewing policy parameters."

"It's gonna be tough to rebuild." Guzman said.

"That may not be an option, Ernie. The city wants to reclaim the island for the park network. In their generosity, they'll give me market value for the land, minus the structure."

Knox stabbed his cane in the dirt. "You know, I get so fuckin' tired of fighting city hall."

"Well, I'm afraid I have more bad news," said Guzman. He took a notebook from his suit coat pocket, "*Muy Perplejo*, very perplexing, yesterday the lab reported that the vaginal swabs from the Warren rape kit reveal no foreign hair samples, or semen. What we have are traces of water-based glycerin, a lubricant with associate compounds. *Anticonceptivo*, my friend."

"In English, Ernie," said Knox.

"Leon is into safe rape, hermano. He wears a condom, and has removed the pubic hair on his genitals and groin."

A look skyward preceded an utterance of frustration. "Some day," said Knox. "I may have to kill that son-of-a-bitch."

"But not today," said Bass.

• • •

RELEASED ON BAIL, Leon had reason to be concerned. Prosecutor DeAngelo was preparing to lock him up, and Gregor Duchak was a man who knew too much.

Leon waited patiently near the reflection pool on the ground floor of the Hennepin County Government Center. At 6:00 P.M., a late elevator emptied out. After a long day in cramped cubicles the last trickle of ubiquitous office workers headed for buses and parking garages. Samantha DeAngelo, among them, carried a leather briefcase, and a purse on a shoulder strap.

His *Star Tribune* newspaper in hand, Leon fell in with the pedestrian crowd leaving the building, his eyes fixed on DeAngelo.

At Fourth Street and Third Avenue, Samantha paused long enough to cast a furtive glance back before she boarded a Metro Transit bus. At the last moment, Leon entered the rear side door just as it closed. He took a seat, concealing himself behind a large man ahead of him. About eight rows forward of Leon sat Samantha DeAngelo, the woman who was to be his prosecutor. He hadn't figured the angles yet, but going to prison was not an option.

The bus continued on its short route down Hennepin Avenue, as DeAngelo stared unknowingly out of the window. Small, athletic in stature, she had a freshness about her, dark hair, and olive complexion. Leon enjoyed a voyeuristic coveting of her. Somehow, he'd arrange to hurt her.

At Hennepin and Main, DeAngelo stepped from the bus. Again, Leon saw DeAngelo's cautious glance back. Their eyes met for an instant. It was enough where Leon could catch her glance of uncertainty. The bus rumbled on, Samantha DeAngelo gone, for the moment.

• • •

In the early evening, a knock at the front door sounded with a haunting echo. Nikky Rothman and her mother bolted from the sofa of their exclusive Edina home. Both stepped warily from the darkened family room. Light flickered from the flat screen TV, and illuminated their path to the mail desk in the front hall.

Leon's last words shot through Nikky's mind. "I can find you again." Nikky ignored the caution of her mother's hand on her shoulder. Mrs. Rothman went for the phone. Nikky grasped a letter opener and kept the lights off so she could see out. The red glow on the alarm pad assured her that the alarm was active.

Her breathing quickened. One hand on the alarm, the other clutched the opener. She pulled back the sidelight window curtain of the front door.

"God damn it!" Nikky yelled, then caught her breath, and leaned against the wall.

"Nikky, it is me, Gregor."

"Gregor, what the fuck are you doing here?"

"I need to talk to you."

"No, you don't."

"Nikky, you are in danger. Leon, he has done bad things to people."

"No shit. The asshole almost killed me. Did he send you here?"

"No. I came to warn you. I can come in?"

"No. You can go back to Hungary for all I care. Please leave."

"Listen, Nikky—"

She made no response.

"All right," said Gregor. "I can do nothing more."

Footfalls descended the front steps, followed by the slam of a car door. Nikky pulled back the curtain again. Gregor's Saab slipped into the night.

Mrs. Rothman rushed to Nikky's side. "The police are on their way, honey."

"Never mind Mom. It's a false alarm."

• • •

GREGOR DUCHAK HAD been a sub-contract programmer with DataTech, the company that had programed the Packard computers. Unfairly laid off, so he thought, he had his own ax to grind. And, Leon worked that resentment into his own scheme of revenge. The agreement was five-thousand-dollars up front, another five grand due on the backend of the job. In a darkened parking lot, Leon sat in his Camaro, waiting. Tonight was the backend payday, or not.

Gregor had provided Leon with two thumb-drives for a virus attack on the Packard Corporation's finance data. One was a decoy; the second had been Gregor's masterstroke, his logic bomb.

The decoy, Leon planted the night of Michael Packard's home invasion caused an easily detected virus that temporarily knocked out the corporate finance records. The second, the bomb, embedded itself into corporate software. It lurked within the data, awaiting its fateful signal to take down the entire system.

Leon chuckled, recalling the night of his arrest. Appropriate enough, a couple simple keystrokes activated a series of remote servers. As soon at the police activated their emergency lights at 32nd and DuPont, the Packard Corporation's mainframe became toast, the evidence fried without a trace.

From Leon's vantage point, amid a stand of elms, Gregor's upscale lodgings sat perched on the pilings of an embankment above suburban Medicine Lake. At 11:20, in the light of a half moon, a sweep of headlights signaled the arrival of the Saab. It backed into the carport alongside the road, lights blinked out. Gregor, no doubt eager for his final five-grand payment, rushed from the car to the house.

Through the lenses of his binoculars, Leon watched the computer guru work his key in the door. An instant later, Gregor Duchak disappeared in a shattering blast and ball of fire.

• • •

AT 8:30 A.M., Knox parked near the barricades on East Medicine Lake Drive in west suburban Plymouth. Up the street, behind yellow crime scene tape, Lescoe and Guzman stood among a group of officials.

Ashes still smoldering, crime lab, bomb squad, fire department, and Plymouth PD personnel cluttered around the blackened ribs of a house frame. With the aid of his cane, Knox hobbled to the barricade. A uniformed officer raised his hand.

Knox flashed his creds and shield. "Minneapolis PD."

The officer waved him by.

About thirty-yards up a slight rise in the street sat the wreckage of the lakeside house, a hearth and upper portion of a chimney protruded from the debris. Its shape, thought Knox, was curious, like the salute of a middle digit finger to the cops.

Splintered boards, roofing debris, and concrete block spread down the embankment to the lake. Across the street, remains of a large oak door lay at the base of a hill. The burned out hulk of Gregor's Saab sat close by. A bloody red mark stained a tree near the car.

"Knox?" said Lescoe, surprised. "You're on injured leave."

"Just pretend I'm not here, LT. What have we got?"

"Nothing good, I'm afraid." She nodded to Guzman who led Knox to the side of the roadway. Lescoe continued her liaison with the suburban cops.

"Remember Gregor?" said Guzman.

"Leon's buddy at the Café."

"Not anymore." Guzman pointed to the bloodied tree. "Gregor became impaled on that elm. His wristwatch stopped at 11:23 P.M. So did Gregor. He's on a pan at the ME's."

"Let me guess," said Knox, "Gregor arrives home, opens the door, turns on the light, and gets his ticket punched into the hereafter; Walt Meyers, all over again."

"That's about it, amigo."

"Witnesses?" Knox asked.

"A neighbor up the hill was at his kitchen window. His place overlooks Gregor's house and the lake. The guy took a sip of water about 11:20 P.M. He saw Duchak's car pull into the carport at his house. The next thing the guy knows, his windows blow in, and he's picking glass splinters out of his PJs."

For a moment, Knox studied the impact of the crime scene then turned away.

"Where are you going, *hermano*?" Guzman asked.

"I'm going for a drive, Ernie."

Cane in hand, Knox stepped off toward the barricades.

"Hey *hermano*, don't do anything crazy."

At 9:45 A.M., Knox parked his car in the nearly empty Bakken parking lot. He eyeballed Leon's house, wanting to see a sign of him, anything to justify kicking in the door.

On a call to Guzman, Knox found that Plymouth PD had no suspicious vehicles, or person reports during the night in the area of Gregor's house. Officers had issued no parking or other traffic citations. There was nothing to tie Leon to the area near Gregor's house that could be reasonably articulated to allow Knox to hook Leon up again.

"Harding," said Guzman. "You better not be where I think you are, trying to do what I hope you're not trying to do, cause we've got nothing yet, man."

"Nah, just checking, Ernie. Talk to you later." Knox realized that his emotions were over riding his better judgment. For the moment, no convincing evidence tied Leon to Gregor's, or to Walt Meyers's death, or any of the other cases, except for Nikky Rothman. All they had amounted to a reasonable suspicion, not probable cause for an arrest on of the other cases. "Passions and protests don't make cases," Jon Bass once said, "facts and evidence do."

But, passion lit the fire that burned inside Knox, passion enough to bring down Leon Love, somehow.

• • •

The historic stone Great Northern Arch Rail Trestle traversed the Saint Anthony Falls cataract of the Mississippi River. Now integrated into the paved walkway of the city riverfront, Samantha DeAngelo stood at the steel railing, the towering buildings of downtown Minneapolis in the background. Sam's arm fell gently around the shoulder of her daughter, thirteen-year-old, Jena. Their usual Saturday morning sojourn along the riverfront found the might of the Mississippi sweep down the spillway of the falls sixty feet below, mist dampened their faces.

"Hello, counselor," said a voice from behind.

A shiver spiked up DeAngelo's spine. She turned. Leon Love stood not ten feet away.

It took a moment for Sam to conceal her surprise, deny Leon the pleasure of what she knew he intended, intimidation. Her eyes tensed to cast as much of an icy don't-fuck-with-me gaze as she could muster.

Above the roar of the river, "Move along Mr. Love," DeAngelo ordered.

Leon sauntered a few steps away, stopped and turned. "Pretty daughter you have there. Jena, isn't that right?"

DeAngelo reached into her shoulder bag. Her hand grasped the trigger on the canister of habanera pepper spray.

"Now, Mr. Love, move off."

Leon's eyes drifted toward Samantha's bag, accompanied by a snarky smile. "See you in court, Miss DeAngelo."

Not until Love reached the end of the stone bridge did Sam release her grip on the pepper spray.

"Mom," said Jena. "I saw that man at the Ortman Street Park a few days ago."

Sam hit the speed dial on her cell phone.

"Harding, I need to see you."

Forty-nine

Knox curbed the Camry on the cobblestones near Francine's on Main. Across the Mississippi River, downtown bustled in the late July morning. Through the French doors open to the street, Knox entered the European bistro and found Samantha at an indoor table. She sipped a glass of iced tea. Jena savored a soda.

"Harding, thank you for coming," said Sam.

Knox hooked his cane on the back of a chair and sat down.

"You remember my daughter, Jena?"

Like her mother, Jena had dark hair, a beautiful Mediterranean complexion, and doe-like brown eyes.

"Hello," said Knox. "We've met but you may not recall."

"I remember, at Mom's office. I have seen you on TV, and your picture in the paper, too. Mom has told me about you."

Knox looked at Samantha, her face a blush.

"She knows, Harding, that we have a *working* relationship, that you catch the bad guys, and I prosecute them."

Jena looked up from her soda. "Mom said you hook 'em up and she sends 'em up."

Knox cast a furtive smile at Sam. "Oh, Mom says that, huh?"

"Jena knows about my work, Harding. Now, she knows about Leon Love."

A waiter arrived at the table. Knox ordered coffee, Sam freshened her tea.

"So, tell me about the bridge, Sam."

She told Knox of her encounter with Leon Love only an hour before, a glance from the bus a day earlier.

"There was no physical contact," said Sam, "no threats, curses, fighting words, nothing except his presence, that snide smirk when he said that he'd see me in court. He knew Jena's name, and that really creeped me out."

"Did you discuss security measures with Jack Griffin?"

"Yes, but I don't want to be hobbled twenty-four hours a day by some man following me with a gun. I've taken precautions, new locks, pepper-spray in my purse, and 911 on speed dial."

"Leon is trying to jerk your chain, Sam."

"I know. The Rothman complaint was issued, and Love is now out on bail."

"I hope he's not stupid enough to try anything with you before his court date. Keep Jena close and the pepper-spray handy."

When the coffee arrived. Knox took a sip. "Have you seen the news, Sam? There was a home explosion in Plymouth."

"No, what about it?"

"You have a prosecution witness on the Rothman case, Gregor Duchak."

"He's a computer programmer," said Sam. She paused, making the connection. "Oh, Jesus, Duchak lives in

Plymouth. We've been looking for him since you've been in the hospital."

"He's in repose on a pan at the ME's."

Samantha uttered a dispirited sigh, and looked toward her daughter.

"Mom," said Jena, "Will the man from the bridge come back?"

"No," said Knox as he finished his coffee, "I'm not going to let that happen."

"Harding," said Sam. "I know that look. What are you going to do?"

"Take you home."

"I'm a big girl now. Please don't crowd me on this."

"Sam, you called me. I do the protect and serve thing, remember?"

Samantha rolled her eyes in mock irritation. "Okay, officer, we're a block away, River Place Commons."

"Yes, I know."

DeAngelo cast a perplexed glance at Knox.

Through the security gate, Sam's place sat in a cluster of private condos with manicured lawns and evergreen trees. Knox let her and Jena off at their front door. He called after Sam.

"Remember, lock the doors, put on the alarm, and—"

"You sound like my father. I really can take care of myself."

Samantha continued up the walk then called after Knox. "Thank you, Harding."

Her tone, more intimate than their *working* relationship.

"I'll see you, Sam."

A few blocks away, Knox turned into the parking lot of the Nicollet Inn. He pulled out his cell and hit his contact number.

"Hello. This is Jack Griffin."

"Mr. Griffin. Harding Knox here. I need a favor."

• • •

Alonzo Rico answered his phone on the third ring.

"Mr. Rico, this is Jack Griffin, Hennepin County Attorney. I'm sorry to bother you at home on a Saturday, sir—"

"Well, Mr. Griffin, what can I do for you?"

"It's a matter of mutual interest, your client, Leon Love."

"Ah, yes, Leon. We have an up-coming hearing. Miss DeAngelo, I believe, is the prosecutor assigned."

"It's about Ms. DeAngelo that I'm calling. Your client had contact with her late this morning, the Stone Arch Bridge in Minneapolis. Yesterday, he was on her bus ride home."

"Nothing unpleasant I'm sure, Mr. Griffin, purely a couple of chance encounters."

"A chance encounter accentuated with an intimidating tone from what I understand. He knew the name of Miss DeAngelo's daughter, as well. Now why would he need that kind of information, and why the hell would he mention that to her, Mr. Rico?"

"I have no idea, sir. Perhaps I can have a talk with him."

"Look, Mr. Rico, let's cut the bullshit. I'm aware of your client's background. When you talk to Mr. Love, you tell him from me that if he has one more contact with Samantha DeAngelo, or her daughter, I will personally move to revoke his bail, and make him a personal project of this office."

"Well, Mr. Griffin, now who's intimidating?"

"Just deliver the message, Mr. Rico." Griffin ended the call.

There were more calls over the weekend, Griffin to Chief Ballard, Ballard to Krieg and so on. As a result, Knox found himself assigned to night surveillance. Injured or not, he could handle a radio. Guzman drove the van. Because of Leon's contact with DeAngelo, the County Attorney now had skin in the game, and assigned assisting investigators who went mobile in two more units.

Neon lights cast a purple glow to the curb-front of Louie's Lake Street Lounge, a two star dive known to the 3rd Precinct cops as Louie's Lizard Lounge. Knox trained his binoculars on the Camaro parked in a side lot.

In the murky 1:00 A.M. hour of bar closing, Leon appeared arm in arm with a buxom, long legged barfly. She wobbled down the sidewalk on a set of stiletto heels, like a boozy giraffe in tight leather pants. In the parking lot, Leon braced her against the Camaro and planted a big wet one on her mouth.

"It must be lust at first sight," said Guzman.

Leon stumbled to the driver's door and slid in with his evening fantasy.

"Now we go to plan B, uttered Knox who called communications from a burner cell. Moments later, the call came out over the air.

The police dispatcher alerted the precinct cars. "Citizen reports a possible DUI, dark blue Camaro leaving Louie's Lounge, headed west on Lake—"

Fifty

Outside the twenty-second floor courtrooms, the hallway was nearly vacant of the usual crowd of detectives, uniformed officers, and attorneys that assemble for hearings. It was Friday, an unofficial day of rest in the court system, time to attend to the loose ends of busy calendars, make an afternoon golf date, a country club luncheon, speaking engagement, or chase down a few highballs at the Gavel Bar.

In Court Room 2213, assistant county attorney Samantha DeAngelo huddled with Sergeants Knox, Guzman, and Lieutenant Lescoe at the prosecutor's table. Forensic techs from the state crime bureau, and from Minneapolis PD, sat patiently behind the spectator railing. It would be a half hour before Judge Richard Brunn would begin the hearing; at issue, the determination of sufficient evidence to try Leon Love for the sexual assault, and the kidnapping of Nikky Rothman.

At 8:50 A.M., the courtroom door swept open. Alonso Rico strode in, his battered brief case in one hand, and a sheaf of papers in the other.

Behind the swarthy mouthpiece trailed Leon Love wearing a smartly tailored dark suit, and his customary snarky half-smile.

Rico, like Edward G. Robinson about to pull a .38-roscoe, barreled through the spectator's gate with a stern expression on his face. He strode to the prosecutor's table.

"Ms. DeAngelo," said Rico, "I spent the other morning getting my client, Mr. Love, released from jail on what I assert is a trumped up DUI charge. Orchestrated by officers, I contend, as a tactic to have my client miss this hearing."

"This is harassment, Ms. DeAngelo." Rico pointed toward Knox and Lescoe who stood at the table, "and I shall request an order from the court to restrain the police department from further contact with Mr. Love."

"Counselor," said Knox, "I understand that your client's inebriated, aggressive demeanor is on a squad car dash-cam. He also refused an alcohol test."

Knox felt Samantha grasp his forearm. She put up her left hand as Rico edged forward in rebuttal.

"One case at a time, gentlemen, without the testosterone."

Leon couldn't resist a challenging leer.

"One case at a time," said Rico in a huff. He stepped to the defense table, and waved his arm for Love to join him.

Rico's heavy breathing, beads of perspiration on his forehead, and sweat stains on his shirt collar, caught Knox's attention. Perhaps it had something to do with the article in the morning paper, coupled with having to handle a looser client.

DeAngelo asked. "Mr. Rico, are you ready to proceed?"

"I am, counselor," said the pale, bullish attorney as he pulled a file and legal pad from the tattered leather case.

At 9:15, a bailiff walked into the courtroom. "Judge Brunn is delayed, handling cases from Judge Lieberman who is ill. He sends his apologies, and has rescheduled your probable cause hearing for 2:00 P.M."

Moments later, Rico packed his brief case, and cast a challenging smile toward the prosecutor's table. "2:00 P.M., Ms. DeAngelo." He escorted Leon from the courtroom. Of course, Leon threw one last characteristic sneer as he departed.

At a bank of elevators, Leon and Rico waited among a group of people for a car. A door slid open when Rico's briefcase fell to the floor. His hands tugged at his chest. His knees buckled followed by a compressed moan. Alonzo Rico fell face down across the elevator threshold. Passengers gasped.

Ding, ding, went the warning bells as the doors slammed into the stricken attorney's body.

Knox and Guzman rushed forward along the corridor. They rolled Rico onto his back and pulled him free. As the elevator doors closed, Knox glance up, the mockery of Leon's extended middle finger sent an emphatic message—he would not be back.

Guzman checked the carotid artery, no response. Knox probed for an airway, the throat seized shut. Alonzo Rico had had died before he hit the floor. Next to his body an edition of the *Saint Paul Pioneer Press* headlined Rico's epitaph, "Embezzlement—Saint Paul Attorney—Indictment Pending."

• • •

To NO ONE's surprise, Leon never appeared at 2:00 P.M. In consideration of Rico's passing, Judge Brunn, over DeAngelo's objections, simply issued a continuance for Leon to obtain a new attorney and to reappear. No warrant.

After Brunn's ruling, Knox and Guzman spent the remainder of the day in a futile search. Leon was in the wind.

• • •

THE STREETLIGHTS BLINKED on in an early dusk to a river front evening. At Francine's, the mellow notes of Amos Redbone's jazz quartet filled the easy atmosphere. Absent his cane, Knox hobbled in from the street. Tired, hungry and looking for a drink, he saw DeAngelo at a table. A legal pad and leather case pushed to the side, her hand rested on a half glass of red wine next to an empty plate. He walked to her table.

DeAngelo glanced up, a look of surprise on her face.

"Harding," she said. "I didn't expect to see you here."

"That's my line, I thought you'd be home with Jena?"

"You doing that protect and serve thing again?"

"No, I was just—"

"Sit down, Knox you're blocking the music. By the way, in regard to your protect and serve concerns, I left the office at 7:00. Leon Love is not the only case my team has going. My dad took Jena home to Duluth this afternoon, and you look like you could use, what is it, Crown Royal on the rocks"

"And, a Chianti for you?" said Knox. "The spaghetti was good, huh?" He tapped a finger to the left side of his mouth.

Samantha laughed and wiped a smudge of sauce from her lip. Knox ordered drinks and a meal while he filled Sam in on the search for Leon Love who had vanished, Camaro and all.

After a time, Freddie, the waiter, returned with a salad and chicken-parmesan while Redbone moved through the notes of "Round Midnight" on his sax. A peculiar feeling shuttered through Knox. He had seen this movie before. Only it had been Lara seated across from him, not Sam, and for some reason things began to feel—complicated.

With the music, Sam settled back with her wine, nodding to the beat of Redbone's rhythm, a tranquil smile on her face. Maybe it was the booze and wine, but after a while, it seemed to Knox as if the two of them were the only ones in the room.

"What the hell happened, Sam?"

The soft expression in her eyes said that she knew what he was thinking.

"Time happened, Harding."

"You mean like far, far away and long, long ago?"

Samantha chuckled. "No, I mean you went off to the FBI National Academy in Virginia. I drifted into law school, to the handsome, silver-tongued devil, Michael Mogelson. He said if I helped put him through law school he'd help me do the same.'"

"I guess that didn't work out, huh?"

"Not so much," said Samantha, a sip of Chianti dampened her lips. "After graduation, Michael left for the Silicon Valley. His infamous last words were, 'with my contacts, I can make a fortune out there for us.'"

Knox shrugged. "So, said the silver tongued devil?"

"And, he didn't come back, left me pregnant. Like a rabbit in heat, he fell for some California bimbo named Barbara. I got the door prize; a Wells Fargo check each month to support Jena. A card and another check comes on her birthday, and at Christmas. Once in a while he stops in between flights from wherever to whatever."

"I'm sorry, Sam. I didn't know the details, never thought it was my business."

"Don't be sorry, for either of us. I have a priceless relationship with my daughter. Equally important, you had Lara, and I know you loved one another very much. I could see it when I saw you together. And, that was none of *my* business."

Knox held her gaze for a moment, perplexed for a response. "How are you getting home?" He finally said.

"I took the bus from work. I live only a block away, remember?"

"I'll walk you home, if you don't mind?"

Samantha held up her brief case. "Will you carry my books, too?'

Knox couldn't ignore the unexpected reply, the soft glint in her brown eyes, or perhaps it was the Chianti. "Yeah, I'll carry your books, and pay for dinner."

Upon stepping to the street, Freddie the waiter walked up. "Knox, I almost forgot. A guy was in here awhile ago asking about you."

"Asking what?"

"If you'd been in tonight, or something like that."

"So, what did you tell him?"

"I was busy, said I didn't know, and worked my tables."

"What did the guy look like, Freddie?"

"He looked tired, kind of played out. He wore a dark jacket, baseball cap, light hair, said he was a friend of yours."

"Did he leave a name?"

"No name, but I thought I should let you know."

"Thanks," said Knox, the information put an edge to the evening.

Along the street, the replicate old gaslights glittered against the night. It felt strangely familiar to be walking beside Sam. At the cavernous alcove between Francine's and an arcade building, a steep series of narrow steps climbed into the shadows toward the landing at Lourdes Place. Atop the steps rested the matriarch church of the old Polish neighborhood, Our Lady of Lourdes. Knox cast a cautious glance as they strode by the dank and poorly lit steps, his instincts wary about the man at Francine's who had asked about him.

"Let's keep to the street, Sam. My legs aren't quite ready for the steps."

Sam slipped her arm in his. He pressed it close to his side. Somehow it seemed like their time apart had never happened.

"I'm glad we had dinner together," said Sam as they turned the corner from Hennepin onto Lourdes Place, a narrow cobblestone street, like a scene from and old English movie.

Near the front of church, Knox stopped and looked at Sam. "I don't mean to impose upon your life, but would it be okay if we did this again?"

Sam dropped her arm from his, and reached for his hand.

"Sergeant Knox!"

The shout echoed from behind, from the shadows at the top of the alcove steps. Knox pushed Sam toward the church, and pulled his .45-caliber Beretta.

The first shot boomed like thunder in the confines of the narrow street. Knox saw the muzzle flash. The slug burred past his left ear. He went right into a crouch. A flash of pain lashed his body, remnants from the hit and run.

The shooter stepped into an angel of light, and fired once more. The round zinged off the street near Knox.

Knox fired three times, then silence.

"Sam?"

"I'm all right, Harding."

"Stay down," said Knox. He crept like a cat along the backs of vacant buildings, Beretta ready.

In the dim setting, the shooter's gun, a Colt semi-auto, lay on the cobblestones. Two steps into the darkness, a figure lay face down on the stairway, arms outstretched, and hands empty. Knox nudged the body. No movement. He slipped his fingers to the shooter's carotid artery. No pulse.

There was a bullet hole center mass in the back of the shooter's jacket, a second through the right shoulder. Knox looked at the face, partially obscured by a baseball hat.

"Oh Jesus, Knox, is he dead?" DeAngelo asked. Her approach guarded.

"Yeah. He's Chuck Leyland, the ballroom shooter's son, the guy who probably ran me down."

"Are you alright, Sam?" Knox stood, still holding the Beretta in his hand.

"Do you think you can put that thing away, now?" Sam nodded at the gun.

Knox shrugged. "Sure."

"Good, I'm a little shaky," said Sam. "I think there's a bullet in my lap top. I'm going to sit down on the steps by the church."

Sirens echoed along Hennepin Avenue.

"I have to call this in, Sam."

"Harding, somehow, I think they have the message."

Fifty-one

It had been three days since Chuck Leyland met his fate in the alcove on Lourdes place. Meetings with Maurice Mancel preceded the process of the Internal Affairs depositions. Not lost in the process was Samantha DeAngelo, who reminded Knox that being in the middle of a shoot-out, a bullet put through her twenty-one hundred dollar laptop, left her a little, well, unsettled. She needed some time away.

When Knox picked up copies of his statements from Internal Affairs, he saw Mrs. Neil Wallace being escorted into Chief Ballard's outer office.

• • •

Ballard closed a large three-ring-binder a portion of the Leon Love case file. The investigation into the bombings, assaults and computer sabotage, and two murders would continue. But the need to resolve an important loose end was critical. In shirtsleeves and braces, he stepped to the office window, a cup of coffee in hand, motive on his mind.

Ever since Ballard had arrived in Minneapolis, Neil Wallace had been a colleague in efforts to reduce crime in the city's minority communities. Given the controversy of Wallace's death, he now faced an awkward responsibility to tread a thin line between police chief, and being family friend.

Back at his desk, he slipped into a double-breasted navy blue blazer when Mrs. Cohan announced the arrival of his guests.

"Please, show her in."

The widow wore a taupe colored skirt and jacket, her demeanor poised, but guarded. She introduced the tall, handsome black man at her side.

"This is Lamont LaCroix, my attorney," said Mrs. Wallace.

In his late thirties, tall, athletic, in a blue pinstripe suit, and thin wire spectacles; LaCroix carried a thin black leather case. He was the perfect picture of a GQ magazine ad.

"Good morning, Chief," said LaCroix as the two men shook hands.

LaCroix set his case next to a chair in front of the chief's desk. "Mrs. Wallace informed me that you wanted to discuss an investigation associated with her late husband. I thought it appropriate that I accompany her, you understand."

"Yes, thank you for coming."

Ballard took a seat at his desk, Wallace and LaCroix in two chairs.

"Mrs. Wallace, Shelia," said Ballard, "I'm still terribly saddened by Neil's death. We had always worked well together, and I miss him. I hope the grand jury proceedings allowed, in some way, a degree of closure for you."

"Chief, my husband is gone. His death was played out before me on a fifty-five inch TV screen in front of twenty-five strangers of the grand jury. Closure is not a word I can apply to that proceeding, or to Neil's death."

She avoided calling Ballard by name, as had been the custom of their familiarity before the shooting. Instead, she addressed him by his title, her attitude cool, distant.

"Chief Ballard," asked LaCroix, "you say your department is conducting inquiries associated with the aftermath of the Packard Center shootings. How does that involve Mrs. Wallace?"

Ballard pushed a photograph of Leon Love across the desk to Mrs. Wallace, careful to study her reaction.

"Have you seen this man before?" Ballard asked.

She studied the photo then pushed it back across the desk.

"The BCA people showed me this picture. As I told them, I don't know this person."

Ballard took the photo back and continued. "Sheila, do you have any recollection of a woman from Madison, Wisconsin, a woman named Lucile Love?"

Mrs. Wallace cast a concerned look at LaCroix.

"Chief," said LaCroix, "I must insist. Where is this going?"

"Counselor, what association did Neil have with an attorney named Alonso Rico, and a company named Hiawatha Holding?"

LaCroix leaned forward in his chair to assert his advocacy on behalf of his client. "Chief—"

Ballard held up his hand, LaCroix retreated. Then Ballard exposed the revelations of Wallace's extended dalliance with Lucile Love, the progeny of that relationship, Leon Love. The department wanted Leon, suspected in a number of violent crimes, even murder.

Mrs. Wallace sat quietly. There was no surprise, shock or anger in her features. Finally, she began to speak. "Chief, let me say—"

LaCroix reached for her hand. She pushed it away.

"Chief," said Mrs. Wallace with affirmation, "my husband was an educated and influential man. He took care of his community, earned positions of respect for himself, his family, and I might add his race, as well."

"I know that as well as anyone," said Ballard. "But I have an obligation to find facts with regard to Leon Love. There are issues of motive, revenge for the death of Lucile Love, your husband, and the violence caused to others that cannot be ignored."

"Chief, those matters do not involve me. First, Leyland, a disgruntled drunk, and your policeman, caused the death of my husband. Now, you insult me, and the memory of my husband by telling me he has a son that has come here to add to that insanity?"

"The DNA results in regard to Neil's connection to Leon Love are irrefutable," said Ballard. "And, our investigation compels us to find Leon to prevent even more tragedy."

"Then, you look elsewhere, because I don't know that person."

Lamont LaCroix escorted Sheila Wallace from the office. Ballard's intuition told him that Mrs. Wallace's ire, and ignorance about her husband's affair appeared genuine. Wallace's mistress, Lucy Love, and his investment-swindling associate, Alonzo Rico, would remain unresolved questions in the widow's mind. Meanwhile, Neil Wallace's dangerous, forsaken son lurked somewhere out in the shadows. In death, the double life of Neil Wallace had only added to the pain endured by those he left behind.

• • •

In the old warehouse district of downtown, Knox pulled into the garage around 6:00 P.M. Large, folding doors closed behind as he parked in the numbered spot for his sublet loft apartment. His cell phone rang.

"This is Knox."

"I see you met Chuck Leyland."

It took a millisecond to recognize the voice.

"Yeah, at first I thought it was you, Leon. Maybe next time, huh?"

Leon chuckled. "Maybe so, Sergeant. I'm still not finished."

The call ended, and in a subconscious reflex, Knox cast his glare into the shadows of the garage. There was no one.

He gathered up his satchel, a bag of Chinese takeout, set the alarm on his car, and went to the elevator.

At the loft door, a clear strip of cellophane tape between the door and door jam was still in place, a good sign. He opened the door, and a sniff of air revealed the lack of gas in the atmosphere, another good sign. A little paranoia was a respectable thing to have with Leon Love on the loose. The routine had become a ritual since Walt Meyers's death in Wisconsin. Knox went to the refrigerator and took out a beer; time for dinner.

In the middle of egg-foo-young, the cell chirped again. Knox slammed his fork onto the table. "That soon-of-a-bitch," he grumbled. "He can never leave me alone. But tomorrow—"

Knox checked the name on the screen—Sam DeAngelo.

Fifty-two

A SLOW, CONTAINED tension framed the tenor of Sam's voice.

"He's here, Harding. Leon is here in Duluth."

Knox felt the measured strain of her words. "Okay, Sam, tell me."

"A few minutes ago," she said, "Jena and Dad left the Skyline observation tower that overlooks the city. Jena saw Leon watching them from a van and told my father. Before Dad could get a number, Leon drove off in a beat up utility van, gray primer and body rust, a Wisconsin license. Dad couldn't get the number and called me. Now I'm calling you."

"Sam, did you bring a copy of Leon's file with you?"

"Yes, but there is still no arrest warrant."

"Call Detective Felstuhl, Duluth PD, give him Leon's background. I'll be up there as soon as I can."

The next call Knox placed was to Deacon Hubbard, a pilot for the Minnesota State Patrol at Holman Field, the Downtown Saint Paul Airport.

"Hub, Harding Knox here. Have you got anything going north? I need a lift to Duluth. I've got a scumbag stalking one of our county attorneys."

"Hey, Harding, yeah, we're on stand-by for a medical package to Duluth. When it arrives, we go. If you're not here, I leave without you."

One eye in the rearview mirror for any troopers, Knox blitzed down Interstate 94 through Minneapolis toward Saint Paul. Tires screeched as he turned off the interstate, sped down the Lafayette Freeway to the airport, and the MSP hanger. Gear bag in hand, he hobbled quickly around the hanger as the rotor of the Bell Ranger whirled, and the bird moved off the pad.

The chopper hovered toward the taxiway, then made a surprising rotation; Hub, at the controls, settled the copter to the pavement, the co-pilot waved Knox forward. Amidst the turbulent down draft, Knox grabbed a door latch, hurled himself inside the bird, slid the door shut and pressed the lock.

A gasp for breath, Knox strapped himself in and put on the headphones that lay on the bench seat.

"Welcome aboard State Patrol Airways," said Hub with a wise-guy flare, "the Ranger Flight, non-stop to Duluth. Fasten your seat belt, no talking until we reach cruising altitude."

The turbine engine whined, and the rotor whirred. The bird tilted forward and proceeded along the taxiway. Through the headphones, Knox heard the air traffic controller acknowledge clearance as the Ranger ascended into the pre-dusk skies above the Twin-Cities. Hub turned the Ranger north as the metro landscape swept by below.

"From here on," Hub said, "we just follow Interstate 35 all the way to Duluth-Superior, dead reckoning navigation."

Dead reckoning, something about the term bothered Knox, like dead on arrival. He checked the clasp on his seat belt and called Sam on his cell.

In little over an hour the Ranger dropped over the ridge of Skyline Drive. Perched on steep slopes below, like San Francisco of the North, Duluth, Minnesota rested along the shoreline grades of Lake Superior. The docks of Duluth-Superior provided the stage for the largest inland seaport in the United States.

Hub banked the Ranger over the expansive port. Below, bathed in amber light, the spectacle of the historical aerial lift bridge spanned the only channel into Lake Superior. Anchored on each side of a narrow channel, skeletal-like steel towers supported a two-lane bridge deck that raised and lowered, allowing the arrival and departure of ships to the harbor. As Hub made his approach to the Duluth International, a 700-foot ship plied its way under the bridge into the vastness of Lake Superior.

The Bell Ranger settled onto the landing pad near a fixed wing Cessna. A maroon state patrol car, emergency lights flashing, rolled up to the chopper. The co-pilot handed the medical box to the driver who signed for the parcel and sped off.

Hub shouted to Knox, as the chopper turbine wound down. "That must be your ride." He pointed to a shapely dark haired woman in jeans and blue jacket who leaned against the hood of a green, vintage, fastback Mustang.

"If you need a lift back to the Cities," said Hub, "I'll be here until tomorrow."

Knox shook Hub's hand, patted the co-pilot on the shoulder and trod toward the Mustang, gear bag in hand.

Sam looked up at the tired, disheveled cop with a limp. "I'm impressed, Knox. I ask for help and you bring a whole damn helicopter."

"It's all I could do, Sam. The Bat Car is in for repairs."

"That's okay. It's Bat Man that I need. I'm really glad you're here." She motioned Knox to the car.

Knox slipped his bag into the back of the car and settled into the passenger's seat. He breathed in the scent of her perfume, still attempting to rationalize his attraction to Sam over his loss of Lara. Part of it, he knew, was Sam's alluring air, and self-confidence, now faded to an uncustomary vulnerability. Part of it too, was his loneliness.

Sam rumbled away from the hanger in the '68 Stang. She glanced at Knox, as she moved through the gears.

"It's Dad's hobby car, a stick. His pickup is in the shop."

"Where's Jena?" Knox asked.

"She's with Dad at the house. I spoke with Felstuhl," Sam said as she turned out of the airport. "He has a BOLO out on Leon. A stop and hold for stalking."

"It's a BS maneuver for now," said Knox, "but it'll be enough to get his attention, enough for us to find out where he's at."

Fifty-three

Deep within the bowels of the ship, four V-20 electro mechanical diesel engines revved to power. Within its cavernous holds, the one-thousand-foot Great Lakes behemoth bore nearly sixty-thousand-tons of Mesabi taconite ore. From the computerized bridge five stories above the main deck, the brush-cut Captain Kolstad eyed the Furuno weather radar and Navnet display. A light westerly squall threatened passage for the course through the harbor. The first mate made the call alerting harbor security the ship was in transit. Kolstad gave orders to cast off.

Lines let loose, bow and stern thrusters engaged, the 105-foot wide hull of the *Superior Star* slowly pushed away from CN Dock Number 6 into the Saint Louis River. Beyond the industrial yards of Rice's Point stood the lighted towers of the aerial lift bridge, and the dark expanse of Lake Superior.

• • •

Knox sat in the passenger seat assessing Sam's skilled movements through the gears of the old muscle car. As they cruised through the city, a large freighter was outbound through the Saint Louis River Basin. Lights from the lakefront entertainment district at Canal Park reflected off the surface of the city's harbor. The scene reminiscent of times Knox had spent in Duluth with Sam, times before Lara.

"The Radisson Hotel, Canal Park, the Blues Festivals, you and I," Sam said. "So much time between now and then."

"Damn it, how do you do that?"

"Do what?" she said.

"Know what I'm thinking?"

"Maybe, because I was thinking it, too," said Sam.

Knox caught the glance she gave him. It was the kind of look that could melt the ice in a glass of good whiskey. But, the whiskey and Sam would have to wait. Leon was still out there, somewhere.

• • •

Leon concealed the van in a greenway behind a vacant house. The lawn sign read Skyline Realty, Home For Sale. He had scouted the place long before he followed Jena and old man DeAngelo to the observation tower above town.

From his vantage point, like a panther scouting its prey, Leon crouched in the dark and watched Tony DeAngelo's home.

Not wanting to get his ass kicked, or worse, Leon had sharpened his research technique. Samantha's father was a retired locomotive engineer. As such, the old man had to be considered with caution, barrel chested with muscular arms; he had the agility of someone younger than a man in his late 60s.

At night DeAngelo tinkered with the old Mustang parked in the drive. Later, Samantha, the old man, and thirteen-year-old Jena spent evenings relaxing on the three seasons porch at the back of the house.

Tonight, Leon could see the Mustang and Samantha were gone. Jena sat on the back porch in front of a television, alone. The old man was nowhere to be seen. The sense of revenge welled up within him. He never could get to Knox for killing his father, Neil Wallace. But, he could get at both Knox and DeAngelo for trying to lock him away. He could get Jena DeAngelo, and introduce her to a man's needs in the process.

In a rush of adrenalin, Leon pulled a black ski mask over his face, anticipating the thrill of grabbing the girl. He bolted from his place of cover, and leaped up the wood stairway to the deck. The flimsy lock on the porch was no obstacle. Leon seized the handle, broke open the door then launched himself into the porch at Jena who lay on a sofa with her popcorn.

Popcorn sailed through the air, accompanied by a curdling yell. "Grandpa!"

Jena kicked and screamed as Leon forced her to the floor, He slipped a zip-tie around her wrists and pulled tight. In the next instant, Leon felt a hand grab the neck of his hoodie. Yanked to his feet, Leon gaped into the fury of a pugilist-like face.

It was simultaneous, Tony DeAngelo's attack and the jab of Leon's equalizer. The knife cut into the old man's ribs.

DeAngelo's grip faded, his eyes swelled in shock, and he collapsed to the floor like a bag of rocks.

Jena cowered in terror.

"You're with me," said Leon as he mashed a patch of duct tape over Jena's mouth. Through darkness to the trees and van, Leon scrambled, half dragging Jena behind. Voices called out from the near-by houses.

• • •

SAM DROVE INTO a cul-de-sac neighborhood near Lake Superior College. Out of the window, Knox stared at the neat front lawns; homes that sat in cozy cul-de-sacs, a neighborhood that gave you the impression you could leave your doors unlocked, where bad things seldom happened.

At her father's home, Sam turned into the drive. Knox glanced down the street at a boxy gray van, and the flash of taillights. Tony DeAngelo stumbled from the front door of the house, hand to his side.

"He took her," Tony gasped. "He took her," and pointed toward the van that rumbled away.

Sam jumped from the Mustang and ran to her father. Knox scrambled to the driver's seat. "Call 911," he said and raced off in the direction of the vanishing taillights.

On Haines, through light traffic, Knox sped after the lone gray van. He picked up his cell.

"Duluth police, do you have an emergency?" The dispatcher asked.

"Sergeant Knox, Minneapolis PD. On Haines headed toward I-35, I have a gray late '90s van—agg-assault, kidnapping. From the DeAngelo residence near Superior College."

The dispatcher paused in response, Knox moved through traffic to get a license number. The Wisconsin plate on the van was obscured with grease and dirt.

"Sergeant, we received a call from DeAngelo's. We are moving cars into the area. Do you have a license number?"

On his cell, Knox explained the issue with the license plate, described the car he was driving, and a change in the direction of travel, north on Michigan Street.

• • •

LEON LOOKED BACK at Jena trussed into a moth-eaten captain's chair in the rear of the van. Her hands buckled in front under a grimy seatbelt, she strained for the buckle.

A police monitor sat on the console of the van. Leon turned it on. The last words of the dispatcher exploded in his ears; kidnap…armed suspect…aggravated assault, and a description of his van. *Fuck, they're on to me.*

Gripped by panic, Leon turned toward the Saint Louis River. He could dump the girl then make a run for Wisconsin.

On the radio he monitored the acknowledgement of city, county, and state police cars moving into the area.

Sweat slid down Leon's neck into his black hoodie. His heart raced. He slammed a fist into the dash of the truck—"Fuck!"

• • •

"Sergeant Knox," said the dispatcher, "You are to take no direct action, sir."

Knox rolled his eyes, having heard that admonition before.

The dispatcher continued, her alert to responding cars. "Off duty Minneapolis Police sergeant is following kidnap suspect vehicle, late '90s gray van, unknown Wisconsin plates, north on Michigan from Haines. The sergeant is in a green '68 Mustang."

Leon couldn't believe it. A glance in his mirror confirmed what he heard. A set of headlights to his rear, the flash of police emergency lights farther back.

"Knox, that fucking bloodhound!"

Leon took a quick look back, Jena strained for the seat belt buckle. She rubbed her face against her shoulder in an effort to remove the tape from her mouth. Leon accelerated the van, deciding to lose Knox and the cops in the neighborhoods.

"North toward Enger Park," said Knox.

"Squads have you, Sergeant. You are to break off. Copy?"

Knox closed to within three car lengths of the van. Leon made a turn then another, an attempt that failed to evade Knox. Up and down the slopes south of downtown, Knox slipped through the gears, using breaks, acceleration, and the sway of the Mustang's weight to maneuver through corners and handle the hills—Steve McQueen in *Bullet*.

Emergency lights flashed, the cacophony of sirens, *whoop, whoop, whoop* filled the night. Leon turned into downtown

Duluth when Knox saw her, Jena's face framed in the back window of the van.

Knox fought to maintain position, and again hit 911 on his cell. The delay in the dispatcher's response was maddening.

"She's in the van," said Knox. "The girl is in the van!"

"Understood. Break off your pursuit, Sergeant."

Out of the fucking question.

Then, the night lit up bright as day, a light from above and the *whump, whump*, of chopper blades. "Police, stop your vehicle," announced Deacon Hubbard through the chopper's loudspeaker.

The van kept on its reckless course.

• • •

A LIGHT DRIZZLE spattered the wheelhouse windows as *Superior Star* churned into the Rice Point Channel. From the bridge, Captain Kolstad saw the blur of emergency lights dash among the streets of Duluth. The distant sound of sirens echoed across the water.

Kolstad checked the Auto ID and Navnet Systems, and eyed the marker buoys through binoculars. His way clear of ships, the first mate radioed the *Star's* ETA to transit the lift bridge.

• • •

PURSUED BY KNOX and four police cars, Leon careened into downtown Duluth. The light rain blurred his windshield as his hands gripped the wheel in desperation. Then a glance at the harbor revealed an escape.

The ship, Leon thought. *Get across the bridge before it goes up for the ship. Leave the cops behind, dump the girl and get away.*

Toward Canal Park, Leon skidded through a turn and sped down the steep incline of North Lake Street. Lights flashed in his rear view mirrors. The rain was blurred across his window by a single, miserable wiper blade, the way ahead unclear.

Police blocked the exits to I-35 and Railroad Avenue. Two marked cars blocked the entrance to Canal Park. Leon had no place to go. Knox anticipated the plan. The PD was going to take the van. He applied a soft brake and crossed over the interstate. At the entrance to Canal Park, two officers tossed spike strips onto the street and dashed for cover.

Leon gripped the wheel, clinched his jaw, and hit the gas. *Boom!* The van hit the spike strips, and bashed through the two-car roadblock.

Running on flats, the wrecked van sped onto South Lake into the bustling Canal Park entertainment quarter. Through a rain streaked, web-cracked windshield, Leon glimpsed the sight of tourists scurry out of his way through the drizzle. The van careened along the street in the wrong lane. The aerial lift bridge in sight, a recorded closure warning wailed out, lights flashed, bells clanged, and the barricades began to lower.

On a wrecking-ball trajectory, Leon roared by Grandma's Restaurant, the bridge just yards away. Frantic, he wrestled the steering wheel to steady the van. He stomped down on the accelerator, traction faded, sparks flew from the van's wheels.

In the distance, through the rain, the shadow of the approaching ship loomed. Police cars, sirens, and Knox still in his wake, Leon smashed through the barricade onto the street level bridge deck. Three-hundred-eighty-feet away lay the hope of escape.

Suddenly, the van skidded. Leon turned the wheel to compensate. The battered gray hulk screeched along the metal deck, jumped the curb, and smashed into the safety railing. The left front wheel of the van teetered into space. Steam rose from the engine. Leon struck his head—"Fuck it!"

• • •

THE THOUSAND-FOOT *SUPERIOR Star*, at five knots was on final approach to the lift bridge, and its departure from the harbor.

Through binoculars, Kolstad saw the emergency lights in Canal Park. A helicopter, its intense light illuminating the bridge, swooped low over the ship.

"Captain, *Superior Star*," said the bridge master over the radio. "We have an emergency, abort your approach?"

"Negative. We go aground or take out your bridge."

There was a long pause. The gray van remained pinned to a tangle of steel, one headlight stared into the light rain, but the bridge began to rise.

Knox gaped at the silhouette of the ship's approach and bailed from the Mustang. With an injured leg, he leaped into the air. Hands gripped the grimy, steel grate of the rising bridge deck.

The chopper hovered, its 40 million-candle-power spotlight, a white, bright sun illuminated the raindrops that fell like a cascade of diamonds. The iron red hull of *Superior Star* bore down. Slowly, the bridge continued to rise.

Knox swung helpless in the blowing rain. With one last strain, he pulled himself onto the deck, his arms and body aching. The two-lane steel platform finally shuddered to a stop. Knox found himself starring one-hundred-thirty-five-feet to the churning water below. "Oh shit," he muttered.

He jerked his focus back to the van, now framed by the intense light of Hubbard's chopper.

Flames licked out from the engine as the rear doors of the van burst open. Leon stumbled out, Jena DeAngelo in his grip. Like Bat Man's Joker, a defiant grin cut across his bloodied face.

Knox lined the sites of his Beretta right between Leon's eyes.

"Well, Knox!" Leon yelled over the din of the whirling chopper blades. "It's been a-hell-of-a ride."

"Let the girl go. The ride is over, Leon."

"Not quite." Leon wrenched Jena close. The duct tape gone, her eyes filled with tears, the glint of a knife blade at her neck.

"Look around, Leon. You have no place to go. Put down the knife."

Leon stood his ground, the knife at Jena's throat. The megalithic *Superior Star* edged to the bridge.

Then with a muffled growl, the gas tank to the van erupted. Three piercing blasts shattered the scene, the horn of *Superior Star*.

Knox fired.

Leon fell against the railing, loosing his grip on Jena. The round creased the left side of his head. Her hands still bound, panic in her eyes, Jena crawled across the wet steel deck. Knox rushed to her, Leon charged, knife in hand.

Knox fired again. The .45-caliber slug smashed into Leon's left shoulder. Over the rail he went, the bow of *Superior Star* passing into the channel.

More from instinct than compassion, Knox scrambled to the edge of the bridge, squeezed under the bent rail and reached out. Just out of reach, Leon clung to a slippery steel strut. Far below, the *Star* maintained course.

The one-hand death-grip his only lifeline, Leon twisted in the wind and rain. He looked up at Knox, eyes wide with fright, blood streamed from the side of his head. He cried out—"You're a cop, save me!"

Knox looked into the desperate eyes, Leon Love, the length of a hand beyond reach.

"Sorry, Leon. It ain't gonna happen."

The powerful, pulsing throb of the ship's engines drew nearer. Leon slipped his grasp. Like a flailing rag doll, he tumbled into space through the rain. The primal scream stopped as he disappeared into an aft funnel of *Superior Star*.

The van afire in the background, Knox collapsed against the bridge railing, a gasped for breath, his body spent. Jena crawled into Knox's arms. With the knife Leon left behind, Knox severed her bindings.

Maybe he could have reached farther to save Leon Love. On the other hand, he saw no need. Like Dale Allen

Nichols who danced to his death at the end of a rope, Charles Leyland, and his son, Chuck, both took a bullet: all had left misery in their wake. Justice, or was it vengeance, had achieved its resolve, the world better off without them.

Deacon Hubbard hovered above, the chopper's beacon turning night into day.

Knox knew that the deaths of Lara, Swede, Neil Wallace and Walt Meyers would remain like four drops of blood indelibly spattered upon the pages of his life. He drew Jena to him. In that instant, the essence of life replaced the sense of peril and anger that Knox had harbored for so long, the pursuit of vengeance, over.

"Is he gone, Knox? Jena asked. "Is it okay?"

The bridge shuddered as it began to descend. Knox tightly closed his embraced and whispered, "He's gone, forever."

The van smoldered, and Knox held Jena in his arms near the bridge rail. *Superior Star* sailed beyond the channel lighthouse, a Coast Guard launch in its wake. Knox looked toward the street below. Sam and the cops waited, the rain had turned to mist.

Two and a half minutes later the two-lane bridge slammed to a stop at street level. Jena ran to the waiting arms of her mother.

Sam reached out for Knox. For a moment their eyes held one another.

"Sergeant Knox, I presume," said the captain from Duluth PD. He stepped forward, his tone less than pleased.

"Yes, sir."

"Well Sergeant, you're a long way from Minneapolis, and have a lot of explaining to do."